HARPER'S FORTUNE

HARPER'S FORTUNE

M4RRY M3

F. C. Clark

Matador
9 Priory Business Park,
Wistow Road, Kibworth Beauchamp,
Leicestershire. LE8 0RX
Tel: 0116 279 2299
Email: books@troubador.co.uk
Web: www.troubador.co.uk/matador
Twitter: @matadorbooks

ISBN 978 1789018 554

British Library Cataloguing in Publication Data.
A catalogue record for this book is available from the British Library.

Printed and bound in the UK by TJ International, Padstow, Cornwall
Typeset in 11pt Aldine401 BT by Troubador Publishing Ltd, Leicester, UK

Matador is an imprint of Troubador Publishing Ltd

Mum
Thank you for all your support and
encouragement.
Love you always.

Acknowledgments

Firstly, I would like to thank my amazing husband; here we go again my darling.

Of course my three babies, love you forever.

Thank you, to all my family and friends for your endless support.

A huge thank you to everyone who has read Harper's Fate and fell in love with Kate and Luke.

A massive thank you to all my Facebook friends and followers, who have liked, shared and spread the word – I am truly grateful.

To the girls I have met on Instagram, thank you for your support.

A special thank you to Erica and Sophie at EKC.

To Luke and Brendan at FMC – sorry and thank you!

Lastly, to my editor Jane Hammett thank you for your guidance.

1

'Katarina Varizin?' the tallest man asks, in a strong Russian accent.

'Kate Harper.' I correct him.

'You follow us,' he says.

I nod.

He leads the way and his associate trails behind me.

I stop before I enter the cabin.

Holy shit, what am I doing?

I'm ushered to a seat and fasten my seatbelt, gripping my bag tightly. The first man faces me, while his friend sits next to me. I study them. Both men are dressed in identical black clothing, with matching stern expressions. Within minutes the plane begins to move. Fear rises in me, but it's too late to escape.

When the plane reaches cruising altitude, both men unfasten their seatbelts. One moves to the rear of the plane, while the other disappears to the front. The first man returns.

'Water.' He hands me a plastic bottle, and resumes his position in front of me.

'Thank you.' Panic makes me need to speak. 'How long is the flight?'

He holds up three fingers.

'Three hours?'

He waves his hand from side to side.

'Longer than three hours?'

He nods.

Silence again.

'How long have you worked for Ivor Varizin?'

He glares. I'm not sure if he understood the question or is just unwilling to divulge information. He holds up a hand, his fingers spread wide.

'Five years?'

He nods again. *Jesus Christ. I admit defeat. I'll stay silent from here on.*

We continue the journey in silence, both men seated close to me. I look out of the window, watching England slowly disappear. My body is cold from shock. I unzip my bag and reach for Ivor's letter. The words are clear: Ivor Varizin is our biological father! I close my eyes, recalling Harry's face, watching my sister crumble in my arms. I should be with her and Mum, waiting for Dad to wake, not here.

I put the letter away and clasp my arms around my bag. I can't think straight; thoughts of adoption and money circulate in my mind, but the only thought that remains strong is Luke. Longing for his protection, I bring my scarf to my nose, inhaling the scent of him, the Sutton scent. Tears leak from the corners of my eyes.

Someone nudges my shoulder and my eyes suddenly open wide. *Crap! I fell asleep!*

'Are we here?' I ask.

The first man nods.

Despite feeling terrified, I can't ignore a small rush of curiosity.

The door opens and the warm air hits me. The day is sunny and the sky clear blue. I follow the first man down the metal steps. The plane is standing in what looks like an abandoned airfield. There is no passport control. *Where the hell am I?*

A black four-by-four waits nearby, with another man dressed in matching clothing. I climb in the back seat. The first man slides in next to me and the other two men get in the front.

The four-by-four moves fairly quickly along the poor roads. I strain to see outside: there is dense foliage and heavy woodland on either side. The long journey allows me to think of some questions to ask the man I'm about to meet.

Eventually we arrive at a set of large metal gates manned by yet more staff, carrying guns. The colour fades from my face and bile rises in my throat. I swallow hard as the gates open.

In the distance stands a large house – actually, it's not a house. The only words to describe the property are 'stately home'. I remember the first day I arrived at Luke's enormous house, but this leaves me floored. The car drives slowly down the long gravel driveway. I'm lost for words. My biological father lives here?

The car stops. My anxiety levels rise. Another man ushers me out of the car towards the gothic front door, while scanning around us. For what, I don't know. I step forward and enter a world I'm not accustomed to, nor wish to be. The house is huge: the hall is twice the size of the house I used to share with Harry. Large paintings and rugs hang from various walls, and an enormous dark-oak staircase sweeps around the edge of the hall, continuing high above us. With no time to absorb any more of my surroundings, I'm led further into the house – before I come to an abrupt stop.

A man appears in front of me. He must be in his late fifties. He's tall, with thick dark hair that has a generous helping of grey streaks. He is striking and has strong dark eyes. He walks towards me, his hand extended. I stare at him as our matching eyes meet.

'Katarina, pleased to meet you, and welcome to Russia. I am Ivor Varizin.'

I'm nervous; still, I take his hand in mine. 'Kate.'

He nods, accepting that I'm not Katarina; Kate is the only name I've ever known. We size each other up, and I can't help but look for similarities between us. Harry has the same hair as him, and we both have his eyes.

'Come. You must be tired after your journey.' He speaks to one of the men in Russian and gestures for me to follow him. 'How was your flight?' His English is clear, his accent faint.

'OK,' I answer, taking in my surroundings once again. We move towards the rear of the property and enter a large room. The grandness is breathtaking – there is dark, heavy furniture and a vaulted ceiling with intricate plaster mouldings. The room is austere, but a roaring fire softens the masculinity.

'Sit, please.'

I lower myself into the huge, brick-coloured sofa.

A servant enters with a silver tray.

'You like coffee, Kate?'

'Yes.' I look around the room. 'These pictures – are they of your family?'

A smile spreads across his face. He appears pleased with my question. 'Yes, and your family too. Some date back many years.'

I raise my brows. Wow! Mum has a 'keep calm and drink tea' picture on her wall. There's no comparison.

'Do you take milk and sugar?'

'Just milk, please.'

He pours the coffee from a large silver pot and passes it to me.

'Thank you.'

'I apologise for meeting you under these circumstances.'

My head is full of questions. 'Did you know my dad was attacked this morning? He's in hospital, fighting for his life.' I watch him closely.

'Yes.'

I take a deep breath. *Christ, has he been watching my entire family?*

'Did you do it?' *Even if he were involved, would he tell me?*

'No! I would not hurt the man who has protected my daughter.' He scowls at my question.

'I had to ask.' Our eyes lock. 'I have no reason to trust you.'

'Katarina – sorry, Kate. I understand your need for questions and your reasons for not trusting me.' His lips curl. 'You are like your mother.' He looks down at his coffee, clearly struggling with some emotion.

'I wouldn't know; I've never seen her.' I can't help but feel hostile towards this stranger – my father.

'You speak your mind, like your mother.' He smiles warmly.

'How did she die?'

Ivor takes a deep breath. 'Kate.' His eyes meet mine, allowing me to see his pain. 'The official paperwork says she committed suicide. But this is not true. She was one of the strongest women I have ever met' – he places his hand over his heart – 'in here. I know someone killed her. I was in prison when she died.'

My face drops. 'She was murdered? Fuck!' Shit – I hope he doesn't understand English swear words. However, the raising of his brows indicates he does.

He nods. 'Yes.'

'Why?'

'Money, greed, or revenge – I wish I knew. As I said, I was in prison when your mother gave birth to you, and I was still there when she died. My family have had many enemies over the years. I accept vengeance may be the reason for her death. Her file… It does not speak the truth.'

'She died in London?'

'Yes.'

I can't take much more; I feel overloaded by emotion. I pick up my coffee, hoping the caffeine will wake me from this nightmare. The heat trickles down my throat, confirming this is real and not a dream.

'When you say files, do you mean death certificate?'

'Yes.'

'Maybe she was weaker than you thought.'

'Please do not use words to hurt me.'

'Hurt *you*! Oh, forgive me, please!'

He looks at the fire.

'Let's get on with it, shall we? You want my money.' A direct approach is all I can offer.

'I have no need of your inheritance. Look around you. This is about your safety.' Ivor's dark eyes connect with mine. Somehow, I know he's telling the truth. Call it a gut instinct. 'Your mother and I set up the fund when you were born. It was Katenka's wish that you would receive the money on your twenty-seventh birthday.'

'But why twenty-seven? Seems a bit odd.'

'She wanted you to find your own path – not to have the money too young.'

'I *was* finding my own path until yesterday, my twenty-seventh birthday!'

'Money can change your direction,' he says.

'And bring problems to your door. Literally.'

Ivor looks directly into my eyes. 'The people who attacked you are no longer a threat. As for the attack on your father, I will deal with that too.'

Deal with it? Shit – what does he mean? I'm guessing they won't be having a chat...

'I wanted to ask about Harry.'

He looks puzzled by my simple question.

'The trust fund has only been left to me – there's nothing for Harry. Why not?'

He raises his hands. 'I assume your mother died before your sister was added to the fund.'

'Oh.' Why does he seem disconnected from her name? Perhaps I'm reading too much into every detail – it's been a long day.

A man enters the room and leans down to Ivor, speaking in a low tone. *Hey, I don't speak Russian – there's no need to whisper!*

'The man from the bank is on his way. You must learn the code for your account.'

'Code!' I swallow hard. *Is he kidding?*

'Yes. I have a passport here for you as ID, but you need to input a code to activate your account.'

'Oh.' A passport – how the hell did he manage to get me a Russian passport? I'm too afraid to ask. Besides this could potentially go tits up. My head is all over the place – how the hell am I going to remember a code?

He hands me a piece of paper with a long line of digits.

'Is this why I couldn't sign the money over from London?'

'The bank has strict rules and, due to the amount of money involved, there were stipulations attached to the trust fund when we set it up. A physical presence is needed, and you must remember these numbers – it is very important. You will also have to sign your name as Katarina Varizin; your signature is on the passport.'

'OK.' I gaze at the numbers. He wasn't lying.

'I have to leave you for a moment, but please do not be afraid. I understand how frightening this is for you.' His eyes lock on to mine, offering me warmth.

'I need to call home; they're expecting to hear from me.'

'Yes.' He looks at his watch and then rubs his jaw. 'You have thirty seconds.'

I frown.

'I do not want your number to be traced – once again, this is for your safety.'

My number traced? Shit. Who is this man?

I nod.

He exits the room and leaves one of his sidekicks watching me. This place is henchman city: everywhere I look, another man appears.

I keep my scarf securely around my neck and slip off my jacket, placing it in my bag. I grab my phone and dial Kiki's number.

'Kate, thank God. Are you OK? Please tell me you're safe,' she says. I can hear the relief in her voice.

'I'm fine. I only have thirty seconds, so have to be quick. How's Dad? Have the doctors seen him?'

'They've just finished their rounds. Nurse Kelly says he's stable. She said stable was good – I guess that means he hasn't gotten any worse.'

'I guess. How are Mum and Harry?'

'They're fine. Barney is providing the entertainment – say no more! He told your mum that you have sickness and diarrhoea.'

'Cheers, Barney!'

'It stopped her asking questions.'

'And Luke?'

'No, nothing – has he called you?'

'No. Text me – keep me updated.'

'Sure.'

Ivor's man checks his watch. Is he timing me?

'I have to go – love you.'

I end the call and wave my phone from side to side. Satisfied, the guard returns to his post in front of the door.

I place my phone in my bag. The time has arrived. I scan the digits: 309010024189. Hell, I can barely cope with four. Jeez. *Think, Harper, think. Food – it's the only way.*

9

I break the numbers down into ingredients. Sugar 30g, flour 90g, butter 100g, eggs 24, and baking powder 189 teaspoons… I repeat the ingredients for a Russian Victoria sponge cake over and over again. On a piece of paper I copy the name Katrina Varizin. That part is easy!

Feeling jittery, I move towards the door and attempt to open it, but the man appears at my side, placing his hand over the door.

'No.'

'Where is Ivor?'

His fixed gaze is blank. Can he understand English?

'Where… is… Ivor… you… moron?'

Nothing. Not even a blink of an eye.

I bang on the door.

'Sit,' the henchman commands.

'I don't want to sit – do you understand that?'

'Sit.'

OK. This isn't going well.

'Whatever!'

As I sit back down, the door opens and Ivor appears.

'I apologise. I had business to take care of. How is Malcolm?'

'Dad is stable.'

Ivor's expression alters hearing me say the word 'Dad' – I'm not willing to extend the title in his direction.

'Your henchman wouldn't let me open the door.' I fold my arms.

'He is ordered to protect you. This is my request. He does speak English and will understand the word "moron".' Ivor offers me a look, like a father chastising his daughter.

'In that case, it's rude not to answer when you're being spoken to.'

Ivor smirks. 'You are a vision of light, Kate. You have the spirit of Katenka – fire in your core. Your mother would be very proud of your ability to speak your mind.'

'I always have.' I turn and walk towards the fire. The heat warms my body, but no fire can thaw my feelings of abandonment.

'Have you remembered the code?'

'I think so. When is the man from the bank coming, and when can I go home?' Ivor looks wounded. Does he think I want to be in his company? Maybe I do, but not like this, under duress.

'Half an hour, then I have a meal for you. The plane will leave at first light tomorrow, returning you to the UK.'

'Oh.'

'Once we have dealt with the money, I would like to show you some things that you may find interesting.'

'OK.' Yet again, I sense warmth coming from this man. Does he care about me, or the money?

'Come – let's go to my office.'

I follow in his footsteps, captivated by his home.

Ivor's office mirrors the house: it is large and austere, with another open fire roaring against the far wall. It may be summer, but the house feels cold. The focal point is a large, wooden desk. He walks to a chair and holds it for me.

'Can I ask what you're going to do with the money? Let me be clear, I have no interest in it,' I say.

He nods. 'It will disappear. Stocks and—'

I hold my hands up. 'On second thoughts, don't tell me! What I don't know won't hurt me, right? What are the chances of the men still coming after me? They might use me to get to you.' I rub my forehead. My life since this morning makes no sense: my mother is dead, I have a Russian inheritance… God, I feel sick.

'The account will be closed.'

'And that's enough?' I don't buy that. 'You're certain they'll stop.'

There is a knock on the door. Ivor responds in Russian, watching me.

'We can discuss this again shortly.'

I nod. I have nothing left to say.

The door opens and the guest of honour enters – the man from the bank.

'Katarina Varizin.' He holds out his hand. I shake it.

'Katarina, this is Mr Akulov.'

I nod.

Mr Akulov prepares his laptop and various forms for me to sign, then gestures for me to enter my code.

I close my eyes to think. Here goes – Russian Victoria sponge cake. Sugar 30g, flour 90g, butter 100g, eggs 24, and baking powder 189 teaspoons. The screen accepts the code. I watch the digits alter until all that remains is a flashing zero.

Job done. I want to go home. Mr Akulov shakes my hand and Ivor walks with him to the door.

'Kate, you have done well. From this point there should be no further threat.'

'I hope you're right. I need to check my phone. I'm waiting for an update on Dad.'

'Yes, of course.' Ivor bellows a command. The same man as before walks me to the large living area.

Oddly, I have no calls or texts from Luke, just a message from Kiki.

Dad is still stable. Nurse Kelly is pleased. X

No mention of Luke!

I hear the door open and turn to see Ivor.

'Our meal is ready.'

I grab my bag and follow Ivor to a very grand dining room. The delicate sound of classical music playing in the background leaves me feeling relaxed – considering the situation.

Ivor pulls a chair out for me, while a man places two plates of steaming food on the table. It looks like a stew.

'Enjoy. It is a classic: Rassolnik. Do you like to cook?'

'Yes.' I taste my first mouthful. It's good – I didn't realise I was hungry. 'This is lovely.'

'I cannot cook. Your grandmother – my mother – tried to teach me. I detested the kitchen. Your mother loved to cook – this was one of her favourites.'

I place my fork on my plate and look across at him.

'Were you happy – I mean, when you got married?'

'Yes.' He takes a deep breath and sits back in his chair. 'I was sent to prison for a crime I did not commit; it was a conspiracy against me and my family. Corruption is big business in this country – money can buy most things.'

'And now... the people who wronged you – are they the same people that want to hurt me?'

'Please, Katarina...' He holds his hands up. 'Kate. Without money you become less... how can I say it? You lose power.'

'What about you? Do you come at a price? Will it cost me my life?'

'On paper, I do not have children.'

'Oh. But they know about me and my trust fund, so clearly there is a paper trail. I had the shit kicked out of me, so someone knows who I am.'

'Yes, and as I told you that someone has been dealt with. You are no longer wealthy, and your paperwork has been destroyed.'

'Destroyed! Was that to make your life easier, wiping us out of your life? Besides, they found me once, maybe they'll find me again.' The attack feels like yesterday, not days ago. I shudder at the memory; it's even worse that Ivor knew.

Ivor shakes his head. 'Not possible.'

Should I ask how he knows this? No.

'Lucky for you – I'll disappear out of your life.'

'Luck is not something I possess. I have lost everyone I have loved.'

'Me included,' I mumble.

Ivor pours some red wine. He holds up his glass.

'Kate, it is an honour to meet you.'

I raise my glass, but I can't reciprocate.

'Do you have any questions about your mother?'

'Where do I start? This is a major shock. I celebrated my birthday yesterday with my friends and family, and now… everything's gone, everything's changed.' I hate him, and my dead mum, for doing this. I swallow my emotions. 'My entire life has… you've… ruined it.' I lower my head, feeling desolate.

Ivor places his hand over mine.

I look up. Our dark eyes are identical; distance or no distance, he is part of me. 'Sorry,' I whisper. I want to hate him, but I can't.

He shakes his head and tries to smile. 'You have every right to be angry with me.'

'I'm angry with everyone.' Mum and Dad too. They knew – how could they have kept this from me and Harry?

'I know I have upset you, but that was never my intention. You must not reject those who have cared for you over the years.' He removes his hand and clasps them together, resting his elbows on the table.

'OK. So – if there was no trust fund, I'm pretty certain this…' I gesture, 'would not be happening.'

He watches me for a second. 'I would like to think that this would have happened at some point.'

I shake my head. No. 'You could have contacted me a month ago – a year ago.'

'Russia is a very different country to your home. Your safety is my priority; I know that your mother took you away for the right reasons. If she were alive today, life would be very different for us.'

'I don't see how. She put us up for adoption.' I shake my head. I can't believe I'm saying this.

'You must understand she was protecting you – that is what a mother would do.'

'No… I don't think I could ever leave my babies. No – never.'

'No!' Ivor speaks sternly, shocking me. 'She had a kind heart. To give you and your sister away would have caused her great pain. Do not speak in that way – do you understand?'

I have no control over the tears rolling down my cheeks.

'Kate. Please.' He gently touches my face. 'This is difficult for me, also. Let me show you some pictures of your mother.'

'OK,' I respond softly.

We move towards the hall and stand in front of two large doors. Ivor uses a key from a chain around his neck and unlocks the doors. He walks towards the wall and flicks a switch, turning on a beautiful chandelier in the centre of the room.

He looks at me. I slowly move to the panelled walls. *What the fuck?*

'How did…' I can't speak. The room is huge. The walls are covered in pictures of *me* – at every stage of my life.

This is surreal! How has Ivor documented my entire life?

'Kate?' Ivor is waiting for a response. 'I have shocked you.'

I bleakly look at him. 'No shit.' Am I supposed to be impressed?

'Kate, this is all I have of your life.'

'If you wanted to know me, why didn't you just contact me?' I fold my arms and continue to absorb all the pictures. 'I would have accepted you. But you didn't contact me until money was involved.'

'I repeat. I do not need your trust fund. My old enemies would have hurt you. I could not allow that to happen.'

'Maybe. Incidentally, I don't want it back.'

'My words do not mean much to you, but they are all I can give you.'

'This is really difficult for me, so forgive me for not taking your word as gospel.'

He nods.

Strangely, many of the pictures were taken inside Mum and Dad's house.

I tap a picture. 'How did you get these?'

'Christina Sampson has been sending them to me over the years. The others have been taken by men that I have hired.'

All I heard was *Christina*... Aunt Christina, Dad's sister! 'What? Why does Christina send you pictures?'

'I pay a fair price for them.' He walks towards me, his hands in his trouser pockets.

I stop.

'You pay her? Fuck! Jesus, I can't believe what I'm hearing. She told us she didn't know you. This looks pretty friendly to me.' I move to the next row. 'These pictures were taken in my mum's house. I was about five, I think.'

'Six... you were six – and please do not speak in that manner.'

I shake my head in disbelief. Does he think he can tell me what to do? No way; he's not my dad.

'When did this start?' I move across the room.

'After I was released from prison. The company that was used for your adoption belonged to Malcolm's sister. I knew I could have photos of you.' He watches me closely, as I crumble. 'Kate, I had the paperwork of your adoption destroyed – there was no trail in London. I could not risk certain people knowing you existed.'

My world has been shattered. How could Christina lie to us?

I continue the tour of my life. Some of the images were taken very recently. I stop at an image of Luke; my finger traces his face. God, I miss him.

'You have made a good choice in finding yourself a man – he seems determined and strong.'

'He is.' *Strong? I'll go with controlling, and thanks to you he'll be extremely pissed off.*

'You don't have many pictures of Harry – is that because of the trust fund?'

He moves forward, closing the distance between us.

'Kate, Harry is not my daughter... I thought you would have worked out the dates of her birth. I was in prison when she was conceived.'

Shit, he's right.

'The dates didn't enter my head. Crap! So if it's not you, then who is her dad?'

Ivor takes a deep breath, almost waiting for me to solve the mystery.

'Do you know who it is?' Then a thought hits me. 'Dad!'

'I believe Katenka and Malcolm had an affair. I have no proof of this, and accept that she needed happiness. Malcolm seems like a good man.'

My eyes glaze over and my legs weaken, making me stumble.

'Kate!' Ivor grabs my waist and guides me to a chair. He sits next to me, taking hold of my hands. 'This is too much for you.'

'What do you think?' The evidence is clear – tears are streaming down my cheeks.

He moves his chair nearer and places an arm around my shoulders. I sense he is unsure how to behave, but I feel comfortable enough with him to lean my head against him.

'Kate, I am sorry.'

'It's fine. Actually, it's not. I'm really cross with you.' I sit up.

He stands and walks towards a glass trolley, pours two drinks and resumes his seat next to me.

He passes me a tumbler. 'Drink this.'

'Thank you.' I down it. The burning sensation takes my breath away – whisky, I think. 'I'm angry at a lot of things today, Ivor, not just you.' He looks at me, uncertain of my state of mind. 'My dad – well, I have no idea how my dad is, because I'm here with you. Let's not forget my mum left us, and now she's dead. Oh, and my sister is now my half-sister because my dad had an affair with my birth mum. You would be right in saying my life appears to be completely...' Fucked. God, I want to scream. 'Why haven't you contacted me? I don't get it.'

His face softens. 'I had my reasons.'

'I bet you did,' I mumble under my breath.

He stands and collects a box from the corner of the room, and places it on the table.

'You may find this interesting.'

'What is it?'

'Information about your mother.' He removes the lid. 'It is up to you if you want to look – I understand if it's too much.'

I deliberate for a moment. Of course it's too much, but not knowing where you come from has to be more painful than knowing. I stand and take a deep breath. Here goes. Instantly, I'm drawn to a picture. I sit back in the chair and examine the image of a beautiful young woman with blonde hair.

'You look like your mother.' He smiles with pride.

Tears roll down my cheeks as my finger traces the picture in my hand.

'If this is all true, then I feel cheated for not knowing her.'

'I have no reason to lie.'

He reaches inside the box and removes a small photo album.

'This, you must see.'

He passes me the album. I flick through the pages. Immediately, I see that Ivor and Katenka look happy. They almost look like Luke and me. She was blonde and Ivor is dark.

'You look happy.'

'We were, but it was taken away from us, and from you.'

'I guess.' Part of me can't let myself think of what ifs. If Katenka hadn't come to London, there would be no Harry – a thought I really can't accept.

He passes me more pictures, this time of their wedding day.

'She was beautiful. What about your family?'

He shakes his head. 'I have no family.'

'None?'

'No. My parents died many years ago. I was their only child.'

'Oh.'

'My mother loved Katenka. You have the same ability as she – to light up a room. This is a gift from your mother.' He looks away. I hate to admit it, but I pity him, living alone with no love – not a love like these pictures display.

Ivor stands and pours himself another drink. 'Kate?' He holds up the decanter.

I shake my head. I'm already feeling confused.

'Ivor, I need to ask – what do you want from me?'

He returns to the chair. 'I need you to be safe. If I enter your life that may alter.'

'I thought that, now we've met... maybe you would want me in your life.'

'I wish it were that easy,' he says.

'I've survived this long without you... just say it how it is. Trust me, I can take rejection.'

Firm lines form across his forehead, and once again his temper returns.

'Rejection? No! I have kept you away from my life for good reason.'

'Safety! So you said.'

'My family have old enemies, who would enjoy...' He shifts in his chair. 'I have lost your mother. If they hurt you, I would have nothing left.'

'Nothing left?' I almost laugh out of anger. 'All you have are some old pictures locked away in a room.'

'That is my life, Kate.'

Christ, it's true – this is all he has. 'It was your choice, and you seem like a man who knows his own mind.'

'Losing your mother was too painful for me. Knowing you are safe and happy gives me peace.'

'You still haven't answered my question. Are you entering my life now?'

'No.'

'When?'

'I do not know; give me time.'

I hold back tears of disappointment.

'Kate, I want you to have this.' He places a wedding picture in my hands. 'I will see you again – one day.' His knuckles tenderly brush my cheek. 'I want you to return home, happy in the knowledge that you and your family are safe.'

I take the picture and stand, feeling confused about the man I want to hate because he abandoned me, yet my heart wants him to be part of my life.

We leave the room. I shall never forget it. My silent footsteps follow Ivor's towards the staircase. I can't help but feel empty – a lost daughter.

He turns to me. 'I have prepared a room for you.'

'Thank you.'

I follow Ivor up the wooden staircase. The house smells old, and I'm not sure what the scent is – maybe wax or oil.

'Is this your house?'

'Yes. It has been in my family for many generations.'

'Oh. It's stunning.'

He looks at me. Perhaps he's pleased that I'm appreciating my heritage.

'Here is your room. Do you need anything?'

'No, thank you.' I stand awkwardly in front of him.

He opens the door. 'I will not be here when you wake. The man who escorted you today will return you home safely.'

I look up into his dark eyes.

'When you're ready.'

I can no longer speak; my emotions grip my vocal cords. I reach up and kiss his cheek, and then bolt into my room.

The door closes and I crumple to the bed. My tears fall hard and fast. My sobs develop into a painful silent wail.

A knock at the door shocks me into stopping. I stand and try to compose myself, wiping away my tears with the back of my hand. I open the door to a man carrying a tray with a jug of water and a glass. He walks past me and places them on a table, and immediately exits. Short and not so sweet! *I assume communication skills must not be a requirement to get a job with Ivor.*

I find my bag on a chair and place the photo Ivor gave me inside. I look at my phone. I have no missed calls from my Luke, but another text from Kiki.

Hi, babe.
Doctors are pleased with Dad's progress. Will keep you updated. Hope U R OK. Love you. XOXO

That sounds positive, although it's odd that Luke hasn't tried to contact me.

I move to the bathroom and study my reflection. Not only do I look like crap, I look nothing like Susan or Malcolm. I run my hands through my long blonde hair and wash my face. Feeling unsettled, I return to the bedroom and down a fresh glass of water. Drained of energy, I move to the bed and look at my watch. *Is that the time? Crap! My body thinks I'm still in England.* My hand touches the gift Luke gave me yesterday – my watch – but the weight of my head is almost too much to bear. I lie down on the bed. The room begins to spin and I blink hard to focus. I feel drunk. I try to move my scarf to my face, inhaling Luke, but I can't. I have no energy. I lose my grip. The scarf falls from my face.

I slowly raise my head. An intense pain at my temples commands my body to wake. I attempt to blink, but can't. I'm in complete darkness. I try to speak, but can't. Panic and fear begin to swirl within me. It increases when I try to move my arms. They remain tightly locked at my side, and my legs are restrained at the ankles. *Holy shit, I'm tied to something.* All I can move is the tips of my fingers. *I'm tied to a chair!*

Tears start to fall as I realise I am in grave danger.

Why would he do this?

I struggle to believe that my father would want to cause me pain. Then my thoughts are interrupted by a muffled bang. My heart beats frantically as I hear the door open…

2

I hear footsteps and turn my head. I can feel someone close to me. *Oh Christ, this is it, my life is over…* A hand moves across my jaw, and the roughness of someone's face brushes against my cheek.

'Do you know how fucking angry I am with you?'

Luke! My heart leaps. My blindfold is removed. I try to speak, but I'm still gagged. I close my eyes, relieved that I'm not dead, but I don't understand what's happened.

He leans forward, into kissing distance – the danger zone.

'My security team called, wondering why I hadn't informed them that you were in Russia.' His dark eyes pin me to the chair. 'There must be a mistake, I said – my girlfriend is in London with her friends.'

I'm confused. SGI Security – Luke's company. They fitted the alarm at Harry's house! What the hell is going on?

'It took me two seconds to get Kiki to tell me what had happened. She informed me that you got on a jet with two men – no, what she said was "two scary Russians" – to sign away an inheritance. Is that a precise breakdown of the story?'

I nod, remaining silent.

'Do you understand how dangerous this is? I'm so fucking angry, Kate.' His temper is scorching me. This is a Luke Sutton Code Red – a burning fire of fury.

I scowl at him.

'Don't look at me like that. You've lied to me and put yourself in a situation that you can't get out of!' He glances at me, tied to the chair.

Unfortunately, he has a point. I try to move, encouraging him to untie me.

'Do you know how tempting it is to leave you tied up? At least you would stay out of trouble. Once I remove the gag you have to stay quiet – do I make myself clear?'

I roll my eyes.

He pulls at my chin. 'Do I make myself clear? I need to get us out of here alive. Are you hurt anywhere?'

I shake my head.

He pulls a knife from his belt. I raise my head and take in his appearance. He's wearing black military clothing. Holy shit, he's carrying a gun. My breathing hitches and my eyes widen.

He registers my look of panic. 'I'll explain later. You're in safe hands.'

My arms are free first; my legs follow. I reach up to untie my gag.

'I've got this.' Luke unties the cloth and throws it to the floor.

I lock my arms around his neck, needing to feel safe. I wince in pain. 'Ow, my head.'

'Look at me.' He pulls a small torch from his pocket and shines it in my face – because that helps with my pounding headache. 'Your eyes are bloodshot – pupils slightly dilated.' He takes my wrist and uses his fingers to find my pulse. 'Your pressure is low – did anyone give you something?'

'Like what?' I try to read his expression. 'Drugs?'

'Your body is responding to something.'

'No, only some food and a few drinks – nothing else. I felt odd earlier – I couldn't move my arms and legs.'

'I'll carry out some tests later.'

Tests. Later!

'Why would he drug me? Ivor…' I shake my head. 'No.'

'I don't know.' He takes a deep breath.

'You said you've spoken to Kiki.' I look down, feeling guilty about lying to him. 'Did she say how my dad was?'

'I spoke to the doctor. Malcolm is stable.'

'Thank God.' I close my eyes, holding back my tears. 'Luke, I didn't know what else to do. After what happened to Dad, if anything happened to you or Harry…' I take a deep breath, pushing away the unwanted thoughts. 'I had no choice.'

'There's always a choice.'

'I still don't understand how you found me.'

He takes hold of my wrist. 'I told you I would always be with you.'

My forehead creases.

'Your watch has a built-in tracking device – it's part of my security measures.'

'What?'

'I'm not prepared to take risks with the people I care about. I'm worth a lot of money.'

My tears cease. 'Are you shitting me? Did you intend to control and monitor my every move?' I can't hide my disbelief. I'm pleased to be rescued, but confused by the news that Luke is able to track me 24/7.

'Don't you dare sit there and argue with me – that watch has just proved my point, as I'm now going to save your tight little arse.' His dark eyes hit me again. Seriously pissed-off Mr Control Freak Sutton is now my companion, and will not be departing for some time.

I fold my arms. This is fucking madness!

'Do you care to explain yourself? You look like a bloody 007 wannabe… And the watch! I thought you were being sentimental with your gift, not controlling. Clearly, you've done this before.' What other bloody secrets is he keeping from me?

His body stiffens.

'Are you joking? You want an explanation? Do you know how many men are out there?'

'No.' Men – what men? Ivor's men?

'We'll discuss this later. I have some questions for you regarding your lack of honesty.'

'Oh, really? Well, you can talk. I know on your dating form you stated you were a controlling gazillionaire – but clearly you forgot to tick the "wannabe special agent" box. Oh yes, you failed to mention that small detail. No, because they don't do dating websites for control freaks.' My voice rises, matching my temper.

I look up to him. Am I scared? Hell, no. Bring it on, Sutton!

'Have you finished?'

'For now.' I meet his dark, almost black, eyes. 'Actually, no, I haven't. I don't understand. You have guns and…'

My heads hurts. I feel confused.

'I would like to get you home in one piece so, I repeat, have you finished?'

I nod.

'Good. I suggest you remain silent.'

Whatever – you controlling lunatic.

He helps me to stand. 'Can you walk?'

'I think so. I feel unsteady.'

'You'll get stronger when the drugs wear off. Listen to me very carefully. When we leave this room, you need to be quiet. If you need me, pull my arm. I will signal to tell you what to do. Understand?'

I nod again.

'Good – that wasn't too difficult, was it?'

Luke pulls my arm to leave. I stop.

'My bag.'

'Sorry?'

'I need my bag and my scarf.'

'Leave it.'

'No! I have a photo inside it. Plus my favourite lip gloss I bought in France.'

Luke fires me a look. 'Fucking lip gloss! I'm trying to save your life and you want your bag. Why don't we call for a fucking bellboy?'

Wow, is there a temper beyond Code Red? If so, I have just pushed the release button.

'Luke, you're scaring me. You have a gun, and Ivor… ' I close my eyes. It's too painful to admit Ivor left me tied to the chair. 'I just want a picture Ivor gave me.'

He places his index finger under my chin. 'Where is your bag?'

'I don't know.'

Luke looks around and then lowers himself to the floor. He pulls the bag from under the bed.

'Here.'

'Thank you.' I shrug it on, and link my scarf round my neck. The Sutton scent hits me – although I now have the real-life version standing in front of me.

Silently, we make our way towards the door. Luke stops before he opens it. He grabs my face in both hands and kisses me urgently. Instantly, my fingers run through his short dark hair. He pulls away and places his forehead on mine. Our eyes meet. There are no words, just a sigh of thankfulness that I'm breathing.

'Remember, no noise from this point, OK?'

'OK.'

He pulls out a gun and holds it ready in front of him. What the hell is going on?

He quietly opens the door, checking the corridor. Before we leave he uses his fingers to indicate eyes up and forward. I stumble over something in the doorway. Fuck! A body, a bullet wound in its forehead, lies in my path. I gasp. Luke beckons me to come with him. I shut my eyes and step over the body. He keeps us close to the wall as we silently move down the staircase. He stops, his gun ready, as we turn the first corner. No activity. We continue to descend the stairs.

Suddenly, we hear a voice. Luke tightens his grip on my hand and quickly takes me to the last set of steps. I have no time to think. My palm is sweaty and my heart beats frantically, but he appears calm; every step is deliberate. At last we make it to an empty room, and he pushes me hard up against a wall. My breathing is erratic. His eyes lock on mine, and he nods, gesturing for me to mirror his actions. Silently, I exhale.

From where we hide, we watch two Russian men talking as they amble past the doorway.

The house is deathly quiet. I'm not sure of the time: the sun is up, but low. Luke guides me to the rear of the house, the room I first sat in with Ivor. How does he know where to go? This isn't luck – this is careful planning!

Luke carefully pushes open the door. My eyes lock on a man looking out of the window. Lying six feet away from him is a body, sprawled on the floor, dressed in black. One of Ivor's men? I can't take much more.

Luke holds his fingers to his lips. He stealthily moves towards the unsuspecting man at the window. As soon as the man realises he's not alone, and attempts to reach for his gun, it's too late. Luke grabs him in a head-lock. There is a crack, then the man slumps to the ground. How can Luke, my boyfriend, be responsible for this?

'Did you break his neck?'

'Yes. I told you not to speak.'

Holy shit!

'We need to keep moving.'

'But…'

'Shh.' His finger touches my cheek. I recognise his touch, but who is he? I feel like I don't know him any more. What the hell is going on?

I swallow hard and avoid looking at the floor.

Luke slides open the sash window. He shifts the shoulder strap attached to his gun before he straddles the windowsill and leaps out. I follow. *Where the hell has he learned to act like this?*

He tucks me in behind and holds his gun in front of him. He stops and places his finger to his lips. I lean against the wall, bewildered at everything that is happening, while Luke disappears for a few seconds. He returns and grabs my hand. He tilts my chin and points to his eyes. *Don't look down, don't look down…*

We reach the far corner of the building.

'We're going over there to borrow a car.' Luke points to the cars lined up on the drive. 'Follow me.'

I nod. I'm lost for words. We run to the cars and he hides me behind one of the vehicles. He slides his rucksack from his shoulders and removes a small black box, about eight inches square.

'Hold this.' He touches his ear. 'Sutton.'

What's he doing?

'Outside the main building… Four vehicles.'

Silence again. His eyes dart to mine. *Who's he talking to?*

'Three detonators. I'll take one. My ETA at the LUP…' He looks at his watch. 'Thirty minutes. Over and out.'

He removes what looks like green putty from his rucksack and rests three pieces on the ground. It smells strong – almost like almonds. He then takes out three small boxes with a digital display, connected to thin metal rods, like pencils. He pushes each box and rod into the three pieces of putty. Carefully, he places the putty on the underside of the three cars.

He scurries back.

'What are you doing?' *Do I want an answer? No.*

'Explosives. Making the cars into loaded weapons.'

I try to breathe.

'Trust me. I know what I'm doing.'

Oh, I can see that, Commander Sutton!

'Listen, I'm going to unlock the car, get in the driver's seat. Once the car starts, be prepared to drive fast.'

'What! I can't!' I shake my head.

'You can drive?' He looks at me.

'Yeah, but here? I didn't bring my licence with me. What if we get stopped by the police? Luke, I can't.'

He holds his gun in front of my face, frustrated.

'Do you think I have a licence for this?'

'I guess not. Luke, I can't think straight.' I'm lost.

'When I say drive, drive fast. Pass me the box.'

I do as he asks. He opens the box to reveal a small laptop, which he switches on then types in a code. A screen appears.

'This blue dot is us.' He points to the screen. 'We need to drive to the next blue dot, here. Keep your eyes on the road and the direction of the dot. Understand?'

'Yes.' *No.* I don't understand. I want to be at home, making French toast, not here with explosives and dead bodies.

Seconds later the car is open. I quickly scramble in and slide into the driver's seat. Luke follows me. He has a small electrical device with a digital display and watches it closely.

'Luke! Oh my God, someone's coming – actually, there's more than one.' Seconds pass and he pushes the start button on the dashboard. The engine roars.

'Go, go, go!' There is no time to hesitate – men are running towards us with guns.

I slam the car into gear and drive. I've never driven a four-by-four. Luke places the laptop in my view and climbs into the back.

'Remember – keep your eyes on the road, and the dot.'

'This looks like the way I came in yesterday – there are some massive gates ahead.'

'They're open.'

'Are you sure?'

'Yes.' His eyes meet mine in the rear-view mirror. 'Trust me.'

I do trust him – with my life.

Next, Luke kicks the rear window to break it. There are other cars following us. Shit! We approach the gates, which – luckily – are open. More shocking are the dead bodies surrounding the entrance.

'Floor it, baby. Keep your foot down until I tell you otherwise.'

Suddenly, there is gunfire. I glance in the rear-view mirror at the three cars, which are gaining on us.

'Kate, take your foot off the accelerator.'

'What?'

'Just do it. I need to get closer to set off the detonator.'

'OK.' *No.*

I see in the mirror that he is holding another device. Is it a mobile phone?

'One, two, three.' He pauses as we slow. 'OK, floor it.'

The explosion takes out the first vehicle. The noise is deafening. I automatically look into the mirror. Flames and smoke cloud the sky, and pieces of debris float in the air.

'Well done; there are two left.'

My eyes flit between the mirror and the two remaining vehicles. I try my hardest to sustain my speed and keep control of the car.

'Do you know where we're going?' I ask.

'Yes. Keep your eye on the dot. Is the gap closing?'

'I have problems with technology – you, of all people, should know that.'

'Yes, you do.' I can hear a small smile in his voice. 'OK. Listen, I'm going to take out the last two vehicles together.'

'I can't believe you kept this side of your life a secret. I know you like to withhold information, but this is seriously keeping me out of the loop.'

I catch his stern reflection in the rear-view mirror.

'You're questioning *me* about honesty?'

'Looks like we have some serious discussions ahead of us.'

'I have to keep you alive first.' He continues to fire out of the rear window. How much longer is this going to continue? I can't take much more.

'OK, on my count, drop a gear then floor it. Ready?'

'Ready.' My shoulders hunch.

'One, two three, drop and floor it.'

He repeats the same procedure as he did moments ago. The two remaining vehicles disintegrate. Jesus, the noise is deafening. The aftershock causes me to tremble. Is it shock or adrenaline? Maybe both. Luke joins me in the front, lifting up the black box to register where we are.

'Not far to go – carry on.'

Tears roll down my cheeks.

Luke places his hand on my hair. 'Shh, it's OK – we're nearly at the safety point.'

Safety point? I don't understand what is going on. I use my hand to wipe my face.

'You've done well. Your driving skills are moderately satisfactory.'

He looks at me, knowing he can make me smile. 'I know you've had the wind knocked out of you, but I'm here now – this is my problem too.'

I nod. I'm too weak to speak.

Luke taps his ear and speaks. 'Sutton. In five. Over.'

'Kate, slow down.'

From nowhere, two motorbikes appear.

'Shit. Luke?'

'They're here for us. Stop the car.'

I stop the car, and Luke presses the stop button on the dashboard. I remain seated, waiting for my next set of instructions. Luke gets out of the car, and goes to open my door.

'Let's go.'

He holds his hand out for me.

The men remove their helmets and move towards us.

'Kate, I would like to introduce you to James Sullivan and Scott Parker.'

'Hi.' They look identical to Luke, with matching outfits and guns. They are tall and well-built. The blond man, James Sullivan, looks rugged, but he has a nice smile. Scott Parker's features are hard, although his chocolate skin and shaved head are certainly striking.

'I took out three vehicles. Any sign here?' Luke asks.

'No. Both locations are clear.'

'Good.' Luke looks at me. 'Ever been on the back of a

bike?' He arches his brow and flashes his best Sutton killer smile.

'Nope. Never wanted to.'

'It must be your lucky day. Do you have a jacket in your bag?'

I nod.

'Put it on.'

Still feeling numb, I grab my jacket and slip it on without question.

James Sullivan passes me a helmet.

'Allow me.' Luke slides the helmet over my head, then does the same for himself. 'Can you hear me?'

His raspy, sexy voice echoes in my ears. 'Yes.'

Luke passes Scott Parker his rucksack, while James Sullivan walks towards the vehicle we arrived in. I watch him plant the same green putty. I'm guessing he's going to destroy the evidence.

Luke straddles the bike. He helps me to climb on behind him. James and Scott share the other bike. The engines roar as we head off. Within a few seconds, there is another explosion.

'Kate, hold on – this will be rough.' Luke talks to me through his mic.

'OK.'

I grip him tightly. The bike hits a rough piece of road and almost throws me off. Luke reaches behind him to steady me. 'Jesus, hold on – these roads are bad.'

Before long the surface changes. The bikes glide across a field towards a farmhouse. Next to the house sits a metal hut, with two large doors that open and automatically close behind us as we ride inside. A dark corridor lights up in front of us as we descend towards another set of doors, which silently open. We ride directly into a large room. *What is this place?* I wonder.

Luke stops the bike and climbs off. He removes his helmet and passes it to a man dressed in military clothing, then removes mine and lifts me off the bike.

Next he takes my hand and leads me to a room where James Sullivan and Scott Parker are waiting. I sit down.

A young man enters the room. 'Sir.' He looks at Luke.

'I need the medical and drug-testing kit, strong coffee and some food.'

'Yes sir.' The young man exits. I look across at Luke, puzzled. This must be his dream job – commanding people.

'Now then, Kate, you gave Sutton quite a fright.' James looks at Luke. 'I don't think many people would have put themselves in this sort of danger – rather brave of you.' He extends his hand. 'Let me officially introduce myself. I'm James.'

I shake his hand. 'Hi.'

'Brave is not the word I would use.' Luke glares at James.

Scott nods, using his two fingers to salute me.

I remove my jacket and look around the room, which is filled with computers. 'What is this place? Some kind of secret army hideout?' This is definitely a military operation. Luke Sutton, what is going on?

James laughs. 'It's no concern of yours.'

'Oh.' *Well, that told me!*

'Luckily for you, we were not far away… That's all you need to know,' James says.

The young man returns. Luke takes the medical kit and wraps the blood pressure cuff around my arm. It tightens.

'Still low – the same as earlier.' He slides his hands into a pair of white medical gloves. He then places a tourniquet around my other bicep and opens a container, taking out a needle.

'What are you doing?'

'I need a blood sample.'

'I hate needles.'

Parker looks to Sullivan and sniggers. I'm not in the mood to be ridiculed. 'Is this really necessary? I think you're being a little over-cautious – as usual.' I can't help but feel hostile.

'If you hadn't put yourself at risk, then I wouldn't need to take blood.'

'Fine!'

He takes some blood and places it in various vials.

'You need to use the bathroom.' Luke places a plastic pot in front of me.

What? 'No, thank you.' I know what he wants me to do.

Luke lowers his gaze to meet mine. 'I'm not bloody asking you; I'm telling you.'

'I don't take orders.'

Furiously, he points at my face. 'Kate, I'm warning you – do not fucking push me after the stunt you just pulled.'

'Stunt! Oh my God, Luke – actually, who the bloody hell are you? Some things don't lie, like your bloody temper. Tell me, are you going to shove something up my arse?'

Oh fuck! I have no filter. Can I blame the drugs? I have no time to think: Luke picks me up and puts me over his shoulder. 'Put me down!'

Luke grabs the pot. I try to move, which is pointless; he is far too strong for me.

'No. Stop moving.'

We arrive at a bathroom. Luke places my feet firmly on the floor and closes the door behind us.

'Excuse me!' I place my hands on my hips. 'I think I can manage to go to the toilet alone.'

'You can't be trusted to go anywhere on your own.'

'Is that so? I'm here because I thought I was doing the right thing.'

'No – all you've done is put yourself in a lot of danger.'

Luke undoes my jeans. 'I need a sample to test the drugs in your system – it's that simple. You may need some drugs to counteract what you've been given.'

'Fine. Turn around.' I scowl. 'Luke, this is embarrassing.'

'Kate, I know your body inside out. Fuck, I've had my mouth on you enough times. Watching you piss in a pot is immaterial.'

'Not for me. How can you be so matter-of-fact?'

He laughs. 'Because I love you.' He pulls me to him and kisses me hard. My arms lock around his neck, and he cups the base of my arse. He pulls away. 'Now piss in the pot.'

'Oh, so romantic.' I shake my head. 'Fine, turn around.' Within a few seconds the deed is completed. 'Finished.' I pass Luke the pot.

'Wasn't so bad, was it?' He smiles, enjoying my embarrassment.

We return to the room with my pot of piss. I sit down and watch Luke test the sample.

'Some form of Flunitrazepam – my guess is half a milligram, as you're fairly steady on your feet.'

'What's that?'

'Have you heard of Rohypnol, Kate?' James says.

I feel the colour drain from my face. 'That's the date-rape drug! I don't understand – it can't be Ivor.' Feeling incredibly vulnerable, I wrap my arms around my torso.

'It's also a sedative, like a benzodiazepine.' Parker says.

'So, would I remember if they did anything to me?'

Sullivan looks across at Luke and then at me.

'Your memory would be sketchy. Do you think anything happened?'

I shake my head. 'I don't think so. I'm still wearing the same clothes. I just remember my body feeling heavy, like I was drunk. But I feel OK, just tired.'

'I think it was to prevent you from running away.'

I understand James Sullivan is trying to relax Luke and ease my mind.

Parker pulls his chair round to face me. 'I need to debrief you, ask you some questions. Sutton has filled us in with some of the details regarding your Russian parents. Did your father say anything to you – tell you where he was going, give you any information at all?'

'First of all, he's not my father.'

'He is your biological father,' Parker says.

'They say any prick can make a baby, but it takes a real man to be a father. Therefore, if you're referring to the arsehole who may have tied me up – no, he didn't say where he was going.'

Parker sits back in his chair. 'Bloody hell, Sutton, you've got your work cut out for you.'

'Tell me about it.' Luke raises his brows.

'Look, for what it's worth I don't think Ivor tied me up. I can't explain why. Anyway, he said he was going to leave early and I wouldn't see him again.' Feeling awkward, I fidget in the chair. 'He told me I would leave at first light. I had to input a code to transfer the money across – is that useful?' The men look at me. 'I think I can remember it.'

'Here, write it down.' Sullivan passes me a notepad and pen.

'Fine, give me a minute.' I make a start. 'Russian Victoria sponge cake.' Luke smiles. 'Here goes: sugar 30g, flour 90g, butter 100g, eggs 24 and baking powder 189 teaspoons. There you go. I wouldn't use these quantities – your cake will be shit.'

Luke places his hands on either side of my face, allowing his lips to show his appreciation.

'What can I say? My girlfriend loves to cook.' He passes me a coffee and a sandwich.

Parker sits at his desk and inputs the code. 'There's nothing in the account – it's empty.'

'Ivor mentioned holdings and stocks – something like that. I didn't really understand.' I take another bite of the sandwich as the men watch me.

'Did he say anything else?' Parker asks.

I shake my head. 'No, other than he thought my mother was murdered. Apparently, he was set up and has some long-standing feuds with another family. I asked him about payback for his wife – my mum. He said he's dealt with some, and he needs proof for others.'

The three men remain silent.

'Do you know him? He did seem quite nice. I know he might have tied me up, but his eyes were sad. I felt sorry for him.' I look down at my hands, confused at my feelings towards a man I don't know. 'He reminded me of you,

Luke, strong and controlling, but I'm sure he wanted to protect me. He told me he liked the look of you.'

'Kate, you've just compared me to the leader of one of Russia's biggest corrupt families.'

I nearly spit my coffee out. 'What? Ivor?'

I know Christina said the family was corrupt, and I admit the situation was scary, but I didn't fear Ivor.

'Sullivan said they've been collecting intel on him for a few years.' Luke moves next to me.

'Years? Did you work here?'

'Kate, drop it.' He looks exhausted. I reach for his cheek.

'You have to let me in, Luke. You can't bring me to a place like… whatever this place is, and not give me something back.'

'Sharing is not always an option, Kate.' Parker offers me his point of view.

I meet his glare. 'Neither is lying to me. I tell you what, just take me back to Ivor's house. I'll find my own way home.'

'Enough – this isn't the time or the place, Kate.' Luke's dark eyes lock on mine, and for a split second we are alone. Today is about more than him rescuing me; this is his past saving me, a past he's kept from me. Why?

He sits back in his chair, breaking our connection. 'What do you mean, he liked the look of me?' Luke asks, moving next to me.

'It was a bit creepy. He had a room that was filled with pictures of me, from when I was really young to now – and there were pictures of you.'

'Fuck.' Luke stands and rubs his chin, taking in the information. 'OK – my gut instinct, this was already a war

43

zone before we arrived. But we need to do a clean sweep. There's no way these pictures can circulate.'

'A clean sweep?' I gauge all the men. 'You mean, blow it up?'

'I agree. Kate, it's for your safety.' Parker tries to justify himself.

I stand. 'No – no way. You can't do that. The house is old and historical. If Ivor is my father, which seems likely, then you can't do that – the house is full of paintings and… history.' I look at Luke. 'Suppose one day in the future – way, way in the future – we had children, then I would want them to know about their ancestors. I know he might be shady, but he did seem to care about me.'

Sullivan looks at Luke. 'We can do a manual sweep. It's your call, Sutton.'

'Luke, please don't damage that house – it's not ours.'

'Fine. Send in the team, collect every scrap of photo evidence. I want a thorough cleanse of the entire house, outbuildings – the entire estate.'

'I'll go and get the team ready.' Parker leaves the office.

I walk over to Luke, slip my arms around his waist and place my head on his chest. His strong arms tighten around me as he lowers his face to my hair.

'When can we go home?' I look up at him.

He reaches down and gently kisses my lips. 'Soon, baby.'

Sullivan stands up.

'I'll go and check the plane's status.'

At last we are alone in the office.

'This has been the worst nine hours of my life. I never want to go through that again.'

I look up at his face. 'I'm sorry. I was scared about what might happen to everyone, including you.'

'You walked into a war zone with no thought of your own safety. Never do that again!'

'Never.' I sigh. 'Luke, I don't know what to do. Harry and I are adopted, and our real mum is dead – murdered. You're not who I thought you were…' I pause. 'Ivor is not Harry's dad – that's why the trust fund was left to me. Everything's changed. I'm so confused.'

Luke releases his hold on me and sits down, pulling me into his lap. 'You assumed Ivor was Harry's father?'

'We both did. Ivor thinks that Dad had an affair with Katenka.'

Luke's brows shoot up.

'I know! This is a bloody mess. I can't take much more… my head is going to explode.'

'We'll sort it out – together.'

I lean my head on his chest. 'What about us? I can't pretend I didn't see you break—' I swallow my words.

'It kills me that you know.'

'Weirdly, I can see you here, at a place like this.' His need for control starts to make sense; Luke Sutton was built for this. 'I don't understand why you haven't told me.' I look up at him and pull his face towards me.

'This isn't right… You don't belong here, Kate.'

'Your past is your past.' *His past involved killing people.* He knows this isn't over; I need more than his limited explanation, but I am too exhausted for a fight.

After a while we leave the hidden underground bunker. I follow Luke closely, his hand gripped firmly around mine. I have no intention of letting him go. I inhale the morning air and squint at the blinding sunshine. We continue to walk past the farmhouse. To the rear of the property is a flat field where I see a small transport plane. Definitely not a private jet – quite the opposite.

Sullivan places his hand on Luke's shoulder. 'I'll be in touch with the lab results.' He turns to me. 'Any chance of staying out of trouble? Sutton's getting too old for this shit.'

'I'll try.' I reach up and give him a kiss. I turn to Parker and plant a kiss on his cheek too. 'Thank you.'

'No problem.' Parker is unmoved. 'Sutton, have a safe flight. All paperwork from the sweep will be delivered as soon as we have it.'

Luke gives both the guys a manly hug. Their history is plain to see: they seem to have the tight bonds of true friendship. 'I'll let you know when we arrive in London.'

We climb the steps to the plane. Inside, it is basic.

I turn to Luke. 'Not your usual five-star mode of transport.'

He laughs. 'I assume you prefer my jet.'

'Yes. I bet there's no office on board?'

'No.' He laughs.

Four men join us. They look fairly young. I wonder if Luke was part of a team like this. Is that how he came to know so much about blowing up cars, and killing people?

It's incredibly loud inside. I feel exhausted, though, and I don't think any amount of noise can keep my eyes from closing. I rest my head against my seat, while gripping Luke's hand.

'Kate… Kate… wake up.'

My eyes open.

46

'We're nearly home.'

'Good.' I yawn.

'Stand up.'

I look at Luke, half asleep.

'Kate, stand up.'

I do as I'm told. Luke bends down and lifts my legs, one at a time, sliding them into a kind of harness. He does the same with my arms, then tightens the straps.

I may be sleepy and drugged but...

'Luke!'

He pulls my face to his and gives me a kiss. 'Do you trust me?'

'Yeah... But, this is a harness, right?'

'Yes.'

'So that means...' Before I have a chance to finish, Luke lowers goggles over my eyes. 'Holy fuck! Luke, no!' I shout at him, begging him to understand what he's asking of me.

He lowers goggles over his eyes too.

'Ever jumped out of a plane, baby?'

'No, and I don't want to... Luke, I can't jump, are you shitting me?'

'No, I'm not shitting you, and yes, we are going to jump – together. Like I said, do you trust me?' He looks at me, waiting for a response. After all these weeks, he's finally found a way to silence me. 'We illegally entered Russia, so we have to return to England undetected too.'

Before I have time to think, Luke connects my harness to his chest. This can't be happening. I have no desire to jump out of a plane – and never will. From the corner of my eye, I notice the other men on the plane signalling for Luke.

'My bag,' I shout.

'Sullivan will bring it with him to London.'

'I'm scared.'

'I've got you.'

The door at the side of the plane opens. Luke begins to walk us to the edge. My heels dig into the metal floor, leaving Luke no choice: he picks me up and carries me to the edge of the plane. I glance at the young soldier counting us down. Holy shit, I can't look.

He jumps and we begin to free-fall. The intense pressure feels amazing, and truly terrifying, at the same time.

'You're doing well,' Luke shouts.

Silence. I can't speak; I can just about breathe.

We continue to free-fall: just the two of us gliding in the air, no guns or explosions. My eyes open wide, looking at the view. The feeling is frightening, and breath-taking. Still, I was not put on this earth to evade hostile forces and jump from planes...

Then Luke reaches up and pulls a cord. The parachute opens.

'Are you still with me?'

'Just about.'

'Amazing feeling.'

'I guess... No, I don't want to do it again.'

Very quickly, the ground grows closer.

'Kate, lift your legs when I tell you.'

'OK.'

The ground is only metres away.

'Kate, lift them now.'

I do as he asks. As we reach the grass, Luke breaks our fall. His back hits the ground and I land on top of him.

My entire body relaxes, and relief washes over me. Luke pushes me up to a sitting position and unclasps our harnesses. Within minutes he has removed his own harness and goggles, leaving the parachute discarded on the ground. He stands and helps me to join him, unclipping my harness.

He pulls me to him by my jacket and kisses me with more passion than ever before. A kiss of life!

'You did well, baby.' Holding my face in his hands, he reads my eyes. 'Not something you want to repeat?'

I shake my head. His lips cover mine again, offering me tenderness.

We gaze across the field towards the sound of a car. From the distance I recognise Luke's black Range Rover – and his driver. Within seconds it draws up and Max comes running towards us. I can't help but smile as he sidesteps Luke and pulls me into his arms.

'If you ever do anything like that again… You don't want to know what I'll do to you.' He pulls away to see for himself that I'm safe and well. 'Kate Harper, you're a pain in the fucking arse. Christ, I knew you were up to no good… You and your lunatic mate – Kiki.'

'I'm sorry, I had to go… I didn't mean to lie.'

'Jesus, Kate, you've aged me another ten years.'

'What about me?' Luke stands with open arms.

'You do this shit all the time, Sutton. This girl is…'

Alive. I'm alive.

Before long, Max weaves through the rat runs of London. The closer to South Kensington we get, the calmer I feel. Luke says that Mum and Harry, along with Kiki, Molly and Barney, my three closest friends, are staying at his house. Controlling or caring? Either way, he has kept them safe.

The large gates open to Luke's impressive home – which I have nicknamed the palace – and the Range Rover stops outside the large black door. I step out with Luke at my side. Luke's home is now my home. God, I love it here. He squeezes my fingers. I turn to him.

'Are you ready to face everyone?'

'No – listen, I just wanted to say, I appreciate what you've done for me.'

Before he can speak, I press a kiss to his lips. 'I don't know what to say to Mum. She lied to us our whole lives…' I shake my head.

Luke pulls me close. 'She loves you both.'

I raise my head and look for strength in his dark eyes.

'I love you more than anything in the world.'

'I'm here for you.'

Luke inputs the security code and the large black door opens.

I walk through to the kitchen, and conversation stops dead. I glance at everyone. Mum and Harry look tired and emotionally drained. Standing to the side is Kiki, using Barney for support. Molly leans against the worktop, her hand resting across her stomach, protecting her baby. The sight is too overwhelming.

As I turn my head, I meet Aunt Christina's eyes – the woman who sold the photos of me to Ivor.

3

My eyes lock on Christina's. 'We need to talk.'

Mum comes bounding towards me. 'Kate.' She places her hands either side of my face as tears roll down her cheeks.

I gaze across to Harry, who nods, confirming that Mum knows exactly what went down yesterday.

'I'm fine, Mum, but I need a minute with Christina.' She looks empty and sad; I guess her world has been crushed too. I place a kiss on her cheek. 'Give me two minutes and then we can chat, OK?'

'OK, darling.' Mum looks at Harry, a little confused.

Christina follows me towards the grey lounge.

'You know why I'm pissed off, so don't stand there and act bloody clueless.'

'Kate.' Her face falls.

'How much did he pay you? I hope it was worth it.'

'Kate, it wasn't like that.' Christina's emotions grow as she realises I know about her deal with the devil – Ivor.

Luke moves to my side, taking my hand. 'What's going on?'

I look at Luke. 'The photos in the creepy room – she sold them to Ivor.' I take a deep breath. 'Obviously, It's been going on for years.'

'You don't understand… I gave him the photos so he wouldn't contact you.' She moves closer, bridging the distance between us.

'OK, so what about the money? Or is that in a bank somewhere?'

Christina looks away.

'No, of course it's not. Why does money fuck with everyone's moral compass? Did you really feel the need to sell out your own brother? I hope for your sake it was worth it.' I shake my head. 'You need to go. I can't even look at you.'

'Kate – I'm sorry.' Her eyes fill with tears and regret.

'I suggest you leave before I remove you myself.'

'Kate! That's enough,' Luke commands.

'Don't defend her! I've had the worst twenty-four hours of my life. Sorry, but I'm not in the mood for forgiveness. Luke can show you out.'

I go back to the kitchen. I can hear Luke talking, then the door closing. Thank God.

In the kitchen, everyone swarms round me. 'Sorry, I needed to ask Christina about… some paperwork.' That's all I can think of.

Mum takes my hand and ushers me to the sofa.

'Let me look at you.' Tears roll down her cheeks. 'I'm so sorry, darling.'

My arms lock around her. 'Everything should be fine now.' I release her and take her hands. 'Dad – Luke said he's stable.'

'Yes, he is. But it's not fine. I didn't know much about your… your real dad… Katenka – your…' Her words trail off. 'Sorry. It's so painful to watch you girls go through this; I never thought this day would come. Your birth mum said your father would never contact us or you, and until last night I believed that.'

'He's gone. It's just us.'

'I don't understand. Harry said there was money and—'

'The money was never mine. Like I said, he doesn't want me – us. He's not part of our lives.'

'But you'll both want to see him.' Mum's voice is barely a whisper. 'Your… real mum.' She tries to find the right words. My real mum is dead.

I shake my head. 'Don't, Mum. I can't think straight. Our lives aren't what we thought they were.'

Ashamed, Mum bows her head.

'You're still our mum, that will never change.' I look at Harry for solidarity.

She sits next to Mum.

'Let's take it slowly,' Harry says. 'I'm struggling to process it all.'

'All I can think about is Dad lying in hospital. Honestly, my head is about to burst, Mum.'

'I know, darling. He idolises you both.'

Tears roll down my cheeks. 'I'm so angry right now…'

Mum hopelessly looks at me. 'How can I make this better? Ask me anything and I will answer the best I can.'

I rub my forehead, trying to ease the tension. 'I've run out of questions.'

'We need to sit and talk openly. I need to know if you

were ever going to tell us,' Harry says. 'Not today... but when we all feel up to it.'

I shake my head. 'Never' is the only word racing through my head.

'We lied to you,' Mum confesses. 'I need you to understand we never meant to hurt you; it was part of the...' Tears roll down her cheeks.

'You had your reasons.' My words are to ease her pain, not mine. Can I forgive them for lying? 'Honestly, I can't believe what's happened. I need some time to figure out who I am.'

'Kate, you mustn't say that.'

'She's right, Mum, I feel odd too.' Harry says.

'Oh God, this will kill Dad. He'll never forgive himself that you've found out. He promised...' Once again her words trail off.

'He's too fragile to talk to him about all this at the moment. Harry's right; we need time.'

Mum nods. 'Kate... Harry.' She holds our hands. 'I can't lose you both; it would...' Her tears are filled with the fear of losing her children, the children she longed for all those years ago.

I break free and stroke her face. 'You'll never lose us.' I lovingly kiss her cheek. Yet I can't stop thinking of Ivor. Why? He doesn't deserve my head space.

Luke stands at the doorway and points to his watch. For once he has a point – I am exhausted. He disappears into the office with Max.

'Let's concentrate on getting Dad better and on his feet. In time we will talk about this – and our...' I look at Harry. 'The adoption.' I need to cry. I have to be alone.

'You're right. Dad needs to mend and then we can start to put together our family.' Her eyes are full of sadness. I can't rescue her; I want to run away and forget about the last twenty-four hours.

Barney has been there, silent, all along. He comes to my side. 'What's going on with lover boy? He looks like an extra from *Mission Impossible*.'

I can't help but smile.

'I don't even know where to start. Come over next week.'

'You got it, babe.' He kisses me on the cheek.

'Hey, you.' Kiki sits on the edge of the coffee table in front of me. 'Jesus, Kate... I can't believe you went.' To hear her voice again is a relief.

'Me neither.' I take her hands. 'I can't imagine what Luke said to you – I'm sorry.'

'Nothing I can't handle; that's what best friends are for... He knew something wasn't right, like he sensed you weren't with us.'

'Yes, that'll be his security team. They're there to sense my every move.' I lovingly stroke my watch.

'What are you talking about?'

'Let's save the love story for another day – my brain is fried.'

'OK. What about everything else?' I know she's inquiring about Ivor.

'Honestly, I don't know. Lunch this week for a catch-up?'

I stand and walk over to the kitchen island. From here I watch everyone. Thankfully Harry has the support of Molly, her pregnant best friend. Mum is comforted by Luke's housekeeper Rosie, the most adorable woman I know. Poor Jerry, Rosie's husband – my little piece of Ireland – is unsure about Barney and his over-the-top gayness. I sigh with relief that they are all safe. Despite the last few hours, life in the palace remains the same. How can it, though?

I feel like lightening the mood around here, and the only weapon for the job is food.

'Anyone hungry?'

The next thing I know, everything goes dark. Then I hear, 'Kate, Kate.' I'm lying on the sofa.

'Max, get my medical kit.' Luke studies me. 'Does anything hurt?'

'No,' I manage to say, although I feel woozy.

Max returns with the bag.

'Check my email for the lab results. If they're not there, get hold of Sullivan and find out where they are.'

The room is silent. All eyes are on the man dressed in black playing doctor. He takes my blood pressure first, followed by my temperature and oxygen levels.

'Keep still,' Luke orders.

'Is she OK?' Harry asks.

Luke stands and runs his hand along his jawline, obviously feeling troubled about sharing too much information.

'I found Kate in a house in Russia… She had been drugged.'

Horror sweeps across Mum's face, and I'm grateful he has refrained from saying how he found me.

'Fuck!' Barney pushes his hands through his hair, panicked.

'She still has the sedative in her system.'

'I don't understand why.' Mum moves closer to me. 'Why would anyone do that? I can't take much more, what with Dad in hospital, you drugged... I think we should call the police. What about the officer who came to see us in hospital?'

'We can't do that, Susan. Kate and I both entered Russia illegally. I'm taking care of the situation. You have to trust me. Can you do that for Kate?'

'But someone needs to tell the police in Russia, or wherever the hell she was, that she was kept against her will. Luke, this is wrong.'

Luke moves closer to Mum.

'I agree with you, but it isn't quite that simple. Ivor – Kate's biological father – might have been responsible, and he is nowhere to be found. I have friends who are experts in finding people. The main thing is she's here with us and we're all safe.'

I try to sit up. 'I'm fine.'

'No, you're not fine, you should be in bed resting after what you've been through. Luke, tell her.'

Oh great, give my control freak boyfriend more ammo.

'I think we should give Kate some space,' Kiki says.

'Kiki's right – Kate needs time to process the last twenty-four hours. You all do. It's safe for you to return home, but be vigilant and call me if something doesn't feel right, OK?'

For the first time, we're alone. Luke takes my hand and walks me to the bathroom. My tears begin to fall as I feel my weary body flagging.

'Hey.' Luke pulls me into his arms.

'I was so scared.'

He looks at me. 'I'm pissed off at you, but fuck me, Kate, your strength has left me floored.'

'Me? You have serious explaining to do.'

'Later.'

'Don't sidestep me. Christ, Luke.' I take his hand and place it over my heart. 'You killed someone in front of me... You didn't even blink.'

His breathing alters, and his eyes close.

'We can talk once you've rested.'

'You can't back out of this – I need some answers.'

There are no more words, just my lips greedily taking what I need from him. No matter what I have witnessed, I seem to need him more than ever. Luke pulls away, taking my face in his hands.

'Jesus. I want to be inside you more than you know. But you need to rest. The shock will hit you... Trust me, I know what I'm talking about.'

I look down, feeling rejected. I turn to walk away. Luke pulls me into his arms and holds me tightly.

'Argh.' An intense pain in my ribs bites me.

'The jump may have hurt you – that's another reason you should be resting.'

I shake my head. 'You can't wrap me in cotton wool. I need to breathe... I need *you* – that's when I feel safe.'

'I can't argue with that. At least if you're under me I know where you are. I love you.'

'I love you too.'

'Shower, food and bed,' he commands.

Luke turns the shower on and then removes my Converse, followed by my socks, jeans and T-shirt.

As he removes my bra a small piece of paper falls to the floor. It slipped my mind that Fiona gave it to me – Christ, it was only yesterday morning at Pete's bar, and yet it feels like a lifetime ago. It's a bonus to have a friend like Fiona who's from the same country as my biological father!

Luke picks it up. 'Did you have an offer while in Russia?'

'No, I bloody didn't. If you must know, Fiona gave me the name and address of her Russian friend. She said he owed her a few favours and I could call if things went tits up.'

'Undoubtedly things did, but why put it in your bra?'

'I thought if I needed help, the chances are I'd be on the run, so it seemed like the safest place.'

'Lucky you, having a Russian friend.'

'Says you, who had friends in a secret hideout in Russia.'

Luke laughs. 'What am I going to do with you? As for your plan, which may I remind you did go tits up,' his hands move over my bare breasts – not fair and stop teasing. 'Unfortunately, the address was no use to you because you were tied up.'

'You've done this before, but I'm new to this. Once again, you don't play fair – and if I'm not allowed to have you, then stop fingering my tits.'

After my shower, I lie on the sofa in Luke's office. He makes me feel safer than anyone else in the world. I can hear him working, and the fire is keeping me warm. The flickering flames remind me of the night in Ivor's house. Why did he do this? Why did he leave? Silently, tears roll down my cheeks.

'I thought you were quiet.' Luke lowers himself to the sofa. 'Talk to me.'

I sit upright. Luke slides in close to me.

'Ivor,' I say.

'Do you want him in your life?'

I nod.

'Honestly, Kate, I'm not sure that is the safest option.'

'Maybe not, but when I saw him I could see the pain in his eyes. Losing his wife and his… me.' Tears trickle down my cheeks. 'It makes no difference how I feel: he told me he couldn't be part of my life, apparently for my own safety.'

Luke pulls me closer.

'Rejection is shit,' I say.

'Maybe it's not rejection; maybe he's just putting the safety of his daughter before his own needs, the same way Katenka did.'

'My head is all over the place. I'm not who I thought I was. Who am I, Luke? I don't even know where I belong any more.'

He turns my head to look at him. 'You're still the same person you were twenty-four hours ago. The very same woman I want to lock away in a tower. Obviously, for my own personal use.'

I can't help but smile. 'Obviously.' I move closer. 'I've decided not tell Harry that Katenka may have been murdered. Besides, I have no proof.'

'I agree, there's no need to distress her over a theory we can't back up. A theory that has come from your estranged father.'

'It could be true – seriously, I have no idea what's real any more.' My hands skim his chiselled face; even now he takes my breath away.

'This is real.' He lowers his lips to mine.

'James and Scott – they looked familiar… I'm sure I would have remembered two good-looking men at the palace.'

'Is that so?' He smirks and takes my hand, brushing my knuckles against his lips. 'Toulouse – the same night you were spying on me.'

I laugh. He did catch me red-handed watching him at the club that night. If a fight hadn't broken out behind me, he would never have known!

'I wasn't spying! I remember seeing you with some men. It makes sense now… Is this why you donate so much money to Help the Heroes?'

'They deserve it and I can afford it.'

'OK. So let's talk about the herd of elephants in the room. Your little secret, which is anything but small. Luke, you have to let me in.'

'No.'

'No!' I nudge his shoulder. 'You really think that you can give me a no? I deserve more than that.'

'Kate… We worked together for a number of years, they stayed, and I left to start Sutton Global.' He shrugs.

'OK – when did you work with them? That building you took me to, is that where you worked? I can see you there, all commanding and telling people what to do.'

'Commanding!'

'It's in your DNA, Luke, believe me!'

'I started to go off the rails in my teens, and Max took me somewhere that turned my life around. I went AWOL for a few years and didn't see my family. That sums up my life – at least, the parts you're allowed to know about. As for the building, the less you know the better.'

'I knew there was something between you and Max – he really cares about you.'

'We've known each other for a very long time. The rest is history. I can't discuss it with you.'

'Can't or won't?'

'Both,' he bites.

'Confidential? What do you mean? Like the SAS?'

'Something like that, so please don't ask.'

'OK. So you can't tell me for whatever reason, but holy fucking hell, this is some serious fucked-up shit!'

Luke grins. 'I see Russia hasn't affected your mouth.' He takes a deep breath. 'You saw what I was involved in; I never wanted you to find out.'

'Killing people!'

'Kate, I've only killed people when following orders.'

'What, like on an order from the government? So does that make it OK?'

'You have no idea what you're talking about,' he says.

'That's because you won't tell me.'

'Stop provoking me into submission; it won't work. Jesus, if what you saw affects us, then…'

I straddle his lap.

'Looking for you was the longest mission I've ever had.'

'I do have a question, an army question.'

'Kate… No more.'

'Where were James and Scott? I mean, they didn't come with you to Ivor's house. Wasn't it a bit risky on your own?'

'Firstly, no more means shut the fuck up.'

'Oi. You can't say that.'

'I can, and secondly it was my choice: they were waiting

if I needed them. Technically it was a low-risk mission, and going in undetected was by far the best course.'

'I was low-risk?'

'Kate Harper – low-risk? Not you – the mission was planned: they were watching various points of interest, perimeters etcetera. But entering the house solo was a calculated decision; my choice.'

'I guess you know what you're doing. So, your body… I mean, you don't have any scars… You must have dodged some bullets in your time, but you don't even have a scratch. Have you ever been tortured?'

'Do I need a gag? Baby, don't push me into a corner. No more means no more.'

I need to change the subject: dead bodies and lies are weighing heavy on my head and heart.

'As I see it, you have a choice.' I draw my lips inward.

Luke laughs. 'No baby, you have a choice. What would you like to eat? You are not moving off this sofa and I can only cook sandwiches! What takeaway would you like?'

'Soup.'

'Soup? You need more than soup.'

'I haven't finished! Vegetable soup, fillet steak with mushrooms and rocket salad… Also my birthday cake, if there's any left.'

'Being hungry is a good sign.'

'Not for food.' I lean forward and kiss him, locking my arms around his neck.

As always, his body responds to my touch, but he tries to pull away. No. I need more. My hips begin to move against his erection. Luke holds me still.

'Baby… This kills me.' He strokes my hair. 'You're exhausted. This is not the right time, trust me. I need to take your blood pressure again.'

'Jesus, Luke, I'm fine! I need some normality and, bizarrely, that's you!'

'She's back… My Kate and her razor-sharp tongue.'

The sunlight filters through the shutters. I unpeel my face from the duvet to find I'm in the middle of Luke's huge bed doing an impression of a starfish – alone. I move my watch closer. Shit! It's almost midday.

Standing at the bathroom sink, my reflection shocks me. Holy shit! I need a full makeover. If this continues Luke will send me back to Russia. I splash some water on my face and brush my teeth. My long blonde hair is wild – as usual, Roller Girl, my 70s alter ego, waves from the mirror. I pull my hair back into a ponytail.

I make my way downstairs. Two voices echo in the hallway. I walk into the office. Luke and James Sullivan are there.

'Morning.' Luke flashes his best Sutton smile, hitting me hard – not my groin but my heart.

I join them at the board table.

'Morning, hi James.' I stand behind Luke and put my arms around his neck. 'I can't believe it's midday – you should have woken me.'

'You needed to rest. I told you the drugs would make you sleep.'

I kiss the top of his head. 'I guess.'

'Sullivan has returned your bag and the boxes of pictures from Ivor's house. Also your blood test results have come back clear.'

Boxes! I guess there were a lot – this doesn't feel real.

Luke moves his arms. I pull down the hem of Luke's T-shirt, which I'm wearing as nightwear, then sit on his lap. 'Any sign of Ivor, then?'

'No.' James shakes his head. 'But we found a flight plan to the Cayman Islands.'

'Leaving me in the crap while he enjoys the sunshine… What can I say? True father material.'

'There's no sign of the money.'

'I don't want it, anyway… Are you hunting him for any reason?' I need to know if he is a threat or just a person of interest.

'Not really. We always keep an on eye on past cases. At the moment, his businesses are all above board, and have been for some years.'

'How creepy was that room with the photos? Bloody odd.'

'I've seen worse.' James smiles.

'I can imagine. OK, so what now? Am I at risk, I mean from Ivor? Although I don't think he would hurt me, he could have done at any point.'

Luke holds me tightly.

'I can't answer that. We don't know what information they have on you. We do believe this was part of the reason you and Malcolm were attacked. There is nothing connecting you to Ivor on paper – our intel couldn't trace you. It seemed that you disappeared along with your mother. Incidentally, Ivor was right: her official cause of death was suicide.' James takes an envelope and slides it across the table. 'This is her post-mortem report.'

My body almost freezes. It's as though she's here – if only in a letter.

'There is no information on you or your sister, so someone must have cleaned the records years ago. We assumed that Ivor didn't have children.'

'Where does this leave Harry and me? What about our birth certificates and all that stuff? Was the adoption even legal? Christ, what a mess.'

'My lawyers are going through all the paperwork, and they've already made contact with Christina,' Luke says.

I turn to him.

'You don't have a choice; we need her at the moment. Safeguard your mum and dad.'

'Yeah, right, because she thought of that when she was taking money from Ivor.'

'Kate, Luke's right... She was there when this went down.' James picks up his coffee.

'Do I need to worry about my parents? Are they going to be arrested?'

'No. The original documents are clear: Katenka signed you and Harry over to Malcolm and Susan. Their surnames were extended to you both and somehow, it has never been questioned. My guess is that Ivor had some part to play in that.'

'He said that my paperwork was destroyed... But whoever has it in for him found me, I mean when I was attacked.' I turn my head to Luke. 'And he said he'd dealt with them.'

'I'm sure he did.' It's clear Luke hates Ivor.

'Russian money can buy almost anything,' I say.

'Something like that... Look, the long and short of it is, Ivor cleared all the records at his end and your adoption in the UK was legal, just very well hidden,' James says.

'I can't even remember the last time I saw my birth certificate.'

'Why would you query it?' James says.

'Maybe one day it would have come up. God knows.' I turn to Luke. 'Something has been bothering me about the men at the house. Ivor's men were dressed in black – almost like a uniform. But the man on the floor outside my room – he was dressed differently, and the other man you…' Luke runs his hand up my back. 'What I'm trying to say is, I don't think they were all working for Ivor.'

James smiles. 'You're observant, I'll give you that, Kate. We did pick up another militia group, Chekhol; they're part of an organisation that we've come into contact with previously. Their tattoos indicate they're from another part of Russia. The Chekhol and Varizin families were at war many years ago, over land and drugs, but, as I said, the Varizin company is clean. What they were doing there is unclear. We assume they were planning to take down Ivor. It looks as though Ivor's men and the Chekhol gang engaged in their own battle, which I am sure had nothing to do with you – you being there could have been a surprise bonus. But we won't take that for granted; I'm looking at every possible scenario.'

'Maybe I'm right, and he didn't leave me to die. He did say he was leaving early, and you never saw him there, did you? It makes sense, right?' I draw my lips in; I don't want it to be Ivor.

'If the feud is between the two families, then there's a chance Kate was caught in the crossfire, and nothing more.' Luke draws me closer.

'Possibly. We don't know. As no one was left alive, we have no means of knowing what their intended target was.

The positive to that is it's unlikely any information got through. Sutton, I'm on this; there is not a chance I won't find out. '

'Ivor did say that I could only talk on the phone for thirty seconds.' I turn to Luke. 'That's why I couldn't call you.'

'I thought you couldn't call because you had lied to me and flown to Russia.'

'Tell me, how long do you plan to hold a grudge?'

'You've not seen anything yet.'

'Leave it all with me. I hope to have some intel over the next seventy-two hours,' James says.

I lean on Luke's shoulder, no longer wanting to be part of this conversation.

'I need normality – this is way over my head. Thank God I start work on Monday.'

'No,' Luke says.

I sit bolt upright and our eyes meet. Dark and difficult meets dark and forceful. 'Don't even go there, Kate. You'll be here resting, plus I need to sort out security for you. You heard Sullivan – we still don't know what information they have on you.'

'No, I heard Sullivan say that they probably didn't even know I was there. You're twisting this, Luke. You can't lock me up.' Why does he behave like this? I think it's more than just the army – this is deep-rooted.

'If I need to lock you up, I will. We still have no indication if they wanted you or Ivor. You're still a possible target.' His eyes darken as he thinks he is losing control of me again. 'May I remind you that you were attacked and your home was broken into?'

'No! Lucky for me, it's firmly locked in my memory. Luke, I need this. You know how much this new job means to me. Anyway, I don't have the money, and Ivor's playing hide and seek. I'm no use to them.'

'Kate, I'm not taking that chance. Your dad is in ICU – do you think I will let that happen to you?'

I take a deep breath and close my eyes; I can still hear the machines bleeping, keeping him alive.

'Of course not.' I need a different tactic. I place my arms around his neck and kiss him gently on his cheek. 'James didn't say I couldn't go to work; that's your version of the situation. It will kill me, and us, if you don't let me do this. I need normality – it's the only way we can survive.'

'Jesus, you drive me mad.' Luke rubs his forehead, frustrated. 'You can go if I take you and pick you up. No walking the streets – not until we have more information about what went down in Russia. There will be extra security.'

'Fine. See, a compromise wasn't too difficult!' I give him a quick kiss on the lips.

'Don't push your luck. I'm trying to meet you halfway; this goes against my better judgement.'

I look across to James. 'You think I'll be fine.'

'No way. I'm not getting involved with Sutton and his woman; you're on your own.' James stands. 'I need to go.'

The day disappears and the evening draws close. Luke opens the door to Harry and her French fiancé Raymond. *Crap! I'll have to tell her about Dad.*

Harry and I sit alone in the grey lounge with a glass of Caymus.

'Spit it out! You've been jittery all night – actually, since you returned from Russia.' She takes a sip of wine. 'I'm still amazed you went. Christ, I can't imagine what you've been through, and to think I let you go… Don't worry, my shit sister award is in the post.' Harry looks down at her glass.

'Don't you dare think you've let me down – no one forced me to go. Besides, you were in shock.' I shake my head and drink some wine for Dutch courage. 'I have something to tell you. Ivor told me he was in prison when I was born, and he was still in prison when you were conceived.'

Harry's expression alters.

'What do you mean? He's your father, but not mine?'

'Ivor thinks…' I look at the fire for strength, 'that Dad is your real dad – apparently he had an affair with Katenka.'

'Fuck! Fuck.' This tips Harry over the edge. 'What the fuck?'

I move closer. 'At least you have a dad who's caring – that counts for something, irrespective of how it happened.'

'Oh my God, Kate, what about Mum?'

'I'm guessing she's in the dark. Christ, it would kill her if she found out Dad had an affair.'

'Totally…'

'I think you should talk to Dad.'

'We said we wouldn't.' She twists the stem of her glass between her fingers.

'I don't mean today or tomorrow, but in time. I think he would want to know. I'll support your decision.'

She looks at me for guidance. 'What about you? How do you feel about this?'

'I won't lie. I'm numb. Ivor did seem nice. I can't explain it. I asked him why you had no inheritance, and he said he assumed Katenka died before she had the chance to change it.'

'I don't want the money, anyway.'

'I know. I have some pictures to show you of Katenka. I haven't had a chance to unpack Ivor's boxes, which arrived this morning from Russia.'

'What do you mean, Ivor's boxes?' Harry looks confused.

'Christ, Harry, it was bloody odd. God, it makes me feel sick. Ivor had a room that was covered – and I mean covered – in pictures of me, throughout my entire life, and obviously the photos included you. That's when I discovered that Dad is probably your biological father. Ivor assumed I had already worked it out – he told me he was in prison when we were both born and when Katenka died. I think, with everything that had happened, I struggled to remember my name, let alone think logically.'

'Christ, Kate… I was in bits when you flew to Russia. I couldn't even speak, let alone put facts together.'

'The worst part was that some of the photos were taken in Mum and Dad's house – our house.' I shake my head. 'Ivor paid Aunt Christina for the pictures.'

'Are you joking? Paid her? She acted like she didn't even know him. Is that why you were off with her?'

'Yeah. You know I said I needed to talk to her about paperwork…'

'Sort of. Jesus, I take it you haven't told Mum?'

'No, of course not. I don't think they had any contact other than the photos and money. Apparently, it was all done to keep us safe.'

'Bullshit!'

'Money fucks with your brain.'

'What a bloody mess.' Harry rubs her forehead, apparently trying to ease the tension, but no amount of rubbing will alleviate the strain. I feel the same.

I reach for the photo Ivor gave to me. 'Here.'

Harry takes it. 'Oh my God, you look like her.'

'I know, it's weird. I kept looking at it when I was at Ivor's house, thinking you're dark like Dad and I'm blonde like… her. Ivor had a hard time looking at me. Apparently, I speak my mind like she did.'

Harry produces a small smile, the first I have seen tonight.

'I guess we'll never know. Keep the picture – there must be more in the boxes.' I reach for Harry's hand. 'We still have each other, and the same mum.'

I watch tears trickle down her cheeks.

'Kate, I don't know what to think any more, I'm so confused.'

'You have Raymond and the wedding to think about. Besides, Dad is your dad.'

'I feel guilty that you have no parents in your life.'

'I have you, and Luke. Mum and Dad are still our parents, aren't they? They were there for us when we were little – and still are. Blood doesn't necessarily mean anything. Maybe Katenka giving us away was the hardest decision of her life.'

Harry nods. 'You're the strongest person I know.'

'No, I'm definitely not strong; I'm holding on for dear life.'

We will keep this secret for the time being.

A gentle kiss on my neck wakes me.

'How are you this morning?' His voice gets me every time.

'OK.' My eyes scan his body. 'You're dressed.'

'You're wide awake.' His killer smile pins me to the mattress.

'Word of warning – I'm back on track. There's no need to wrap me in cotton wool.'

'Is that so? Feeling frustrated?'

'Yes.' I sit up to face him. 'I suggest you stop playing doctor and resume your role as sex god, or I'm off to Russia to find boob man. I can't remember his name; you stole his number from me.'

Luke's face softens when he laughs. 'Boob man!'

'Yes, Fiona's Russian friend, remember my emergency number in my bra?'

'Argh – boob man! If you mention going to Russia or anywhere else for that matter, you will – and I'm serious when I say this – be locked in this house.'

'Fine! Anyway, what's kept you from your duties this morning?'

'A meeting with the extra security staff.'

I can't help rolling my eyes.

'Part of my deal... Work equals tight security. Until I have intel on Ivor's whereabouts, you're under house arrest.'

'OK.' I look at my watch. It's ten thirty. 'Bloody hell, look at the time – I'm supposed to be meeting Harry and Mum at the hospital at eleven.'

'Rest is what you need.' He bends down and kisses my nose.

'And to see my dad… Look, you stay here. I'll take Max, if he's around.'

'Max is already on standby for you. For some reason, he would do anything for you. You've taken over my staff.'

'What can I say? I've charmed them. Maybe you should try it sometime.' I offer him a wink.

'You have far too much to say for yourself this morning.' He lies beside me and prods my waist. 'You're the biggest pain in my arse.' I try to stop him, but I can't help laughing.

'Luke, stop… No more, I give in… Lock me up.'

He holds my hands above my head. 'What shall I do to you now?' Playfully, Luke nibbles at my neck, and I giggle. Suddenly my humour fades, turning into desire as he threads a necklace of kisses along my jaw. His tongue gently brushes against mine. God, I'm hungry for him. But then his phone ringing stops his touch. *You have to be kidding me!*

He pulls away. 'I need to get this.' He stands, tenderly skimming my cheek with the back of his hand. 'Yes,' he says abruptly to the caller. I know I've lost him. He moves away from the bed. 'Hold, please.'

'It's fine. Go – I'll meet you downstairs.'

'Sorry, baby.' He plants a kiss on my lips and disappears.

Out of the shower, I feel the need to make myself look human. I enter my second-favourite room in this house: the walk-in closet. I scan my wardrobe, which is still waiting for my clothes from Harry's house. I decide on cream jeans and a coffee-coloured camisole top – a mating call for my Sex God, I hope! I layer my outfit with a cream cashmere cardigan (another gift from Valerie, Luke's personal stylist), tan shoes and my cream Chanel bag.

The office doors are open, with various voices filling the room. Men, lots of strange men. The conversation stops as I appear in the doorway.

Luke stands up. 'Gentlemen, this is my girlfriend, Kate Harper.'

I offer a small wave. 'Hi.'

Luke walks towards me and guides me to the hallway. 'You look beautiful.' He scans my outfit.

'I think it's safe to argue I looked like crap. It really wasn't a challenge to look better.'

Luke rests one hand on the wall and uses his other hand to brush my silk camisole top. 'You're wearing underwear.'

'Your observational skills are commendable, Mr Fashionista Sutton.' I raise my brows. *Challenge me, Luke – knock yourself out!*

He produces his one-sided sexy smile that hits a nerve, causing my clit to scream his name – slowly...

'My impertinent Kate is back! Welcome home, baby. As for allowing you to wear this – today it is acceptable.' He stifles a smile, knowing humour is the key to my heart.

'Oh, really! Why, thank you, sir... do you have any other requests?' I giggle and link my hands around his neck, letting my fingers play with his hair.

'I have a list that you may find useful.' He smiles and brings his face closer to mine. 'I would suggest using "sir" more frequently.'

I laugh and shake my head. 'Would sir like to kiss my arse?'

'Is that a request or an invite?'

'Whatever! I would like to point out you have a room full of men waiting for their commanding officer.' My hand skims the swelling pushing against his zip. 'Looks like you've got a long, hard afternoon ahead of you.' I rest my hands lightly on his chest and give him a quick peck on the lips.

He runs his thumb across my lower lip, leaving me no option other than to take a small bite. His eyes darken and his tongue skims his lower lip. God, he looks hot.

'I need to be inside you.'

'I have to go… Maybe you can fit me into your schedule later.' *Wow, did I shower in bravado?*

'Are you trying to push my buttons, Kate Harper?'

I lean closer to him. 'The only button I have for you is play – you should know that.'

Max arrives in the hall. 'Ready, Kate?'

'Yes.' I reach up and give Luke a kiss. 'Can't wait for my appointment later.'

He stifles a laugh, and is now frustrated. Thank fuck for that… payback is always so damn sweet.

'Stay out of trouble,' he says to me. He turns to Max. 'Call me when you get there and when you leave.'

Max nods. Not wanting to let my bravado shower gel down, I give Luke a salute as I leave.

We remain at the hospital most of the day. The atmosphere is odd, or maybe I just feel uncomfortable, but I smile and try to appear normal. However, my mind is in Russia, or the Cayman Islands. Fury and abandonment keep me quiet. I'm not only feeling confused about Ivor, but also guilty for wanting to know him. My dad lies in a bed, having been badly beaten, and I want the man that doesn't want me – his daughter.

Five o'clock arrives. Max returns me safely to the palace. The black door opens and I'm home. I head straight to the office – and Luke. Instantly, he hugs me.

'Look at me.'

I raise my head for him to read my eyes.

'Talk to me.'

I shake my head. 'I have nothing to say… I feel so lost.'

'Ivor?'

I take a large breath. 'I was jealous of Harry today; she has her dad. I have… I'm so alone.'

Luke places a tender kiss on my lips. 'I can't pretend to know how you feel, but I need you more than you realise.'

'You're my saving grace, Luke. If anything happened to you, I would…' I shake my head and look down at the floor. 'It would kill me, I love you so much.'

'I'm here. Nothing is going to happen to me.'

My lips make contact with his, hard, while my hands slide down his chest and hastily unbutton his shirt. Within seconds his upper torso is naked, allowing my lips to layer kisses across his muscular body. Luke slips off my cardigan and slides his hands under my camisole top, reaching for my erect nipples.

My hands move to his waistband. I drop to my knees and pull his jeans and boxer shorts down his powerful thighs. His erection stands to attention. I take his entire length into my mouth. My body has no sense of time, just one of need – my need for Luke. My mouth works quickly, and he grows thicker and stronger every time I sink lower.

Luke's breathing quickens. I can hear the noise he makes when he loses himself to me. I continue to work fast, sucking and licking. I run my hand up and down his shaft, increasing the pressure, ensuring his body surrenders to me.

'Kate.' He tugs my shoulders. 'Kate… No more. I want you, but not like this.'

I don't want to listen. I need him to want me – the only person in the world who won't leave me – ever.

'Stop… I'm going to come – stop.' His strong arms ensure that I release him. I stand.

'Jesus!' His hand rides up to the nape of my neck. 'I want you but not like this.' He tenderly strokes my cheek. 'I love you.' The tone of his raspy voice arrows to my heart.

I nod. Our eyes lock. Dark and appeasing meet dark and demanding.

Luke places his hands on either side of my face and kisses me hard. He must be able to taste himself on my tongue. He removes my top and bra and then works at my jeans, then drops to his knees and strips me naked.

His kisses begin at my calves and work up until he reaches the apex of my thighs. Gently his fingers slide inside my sex. My eyes close and my breathing shallows.

'You're so wet.'

I lower my gaze and watch him devour me. His tongue flicks against my sensitive clit. My arse rests against the table for support, and my legs are weak.

My sex god knows me better than I know myself. He stops and pushes me back on the table, taking my legs and spreading them wide. His tongue continues to brush against my clit, while the pressure of his fingers increases. The first crash hits me hard – my breathing labours and my legs quiver. All I can do is groan – loudly.

Luke slides me further up the table and stands between my thighs. I can feel his hardness pushing against my sex. My hands slide down his back, drawing him to me. The head of his thickness slides into me slowly. But fast and hard is what I need – one full thrust and that's what he gives me.

'Look at me, Kate.'

My gaze falls to his.

'You have me.' He places his mouth over mine, giving himself to me.

He cups my arse, offering him the access he needs to work me harder. I can feel myself begin to climb. As I lose myself to him again my body grips him. I can't let him go.

'Oh my God… Luke.' My orgasm bursts over me. 'Don't stop.'

'I'm with you.' He hisses the words I love to hear, prolonging my orgasm.

My body tingles with the aftermath of multiple orgasms, but I still need Luke. His eyes lock on to mine as his lips skim my nose.

'You have just fucked with my hotel plans.'

'I thought I would offer some additional input.' I giggle.

'It's music to my ears to hear you laugh.' Luke slides out of me and helps me to stand. He lifts my chin.

'I need you more than ever now.' Tears roll down my cheeks.

'Us forever, baby.' He kisses me tenderly.

4

'Fuck, I can feel you coming, Kate.'

My ankles tighten around Luke's waist, and my back grinds against the wall of the shower.

'Yes,' I whisper.

He thrusts twice more and gives himself to me. He's hot and sexy as hell.

Luke slides out of me, and lowers my legs. His lips deliver soft tender kisses, a sign of appreciation for a morning of hardcore sex.

'How are your nerves?' His hands travel across my sensitive nipples.

'OK for now, but we can't have sex all day; I need to go to work!'

Luke smiles. 'If you worked for me, we could stay in bed all day.'

'Tempting as that sounds, home accessories excite me a little more than – whatever it is that you do.'

'You could work directly under me.'

'I did this morning!'

My hands slide down his back and grip his firm arse, and my head rests against his heart. Orgasm over, my anxiety returns.

After we have showered and dressed, Luke and I head outside to start our days in the professional world – Luke in search of world domination, and me to cope with my first-day nerves. As ever, we're worlds apart. We are greeted outside by Max – and a new face.

'Kate, this is Jack Thomas – he will be working with Max.'

I hold my hand out. 'Pleased to meet you, Jack.'

'You too, Miss Harper, and call me Thomas.'

'OK, and call me Kate.'

He's dressed in a dark suit with a grey shirt, and is maybe in his late forties, slightly younger than Max.

'I think Thomas would rather call you Miss Harper.' Luke's response whips out.

I shake my head. 'Fine!' I walk pass the three men and get in the black Bentley.

Luke slides in next to me. He immediately takes hold of my hand, skimming his lips across my knuckles: a green light for me to move closer.

'You understand the security rules.' Yet again he repeats the plan of action. This must be due to his military training… Or then again, maybe not!

I sigh. 'Yes. I'll wait for Max at all times, and won't go outside alone, or collect two hundred pounds when I pass go!'

'There's a time and a place for your humour – and it's not today.'

'Jesus, Luke, lighten up… I've got it, don't go anywhere alone. Sorry, Max, you're in for a real treat today – lunch with Harry.'

'No Max – no lunch. You're lucky you have him; I had two others in mind for you.' Bullshit! Luke trusts Max with his life – and now mine.

The journey takes about thirty minutes, just enough time for my nerves to kick in. We pull up at Pacific Tower, the home of Hudson Bay Interiors, my new employer. *You can do this, Harper – this is your dream job.*

Wow! The building looks bigger than I remember. I feel excited – and nervous.

'You'll be fine – just be yourself. A word of advice: remember to filter what pops into your pretty head before you speak, just for today.'

I look across at him. 'I use my filter for most people except you.'

'Call me. Let me know how your day is going. I'll collect you later.'

I lean to his mouth and kiss him. 'I love you.'

'I love you too.'

Max and I stand side by side on the pavement. I watch the man who holds my heart disappear into the distance. This is it; the world of interior design is waiting for me on the fifteenth floor.

We walk towards the building.

'Will you be loitering all day?' I ask.

'Loitering!' Max looks at me.

'I could have said stalking.' I can't help but laugh – at myself.

'Neither.' He continues to walk with me, checking for Russian mobsters, under strict orders from his commander-in-chief, Mr Control Freak Sutton!

We enter the large revolving doors.

'I need to collect my security pass.'

'OK,' Max says.

As we approach the desk, the security guard looks up. Something feels odd, almost familiar, about him. Before I can say anything, he speaks.

'Miss Harper, Max.'

I turn to Max. 'What's going on?'

'It's part of the security measures.'

'Measures!'

Max guides me away from the desk. 'Luke provides the security in this building. Actually, SGI Security now has the contract for Pacific Tower.'

'Are you shitting me? Since when? Christ, what's his problem, and when was he going to tell me?' I fold my arms and tap my foot against the marble floor. 'Oh my God, I want to scream at him! He is seriously fucked up... Too many parachute jumps must have affected his brain. I would love to walk out of this building right now, but he knows I won't do that because I want this job. Christ, he's relentless.'

'Protection.'

'Protection, my arse! You know what, Russia has given him the perfect excuse to watch me like a bloody hawk.'

'Jesus, Kate, don't be so fucking dramatic.'

'Dramatic... that's unfair.'

'*Unfair* was you flying to Russia and me watching Luke die a thousand deaths. You can't win this round.'

Frustrated, I sigh. 'Tell me, was that man at the palace yesterday? Don't bullshit me, Max, I know I recognise him.'

Max nods. 'They're here for your safety.' He places his hands on my shoulders. 'Don't overthink this. I know Luke can be controlling, but he's trying to protect you.'

My first day is already going tits up!

'Kate, we still don't know where Ivor is.'

'I get it, but why didn't he tell me? Christ, he keeps me out of the loop and it pisses me off.' I look away, feeling dismayed.

'Do you want to go to work or not?'

'Yes.'

We return to the security desk and receive our passes, and move towards the lifts.

'Are you going to be sitting at my desk? This is going to be fun.'

We enter the lift alone. 'No! I'll leave you on your floor and collect you at lunchtime.'

'Of course you will.' I'm so fucking angry.

We arrive at my floor.

'Goodbye, Max.' I step out and blow him a sarcastic kiss.

The first couple of hours pass quickly as I learn about the various departments, which distracts me from this morning and my need to scream at Luke. Honestly, sometimes he's too much. For the last forty minutes the entire department has been called to sit through a talk from the new security team from SGI Security. The talk is given by the manager who runs the show, another face I recognise from yesterday.

I sit at the back of the room, sinking further into my chair each minute. Any lower and I'll be on the floor. Can anyone tell that this show is for me, engineered by Luke?

After a rundown on how to avoid Russian ancestors from SGI Security (well, it may as well have been! We are told how to exit the building safely in an emergency, and to be vigilant at all times), I return to Christmas accessories, making notes for the buyers on what items I expect to be top-sellers in the UK. Finally I relax and lose myself in home interiors. My thoughts stop as my phone rings, startling me.

I quickly retrieve it from my bag. Caller ID – boss. I'm not in the mood to make polite conversation – kiss my arse, Sutton. My mobile rings a few more times before I receive a text.

> To my impertinent Kate,
> Are you pissed off at me, as you are not answering your phone? I hope you are enjoying your day so far. How is your filter?
> Yours always, Luke... aka trying not to be a controlling boyfriend. x

Oh really! I look around before replying.

> To my controlling boyfriend,
> When were you going to tell me about SGI Security? Don't keep me in the dark. I am not missing you, but still love you.
> Kate, aka pissed-off girlfriend.
> PS: your 'trying' skills are shit. x
> PPS: don't call me at work... Do you want me to get fired?!

One o'clock arrives. I grab my bag and head to the lift with my new colleague Maria, who I've been shadowing. She's sassy and really eccentric, judging by her creative passion and dress sense.

'What do you think? So far, so good?' Maria asks.

'I love the Christmas line. Although it's a bit early for me.'

'You'll get used to it – you're always a season ahead of yourself.'

'I guess.' I get lost thinking about all things festive, especially stars. The lift doors open, dispersing all festive thoughts. Max.

'Kate.' He gauges my mood.

'Maria, this is my friend Max. Max, this is Maria.' He nods.

Maria and I step inside the lift.

'Where are you going for lunch?' Maria asks, while checking out Max and our relationship status.

'I'm meeting my sister at Gino's, and Max will be joining us.' I'm finding the extra security a little overwhelming, Russian father on the loose or not.

'It's nice at Gino's. If you're free tomorrow, we could grab something to eat?' Should I tell her Max will be joining us?

We arrive on the first floor. I need more freedom than this. I'll be the brunt of the office gossip, with Max being called my stalker. Well, if the cap fits…

Max and I head out to the front of the building, where he checks for unwanted Russians. Does he know what he's looking for? I don't suppose they walk around with a sign on their back.

From a distance I notice Harry, and within a few steps I'm in her arms.

'Thank God! Let's go.' I link my arm though hers as I almost drag her to Gino's.

'What's up?'

'I want to scream, that's what's up.'

We enter the café and find a table. Max sits in the corner close by. I look across and smirk. He shakes his head.

'Tell me, why is Max following you?' Harry turns to look at him, tucked away in the corner, ironically standing out from the crowds. 'I mean, I know he's always with you... But not this close.'

'Luke is driving me bloody crazy. Honestly, he's reached a whole new level of control. He thinks I might still be in danger, as they don't know where Ivor is. Because he's so fucking irrational, I have security coming out of my arse.'

'Oh.'

'I'll give you oh! Listen, it gets better! He's got the security contract for Pacific Towers just so he can rely on his own security team when I'm at work!'

Harry begins to laugh. 'He's trying to look after you. Besides, you did fly to Russia. I can only imagine what that did to him.'

She takes hold of my hands.

'It's a bloody nightmare. When did my life become so complicated? I know that it's not Luke's fault.'

'I think he's brave taking you on, especially now...'

'That includes you, and yet you don't have Max stalking you.'

'Ah, he's a nice stalker, like a father figure.'

'It's not funny.' We both giggle.

'OK... Give it some time; you've both got war wounds. Anyway, Ivor is your dad, not mine.'

'Don't remind me... Look, I haven't told you much about Russia or Luke rescuing me.' I look away, feeling guilty that I've held out.

'What do you mean?' Harry's brow creases.

I swallow, wondering where to begin. 'Luke found me tied to a chair, that's when he realised I had been drugged. I don't remember being tied up, just waking up and...' I take a deep breath. 'I was blindfolded and gagged.'

'Shit!' Harry takes my hands and squeezes them tightly. 'You must have been so scared. I can't believe this.'

'I was... I know I didn't tell you. I knew you weren't ready to hear about it and there's no way I would ever tell Mum or Dad – it would kill them.' Out of the corner of my eye I notice the waiter heading our way.

'Hi, can I have a white Americano and a chicken salad? Thank you.'

'The same, please.' Harry says distractedly. 'I can't believe it. Who did it – Ivor?'

I shake my head. 'No. I don't know, but my instinct tells me no. The night before, when we were looking at the pictures, I got really upset.'

'No shit. I think that's understandable.'

'Harry, he was... kind, almost like a father... He was awkward but caring – does that make sense?'

Harry nods.

'I told him I was cross that he's never tried to make contact. He explained he did this for my protection... I believe him, I could see the hurt in his eyes.' My emotions return.

'I can't believe what I'm hearing. Luke – what happened? I mean, how did he find you?'

I hold up my beautiful birthday gift. Harry looks puzzled.

'Welcome to my world, little sis. This lovely gift given to me by my boyfriend, who at the time I thought was being sentimental, has a tracking device.'

'Holy shit! Are you joking?' Harry's jaw hits the floor.

'Well, at least he found you. Maybe among all the madness, he saved your life.'

'Maybe, but let's not indulge him.'

'Oh Kate – you poor love.' Harry struggles to conceal her amusement.

'You can imagine my face when I realised it was Luke who was untying me… Dressed like some 007 agent and carrying a gun. I'm all for a bit of role play, but seriously you could have knocked me on my arse.'

'A gun? Seriously?'

'Seriously.'

'So he's done this before?' Harry asks.

I nod. 'He's being tight-lipped. It's in his past, before he started his business… Harry, he knew how to shoot and hurt people, and I mean *really* hurt people. I know he was saving my life, but it was still a bloody shock.'

'I can't imagine how you feel.'

I look across to Max, who is glancing between me and his newspaper.

'Anyway, he got me out of the house – that's when he blew up some cars, and made me get on the back of a motorbike to escape. Although jumping out of a plane kind of beats the rest of the story.'

Harry laughs. 'What! You jumped out of a plane?'

'Let me rephrase that. Luke dragged me, kicking and screaming, out of the plane.' This time I join her and laugh. 'Not a word, to anyone, not even Raymond. Max is the only person who knows. Not even Luke's family know. If he ever found out I told you…'

'You have my word.' She places her hand on her heart: our gesture for secrecy at any cost. 'I promise.'

Information overload seems to have affected our appetites. We have discussed dead parents and corrupt adoptions – and also clothes, a pain-free topic.

We both stand to leave the café, and Harry passes me some post that has arrived at my old house for me. 'I meant to give you these yesterday.'

I place the mail in my bag.

'Friday, let's meet up for a drink,' she suggests.

'Sure, if I'm allowed out of the prison.'

'Be strong, Kate Harper, and remember he loves you.'

Harry and I part. Max walks close by, carefully scanning the area. His phone rings. 'Yes?' he says and then hands the phone to me, 'it's for you.'

'Sorry, I'm busy.'

He takes a deep breath.

'She's busy!' He remains silent while listening to the caller. He places his phone in his pocket. 'Kate Harper, you're a fucking pain in the arse.'

'And you can tell Luke he can kiss mine.'

We stop in front of the lift.

'I think I'm safe; you can go.'

'If you think I'm going to let you out of my sight, you're mistaken.'

The lift arrives and we step in. I watch the digital display while offering Max silence, his ideal style of communication.

The door opens and I step out.

'I'll see you at five o'clock.'

I walk off. 'Whatever.'

Maria takes me under her wing for the remainder of the afternoon. I concentrate on getting to grips with more products and understanding the demographic demand for them, not just in the UK but globally. It's amazing how stripy fabric, seashells and ceramic starfish can change my sullen mood to one of happiness.

Five o'clock arrives in the blink of an eye. I press the button for the lift and check my phone. No calls or texts – this can only mean one thing. Luke is either busy or pissed off. The lift arrives and the door opens. Holy shit… Our dark penetrating eyes lock together – I'll go with pissed off!

'Kate.' He is wearing his black signature suit and white shirt, a black tie loosely knotted. Shit, he looks hot – I must stay focused!

'Why are you here?' I lash at him.

'I told you that I would collect you.' He moves towards the doors, holding them open. 'Are you getting in?'

I step in and move to the far corner. Luke presses the button and turns to me, placing his hands on the wall on either side of my head. His lips brush against my ear.

'I thought I would relieve Max from dealing with my errant girlfriend.'

'Errant! Excuse me, Mr Control Freak Sutton, you have a lot to answer for.'

His eyes meet mine. 'Is that right?'

The lift stops and the doors slide open, allowing more people to enter. Luke grabs my hips and pulls me in front of him; my arse is now hard up against his groin.

He leans towards my ear. 'Apparently you're pissed off, and now it's my turn. Fuck, you know what that does to me.' He words are quiet, yet so raw.

I can feel my breathing speeding up as Luke's growing erection presses against me. His hands are spread wide on my hip bone, ensuring there is no space between us. His desire is like a cold burst of air washing over my skin. My nipples harden and goose bumps coat my body. Seconds – that's all it takes for him to fire up.

The sound of the lift reaching the first floor breaks the spell, and Luke's firm hold. He clasps my hand and swiftly moves out, weaving among the crowds of workers. He diverts to a corner shielded by artificial foliage. His mouth becomes an attacking force against my soft lips.

He pulls away. 'You drive me insane.'

My hands are in his hair. 'Back at you.'

He kisses me again: a ferocious demand to claim my mouth.

'We need to leave.'

I can't respond; he's sucked the life out me.

The Bentley waits by the kerb.

I look at Max, who is holding the door open. 'Hi… Did you have a good day?' I smirk.

Max shakes his head.

'You can't help yourself, can you? Get in the car,' Luke commands.

'Get in the car,' I softly mimic under my breath.

We sit in opposite corners. He takes my hand and runs his fingers over my skin. His touch is magnetic. I turn. Our eyes lock: dark and dominant meets dark and intractable.

Fuck it! He had me at the lift! My body slides across. We now continue the journey with my legs over one of his and his arm around my shoulders.

'I'm still pissed off, Luke. You should have told me about your little covert operation.'

'Back at you.'

'How so?'

'You question everything I do. Max is here to help you, not for your amusement, and certainly not for you to antagonise him.'

'Really?' I look up at him. 'I told him not to ride up in the lift with me – it's embarrassing. I feel like I'm taking my dad to work with me.'

He lowers his lips to my hair.

'Get used to it. Until I know you're out of danger that's how it's going to be.'

'Fine – but I'm telling you I'm not happy.'

'As ever, Kate Harper, you provide the light in my life and the pain in my arse.'

'Welcome to my world, Sutton.'

I'm first to open the black door. We haven't spoken since our earlier conversation. I swiftly move to the kitchen, and head to the fridge for a cold glass of wine. I hold up the bottle to Luke.

'No. I have to leave for another meeting, which I would have continued this afternoon but I made a promise to collect you.' His dark eyes glare.

Wine has no effect on my mood. 'And you made a promise not to control everything I do! It seems your definition of a promise is different to mine.' My eyes meet his. 'I never asked you to collect me from bloody day-care!'

He has hold of me within seconds. Once again, his speed and agility leave me standing. His clinch is firm, one hand at my neck, the other cupping my arse.

His breath glides across my lips. 'I never promised. I aim to try.' He tenderly kisses me, unlike the passion he displayed earlier. He moves slightly. 'Kate, someone nearly killed your father and the same someone may have been involved in tying you up. I'm not going to take the risk – don't undermine me on this.'

I nod. Maybe he does have a point, and maybe I need to make some adjustments too. I return his kiss, my way of showing him I'm listening.

I break free. 'How long will you be?'

'An hour or two. I'll make it quick.' His Sutton smile merely highlights his chiselled face.

'Before I leave, how was your day?' Luke asks.

'It was good – really good. It feels perfect for me, I know it's my first day, but it feels right.'

'I'm happy for you.'

'I was working on the Christmas line.'

'Already!'

'It's what they do. The products are stunning. I assume you get a Christmas tree?'

'No. I normally go to my parents or I go away.'

'You're in for a real treat, as I love everything to do with Christmas. I have huge plans for this house.' I retrieve my mail and the Christmas catalogue from my bag. I begin to flick through the pages. 'Look how stunning this will be in here… A big tree with lots of stars.'

Luke glances at the picture. 'Whatever you think. I'm in your hands.'

'You will be – later.' I giggle.

Luke's mobile rings, and he checks caller ID. 'Sullivan.' He walks away from the island and towards his office.

I drink some more wine and begin to go through my mail, opening the largest envelope first. I read the name stamped at the top left-hand corner: *Bateman, Gates and Wilkinson, Attorneys of Law, New York.* I can feel Luke at my shoulder.

'She has the letter here.'

I look at him as he moves away.

I open the envelope and pull out the letter. I read it and instantly feel confused.

'I'll let you know. Agreed. Call me with anything else.' Luke places his phone on the island and sits next to me. 'Have you read this letter?'

'Yeah, but I don't understand. The name Bagrov is Katenka's family name, but this letter is from a law firm in New York.'

'That was James Sullivan. He has some new information on Katenka.' Luke takes a deep breath. 'Kate, you're the beneficiary of Katenka's fortune. On your twenty-seventh birthday you inherit your mother's shares.'

'Her shares and her fortune? What do you mean? How? This doesn't make sense – I mean, Ivor didn't say anything about this.' I shake my head. 'Christ, I can't take much more.'

'I assume he is unaware of this. Perhaps there was a clause about the identity of her beneficiary.'

'So, I'm some kind of secret.'

'Possibly.'

'Wow – can my life be any more fucked up?'

Luke skims my cheek with his finger. 'I can't believe I didn't add up the information until now, with everything that's happened over the last few days.'

'Add what up? You're making me nervous!'

'The name Bagrov.'

'What about it?'

'Jesus, I took my eye off the ball.'

'Luke, you're talking in riddles.'

'Sullivan explained that various members of the Bagrov family owned the business. As time went by and people died the shares eventually ended up with Katenka Bagrov – and now you. You own sixty per cent of the company.'

'I don't like where this is going.'

'The company is Bagrov and Cooper.' He looks at me, waiting for my response.

'Is that supposed to mean something?' My brain refuses to compute what he is saying, highlighting why I shouldn't be left a company, let alone a fortune – for the love of God.

'A couple of points. First, it's one of my biggest rivals in business, and second – Cooper.'

I remain stumped.

'The company is run by Philip and Alexis Cooper.'

'Holy fucking mother of Mary – are you shitting me?' My face drains of colour. 'This can't be happening. I must have pissed someone off big-time in my past life. Do they know? She hates me. This just can't be happening.'

'I would think they know now. You're a very rich and powerful woman.' Luke smiles.

'Do you think this is funny? It's not.' I stand and begin to pace. 'This must be a mistake… Oh God, I can't breathe.'

'Yes, you can. Calm down. Take a deep breath.'

'I can't… Business… Me and the word business we just don't go together.' I laugh nervously. 'Too much money brings a shitload of problems, I know from experience.'

Luke pulls me between his legs. 'Kate, this was your mother's company. Sullivan believes the information was made public the exact time you inherited your trust fund. As you know, your shares were released on your twenty-seventh birthday.'

'No mention of Harry?'

He shakes his head. 'No.'

'OK – random question. If I have control of the company, does that mean I can fire the evil Coopers?' Just the thought of Alexis Cooper makes my blood boil and my fists clench, and her father makes my skin crawl.

'It doesn't work like that.'

I move away from his legs. 'Give me your wallet.' I hold my hand out.

'What!' Luke frowns.

'Wallet – now.'

He reaches inside his jacket and passes me his black leather wallet. I take a twenty-pound note.

'You have just bought yourself sixty per cent of Bagrov and Cooper: you can now sack the pair of Coopers and have world domination.'

He takes my face between his hands. 'I appreciate the offer, but it's not quite that simple.' He kisses my forehead.

'Luke, I mean it, don't patronise me. I don't want it.' I look at him. 'I trust you with my life and I'm telling you to take it – please. You promised to protect me, so protect me. I will sign it all over to you – call your lawyers.'

'You have to go to New York for a meeting. I'll come with you.'

'Are you sure Ivor isn't involved in this? I mean, is this his company?'

'No, they are completely different. The chances are he is unaware. Even so, it's beyond his control: this was your mother's company.'

'But you said it was made public, and he seems to know his stuff… Christ, I've seen the pictures, remember!'

'It was only made public to the other shareholders. Yes, if you dig around you could find out, but I don't see how it would benefit him.'

'He might come back.' I secretly pray.

Luke takes a deep breath. 'He may not.'

'You hope he doesn't.'

'No. I think he has too many skeletons in his closet to be part of your life.'

'Says you…'

'Different closet, baby.'

'This can't be happening.'

He stands and takes me in his arms. 'We'll tackle it together.'

I break free from his hold.

'Go, you have a meeting… I'll cook some dinner.' I take a deep breath and move round the island and stand in front of the cooker, my sanctuary.

'I'll cut it short.'

'I'll be fine. I'll cook and then drown myself in the bath.' I smile wryly, trying to cajole myself into some state of happiness.

Luke walks towards me and takes hold of my face.

'Cook, and then we can take a bath together; let me wash away your stress.'

I link my hands around his neck. 'God, I love you, I love to moan at you, I love to argue with you… But I love you more than anything in the world.'

'You are very testing… but you keep me on my toes.' He delivers a quick peck on my lips and begins to walk away. He stops at the doorway. 'I love you too. Stay out of trouble.' He walks away and heads for the black door. I notice Max waiting for him.

Rosie joins me in the kitchen. Even though I have lived here for a while I can't get used to Luke having staff.

'Kate, I didn't want to disturb you, but when you have a minute can we send Adam another email?'

'Sure, let's do it now.' Perfect timing. Fuck me, a business from the grave – Jeez.

'Thanks, Kate.'

'How is Adam?'

'Good. I just feel bad for Jerry.'

I stop in my tracks. 'Adam is your baby, remember that – OK, he's a grown-up baby, but Jerry can't take that away from you. Gay or not, he's part of you both.' What is it with parents abandoning kids? Jerry can't cope with his son being gay so he refuses to contact him. I've been secretly helping Rosie email him. She'd love to see him again.

'Yeah, you're right. I want him back in my life.'

'That's the spirit. I'll win Jerry over – fruit cake should work!' Rosie laughs.

We both enter Luke's office.

Holy fuck! The noise – I recognise the sound… The office floor shakes as the three long windows break, and Rosie and I are blown across the room. I land facedown with debris and shards of glass scattered all around me.

My ears are ringing and I struggle to focus. I cough and squint across the room.

'Rosie?' I shout out. She's lying at least ten foot away from me, motionless.

I crawl across the wooden floor, cutting my arms on the broken glass. My heart pounds. *Please be OK.* Just as I reach her, she comes to.

'Kate?' she whispers.

'Thank God.' I move her hair back from her face. She looks fine, apart from being covered in small cuts.

'Luke…' I try to stand, but my legs are weak.

'What happened?' Rosie asks, sounding confused.

'A bomb.' *Oh God, at my home.*

'*What* did you say?'

'It was a bomb; I know the sound.' Memories of the car bombs in Russia come flooding back.

The room is in utter chaos. I slowly move to the hallway. There is dust everywhere. I make it to the front door and stumble out to the driveway. 'Jesus!' It's destroyed.

Straight away I notice there's no security guard at the gate. This doesn't make sense! Where is everyone? Dense smoke is coming from the far end of the driveway – the garages. *Oh God – Luke!* Quickly, I move, sidestepping pieces of metal and almost losing my footing in the rubble.

'Kate?' I hear, and I turn. Jerry is running towards me.

'Rosie's inside… where's Luke?'

'I don't know. I was in the garden.'

'Luke!' I shout frantically.

As I move further up the driveway the smoke thickens.

'Kate – wait,' Jerry calls.

'I have to find him.'

I struggle to see, and stumble over a large piece of concrete. On my knees, I see the shell of a car. That must be where the explosion went off, Luke's car. A car bomb!

'No!' I scream.

Frantically I scramble to my feet and run to the Range Rover. My hand covers my mouth as tears roll down my cheeks. The car looks destroyed. This is my fault; I brought Russia into his life. How could I do this to him?

Beyond the car I can see a body. My eyes sting and I begin to cough. Careful of the wreckage and flames, I move closer. God, no – two bodies lie on the ground.

'Luke?' I try to scream his name, but it comes out as a croak. 'Luke?' I stop, coughing and wheezing. My chest feels tight. 'Luke…' I whisper, and drop to my knees.

Everything goes black.

5

FOUR MONTHS LATER –
23 DECEMBER

'Kate… Kate,' Harry calls.

I turn, lost in my own harrowing thoughts, as she moves towards me.

'Hey.' She gently wipes the tear rolling down my cheek.

I swallow hard and briefly close my eyes.

'Sorry, I'm just feeling a bit…'

'The explosion.'

I nod.

'Bloody hell, Kate, it was only four months ago… That day will haunt you forever.'

'I know. Let's just forget about it, this is your weekend.'

'No. Don't shut me out… You did that before and I watched you disappear.'

I look at her. 'Disappear?'

'Your eyes were dead… OK, "dead" is probably not the best word… They were sad and empty.'

'It was so hard.'

'I know, it killed me to watch you go through it. How are the nightmares?'

There's no need to answer. I shiver.

'Come here.' Harry pulls me to her. 'Give yourself time; you're not superwoman.'

'Come on, this is about you, the bride-to-be, not me… It'll be the best day ever tomorrow.'

'Agreed… But while you're having a moment, I've eaten every last bit of food. At this rate I won't be able to fit in my bloody dress.' Harry looks down at her inflated stomach.

'You'll be fine. You always eat loads when you're nervous.' I reach for her hand. 'Thanks, and sorry.'

'Never be sorry – your memory is my memory, your hurt is my hurt. That's what we do.'

'I guess.' I pass Harry a glass of champagne. 'Here's to a perfect day for my perfect… well, sometimes perfect, little sis.'

Harry raises her glass. 'Cheers. Here's to the best sister ever, who I adore, and here's to my food baby. Why can't I have the kind of nerves that make you starve?'

I take a closer look out of the window; although it's pitch black I can see a light dusting of snow.

'Holy shit, I think it's snowing.' I lean my head against the window. 'Bloody hell, Harry, it is! Get your coat.'

I grab my coat and head for the door. I look back to see Harry staring at me with tears in her eyes.

'Move your arse.' I walk back and grab her hand and coat.

I scan the hallway, checking for Harry's groom. All clear. We head towards the grand staircase and slip quietly past the reception area. We exit the large glass doors, and run down the stone steps towards the white flakes settling on the grass.

I look up to the night sky, allowing the snowflakes to float onto my face.

'Oh my God, this is perfect. Christmas Eve tomorrow and the most perfect wedding day too. I'm good at organising, but snow… it's a bonus.' I look across to an emotional Harry.

I grab her hand and run to the middle of the lawn. 'You know what's coming.' I chuckle. 'Harriet Harper, do you believe in angels?'

'Kate! We're too old – besides, someone might see us.'

'Good.' I lie down and begin to make an angel shape. 'Harriet Harper, get your butt on the ground.' She relents and joins me.

We raise and lower our arms, our actions mirroring each other as we continue to laugh.

'There's nothing angelic about you!' Harry declares.

'Tell me about it.' I reach for her hand. 'Look at the stars. Do you think she sees us?'

'I don't know. Maybe. Do you miss her?'

I turn and meet Harry's eyes. 'Yeah… But how can you miss someone you've never met?'

Harry squeezes my fingers. I feel abandoned. Will these feelings haunt us forever?

Finally, we return to the hotel reception, cold and damp.

'You go on ahead. I want to give the ballroom one last check.'

'I'll come with you.'

'No… Go and have a bath, the others will be here soon. You won't get a minute to yourself.'

'OK.' She begins to walk towards the large staircase.

'Oi, Harper?'

Harry turns with the biggest smile on her face.

'Don't answer the door to anyone with a French accent.'

'Got it.'

I move towards the ballroom, secretly wanting some time alone. The past twenty-four hours have been testing in many ways. I turn the gold handle on the large door. Wow. It looks amazing, even more so since it's pitch black outside and there are fairy lights on the tables – it looks magical. Harry decided to run with the Christmas theme by using mistletoe for the table arrangements. For the first time in a while, I feel excited.

'Sexy Kate!'

I spin around. 'Well, if it isn't the shag monster himself.' Declan – Luke's younger brother – is at the doorway. Harry decided to invite everyone close to us to her wedding and, even though they aren't related to her, this includes the Sutton family.

'Journey OK?' He pulls me close to his chest. I forget how similar he is to Luke. They're both tall and broad-shouldered; it's just Declan's juvenile take on life that sets him apart from Luke.

'Yeah, although I could have done without the snow.'

'Are the roads bad?'

'It's not settled on the main roads, only the country lanes. So – is everyone here?'

I fold my arms. 'Are you referring to the other shag monster in my life? No, Kiki isn't here. Actually, I want to speak to you about her.'

'Kate, I haven't banged her... yet!' His brows arch.

'Oi, Declan!' I tap his arm. 'Seriously, I know you have the hots for Kiki, and she probably does for you, but I'm warning you... she's off-limits.'

Declan laughs. 'Do you know how hot you look when you're pissed off?'

'Declan, I mean it... I don't want to get caught in the middle.'

'What an image, me on one side and Kiki on the other.'

I hit him again, harder.

'OK... OK.' He flashes the Sutton smile, the sort that knocks you on your arse and slides off your knickers. 'Do you need any help?'

'No. I'm just checking the room.'

'OK. I'll see you later.' He leans towards me and places a kiss on my cheek, then begins to walk away.

'Remember what I told you.'

'Yeah, yeah, yeah... Tell your mate too.'

He hasn't listened to a word I said.

In comfy PJs and with champagne, Harry and I are officially set to celebrate her last night of freedom, then I hear a knock at the door.

'I'll go, just in case we have an unwanted Frenchman.'

Harry smiles, but I know she would love to see Raymond.

The noise from the hall echoes, and I can hear who it is before I open the door.

'Oh my God, you're so bloody loud.' I laugh at the pack loitering in the hallway.

Barney leans towards me for a kiss. 'It wasn't me, babe; these two noisy bitches have done my fucking brain in. I tell you what, the bloody M25 looked more appealing than being with these two.'

'That bad?' I laugh.

He shakes his head and walks past me. 'Jesus H Christ, I need a bloody drink. Come here, Harry Harper... Not for much longer!' Barney takes hold of Harry and swings her in his arms.

Barney immediately finds the alcohol and food.

'Are you coming in or not?' I look at Molly and Kiki.

'Kate, she's driving me mad. I know I'm getting fat – well, the baby is – but she keeps calling me a beached whale.' Molly looks at Kiki.

'Er, that's not what I said.' Kiki rolls her eyes.

'You said I looked fat,' Molly responds.

'No – I said you looked bigger, as in the baby is growing!'

'Kiki, leave her alone, I think you look beautiful.'

Molly drags herself through the door. Being the first in our group to get pregnant, we are all adjusting, but not nearly as much as her waistband!

'You all right?' I ask Kiki, pulling her close for a hug. 'What time will your dad be here?'

'He's just landed at City Airport, and he'll come straight here. The traffic was a nightmare.'

'I thought your driver brought you?'

'He did. You try being in the car with Molly moaning about her ankles and Barney, who clearly hasn't shagged someone for at least twenty-four hours, not to mention the traffic – let's just say it's been eventful.'

We all lie around on the bed laughing and eating, side-tracking Harry from thoughts of tomorrow. I massage

Molly's swollen feet, while Barney indulges us with another one of his love stories. Kiki remains fairly tight-lipped; it's safe to argue her mind is elsewhere.

A knock at the door makes Harry hyperventilate. She wants to see Raymond one last time before they get married. Barney does the honours as doorman, and Danny follows him through. There's no sign of the groom.

'Hi girls, Harry, you OK?' Danny scans the room, and his eyes fall on the woman carrying his child – Molly.

'I think so…' She can't hide her nerves. Danny holds his hand out for Molly. 'Come on. Judging by your ankles, you need to rest.'

'Are you sure you're going to get your feet into Louboutins?' Kiki looks at Molly's swollen feet and ankles.

'Even if it kills me, they'll be on my feet. That's the only reason I agreed to be a bridesmaid – sorry, Harry.' She stands, placing her hands on the base of her back.

'I'd have done the same.' Harry joins her pregnant friend for a 'last night of freedom' hug.

Kiki stands too. 'I need to find my room.'

I offer her a look. I detect bullshit! 'I want a word with you.'

'We're going – see you tomorrow.' Danny and Molly leave.

Kiki returns to the bed.

'I saw Declan earlier… He sort of asked me if you were here.'

Kiki's eyes widen.

'It's no secret you both like to shag everything in sight, but please don't hurt each other.'

'OK – thanks for the lecture. Anyway, it may not happen.' Kiki stands, a smirk plastered across her face.

'Really? You have a plan to take exactly what you want from Declan – please don't stand there and feed me bullshit. Now go, before I lock you up.'

Kiki takes hold of Harry and pulls her into her arms. 'Sleep tight, Harry – love you loads.'

'Don't start me off again.' Harry wipes her eyes dry.

'I had better go too.' Barney stands.

'Stay, there's no rush.' I put my arm around him, needing a hug.

'Actually, babe, there's a cute barman I spoke to when we arrived… When I say "spoke to", I mean he's foreign – fuck knows where he's from.'

'Not much conversation then.' I look at him.

'Who needs to speak when you have something in your mouth?'

'Barney, you're a man slut.' You gotta love Barney.

'Born and bred… Now then, my needs are great, so I will see my two favourite Harper girls later.' He kisses us both and leaves.

We both climb into bed, with the duvet tucked up tight below our chins. I begin to channel-hop, trying to find something to eliminate pre-wedding jitters. *Sex in the City 2* – perfect. After half an hour, her eyelids are drooping, and Harry finally relents.

I lean over and kiss her cheek. 'Goodnight, little sis.'

The smoke is everywhere, blurring my vision. I can't breathe; there's no air. My head is heavy and my body is motionless. I can't breathe. I can't breathe! I can't breathe! Please.

Suddenly, my eyes open and I gasp for air. Bolting out of bed, I rush to the bathroom and run the cold tap, bathing my face. The water cools my face and trickles down my throat. My breathing remains rapid as I inhale and exhale, trying to calm down.

Christ! How long are these nightmares going to last? Fresh air is what I need.

I grab my coat, slip on my Converse, and exit the room. The hotel is quiet – nobody is awake except for me.

The cold air hits me as I walk outside. I make my way across the snow-covered grass to a nearby bench under a huge oak tree. I use my arm to brush away the dust-covered seat and sit, taking in the perfect view, which goes on for miles. The hotel is a former manor house, located on a small hill.

My fingers automatically clasp my wrist, turning and twisting my beautiful watch. I lower my gaze. It's seven fifteen. I knew it was early; the sun is still fairly low.

I look into the distance, noticing a male figure wearing a grey hoodie and joggers. He moves towards me.

'Lovely morning.'

'It is stunning, Kate.' Raymond inhales deeply. 'How is my bride-to-be?'

'Asleep. Are you nervous?'

'No.' He looks away. I agree – I don't see a man full of nerves; in fact, quite the opposite.

'I could sit here forever. However, the bride will be waking up, so I'd better get back.' I stand and brush the dusting of snow from my coat.

'Can you give my wife-to-be a kiss from me and tell her I will see her in a few hours?'

I reach up and give him a kiss. 'It will be my pleasure. She's crazy in love with you, Raymond… Super-crazy.'

He laughs. 'I promise to look after her.' Raymond looks at me with complete sincerity.

'I know you will. OK – wish me luck.'

'Harry… Wake up.' I move her mussed dark hair from her face. 'Harry!' Nothing. 'Oi! Mrs Raymond Leclair, wake up.' A smile spreads across her face.

'It's here! Oh my God.' She rolls onto her stomach and screams into her pillow, and at the very same time there is a knock at the door.

'That'll be our breakfast. Up you get.' I move towards the door.

Harry strolls in to the living area, tying her robe around her. 'Smells good; I'm starving.'

'I ordered the biggest breakfast on the menu.'

'I'm going on a diet forever once today is over.'

'You'll be fine, you haven't eaten that much!' I chuckle. 'I saw your hubby-to-be, walking in the field. I tell you what, he's as cool as a cucumber.'

'I can't think about it.'

'What! Raymond?'

'No, husband-to-be… Shit! This is it.'

'You're not walking down the aisle to die. "This is it" is a bit dramatic.'

Harry pushes her plate away. 'I don't think I can eat.'

'I have something for you.' I stand, move to the bedroom and return with a couple of gift bags. 'Here.'

Her eyes glaze over.

'No more tears.'

'Then don't buy me surprise gifts.'

The first present is in a purple box with silver writing

saying *Asprey of London*. She opens the box to reveal a diamond solitaire necklace, almost identical to mine – which was another birthday gift from Luke. Harry places her hand over her mouth.

'Oh my God, it's stunning. I don't know what to say. Thank you.'

'I knew you liked mine.' I lean on the table, enjoying my view of a happy Harry.

'It's too much, you've given me so much.' She fastens it around her neck, running her fingers across the chain towards the diamond. 'I'm going to wear it today, to keep you with me.'

'You don't have to wear it today. I wanted to get you something – a keepsake of us.' Wow, today is going to be harder than I thought. 'Open the other gift.'

She quickly removes the lid of a black box and empties a velvet bag into the palm of her hand. It's a gold locket. She opens the catch to reveal two baby pictures – us.

'Where did you get this?' she asks.

'I found it in the boxes from Ivor's house. Katenka wore this on her wedding day.'

'How come Ivor had it?'

I shrug. 'I don't know. If I ever see him again, I'll ask.'

Harry reaches for my hand. 'You should keep this.'

'No, I want you to have it.' Christ, this hurts.

'I wish you had Ivor – good or bad, I wish he was part of your life… This is so messed-up.'

'I guess… But let's not worry about it today – today is going to be the best.' I raise my glass of fresh orange. 'Here's to eternal happiness for my little sis and her French hubby, a shit-hot wedding, and not forgetting a happy Christmas Eve.'

'Cheers... To weddings and Santa.' We both laugh.

'Have you thought about talking to Dad yet? I know you wanted to wait until after the wedding.'

She shakes her head. 'Either way it's crappy. Oh, by the way, Dad we know you knocked up Katenka... Or letting him think we both don't belong to him. Besides, he clams up whenever I mention the adoption. How the hell am I going to bring it up?'

'He doesn't mention it to me either. But I'm sure he would want to know. Anyhow, we really don't know what happened between them – Ivor made assumptions, that's all.'

'Maybe... I've decided to talk to him when I get back from France.'

'I'm here for you, whatever you decide, OK?'

'What about the grave?' Harry asks.

'Are you ready to visit?' Will I ever be ready to say hello and goodbye to Katenka?

'No,' Harry whispers.

'Me neither. I guess she's not going anywhere – I mean, it's a bloody grave. Right here, right now is for the living. And speaking of which, you need to get ready.'

'Harry, you need to get your dress on.' I look at my watch. There's forty minutes until kick-off.

Harry appears from the bathroom kitted out in the most beautiful white lingerie set.

Barney wolf-whistles. 'Harriet Harper, you sexy little slut.'

113

'Barney!' Harry slaps him. 'A slut? You cheeky git.'

'You look hot – tell Raymond to use his teeth to get you naked,' Kiki the nympho responds in true Kiki fashion.

'You two and your one-track minds, you're bloody exhausting! Kiki, help me with the dress. So, how was Declan last night?' I ask.

'All I can say is he's good in the sack.' Kiki smiles. Crap! It's not just a satisfied smile, but one that confirms she has feelings for him. Oh boy, this is not looking good!

'Enough sex talk, let's get Harry into her wedding dress. Barney, keep Mum entertained. She's going to be a mess when she sees Harry.'

'Got it, babe.' He leaves us to it.

Kiki and I take hold of Harry's dress, allowing enough room for Harry to step in the centre.

'Ready to look like a meringue?' I ask.

Harry laughs. 'As I'll ever be.'

I hold her hands as Kiki helps guide her feet to the bottom of the dress, then I slide the dress up and over her body. I then begin the painstaking job of fastening the individual buttons that hold the diamante-encrusted bodice in place.

'Bloody hell, Harry, Raymond may have to rip this off you. Don't let him drink too much, otherwise you'll be sleeping in this tonight,' Kiki says.

I move to see the bride – and what a view! I clap and jump. 'Oh my God! You look stunning. And I mean bloody stunning. Mum and Dad are going to melt.'

'I can't speak,' Kiki says.

'That's a first. You like it?' Harry brushes her hands down the bodice.

'Gorgeous, you look…' There are no more words from Kiki, just a thumbs-up, and tears rolling down her cheeks.

'Let's attach your veil and then you're done.'

The diamond tiara sits neatly below her veil, and her dark hair hangs down her back. Lastly, she puts on her Louboutins: I crawl under her dress and slide them onto her feet.

All that remains is for the three of us, and my plus-one, Barney, to dress for the day.

'Molly, sit down and I'll put your shoes on.' I lift one foot at a time. 'How do they feel? Tell me if they hurt.'

I help her up.

'Not too bad – at the moment.'

The four of us look in the mirror. Barney wears his penguin suit as any Italian *Vogue* model would… He looks hot. Our dresses are simple: black strapless and full-length. Except for Molly's, which has an extra panel at the front for her expanding bump.

We all make our way down the grand staircase, Barney on one side of Molly and me on the other. We reach Harry and Dad. Barney walks towards Mum, ready to link her arm through his.

'This is it, girls.' I place Harry's white fur stole over her shoulders and rearrange her veil. Kiki places Molly's black stole over her shoulders, and we do the same.

I pass Harry her elegant bouquet of white roses tied with a white sash, and take two more hand-tied bouquets of mistletoe, which I pass to Kiki and Molly. I take mine too. We're ready for Harriet Harper's final walk.

We exit the large glass doors of the hotel reception. I can feel a sense of trepidation in the air: Harriet is the first in our pack to get hitched. The air is cold and the ground remains covered in white powdery snow: the scene is picturesque.

After a short walk, we arrive at the small church in the grounds of the venue.

'This is it… ready?' I nervously say.

Harry nods. Taking in a deep breath, she touches her diamond necklace, perhaps to give her strength.

'Ready.' I inform the wedding organiser waiting at the door.

The music begins. Mum and Barney are the first to enter. Next are Molly and Kiki.

Harry turns to me. 'Love you,' she whispers.

Dad strides in first, Harry on his arm. They walk slowly, in time to the music. A narrow walkway hides them from view at first, then they turn a corner and the congregation gets their first glimpse of Harry.

The church is old and dark, but the soft glow of the sun seeping through the stained glass windows waterfalls across the bride. I follow close behind her and listen to the gasps of the congregation, agreeing that Harry looks every inch the most beautiful bride.

All eyes are on Harry as she floats effortlessly towards the altar.

I look ahead, and my eyes lock with his. For a split second we're alone. I take a deep breath. Dark and captivating meet dark and spellbound…

6

'I now pronounce you man and wife.' The vicar smiles and looks at the congregation.

The noise ripples inside the church: waves of cheers and celebratory whistles. Harry and Raymond sign the register and then take their first steps as a married couple, followed by Mum and Dad, and Raymond's parents. It's my turn to leave. I clasp the best man's hand. My fingers link with his, shooting a current through my core. How can he maintain this level of power over me?

He leans towards my ear. 'You look stunning.'

My hand grips him tightly as we walk slowly down the aisle. We exit the church and swiftly move towards a large tree, away from all the guests. I have no time to think as his lips meet mine, accepting his firm, yet soft, tongue. My need for this moment – for him – is strong, and he knows it.

I pull away as my eyes dance with his. We don't need words; a silent understanding floats between us.

'Did you have another nightmare?'

I nod. 'It's always the same when you're not with me.'

Luke takes my face in his hands. 'I'm sorry.'

'Don't be. I'm just your crazy girlfriend who can't live without you.'

'I like crazy.' His lips skim my forehead, before he begins to grin.

'What's up?'

'Nothing.'

'Are you withholding information, Sutton? I know that look.'

'You can always read me.'

'Bet your arse I can.'

At last, we return to the hotel. With a Winter Pimms in my hand, my body begins to thaw and relax.

Luke pulls me to one side. 'I have something to show you.'

'Really! And what might that be?' I can't help but laugh.

'My insatiable Kate is with me this afternoon... Are you feeling greedy? Baby, you'll have to wait.'

I tap his arm. 'Oi, I'm not greedy! You, on the other hand, always want to show me something that involves a certain body part.' I fold my arms.

'Point taken... Let me rephrase that: I do have something to show you that doesn't involve my body. But later will be a very different story.' He seductively arches his brow. Crap! I've gone, melted to the floor.

Luke guides me to an empty room at the rear of the hotel. Suddenly I see Max. Max! What's he doing here? I thought he was still in Switzerland with James Sullivan, where he's been recovering ever since the explosion. Oh my God! My heart beats rapidly as I find out I can run in Louboutins! My arms link around Max's neck as tears roll down my cheeks.

'Jesus, Kate.' Max steadies himself as I almost knock him flying.

I stand back and take his hands. 'Let me look at you.' My eyes close for a second, which is all the time I need to remember Max lying on the driveway next to the remains of Luke's Range Rover.

'I'm back in one piece.'

'You look like... you. Christ, you've been gone – how long?'

Three months. I've had silence for three wonderful months.'

I nudge his arm. 'Admit it, you've missed me.'

'No... I had you in my ear for a month in that bloody hospital room.'

'Well, you look amazing.'

'I feel good.' He extends his leg and taps his thigh. 'Sullivan's given my leg a complete overhaul. He knows his stuff when it comes to rehabilitation, Christ, he made me work.'

'I'm just grateful he could help, and now you're back for good – I hope? Can I get rid of Thomas? He's nice, but he's not you.'

Luke places his hands on my shoulders. 'It takes a certain type of person to work with Kate.'

I gaze at the love of my life. 'Oh really, and you're such a joy to work for.' I turn to Max. 'You could move into the house; I can take proper care of you.'

'No bloody way! I wouldn't be here unless I was ready.'

'I guess.' I fold my arms. 'I can't believe you didn't tell me you were coming home. I call you every day – and you say nothing! You knew I was upset that you weren't home for Christmas.'

'Surprise!' Max actually laughs – what the hell has James Sullivan done to him?

'Very funny. So, you were both in on the covert operation.' I turn to Luke. 'Working away – Switzerland?'

'James Sullivan lives in Switzerland, so there was an element of truth. As much as this joyful reunion is touching, we should return to the wedding.'

'Well, I forgive you both… For now.'

The time has arrived for the guests to be seated in the ballroom. The room looks exquisite, with candles burning and fairy lights glowing against the dark green foliage. I watch Harry closely as she enters with Raymond. She glances across at me and mouths 'thank you'.

Once everyone is seated, the newlyweds have the honour of lighting the Christmas tree. Harry and Raymond stand and raise their champagne flutes. The tree stands proudly at the rear of the ballroom – it's a perfect Christmas Eve.

Luke leans to my ear. 'It looks amazing in here.' He places tender kisses on my shoulder, working towards my neck.

My lips make contact with his. I pull away. 'God, I bloody love you.' I bite the inside of my cheek. To lose him would kill me. 'I mean it. I seriously love you.'

'Back at you.'

'So… I don't want to ask.'

'Then don't… Jesus, Kate, every time I speak to Sullivan you think he will give me information.'

'Yeah, but Sullivan still works at… you know where, with Parker – they must have heard something. Four months, and nothing?' I know Luke often speaks to James, which also leads me to question whether Luke will ever return to his previous work – God, I hope not.

'Sullivan has no news.'

I gauge his response, while I remain sceptical. Bullshit, I think.

'What, Ivor, or the…' I draw my lips inward. 'Explosion.'

'Don't torment yourself.'

'I'm not, but you like answers and we don't have any. Are they still watching Ivor's house?' I hope they are.

'Kate, I can't give you the answers you want to hear and make him appear.'

'You don't want him to appear.' But I want him to show up, just to vindicate himself.

'No.' His finger skims my cheek. 'I have no news on him or the explosion. Trust me. So let's just enjoy the day.' His lips softly brush against mine, silencing me. 'So, tomorrow is our first Christmas together.' He sits back in his chair with his arm draped across the back of mine – 24/7 protection, Sutton style.

He makes it clear the conversation is at an end. Until next time, Sutton. I need some answers.

'I hope you like your presents.' I look down at my plate. What do you give the man who has everything?

He pulls my face to his. 'What is it?'

'Nothing.'

'I only want you for Christmas. Besides, I have a plan. We won't exchange gifts until we're alone, OK?' I receive the penetrating glare that only Luke Sutton can give. It makes my body crave his attention. I look at my watch. Too many hours must pass before we're alone.

I scan the sea of guests. The atmosphere is perfect. As usual, my table appears to be the loudest – with Barney and Kiki seated with us, this is no surprise. Across from our table is Luke's family, as well as Max. After the explosion, the Sutton and Harper families spent a great deal of time together at the hospital, so they grew closer. Harry and me hang on to our family. If only Katenka was here too. So, today we are all together, safe and sound.

The evening approaches and the speeches begin. Surprisingly, Luke was asked to stand in for the role of best man. He and Raymond have really bonded over the past four months – explosions and Russian adoptions lead to the most bizarre relationships. I sit back and observe him. The audience appears to be putty in his hand – hell, I know how that feels.

After the speeches there is music, and the bride and groom have their first dance. I feel an arm around my waist. No need to turn to see who it is; his scent hits me. Luke's soft lips leave tantalising kisses on my collarbone, moving towards my ear.

'Shall we dance?' he whispers softly.

I look at the floor: family members have joined the bridal party.

'Yes.'

Luke takes my hand and pulls me tightly to him. My hands lock around his neck as my lips reach his: even with an audience, I can't help but take what I need from him. Maybe I am greedy!

'How long before I can take you upstairs?'

I tilt my head. 'Hours! I'm expected to dance all night…
Maybe you should have dragged me off earlier.'

'Is that so?'

'Yes.' I look deep into his eyes. 'I think you have a very
long, hard night ahead of you.'

Luke laughs. 'My beautiful prick-tease.' I lean further
into him. He knows I'm searching for affirmation of a
different kind.

'I won't apologise for wanting you inside me.'

'And I won't apologise for fucking you – later.'

I love his dirty talk.

'Oi, lover boy, I want to dance with your woman.'
Barney yanks my arm, startling me.

'Sorry!' I shout to Mr Frustrated Sutton.

Within seconds we're in the middle of the floor. The
floating meringue joins us, along with Kiki and Molly. The
band is fantastic, blasting out 70s classics to modern club
tunes. Barney and I lose ourselves dancing.

The party is in full swing, and after numerous dances
Kiki orders shots for us all, including Luke, who is deep in
conversation with Danny and Max.

He leans to my ear. 'Do you want some water? You
have drunk quite a lot.'

'No thank you.' I look at Kiki. 'Line them up.' No
need to turn; I can feel Luke's eyes boring into me. This
is my sister's wedding and I shall get completely pissed if I
want to! Adding to my growing insobriety is a magnum of
champagne, courtesy of Henry Marlow – Kiki's dad. Does
Mr Control Freak Sutton have a point – possibly?

Back on the dance floor, my senses are slowly abandoning
me. Thankfully I have the support of my human pole, Barney.

Later I stagger from the dance floor towards Luke. No amount of alcohol can stop my body from feeling his penetrating glare.

'Hold my shoes?' Without giving him a choice, I place them in his arms. I reach up and plant a drunken kiss on his cheek. 'Love you.'

He tries to stifle a smile, but one side of his mouth curls up. 'You're drunk.'

'Yes, and you're sexy... hot... Love you forever...'

There's no time to think, just dance, for the rest of the night. Thanks to Kiki disappearing, only to return with more drinks, it's official: I have started to behave badly, embarrassing myself. Of course, this will please the man of my dreams.

Harry and I make our way to Luke and Raymond, who are standing at the bar. Having lost my ability to balance, Luke has to catch me as I stumble, which Harry and I find highly amusing.

'Jesus, Kate, you're pissed.' Luke's tone is hostile.

I nod in agreement. Yet again, this appears to be the funniest thing I've ever heard.

I place my arms around Harry's neck, as my laughter turns into tears.

'Harry, I love you... Be happy.'

'I love you too.' Pathetically, we have matching tears. 'I'm not a Harper.'

'I know.' I kiss her face.

My head begins to spin. I turn to Luke.

'You... bed,' his baritone voice commands me.

I can't speak for fear of throwing up. Within seconds Luke picks me up and carries me to the large staircase, in search of our suite. I close my eyes and nuzzle into his neck – my favourite place in the world.

I can hear the door open, followed by Luke lowering me on the bed.

'Stand up – let me unzip your dress.'

Move? He wants me to move? He pulls me into his arms and reaches for my zip. I place my arms around his neck.

'Are you cross?' I giggle.

Luke draws a deep breath. 'No.' He removes my underwear and pulls back the bedcovers. 'Get into bed.' Alone? I may be drunk, but fear and panic arrive.

'Shh, I'm not going anywhere.'

I wearily lie down and feel the protective arm that holds me every night. 'Merry Christmas, baby,' he whispers in my ear.

Next morning, I open one eye at a time, trying to convince myself to wake. Why did I drink so much? I wince when I turn my head, only to see an empty space next to me. I slowly move to the bathroom and catch a glimpse of myself. As predicted, I look a bloody mess.

I pad into the lounge, wrapping the hotel robe around my naked body. Luke looks up from the desk.

'At last she surfaces from her drunken sleep.'

'Was I that bad?'

'Mildly entertaining.' His dark eyes watch my walk of shame.

I clasp my arms around his neck, as he pulls me into his lap.

'Merry Christmas... Sorry, this wasn't how I planned our first Christmas morning together.'

He rubs his nose against mine. 'I assume you mean with a hangover?' He wears a smirk with an underlining message – *I told you so*.

'No – I wanted to be at home, just us, and the tree. Special.'

He places his hand at the nape of my neck. 'Christ, what we've been through lately. This here, you sitting on my lap, is special.' His eyes meet mine. 'Anyway, I have something planned.'

'Planned! What?'

'You'll find out later.' He places his lips over mine. I try to pull away, knowing my breath will not be sweet. Instantly his hand slides in my robe, grabbing my breast, skimming my erect nipples with his thumb. A ripple of pleasure escapes the back of my throat.

A knock at the door hinders our morning of Christmas passion. Luke breaks free.

'Breakfast is here.'

Lifting me off his lap, he opens the door to a waiter. I watch the food being laid out on the table. I'm not sure food is what I need.

I walk unsteadily towards the table.

'You need to hydrate your body. Maybe next time you will listen to me.'

'I don't think there'll be a next time; my head is seriously pissed off at me.' I sit and try to work out what food won't make me throw up.

Luke stands and disappears into our room, only to return with painkillers.

'Take these.'

I frown. 'Always looking after me.'

'It's easy when you give me reason to.'

Luke places food on my plate – a hangover cure. I'm far too fragile to argue: any sudden movement at this stage could have a catastrophic outcome – my head and the toilet!

'This doesn't feel right. I'm the biggest Christmas fan, and this feels nothing like Christmas Day.' I push some scrambled egg around my plate.

'Give it time… Eat.' Luke looks at his watch and continues to eat. 'Christmas lunch will be served at two – we should be done by four, and it's eleven o'clock now. We need to meet our parents and exchange gifts. Max unloaded my car this morning, and I asked him to leave the gifts downstairs.'

I nod, as my mouth is full.

Luke's mobile phone rings, and he reaches across the table and picks it up. 'Yes.' He watches me eat. 'That's fine; we'll join you in half an hour.' He places his phone on the table.

'Sounds like our morning is going to get busy?' I reach for my coffee.

'Yes, but you knew that when the wedding was arranged for Christmas Eve. Although having everyone under the same roof does make it slightly easier: we can escape after lunch.'

'Escape… where?'

Luke taps his nose.

'But I haven't packed for us to stay away.'

Luke stands and drops a kiss on my head. 'We won't need clothes.' He walks towards the bedroom. I can hear him running a bath. This is my favourite Luke, loving and caring. How many hours did he say until we're alone?

The painkillers seem to have done their job – that and a hot bath. I almost feel human – almost! Dressed in a cream lace blouse and cream jeans, I'm ready to face the world on Christmas Day.

I emerge in the lounge. 'Is everything OK?'

'Yes.' Luke walks towards me, scanning my outfit. 'You look beautiful. How's your head?'

I link my arms around his neck. 'Fragile!' I plant a cheeky kiss on his lips. 'Merry Christmas.' I take a breath, thanking my lucky stars – Luke and Max could have died.

'Let's go, they're serving hot chocolate and marshmallows.'

I grimace at the thought. 'Not for me.'

After exchanging presents and reminiscing about yesterday, we all make our way to the ballroom. I sit with Luke on one side and Max on the other – perfect dinner partners. I can't help but feel subdued, not only with the hangover from hell, but I can't stop wondering about Ivor. Where is he, and is he thinking about me?

Luke leans to me. 'What's wrong?'

'I'm fine.'

He pulls my chin. We make eye contact. 'Honesty.'

'Ivor. Do you wonder where he is – I mean, today, Christmas Day?' I feel sorry that he's alone, even though he doesn't deserve the space in my head and heart – I want to see him.

'No! I need to keep you safe.' He looks at his watch. 'Couple of hours and then we'll go.'

I seal his declaration with a kiss. 'And we don't need any clothes?'

The roast turkey dinner arrives. I look up and down

the table, taking in all the faces of everyone who means something to me, all here in one place. Actually, this is the perfect Christmas Day.

I link my arm through Max's.

'How are you feeling today?'

'Good. I just want to get back to normal.'

'Well, I'm pleased you're back. So, tell me, what's James's house like? I know it's in Switzerland, but Luke hasn't said much other than that.'

'Secluded. There's nothing around for miles. I'm not sure you'd like it – there's not enough people to talk to.' His face lights up when he smiles.

'Right up your street, then.' I give him a little shove. 'Do you still feel pain in your leg?'

'No, honestly I'm fine. Do you think Luke would have me back otherwise, especially where you're concerned?' He places his hand over mine.

'I guess not.'

'Luke said you still have nightmares.'

I nod. 'I hate them. He wants me to see someone.'

'I'm sure they'll fade.' Max looks away. 'Christ, you drove me mad in that bloody hospital; I needed to go to Sullivan's just for a break.'

'Just think how much I taught you. You now know all this year's top-selling outfits and what's predicted for spring.' We laugh.

He takes a sip of wine, maybe for Dutch courage. 'You're special, Kate… Very special.'

I plant a hasty kiss on his cheek. 'Too bloody right I'm special, putting up with you – and what with him,' I tilt my head towards Luke, 'I need an award'.

I try to lighten the mood. Four months down the line, the explosion is still raw for us all.

After lunch is over, I stand and move towards Harry, stealing Raymond's chair and sharing it with Kiki.

'I can't believe you're married.' I take hold of Harry's hand and look at her ring. She's definitely married!

'She won't be the last,' Kiki says.

'I don't think so; we're not there yet... Anyway, I can't think beyond the business trip to New York,' I say.

'I forgot you were going.' Kiki says.

'I wish I could... The wedding has stopped me from thinking about it.' My stomach flips.

'Harper, you're stronger than you look.'

I crook my neck to look at Kiki. 'You reckon? May I remind you that Alexis and Philip Cooper hate me? That's a good enough reason for me not to go. Besides, Bagrov and Cooper is thriving – they don't need me.' Not that I can do much to help!

'You'll be fine. Just think of it as a discussion around a dinner table,' Harry says.

'It's just... you know what I'm like. Kate Harper, businesswoman? Even when you say it aloud, I want to laugh.'

The girls join in my amusement.

'You can't put it off for much longer.' Harry takes my hand.

'That's what Luke says... I've sidestepped it so far. Just the thought of seeing Alexis and Philip is enough to make me throw up. Anyhow, I need a job.'

'You're loaded.' Harry says.

'*We're* loaded – I told you, it's just as much your money as it's mine... Christ, take me back to my first day at Hudson Bay Interiors when I was a nine-to-five girl.'

Kiki laughs. 'You worked there for one bloody day.'

'OK – but it felt normal for a day... Explosions and seriously ill boyfriends don't enhance your career.'

'Well then, get stuck in at Bagrov and Cooper. You can do this! Don't let the super-bitch take over – no way are you to sell to them,' Kiki says.

'No – never! Come with me, Kiki, just to kick arse.'

'My pleasure, babe, but you've got this.'

'Anyhow, I won't be alone. I have Tanya, one of Luke's ex-assistants, with me, and she's totally clued up.' I need to change the subject. 'So, Miss Shag Monster Marlow, how is Declan? Obviously, you really like him.' I place my arm around her shoulder. 'I don't want you to get hurt – either of you.'

'It's just a bit of fun. He's invited me to stay with him at Klosters in a couple of weeks. Apparently the entire Sutton family goes every year, Luke too.'

I look at Kiki. 'Luke hasn't mentioned it. But then he's shit at sharing information.'

'He has a lot on his mind – you've both been through so much,' Harry says.

'Bullshit, Harry, this has nothing to do with the explosion. But I hear you... So we're leaving soon, Luke has a surprise for me.'

Kiki nudges me. I place my arms around both of the girls, drawing them closer to me. 'Here's to us, and good girls do win – eventually.'

I can feel him, and smell the Sutton scent directly behind me. I turn to see Luke.

'Girls, I need to steal Kate – we have some celebrating to do.'

Kiki looks at Luke. 'I bet you do. I may have some of my own, Luke – your brother is quite entertaining.'

'Kate, we need to leave.' Luke repeats, ignoring Kiki's remark.

'Did I hear my name mentioned?' Declan arrives at Luke's side.

'Actually, Kiki was just explaining that you know how to entertain.' I laugh, but Luke glares disapprovingly.

'You know me, sexy Kate, Sutton through and through.'

'Say goodbye, Kate,' Luke commands.

Fifteen minutes later, we pull away from the venue, and leave the perfect fairy-tale wedding.

'Where are we going?'

Luke looks at me, smiling. 'I'll tell you in about four hours.'

'Oh!'

Thirty minutes into the journey, the sun disappears, and for the first time it feels like Christmas Day – with just us. I place my hand against his thigh and take a breath.

'I wanted to arrive in daylight.'

'I haven't got a bloody clue where we're going! Your surprises always knock me on my arse.'

'Good.' He smirks. 'I told you I wanted to give you the world.'

'Yeah, and I told you I only want you.' Even in darkness his Sutton smile warms me.

'Are you going skiing?'

'Yes, we are,' he answers firmly.

'We are… since when?'

'My parents hire a chalet every year.'

'And when were you going to tell me?' My hand wanders further up his leg.

'You know now.'

'I hate hearing things second-hand.'

'Can you ski?'

'I'm OK. I won't win any medals, though. Kiki is bloody good – actually, she's a lunatic on the snow.'

'Good to hear; she'll keep Declan off my back.'

'Oh, and just for the record, Kiki and Declan slept together.'

'I know.'

'You do? Has Declan been bragging?'

'Kate, I know my brother, a little too well.'

'In that case, you should know that I know Kiki too well and she likes Declan – a lot. And, let's face it, your brother likes to share his dick. A lot!'

'Jesus, Kate, the words "Declan" and "dick" should not come out of your mouth.'

'Just words, Luke.'

'Not to me.'

'Well, anyway, I've told him not to mess with her head.'

'I would like to point out they're both old enough to decide for themselves.'

'I'm just saying… I don't want either of them to get hurt.'

I yawn.

'Sleep, baby.' Luke touches my cheek. 'I'll wake you when we arrive.'

'By the way – I love you.' No more words are spoken as my eyes close.

'Kate?' I feel a hand on my face.

'Are we here?' I feel disorientated.

'Nearly. I want you to wear this blindfold.'

'Oh.'

Luke slides it over my face, covering my eyes.

The car moves again, but only for a few minutes.

'We're here. Stay where you are – I'll come and get you.'

'OK.'

I hear the door open and then Luke's strong arms lift me out of the car.

'I can walk.'

'It'll be safer if I carry you.'

'Safer?'

Eventually Luke lowers my feet to the ground. I hear him unlock a door, then there's an alarm bleeping.

'Don't move.'

Move – where to?

He takes my hands. 'Small steps.' We continue to walk. 'OK – stop.' He slides the satin mask from my eyes. 'Merry Christmas, Kate.'

7

'Do you like it?' Luke asks.

'I don't understand. Is this your house?' I look around the room, which is covered in fairy lights.

'Ours. I bought the land just before we met. As I said, I wished we could arrive in daylight.'

'You built this house?'

'Zhan designed it… It was completed a few weeks ago, just in time for today.'

'You had this all planned.'

'Yes.'

I move further into the huge room, which houses a large white French bed, and beyond that stands a Christmas tree, at least ten feet high. 'Where are we?'

'Sandbanks – Dorset. My grandparents had a house not far from here.' Luke holds his hand out. 'I want to show you something.'

I slip my hand into his palm. He then walks me to the far side of the room. He presses various switches on the far wall, illuminating the outside deck, and opens one of the full-length concertina glass doors. He gestures; I step out and move closer to the handrail.

'I can hear the sea.' I turn to him.

Luke laughs. 'That's because we're on the beach – can you smell the salt water?'

'I can.' My hands cling to the wooden railings as I inhale the cold fresh air.

He takes me into his arms and kisses me. My tongue swirls against his, stroking him, wanting more. He pulls away.

'I love it, Luke.'

His chest expands. 'This is our hideaway from everything and everyone. It's just for us.'

'I don't know what to say.' My teeth chatter.

'You're cold – let's get you inside.'

We return to the large room. I now feel invigorated, and excited about the house.

'You may notice there's no furniture... except...' No more words are needed. He offers a killer Sutton grin.

'It's a bit hard not to notice! So, is this a romantic gesture, or is my sex god the big surprise?'

'Both... Truthfully, I wanted this house to be ours – yours, for you to choose the décor and furniture.' He holds his hand up. 'As for the bed, it seemed appropriate for you as it's feminine.'

I move towards the large bed in the centre of the room. 'It's beautiful – and huge.' The width can take four pillows lengthways, easily.

'Obviously, it won't stay here, but as the house is empty...'

'Perfect... we can sleep and play right here.' I hold my hands out to him.

'Play? I like the sound of that. You wanted us, and a tree.' Luke's face lights up.

'For someone who doesn't listen to me, you certainly knock me off my feet.'

I pull him towards me, kissing him hard. He pulls away.

'Let me show you around.'

'OK.'

'Obviously, this is the main lounge.'

'The fireplace is stunning.' I walk towards the coffee-coloured stone surround, feeling the coldness against my fingertips. 'It looks French.'

'It is.'

The entire house is painted off-white with dark wood flooring; a winning combination.

I follow Luke to the front of the house.

'As you can see, this is the kitchen – well, a makeshift kitchen. The company are waiting for you to design it.'

'What!'

'It's your domain – as you're aware, I can't cook.' He runs his hand through his hair.

'I guess. I've never designed a kitchen.' I walk towards the makeshift worktop.

'They will help you, but ultimately the choice is yours.'

'Oh.' The room must be at least forty foot square. No pressure, then!

Luke takes my hand as we make our way back to the large lounge.

'Over there are two additional rooms. Once again, you can decide what they'll be used for – although I may need an office.'

'I don't think you will.' I reach up to his lips, not quite touching him. 'If I don't need clothes, then you don't need an office.' I giggle at my man, and the need I have for him.

'You're trouble, Harper.'

'Maybe, but I'm your trouble.'

He takes in my words and releases a contented sigh. 'Let's look upstairs.'

We climb the incredibly wide white staircase with dark wood handrails and reach the landing, where the stairs continue to another level.

Luke moves towards a set of double doors and pushes them apart. 'This is our room.'

'Wow!' The empty room also has full-length windows, with a whitewashed exposed vaulted ceiling. I brush past Luke and move further inside the room. 'I love it. Oh my God, just think what I can do to this room… It's beautiful.' I turn to Luke.

'I was thinking the same – what I could do to you in this room.'

'Really?' I laugh at my boyfriend. 'Are you feeling frustrated?' I bloody hope so!

'Yes.' He walks towards another set of doors leading off the bedroom. 'I know how much you like a dressing room.' A smitten look beams across his face.

This one is slightly smaller than the closet in London, with drawer units in the centre and white open rails, which already contain some essentials. However, a couple of the garments look unfamiliar.

'Have you been shopping?'

'Yes.'

I laugh. 'OK, so jeans and T-shirts I get.' I move closer. 'But this…'

'Exquisite.'

My hand skims the full-length fur coat. 'I assume it's fake?'

'Of course.'

'Hmm – and the sexy black underwear… Is that to wear under the coat?'

Luke pulls me to him, and I enjoy a sense of closeness, and a sense of anticipation for what may happen very shortly.

'This is no use – presents, and then I'm going to have you on our new bed.'

'Christmas Day does nothing for your self-control.'

'No.'

'Luke, I'm blown away.'

'Good… Maybe a smile from you would back up your words.'

'I am happy, but how can I compete with you?'

'Don't overthink this.'

'I'm not.' My hands run down his chest, moving to the button of his jeans.

'Fuck! I can't wait any longer. I need to have you.'

'Marking your territory?' I giggle.

'You're mine, there's no going back now.'

He scoops me up in his arms.

'Luke!'

'No arguing.'

Not a problem.

He carries me downstairs and lowers me by the bed.

'I've fallen for this place. Let's not bother with furniture – this could be our fuck pad.'

'Sweet words from such a beautiful woman.'

'You've corrupted me Luke Sutton.'

My hands begin to unbutton his shirt and my mouth takes control, ruthlessly attacking his lips, demanding that Luke play with me. I fear that my hunger for him will never be fulfilled.

Luke's shirt falls to the floor. His taut chest screams for my attention as my lips slide across every inch of his perfectly toned torso.

'I want you naked, and I want to eat you on our bed – now.'

I giggle. I hope this means at least three courses…

My top and bra hit the floor in record time. Luke grabs both of my breasts and lowers his mouth, sucking and nipping my nipples in turn. I need more. My clit is screaming for some action.

His hands move to my zip and his fingers slide inside my knickers.

'Jesus, baby, you're wet.' His touch moves from the edge of my sex to my clit, and almost gives me my first orgasm. My breathing hitches. Luke moves to my ear. 'Not yet.'

He lowers me to the bed. My boots and clothes are discarded, leaving me bare and vulnerable. I watch him strip. He's hot and naked. His needy mouth works from my ankles up to my hip bone, then he brushes his lips against my pubic area. I sway my hips against him.

'Greedy.'

'Luke, please… Touch me.'

'Where?'

'Just touch me – please.'

He takes my hand. 'Show me.'

Oh, for the love of God!

One hand covers my eyes, while the other slides between my wet lips and brushes gently against my clit.

'Kate, look at me.'

I move my hand from my eyes and watch his hand slide up and down the length of his shaft. I blow air through my lips, needing to come – but not yet.

'Spread your legs, baby, I'm hungry.'

In seconds, his tongue flicks against my clit, and moves slowly down to my sex. Christ! His touch is almost too much to bear. Fast and slow, dipping and sliding. Is this his gift, to torture me?

'No more… please,' I beg, and not for the first time.

'I love taking you close. I could come all over you just watching you.'

His mouth returns and his fingers skilfully slip inside my sex.

The first wave washes over me. 'Luke,' I manage to whisper as my body helplessly buckles under his touch.

As ever, he brings me to a place of greed and demand.

His lips move towards my stomach and then my breasts, with slow, leisurely sucks on each nipple. I'm still reeling from the aftermath of my climax. At last his mouth meets mine, and so does the head of his hardness. I hold my breath the moment he enters me; we remain still. Holy shit, it feels good to take him – all of him.

'I love you.' His low voice echoes through my body.

'I love you too.'

His eyes burn not just with desire, but something different tonight.

'Kiss me?' I ask.

His lips are brutal.

My hands slide down his back, encouraging the deepness that I enjoy. His touch and tempo are spot-on; he understands my body like no other. He takes hold of my leg, and I raise my pelvis to meet his rhythm. Hard and fast sex – merry Christmas to me.

'Don't stop, I need to come.' The start of my second orgasm begins. The sensation is intense. As my breathing increases, I begin to climax. 'Luke… I love you.' I can barely speak.

My nails dig into his skin and his lips make contact with mine as he groans into my mouth. Two more thrusts, and I have him.

Afterwards, Luke lights the fire and we sit on the rug close to the Christmas tree, surrounded by our presents, wearing matching grey Abercrombie T-shirts, wet hair and 'just fucked' faces.

'Hold that thought.' Luke saunters to the kitchen and returns with an ice bucket and two flute glasses.

'Are you feeling up to it?' he smiles, taunting me about last night while releasing the cork from the champagne.

'Funny, ha ha.'

He passes me a glass. 'Cheers, baby – merry Christmas.'

'Cheers, I love you.' I lean over and kiss him. 'Present time… Just a heads-up; there's no house lurking under the tree.'

'Good to know!' He laughs.

I pass Luke some smart black boxes tied with black satin bows: very masculine and very Luke Sutton.

'Where shall I start? I see a perfectionist has been at work.' He smiles as he passes me my gift boxes.

'Crap! Your presents are… Luke, you're the hardest person in the world to surprise.'

'Hey, I love them already… You go first,' he commands.

'OK.' I take one at random, untying the red bow and lifting the lid of the white box. I'm faced with another box inscribed with the words *Aspinal of London*. I open it and laugh.

'I love it!' It's a pink leather notebook with a gold inscription: *EAT ME*. My fingers trace the words that remind me of our early days together. The notes I left Luke from the day we first met. How can two simple words carry so much weight?

'How could I resist?'

'Now open one of yours.' At last I feel excited.

He decides to go for the smallest present. I begin to laugh.

'Am I missing the joke?'

'No, just open it and you'll see.' I take another sip of champagne.

Luke tips the contents of the black velvet pouch into the palm of his hand. Instantly he laughs.

'Great minds think alike.' He holds a set of brushed platinum cufflinks with an inscription: *EAT* on one and *ME* on the other.

'I thought it was a bit of fun – do you like them?'

'I do; they're perfect.'

Next, I begin to undo another gift, a small one this time: a purple box with silver writing. I know the signature look of Asprey of London, having received a similar box on my birthday. I remove the lid to reveal the most beautiful diamond stud ear rings.

'Bloody hell, Luke, they're stunning.'

'They match your necklace.'

I remove the earrings and place them in my ears, modelling my gift.

'Beautiful.'

He takes another present, a larger box, and removes the paper.

'Silly, I know.'

He laughs. 'It's been a while since someone has given me a toy.'

'I know how much you love your Aston. I thought a remote control version might help brush up your parking skills.'

He shoots me a look – oh, how I love pressing a Sutton button. 'I was unaware I needed to brush up my parking skills.'

'It all helps.' I bite my lip.

'How thoughtful of you!' He laughs and glides his hand over the box as he reads the information. 'I'm just a bit shocked.'

'Good.' I relax, watching his face light up.

Luke passes me another gift. I tear off the paper to reveal another box that I'm familiar with: Agent Provocateur.

'Now, Mr S, if my memory serves me correctly, the last time you gave me a box like this it was a joint present.' I lift the lid. Wow! A full-length silk nightdress in the palest of pink edged with cream lace. There's also a matching silk robe. 'I love it.'

'I knew you would.'

I stand up and strip, sliding my present over my naked body. My hands run down the fabric and I twirl.

Luke whistles. 'I can't guarantee I won't remove it within the next hour.'

I sit back and give him a kiss on his cheek.

'Thank you.' I pass him another box – the biggest one.

He shreds the paper in no time. I know he will love this.

'Are you trying to keep me young, Kate Harper?'

'No, simply addressing your mental age.' I can't help but laugh.

'Are you challenging me to a race?'

'Are you ready to lose to a girl?' Who would have thought Scalextric would bring out the competitive side of Luke Sutton?

'We'll have fun with this.' Luke stands. 'I have one more present for you – wait here.'

He returns with a gift the size of a large mirror or picture frame.

'Come here.'

My hands work quickly, removing the paper. A picture looks out at me: us at the ball in Venice – the evening that changed my life. My hand skims the image of us dancing. 'Where did you get it?'

'My mum showed me some images a few weeks ago. I zoomed in on our faces.'

'Look at us! So much has happened since then.' I giggle. 'Just think – we hadn't even had sex or kissed.'

Luke tenderly touches the image. 'That's the point: look at your eyes.'

I nod. 'I loved you even then.'

Luke takes a deep breath. He knows I'm his.

'OK. So, do I take it home or… No, lift it above the fireplace.'

He rests the frame on the mantel.

'You look stunning in this. I'm a very lucky man.' He places his hands around my waist and kisses the top of my head.

'Yes, you are.' I chuckle at myself. 'And you have one more gift.'

I pass Luke his last present. He removes the lid, and picks up a black leather book inscribed in gold with two words: *Harper Sutton*.

'Open it,' I instruct a confused Luke.

He does, and begins to read the first page.

'Dear Luke, you have taken possession of my heart and soul. I will love you forever.' Crap. My face glows.

'I found the notes in your office,' I explain, exonerating myself.

He continues to turn the pages.

'It's your very own cookbook. What do you give to a man that has everything?'

'Cooking lessons. Kate, this is very clever.'

I reach across and turn a page. 'My note with the first meal I cooked for you, followed by the recipe and your note.'

'Lasagne… I never saw you coming, Kate.' His eyes meet mine. 'The day you arrived at Sutton Global… I thought I had everything I needed.'

What! Self-effacing Luke Sutton plays havoc with my heart…

'And now you do: your ex-cook is going to give you cooking lessons… Look what else is in the box.'

Luke produces two aprons, a black one for him with COOK and a pink one for me with BOSS embroidered across them.

'So you think you have the patience to teach me?'

'Will you be a good student?'

His eyes remain fixed on the pages. He shakes his head.

'This is… you can't put a price on this… this is our history.' His lips reach mine, gently kissing me.

We sit together on the rug, surrounded by a picnic of ham and cheese sandwiches, pickles, caramelised onions, crisps and a glass of bubbly. Perfect…

'So tell me, how long are we here for? I assume you have a plan?'

'Until New Year's Day. As for the days we are here, we have no plans – just us, the bed and food.'

'You mean, your idea of heaven.' I roll my eyes.

'You know me far too well, and now we have toys, I think we may never leave.'

'Are you ready for a race?'

'Be prepared to have your arse whipped, young lady.'

'Bring it on, Sutton.'

The bright sunshine filtering through the full-length windows is blinding, but it is the noise ringing in my ears that has woken me.

I roll to the side of the bed, looking in the direction of the racket.

'At last she's awake… Are you up for a challenge?'

'What time did you get up?'

'I've been up a while.' Luke saunters around the room

semi-naked, in grey jogger shorts. He looks at me with his captivating smile. 'Look at my track.'

'It looks… hmm… interesting.' I gaze across to the empty boxes and leftover pipework.

'It's a work of art!'

'Tell me – is this present staying here?'

'No… I texted Declan earlier. He wants a race night when we get back to London.' He flashes a boyish smile.

'Oh!' I sit up and reach for my new pink robe, pulling it round my naked body. 'Are you hungry?'

'Yes.' He says, his eyes remaining fixed on a road layout.

I step out of the bed.

'Whoa – look out.'

I freeze as my foot nearly crushes a box, or what appears to be a handmade jump.

'You've taken over the entire room.' I walk towards him. 'And I was concerned you wouldn't like your gifts.'

He stands and wraps his arms around my body, dipping me. Mr Playful Sutton is with me, I hope for the foreseeable future.

'I told you I loved it – please don't doubt me.' He kisses me, and returns me to an upright position.

'Holy shit… look at the view.' I walk towards the large glass windows and try to open the door.

'Let me… It'll be cold out there.'

'I don't care.'

The bright, sunny morning hits me. The panoramic view is amazing. I head to the steps and walk the short path towards the beach. Instantly the sound and smell of the water makes me feel alive. Luke is right; it's bloody freezing, not just the icy temperature, but the sand beneath my feet as well.

'Oh my God. Luke, it's stunning.' I walk further forward. As it's so early, the beach is deserted. There are few houses, some distance away. 'The house isn't overlooked.'

'That did have an impact on the land price.'

'I guess it would.' I dread to think how much our house was. The houses on either side are just as huge and expensive-looking!

The day passes quickly, and gives way to a cold dark night. Having watched far too many Christmas films with the added sound effect of cars racing, I feel Mr Sutton should cook dinner tonight – something easy from his book.

I move from the bed and place my arms around Luke's neck.

'I've been thinking.'

'Go on.'

'You should cook dinner.'

'Is that so?' He kisses my arms, which are lovingly wrapped around him.

'Yes – something easy. How about bacon chilli pasta? Are you up for the challenge, cook?'

'Always.'

As I thought. Goodbye boredom, hello prick-teasing girlfriend! I swiftly move with a certain amount of excitement and collect Luke's new book and apron.

'I'm going to change. I'll join you in the kitchen.' As I reach the stairs, I say, 'Oh, and if you collect the right ingredients there may be a reward.'

He raises his head and fires me a look. 'And what might that be?' he asks suspiciously.

I tap my nose.

I'm grateful Luke had some foresight and bought me the new underwear. I put on a black lace bra, garter belt and lace-top stockings. I slide up my French knickers, then tie my apron on over them, and slip on black Louboutins.

My heels tap seductively against the wooden floor as I enter the kitchen. My eyes fall to Luke, who is concentrating, which always makes me horny: it does at home and now at Sandbanks. My spell breaks when he looks up at me. I move towards him.

He scans my body. 'Are you expecting me to cook when you're dressed like that?'

'I thought, as you're going to so much trouble, that I'd dress for dinner.' I can't hide my amusement.

'Dress for dinner!' The tone of his voice alters. Is my mission complete? Hell, yes!

I turn and walk towards the larder, where I grab a bottle of Luke's favourite burgundy Caymus wine.

I open the red wine and collect two glasses, pouring equal measures. I pass one to Luke. 'Cheers – happy Boxing Day.'

'Here's to pushing my buttons.'

'I'm not pushing your buttons. But I do feel hot.' I suggestively untie my apron and remove it. Luke moves towards me.

'No!' I hold up my finger.

'No?' Luke suppresses a laugh.

'Let's eat first.'

'I'm not hungry.'

'You're always hungry.' This is hard! Stay focused, Harper.

My eyes lock to his: dark and sexually needy meet dark and sexually teasing…

I blink to break the spell.

'Let's see how you're getting on.' I move in front of him. 'OK. You have most of the ingredients – well done.' I can feel his laboured breathing on the back of my neck. I reach for the jar of rigatoni pasta, causing my arse to push up against him. God, he's ready!

'Fuck, Kate.'

'Concentrate, Luke.' I purse my lips. At last I've kicked the hornet's nest.

His mouth moves to my ear. 'Oh, baby… If you stick your arse out again I will take you now, and it won't be for you.'

Diversionary tactics are needed – for me! I jump up and sit on the worktop, crossing my legs.

'Have you read what's next? So, you need to finely chop the mushrooms, onion, garlic and chilli.'

He listens and begins to chop the mushrooms.

'Well done.'

'Well done?' he repeats.

He loves the game we're playing. He's built to play – and, of course, win.

'You need the large pan and some oil.'

I can feel his dark eyes observing me, slowly working their way down towards my legs. I lean across the book to collect the bottle of wine. 'Sorry.'

'You will be' – threatening talk from Mr Frustrated Sutton – oh, what fun.

I uncross my legs and provocatively re-cross them. 'Do you want me to help you?'

'Help, and how are you going to help?' Luke sounds frustrated.

I reach across him again, this time brushing my breast against his arm. Luke grabs both my wrists, preventing me from moving. His grip tightens.

'So you want to play a game, do you?' His eyes are scorching, a warning he's going to take me.

'No… cooking.'

'Kate Harper, you know I always win.'

I try to remain in control: however, my act is fading rapidly. Giving me no time to answer, Luke claims victory over my mouth, and his tongue begins to move against mine. I willingly respond, as I always do.

He grabs my hips and aggressively removes my knickers. He leaves my mouth. I pant, wanting more.

'This will be quick.'

I nod. My eyes remain fixed on his, watching and waiting for his next move. He roughly spreads my legs. I yank at his waistband and my eyes fall to his erection. Jesus, he looks harder than usual. I lick my dry lips. At the same time, he grabs my hips with one hand and guides his erection to my sex with the other. One thrust and he's deep inside.

'Christ, Luke!' He feels harder than usual.

He withdraws, only to drive into me again, with power. I hold on to the side of the worktop in case I fall. He thrusts harder and harder. He knows I want and need more. I also know he's not going to give it to me. He picks up my hand and places it on my clit.

'Now let me watch you work.' I don't argue; quite the opposite – I gratify his demand.

How does he do this to me? Make me want and need to please him? My hand remains on my clit, working in time with Luke's pounding. He looks from my eyes to my hand. This is Luke Sutton declaring triumph: he's in total control – not me.

My orgasm is on the brink of release as Luke's thrusts become more hard-hitting, touching the area that sends me to a place of incoherency. Shockwaves begin to roll through me as my body jolts.

'Kate, look at me.'

My gaze locks to his as the tremors begin within me. Christ, my clit is on fire! As my orgasm erupts, he drives hard enough to find release. The rise and fall of his chest is visible; I have him, hot and deep-rooted.

'Are you enjoying your cooking lesson?' I tenderly kiss his jawline.

'You're a prick-tease. There's no teaching here.'

I kiss him as he slides out of me, making me wince slightly.

Luke lifts my chin. 'Did I hurt you?' Panic shows in his eyes.

'No.'

He looks away.

'Hey, I'm fine.'

'If I ever go in too – deep or…' His lips brush against my forehead.

'Christ, Luke, you're missing the point… I like it when you're…'

'Rough?' His features alter.

'No, not rough… It turns me on when you need me so much – like life or death.' I pull his face to mine and kiss him. 'I like teasing you. I can't control any part of your life, except this – us, you dripping down my leg.'

'You control me, period, Kate.'

'Last night was different – it was making love, but this is fun too. I like the chase and conquest. Crazy, right?'

'No… Us and sex is always about love; it's what drives me to want you.'

'Me too.'

His thumb skims my lips. 'I would never hurt you.'

'I know.'

Another day arrives, and we both feel the need to burst our Harper–Sutton bubble and get back to the real world, so we leave our love nest and head to Canford Cliffs, a nearby village. We amble through a small high street looking for somewhere to have lunch.

'Over there,' I point across the street, 'the Duck and Goose.'

The pub is perfectly quaint with an amazing open fire. However, I do feel slightly overdressed in my new black faux-fur coat!

We sit and read the menu.

'Too many choices! OK, I'll have the steak and stilton pie and a glass of Guinness.'

'Guinness!' Luke looks at me.

'My dad drinks it.'

'Guinness it is, and I think I'll join you.'

Luke goes to the bar.

My eyes lock on the flickering flames. I take a deep breath and mentally return to the night I spent with Ivor. So many questions remain unanswered. 'Where the hell are you?' is my first question, followed by, 'did you try to kill me – twice'?

'Kate!'

'Sorry, I was miles away.' I reach across and take his hand.

'Anywhere special?' His warm smile almost stops me from answering.

'Honestly?'

'Always,' he says.

'Ivor.'

Luke's brow creases.

'I know it pisses you off, but it makes me so mad. I know he may have tied me to the chair, but the fact he walked away kills me... I don't understand how he could do that.'

Luke brushes my cheek with the back of his hand. 'I understand.'

'How can you? Your parents idolise you.'

'So do Malcolm and Susan.'

'Do they?'

'Why would you say that?'

'They kept a huge secret from me and Harry.'

'For good reason – they love you, and I think you need to spend some time with them.'

'I know they love us, but everything's changed... Christ, Luke, the day Harry and I sat with them to "talk openly" about the adoption, Mum sobbed and Dad left the room after ten minutes, to work on something – apparently. They aren't dealing with it and I can't carry them. God, I have my own issues to work through.' I take a sip of my Guinness. 'Dad struggles to be in the same room as us; it's like he's lost the right to be our dad. They forget they did this – not me or Harry.'

'Give them time. Your dad could have died, and today could have been different for all of you. '

'That makes me feel guilty. You can't hide the fact that *I* did that to him; my inheritance could have killed him.'

'Baby, no! This is not your fault.'

'Er – yes it is! My Russian ancestors and all that goes with them. I'm angry that Dad's brushed the adoption under the carpet, and Mum supports him. Just before Christmas, Harry and I tried to get him to open up, but he just wouldn't. I don't get it. We could have disowned them, but we haven't and never would.'

'Have you thought that he's probably in shock – not only from the attack but also the biggest secret in his life is out there – your adoption? Maybe it's time to sit down with them both again.'

'What's the point?'

Luke gently skims my cheek.

'Luke, it's easier for them to pretend that nothing's changed.' I look towards the roaring fire.

'In some ways it hasn't; they would do anything for you and Harry. For them to carry on as normal is the only way they will get back what they lost, and perhaps get rid of their guilt.'

'That makes me feel worse. I'm judging Dad for befriending Katenka – shame I don't do that to Ivor.'

'You're curious about him.'

'You think? Run, Sutton, run like the wind… You've found yourself a lunatic girlfriend with a shitload of baggage.'

'You're my kind of crazy.'

'Even though I have a crazy Russian father, who I want to find? Help me, Luke – this is a huge deal for me; please don't sidestep me.'

'Perhaps you should spend more time with Susan and Malcolm and less on…' He trails off.

'Ivor? You won't burn saying his name. Look, Mum and Dad know I love them. Clearly, nothing's bloody changed – considering my life has. I need this, not them or Harry. I need this… You know what surprises me? You.'

His eyes widen.

'Don't look like that – you know what I mean. And, for the record, I think you do know where he is, but you're holding out! You have the means to know, that's why I asked you when you got back from Switzerland – you and Sullivan are as thick as thieves but apparently you know nothing. I don't believe you.'

He takes a deep breath, one filled with frustration. 'That's unfair.'

'Is it? Then tell me I'm wrong.'

'You're wrong, and I will never forgive the person who tied you to the chair – that person may be Ivor.'

'My gut instinct, for what it's worth, is that it wasn't Ivor.'

'Don't knock it, my gut instinct has saved me more times than I care to admit.'

'While we're on the subject of missing Russians, I've decided to look into Katenka's death.'

'You've read the coroner's report from Sullivan – it clearly states her death was suicide.'

'I think Ivor was right; something doesn't add up.'

'Gut instinct, again?'

'Don't take the piss… Something's bugging me about this.' I take his hand. 'I need to find out; I don't know how, but I have to.'

Luke leans across and kisses my cheek. 'I'll help you, but I need you to be honest with me – no disappearing to Russia.'

I can't help but smile. 'Never! Besides, I have my very own assassin.'

'Oi, watch it.' Luke gauges the people nearby.

'That reminds me, are you going to dress up in your 007 wannabe outfit?'

'No… Unless it's to rescue your tight little arse – again.'

I watch Luke sleep, and run my fingers through his hair, skimming the small scar on his shoulder from the explosion. Thank God I kept him talking that afternoon; him running late may have saved his life. I close my eyes for a second, and the image of Luke lying next to the burning car is a scary reminder that today could have been very different. He spent years in the military and got no scars; I walk into his life and he now has the scars to prove it. My mind goes over our conversation in the pub, but I'm too exhausted to think about how I can move forward. I hook my leg over Luke's, needing to feel close to him, although Luke buried deep inside me ten minutes ago would constitute being as close as two people can be.

The smoke fills my lungs – I can't breathe. Arms pull at me, stopping me from moving. I scream Luke's name again and again. My heart pumps fast, desperately. Through the grey mist I can see someone moving slowly. I call out his name…

My eyes open. I can't breathe. Luke lies sprawled across the bed next to me. He's safe. I close my eyes; he's safe. I still can't breathe, and gasp for air.

I slide out of bed, wrap my fur coat around my naked body, and slip on my Hunter boots. I open the back door. Shit, it's freezing! I walk across the sand towards the sea. I look down at my watch. It's seven thirty. The sound of the sea is hypnotic. I close my eyes and inhale the salty air. The love of my life is alive and asleep.

A hand around my waist bursts through my thoughts.

'Nightmare?'

I nod.

'Clear morning.' Luke kisses the top of my head.

'Stunning.' I exhale.

'Did you need some air?'

'I couldn't breathe.' My shaky voice indicates the horror show that woke me. 'It was the same as before; you were coming out of the smoke.'

Luke turns me to face him. 'Maybe it's time to see someone.'

'No... I haven't had a nightmare since... the night before the wedding. I'm usually OK if you're with me.'

'That's not a problem. I hate leaving you.'

I link my hands around his neck. 'Let me try and deal with them before you lock me up.'

'Any excuse to lock you up.' My coat opens slightly. 'Kate Harper, you're naked on the beach.' His cold hands slip inside my coat.

'No, I have a coat on, and your hands are bloody freezing.'

He tilts his head and gives me his one-sided fuck me now smile. Shit, I'm now officially ready for him.

'You have a couple of choices.'

'Luke Sutton offering choices? There must be a catch,' I respond sharply.

'Yes… Choices. The beach or,' he looks back towards the decking, 'the sun-lounger.' A wolfish grin spreads across his face.

'They're your choices… in the freezing bloody cold?' I laugh. 'Who said romance was dead?'

Luke's lips cover mine urgently. His touch is caring, but I can feel his need for me. His strong arms hold me close to his chest, protecting me – after all, it's his job. Perhaps he thinks of me as the assignment he couldn't fulfil. His chest expands against mine; I move my head and look up to him. He sweeps the hair away from my face, the look in his eyes suggesting this is more than sex. This is Luke Sutton giving himself to me; no one can touch us when we're together. 'You're safe here; this is our place.'

I nod. A safe haven for him too.

He scoops me up in his arms and begins to walk.

'I'm guessing the beach is off the menu.'

'You were too slow. Besides, I like to have you in private.'

Luke steps up onto the secluded deck and lowers my feet to the wood. Instinctively the connection between us alters. My hands link around his neck, drawing his lips to mine; his tongue is as piercing as the morning sun. His hands wander inside my coat: once again, cold hands on my soft, warm skin.

He moves me towards a lounger and sits down. 'Straddle me.'

'Luke, you must be freezing.' He just has a T-shirt and short joggers to keep him warm.

'I'm fine; just straddle me.'

I spread my legs, lower myself down, and meet his early morning erection.

'Weather conditions don't affect you.'

'No… Suck me.'

'Or your demands!'

My hands yank at his jogger shorts, freeing his heavy erection into the palm of my hand. I move down his legs and lean forward. I gaze up at his face and run my tongue across my lower lip. His breathing quickens before I lick the crown of his hardness. Seconds later, my mouth closes around him.

'Jesus, Kate.'

My hand begins to pump his shaft. His thighs tense beneath me and soft seductive groans echo through his slightly parted lips. The sounds he makes when I have him turn me on, encouraging me to take him to a place he takes me every time I'm close to orgasm. I continue until pre-cum swirls inside my mouth, and I know he's close.

He pulls at my shoulders. 'Baby, I want to be inside you.'

I raise myself off him and wipe my mouth on the back of my hand. He takes hold of his erection.

'Christ… my dick is so hard.'

I nod.

'Lift up.' His hand gently slides inside my sex. 'Good – you're ready, as always.' He holds the head of his erection at my sex. 'Slowly.' I lower myself and groan. 'Don't move – wait.' Luke looks at me. 'Breathe, baby.'

'I am.'

'OK – you have me… Jesus.'

Let the games begin.

The soles of my Hunters make contact with the decking, giving me leverage to thrust. Luke pulls my coat open. The cold air meets my warm skin: it's breath-taking, especially with his fingers circulating over my clit in a small motion with a huge impact.

'You look hot... I want to touch your arse.'

I almost freeze on the spot.

Luke senses my uncertainty. 'Trust me.'

I nod. Fuck!

'Lift yourself off me.' He grips my hips and eases me off him.

He inserts his fingers in my sex, distributing my juices from my clit to the opening of my arse. He repeats this over and over again. It feels naughty – but sexy.

'Take me again.' He guides me in and readjusts his position.

His eyes are scorching, and so is his touch against the entrance to my arse, as his other hand increases the pressure on my clit. I gasp when he inserts his finger. *Fuck!* I pathetically try to maintain my rhythm, but as my body is being manipulated in various places I struggle to carry on.

'That's it... keep going. Look at me. Baby, look at me.'

I raise my head at the same time his hands work harder. The sensation is killing me: my breathing is rapid and my skin is on fire.

'I know you want to come, but just hold off.'

Hold off? Is he joking? I try to slow myself, but I can't. Luke inserts his finger further into my arse.

'Shit... Luke... I can't...' *I'm gone.*

'Give it to me, Kate.'

I close my eyes and ride the rush. He's relentless this morning, and I'm happy to take it.

'Again... Kate, look at me.'

I open my eyes and lick my dry lips.

'Give me another orgasm. You're so wet. Jesus, Kate.'

My nipples harden with the sensations he's arousing in me, and the temperature outside. He fingers my arse again, but faster. 'Is this OK?'

'Yes,' I whisper, as the second orgasm arrives. 'Oh my God… don't stop… Luke.'

'I'm with you,' he says through gritted teeth. 'Fuck… keep going.'

His breathing grows shallow and his jaw clenches. One more thrust and his body slackens. He removes his fingers from various places. I lower my head to his T-shirt. Wow, that was intense.

Luke runs his hands through my matted hair. 'I think Sandbanks has a lot to offer.'

I laugh, still feeling dazed.

'I may have to question your choices.' My arse! What shocks me is that I enjoyed it so much. 'I'm cold.'

'I'll run a hot bath for us both.'

I nod, too cold to speak.

Emptying the fridge, I decide what to cook for our last evening together at Sandbanks. The thought of leaving our safe haven tomorrow hits me: back to reality, and back to dealing with the Coopers. For the first time in months I have felt contented. How can something so simple be so hard to achieve? My emotions swell inside me: having money and a busy life doesn't mean happiness.

Luke's voice distracts me from the task in hand.

'If it doesn't arrive, I can assure you there will be trouble,' he yells. He shuts his phone off, running his hands through his hair. He sees me watching him.

'Problem?' I pass him a coffee.

'No.' He reaches over and gives me a kiss. 'Work issues. How are you getting on with packing?'

'It's nearly done, just some bits left that I'll pack tomorrow… Risotto OK for dinner?'

'Are you asking me to cook again?' Luke drinks his coffee, taking my hand as we walk back to the lounge, the room we have lived in for the last week.

'No.'

'Then risotto will be fine.'

We lie on the bed watching another film. My head rests on Luke's chest, and I relax, allowing my body and mind to enjoy our last afternoon of the year together – it's New Year's Eve. Luke's phone buzzes, and he reads a message.

'I'm going for a run.' He places a kiss on the top of my head.

'OK.'

I stay on the bed as Luke leaves me with my thoughts and my Christmas present, an empty pink notepad. My life is like the notebook: an empty sheet of paper waiting to be filled with hopes and dreams!

Before long the door opens again, and Luke enters, panting.

'Good run?' He nods and leans forward, planting a damp kiss on my cheek. 'You're sweaty.'

'Do you want a shower?' he says in his raspy voice, which is mixed with breathlessness – quite captivating.

I laugh. 'Do I have a choice?'

He tilts his head. 'You always have a choice. But I do have powers of persuasion.'

I'm now wet and ready. I stand, and go with him.

Our last night passes with us both playing with the Scalextric and Luke making an assault course for his remote control car.

'Here's the deal. If you reverse the car in between the boxes, I'll let you drive my Aston when we get home.'

'Oh, really? Well, I'll reverse the car, but I have no intention of ever driving your baby.'

'OK.' For the first time he doesn't fight me. We both know that hell will freeze over before he lets me behind the wheel of the love of his life.

Luke looks at his watch.

'Half an hour to go. I'll get some champagne.'

My head rests against the window. The outside lights show the weather is dismal, with strong wind and rain. With the fire roaring and the fairy lights twinkling, the outside elements have no effect on our peaceful evening.

'Kate.' I turn to see Luke holding two champagne flutes.

I take a cold glass of bubbly. 'Thank you. Cheers.'

'Cheers.'

I take a sip.

'Put your coat on. I want us to go outside to bring the new year in.' He takes my glass.

'It's raining.'

Luke laughs. 'Good.'

'How's that good?'

'Baby, I met you when you were wet – I see this as a lucky sign of our lasting relationship.'

Oh God, the day I arrived at Sutton Global drenched.

'Mr S, are you being sentimental?' I reach up and give him a kiss, and realise I will have to oblige in his little game.

We look identical in black Musto coats and black Hunters.

'Ready?'

'Yes.'

Luke opens the back door. The wind hits me as soon as we step out on to the decking. He takes my hand and leads me along the beach. I guess he really does want to get me wet! We stand at one side of the house. Luke checks his watch. 'A minute to go.'

I place my arms around his neck. 'I love you, Luke Sutton. This has been the best Christmas ever. Thank you.'

'I love you too... Ten, nine, eight, seven, six, five, four, three, two, one – Happy New Year.'

'Happy New year.'

'I want you to do something for me.'

'What?' The rain continues to drench us both.

'Press this button.' He passes me something. It looks like a car alarm. 'Press it now.'

I press the button, and a set of car headlights shines directly in front of us. Luke takes my hand and guides me towards the beam. The car is parked on the verge.

'Holy shit... Luke!'

8

I turn, to see Luke on his knees. 'Will you?'

I stare at the number plate in disbelief. It is M4RRY M3.

'Kate!'

I join him on my knees. 'Yes,' I whisper hoarsely. I can barely speak. His question has shocked me to the core. Luke wants to marry me! Holy crap! The words go round in my head – Luke wants to marry me!

He takes my face and kisses me hard. The strong wind blows the hood of my coat back, allowing the rain to soak my hair and trickle down my cheeks.

He pulls away. 'You won't regret it, Kate... Let me show you something.'

He takes the black key fob from my hands and waves it in front of my face. I notice something sparkling there. Luke unties the black ribbon and removes a ring.

'Kate Harper, will you marry me?' He slips the ring on my finger and takes my hands.

My tears fall.

'Yes.' I lower my gaze to the ring: a simple diamond solitaire – it's stunning.

'I love you, my fiancée.' His face lights up in a way I have never seen before.

'I like the sound of that.'

'Me too. You have possessed me, Kate Harper.' Luke stands and holds his hand out. 'I have something else to show you.'

I place my hand in his as we walk to the car. He presses the button again, illuminating our path.

'This is your last gift.'

'The car!'

'It's a Bentley Continental GT. The number plate was… difficult to get hold of.'

'It's real!' I laugh. Only Luke would be able to find a way to inform everyone that I'm officially off the market.

'Let's go back inside… You're soaking. I would rather you be a different kind of wet, and remain healthy.' He smirks.

'Oi – what am I going to do with you?' I run my hands through his wet hair and kiss him. I have never felt such love for him as I do tonight.

We run back to the house, battling against the rain.

Luke takes my hand, walks me towards the fire, and begins to remove my wet clothes. I watch him as he slips his T-shirt over his head and slides his jogging trousers down his strong thighs.

'Luke Sutton, commando!'

'Easy access.' His best Sutton smile appears.

'I can see that.'

He pushes my wet hair back from my face, and draws me close.

'I will never let you go… You need to hang on for the ride of your life.'

'Back at you.' My eyes lock with his. I know the ride will challenge us both.

Luke guides me to the rug and places himself between my legs. His lips gently skim my stomach and move up towards my breasts. His tongue circles my nipples.

'I could do this all night.' He says sharing his lips between each breast.

'You can, every night.' I draw my lips inwards as my body begins to respond to his simple, yet effective technique.

I open my eyes. 'Luke, promise you'll never stop this.' He moves to my face. 'I mean, needing me.' I run my hands through his damp hair, drawing him closer.

'I will always need you – you're going to be my wife.' His hand slides between my thighs as his fingers dip inside my sex. My breathing hitches. He grips my leg, allowing himself more space. 'You have every part of me, Kate. I have never been this exposed to anyone.'

Oh God. A single tear rolls down my cheek. His dark eyes gleam with happiness, and we both understand our lives from this moment will never be the same. Mr and Mrs Sutton.

Afterwards, we lie in front of the fire, wrapped in each other's arms, the duvet keeping us warm.

'I can't believe you've asked me to marry you.' I roll onto my stomach and look at my ring, touching and twisting it with my fingers. 'Did you ask my dad?'

Luke props himself up on his elbow.

'A while ago.'

'A while ago! How long have you been planning this?'

'I ordered your car a few months ago. Once I got the number plate, tonight seemed the perfect time to ask you, and the rain just added to the scene. Though waiting for your car to arrive was pissing me off.'

'Romantic at heart! I never saw this coming... I mean, I couldn't imagine life without you, but this...' I look at my ring and hold it up, the light from the fire gleams across the stone. 'It's beautiful.'

He takes my hand and kisses my finger.

'It's a perfect fit. This means we're forever, Kate.'

I believe his words.

I laugh. 'Do you know what you've let yourself in for?'

'Our lives will be challenging, I know that, Kate Harper... Or should I say Kate Sutton?'

I giggle.

'That sounds odd. Can I suggest something? I know I'm a bit ahead of myself.'

'Of course.' He gently sweeps the damp hair from my face.

'Venice... Can we get married in Venice? Something small, just us, with our families and friends?'

'Where it began.'

In the morning, I stir to find Luke watching me. My stomach somersaults, remembering last night and the proposal.

'Good morning, husband-to-be.'

'Hello, my beautiful wife-to-be... Did you sleep well?'

'No nightmares.' My arms stretch high above my head. 'Let's stay here forever.'

'We can come here every weekend, but I would like to get some more furniture, although this has been fun.'

'It has. Back to basics, no fuss or frills.' I roll to my side. 'I do have a lot of ideas.'

'Good – decorating and a wedding to plan… you'll be very busy, Kate Harper – or should I say Kate Sutton.'

'I'm not a Sutton yet. You've slept on the idea, it's not too late to change your mind.'

Luke's strong arms seize me. 'Not a chance; you said yes! No going back.' He kisses me while one hand pins my arms above my head. His lips move to my neck, making me laugh. What a joy: Mr Playful Sutton is with me this morning.

'You need to keep this fob in your purse or bag. It activates the push button start.'

'Why don't they have a key?' I sit in the driver's seat of my beautiful new black Bentley.

'Because they don't.' He looks at me, exasperated by my question. 'Push the button, Kate.' I do as instructed, and the car starts. 'As you can see, here are the lights, indicator and windscreen wipers.' He leans across me. 'In the centre is your touchscreen satnav: the car will automatically pick up your Bluetooth so you can call your fiancé.' I smile. 'The car has an eight-channel and an eight-speaker sound system with a fifteen gig storage facility. You can use your iPhone, or discs; it's your choice. This car has a V8 engine: it's quick, so, watch your right foot.' He looks at me, realising he's lost me.

My hands move to the sun visor. I pull it down and lift the flap. 'Nice mirror.'

Luke shakes his head. 'Have you listened to anything I've said?'

'Yeah… Push the start button, I can call my hot fiancé and play music… Of course, there's a fab mirror and a cup holder… Looks like I'm good to go.' I step out of the car and link my arms around his neck. 'I love it; I'm just overwhelmed.'

'A sexy car for my sexy fiancée.' He delivers a cheeky kiss. 'Time to leave – do you have everything you need?'

'I'll have to follow you.'

'We'll take your car. Thomas will pick up the Range Rover tomorrow.'

'Oh… Never short of an order, are you?'

The car runs smoothly. Most of the time, Luke is a businessman, but this is my favourite Luke, when he's perfectly relaxed. Weirdly, watching him drive is a huge turn-on… Is there no hope for me?

'I need to call Mum and Dad when I get home. I feel bad I haven't told them or Harry. Did Mum and Dad expect you to ask me last night?' I gaze across at him.

He places a hand on my leg. 'No. I never told your dad when I'd ask you, only that it would be soon.'

'And your parents?'

'My mum asked me at Harry's wedding; she sensed there was something on my mind. To be honest, she was more surprised I hadn't done it sooner.'

'She has a point; you did take your time.' I laugh. 'Are you still happy with the idea of Venice? It's just that I really don't want a massive wedding like Harry's.'

'Simple… I love the idea. The only stipulation I have is the date – sooner rather than later. It seems pointless to wait.'

'Me too, but I do want our closest people there if that's not too much trouble. I'm guessing the hotel will be pretty pricey?'

'The cost is irrelevant.'

'Anyway, changing the subject, I've been thinking about my future, and making notes in my beautiful Christmas gift.'

'Not content with your mother's empire?'

'Kate Harper' and 'empire' in the same sentence – not funny!

'No. I would rather you run it. But you know that! OK, so, I know what I want to do.' I hold open my pink notepad.

Luke's eyes flit from the road to my writing. 'Harper Jones?' he says uncertainly. 'Enlighten me.'

'Mr Jones's fashion collection; remember the sketches I told you about?'

'In his store room.'

'Yeah. On my last day at the tailor's, he showed me his hidden books. I've told you how amazing they were. Anyway, I mentioned that if I had the money we could bring his drawings to life – Harper Jones. I was joking, but now we can: I have the money.'

Luke remains poker-faced.

'Is that something Mr Jones wants?'

I shut my pink book. 'Honestly, I'm not sure – I'd need to talk to him first. I spoke to him just before Christmas, and I think it would be fun. You know how talented he is. Not only that, but I also thought about asking others to join. I'll need all the help I can get.'

'Others?'

'Maria.'

'Kate, you've only worked with her for a day... That could be a risky choice.'

'No. I think I could work well with her. I met her for lunch before Christmas – she hates her new job and loves a challenge. She would be perfect – and Valerie.'

Luke looks at me. 'Valerie!'

'She's an amazing stylist. Look, it's an idea, that's all. I'm going to invite Mr Jones over for dinner tomorrow – are you OK with that? Not the dinner, but my idea. I know it's a long way from ever being a reality, but I need your support and advice.'

Luke scratches his jaw. 'Of course I'll support you… But any new business is tough and it takes a lot of time and patience.'

'I need something to get stuck into, something that's mine… Nothing to do with you, or Russia.'

He grins. 'Me?'

'I don't need space from you – well, maybe I do.' I chew the inside of my lip.

'Space… How much space are you talking about?' He squeezes my fingers.

'You're missing the point. I don't need space as in being far away from you, but space to figure out what I want to do with my life. You have your empire. I want to do something too. To come home at night and talk about our lives. The only time we had that was my first – and last – day at Hudson Bay Interiors. I kind of want that back.'

'Fair point. OK, Run with your vision, soon-to-be Mrs Sutton.'

'Bloody hell, my stomach flips when you say that… I'm still in shock – as usual you knock me on my arse.'

'You know I love your arse.'

'We just got home. OK, Mum, that's fine.' I walk into Luke's office, holding the phone away from my ear. 'See you soon.' Luke looks up from his desk.

'Are we having visitors?'

I move to join him.

'She wants to come over and congratulate us in person. You must have heard her excitement. Why don't you ask your mum and dad too... Two birds, one stone?'

Luke turns his chair and grabs my hips, pulling me onto his lap. He strokes my hair as his lips meet mine, kissing me with purpose.

He breaks free. 'I'll call them.' He seems preoccupied.

'What's up, Sutton?'

'It scares me that you read me too well, baby.' His eyes gleam. He does love that I can see him, the real Luke Sutton.

'Bet your arse I do.'

'Back to reality now.'

'Reality is crap! Thank you for Sandbanks – it was the best. Just us was perfect.'

'For the first time in a very long time I haven't thought about Sutton Global.'

My eyes narrow. 'You always think about work, it's in you.'

'I was in you for the past week.' His smile gets me every time.

'Oi.' I tap his arm.

'Kate, I've never had that.'

'What?'

'A reason to not think about work. It feels good.'

'Oh.' I wasn't expecting that.

'It's made me realise that I need to balance you and work.'

'Good. I was thinking the same. You need more free time to spend with me – maybe Sutton Global needs a shake-up... Drop Iceman Sutton and thaw a bit. Take cheeky days off – live a little.'

'Iceman!' He laughs.

'Hot iceman.'

'God, I love your mouth.'

'Good, because I intend to do rude things with it later.' I place my hands on his chest.

'I'll call my parents and finish up here.'

I head to the door.

'But you're all mine once they've gone, Harper.'

I laugh. 'All part of my plan, Sutton.' I think I'm starting to control his world!

God, it feels good to be home. My back hits the bed; I lie there staring at my sparkly ring. Shit – I'm going to be Luke's wife! I roll onto my stomach, grab my mobile and call Harry.

She answers immediately.

'Hello, is that Mrs Leclair?' I chuckle.

'Yes it is, how may I help my fab sister?' Harry says.

'Guess what? Your sister will soon be Mrs Kate Sutton!' I hold the phone away from my ear.

'Holy fucking hell! Oh my God...' The words are followed by screams and then silence.

'Harry... Harry... Harriet Harper, are you crying?'

'Yes.'

My tears begin to flow too.

'I miss you. I would rather have told you in person, but there was no way I was going to wait for you to get back from your honeymoon.'

'Oh my God, no way. How did Mum and Dad take the news?'

'Pleased – I hope. They're coming over for a drink to celebrate.'

'I'm so happy for you both. I know what Luke can be like, but, Christ, he adores you, and that's good enough for me.'

'I couldn't be without him.' Never.

'Big kiss to you.'

'Back at you, babe. How's Raymond?'

'Lovely, he's working on a portrait... of me.'

'Naked?' I ask in jest.

'No comment!'

I can't help but laugh. 'Are you kidding me? Is he really painting a naked picture of you? Seriously, this is taking painting by numbers to a whole new level.'

'Maybe.' Harry laughs. 'Don't tell anyone.'

'Don't worry, I won't... Harry, I can't believe you. I take it you're not going to put it above the fireplace in London?'

'No way; I'll leave it here in France.'

'Safest place. I'd better go. I want to call the others and spread the news. I'll see you next week. Love you.'

'Love you too.'

I shake my head at the thought of Raymond painting my sister – naked! A vision I need to eradicate from my mind – quickly.

Kiki is relatively happy about the news, which surprises me, and of course practical Molly knew it was looming. The only person left to call is Barney.

He answers instantly. 'Is that my favourite Harper girl? Happy New Year, you gorgeous creature.'

'It is, but I have to inform you, I'll soon be your favourite Sutton girl.'

'Well, fuck me gently, about fucking time. I tell you what, babe, if he didn't get down on one knee soon, I was going to do it for him… Now there's a thought – on my knees for the Sutton boy… Anyway, back to you and the best news I've heard all year.'

'Barney – it's New Year's Day.' I laugh.

'Well, it's not much of a challenge then, is it? I'm so happy for you – right, we're out celebrating. You name the place.'

'Soon! I have to go to New York in a couple of days: I've got a meeting with the Coopers – what a treat.'

'Now lover boy has put a ring on your finger, you can tell her to shove it up her arse… Look who's no good for him now, stupid bitch.'

'I wish I could take you to the boardroom. Who am I kidding? I mention the word "boardroom" and I melt… I hate this, Barney, it's just not me. I would sooner serve the bloody coffee.'

'Well, tough fucking luck – you make sure you dress to kill. Kate, you're not bloody stupid, so don't let them make you feel that way.'

'Thanks, Barney. So, what else have you been up to?'

'Not a lot. Your mum has been feeding me. I went to a party last night.'

'How's my house?'

'Still standing and rent-free.'

'It's yours, I promised you.'

'I know, babe… but…'

'No buts… I can afford it. Look, I have to go. So I'll see you in about five days.'

'OK, babe. Big congrats to you and lover boy.'

Everyone congregates in the kitchen to congratulate us. Mum and Livy cry, and so does Rosie. Dad looks lost; he should be used to it, though, having walked one daughter down the aisle only a few days ago. He's quiet for other reasons; I know him too well.

Mum and Livy are intent on wedding talk: where, time of year and theme. I look across to Luke, feeling grateful that we've agreed on a simple affair.

He moves towards us, placing an arm over Livy's shoulder. She looks up at him with warmth. 'Oh darling, Susan and I were talking about the wedding.'

'We've already decided what we'd like. I have to say I think my fiancée has made the best decision, as she always does.'

Mum looks at me.

I take a sip of champagne. 'We want a simple day.'

'Venice.' Luke pulls me into his arms. God, he feels safe and – mine. This has to be my favourite place in the world.

'Venice!' Livy looks at Mum.

'Simple and romantic,' I respond quickly. 'Neither of us want a big wedding like Harry. Honestly, we could go to Gretna Green for all I care!'

Luke holds my towel as I step out of the bath. I can't help yawning.

'You look exhausted.' He kisses the top of my head.

'You're upsetting my mojo, Mr Sutton. As ever, you drain me… kiss me.'

Luke gently places his mouth over mine. It's soft and tender, yet he never loses the power to command my body. His arms loosen, allowing my towel to fall. We stand together, naked. Luke stops kissing me and scoops me up in his arms and carries me to our room, placing me in the middle of the bed.

He crawls between my legs, kissing me all the way until he reaches my face.

'I love you… Never leave me, Luke.'

He doesn't reply, but his answer glimmers through his dark eyes.

9

My eyes open reluctantly.

'It's only seven thirty. You have plenty of time.' Luke runs his finger down my cheek. He's dressed and ready for world domination. 'Tea is next to you.'

I bury my face in the pillow, already fretting over my meeting with Tanya. I sit up slightly, wrapping the duvet around my naked body.

'What time did you get up?' I reach for my tea.

'A while ago; I went for a run.' He sits on the bed.

'You have far too much energy.'

'I need my strength to deal with you.' His soft lips gently touch my forehead. 'Other than Tanya, what else do you have planned for the day?'

'I'm going to call Mr Jones, invite him over for dinner. Will you be home or are you working late?'

'It depends how my day goes. After a week away, no doubt there'll be a pile of work to do.'

Luke stands, adjusting his trousers. 'I'll be downstairs.'

I lie back down on the bed and give him a wave.

'Get up, Harper!'

'Not for much longer – Sutton.'

I study my reflection in the French mirror: a fairly short navy lace skirt, navy opaque tights and a tight-fitting navy polo neck, tan shoe boots, and a wide tan leather belt to highlight my narrow waist. Feminine, yet smart. My entire outfit cost about forty pounds, though that doesn't include my underwear, which must have cost Luke triple that!

I enter the kitchen and the noise stops. Luke silently scans my outfit.

'Morning. You OK, Rosie?' I place my bag and coat on the island and move to the fridge.

'Fine, darling,' she says, heading off to the laundry room.

'Toast and fruit OK, Luke?' I ask.

I close the fridge door to face Luke.

'Did I miss the memo that stated my fiancée must look far too sexy to leave our house today?'

'Yes. You also missed the memo requesting my sex god this morning… You've dropped the ball on this deal… Do I have to take my business elsewhere?' I reach up and kiss his cheek.

Luke whistles. 'So, is this why I asked you to be my wife? Simply to push my buttons?'

'Yes. Now sit. I'll make your breakfast.'

Shortly, we finish our breakfast, which we have eaten mainly in silence.

'I called Mr Jones. He's coming over tonight around six thirty.' I look across at Luke, who's reading paperwork and clearly not listening. 'I thought I would go to your office naked… Maybe just wearing my fur coat.'

'Not if you want to enjoy the rest of your life.' His eyes meet mine. 'I was listening; you have a tendency to not allow me to answer.'

'No, I don't!'

He leans to my cheek and leaves a tender kiss.

'Do you realise you're always talking?'

'You know I hate silence.'

'I do. The only peace I get is when you're asleep.' He laughs.

I fold my arms with resentment. 'We don't have to spend so much time together; you can have time out.'

'Not a chance, and don't flip this conversation. If you're with me then I know you're not in trouble.'

'I'm not a child! Besides, I think we should set some boundaries.'

He stands. 'Boundaries?'

I join him. 'Boundaries.'

His eyes darken. 'Is there a point you're trying to make?'

'I love you, but I can't spend all day here, and what else do I have? A group of board members who want me once in a blue moon.'

'Then explain to me why Mr Jones is coming over this evening – your new venture? What the hell are you talking about? What sort of boundaries?' Collecting his paperwork, he heads towards the office.

I follow him. 'I just need something else other than this – us.'

'I have no issue with that, but I will follow close behind you.'

'Lucky me; my fiancé wants to be my stalker.'

'You're lucky you're not tied to our bed.' He plants a cheeky kiss on my lips.

Max draws Luke's black Bentley to a halt outside an impressive glass building, owned by Sutton Global.

We stand side by side in the lift, hand in hand. Luke's fingers skim my newly acquired ring. I raise my eyes to meet his. We both know the ring symbolises more than love: Luke Sutton wants me – forever – and I can't deny I like it.

The doors slide open at the top floor. A sign with large silver lettering, saying *SUTTON GLOBAL INUDSTRIES,* is the first thing I see. It blows me away that the man who frustrates the hell out of me, and can take me with just a smile, runs this show!

Luke's grip remains firm as we walk towards his office, while what feels like the entire staff of Sutton Global follow his every step. Stella, Luke's personal assistant and one of the most important women in his work life, looks up as we approach.

'Kate, happy new year.' She moves towards me and folds me into her arms. Her actions always leave me feeling sad – sad that she was unable to have children. That's why she idolises Luke – he's the son she never had.

'Same to you, Stella, how did you and Richard get on in Yorkshire?'

'It was relaxing, and wonderful to see Richard's family.'

'Stella.' Luke looks at her with his usual stern expression – the boss has officially entered the building.

'Luke, happy new year.' She hugs him, which makes me laugh – internally, of course!

I take Stella's hand. 'I want to show you something.' I walk with her into Luke's large office and head towards the sofa. I remove my fur jacket and place it next to me with my bag.

Luke silently moves to his desk and watches me from his throne. Without a doubt I bring something different to Sutton Global – warmth.

I drop my gaze to my hand, which rests on my thigh, and remain silent. Her brow creases with confusion. At last she looks at my hand.

'Oh my goodness, is that what I think it is?' Her hand covers her mouth.

'Yes.'

She pulls me to her chest. 'How to brighten up a dull January; I am so pleased. You're so good for him, but you know I've always thought that, since the day we hired you to cook... I knew he needed you.' She stands and moves towards Luke. 'You, young man, have made me very happy. Come here.'

Luke can't help but smile. She holds him close.

'This is by far the best decision you have ever made. I can't tell you how proud I am of you.' She sniffs, and a tear escapes.

'Not you as well! Why has everyone cried at our news?' Luke tries to lighten the moment.

I move to join them. Luke places his arm around my shoulders.

'Our news gets better... wait for it! We're getting married in Venice, something small and simple, and we want you and Richard there. You have to be there, Stella, you've been at Luke's side since... well, forever.'

'Of course, we wouldn't miss it for the world. Oh, I almost forgot, how was Harry's wedding?'

'It was stunning.' I turn to mush at the thought of Harry's magical day.

'I don't mean to be rude, but I have to work. Stella can you send a memo informing everyone of our engagement? I would rather they hear it from me before I announce it to the wider world.'

'Yes, of course,' Stella says.

'The world?' I laugh.

'The world of business.'

'Oh.' I just told three friends and my sister...

'Ladies.' Luke nods towards the door.

'I'll wait for Tanya at your desk, Stella.'

Stella and I both turn to leave, but Luke pulls at my hand. 'Don't distract my staff.'

'I won't. Oh, and just so I'm clear, does that include you?'

'No. Distraction from you is acceptable.' He kisses me hard on the lips. The Bagrov and Cooper meeting with Tanya at Sutton Global might not be as dull as I thought...

I perch on Stella's desk showing her and Tanya, Luke's ex-assistant and now my personal assistant, photos from Harry's wedding. I lose all track of time. Suddenly Luke emerges from his office.

'Stella, I requested a file... But I see you have a distraction at your desk.' He exhales and glares at me.

I try not to laugh. God, he would drive me mad if I worked for him. Stella deserves a medal.

'My fault – apparently I'm more entertaining than your mergers!' I move off the desk and walk towards him. Placing my hands on his shirt, I reach up on tiptoe, allowing my lips to brush against his ear. 'I'm horny, in your office – does that count as a welcome distraction?' I slip away and enter his office. 'Tanya, shall we make a start?' I turn and catch a flash of a frustrated Sutton. Wow! To say I feel hypnotised is an understatement.

Tanya and I sit at the board table at the far end of Luke's office. She organises the paperwork for New York, and I watch and admire her skill. I must take note! Her phone rings, which allows me a few minutes to send a formal complaint to Luke.

> Dear sex god,
> I would like to point out that my needs have not been met today and, as I said earlier, do I need to take my business elsewhere? In the meantime, I shall sit here and think of you at your desk – and me on my knees, yum yum!
> Love from your deprived fiancée.

I hit send and glance across at him. I count: one, two, ping! He looks at his phone and then continues to work. Ouch! Not even a smirk on his face. Perhaps, he needs one more message.

> Dear sex god,
> Do you need me to fuck with your paperwork? Just a thought, while I Google male escorts for hire!
> Love from your frustrated fiancée.

'Kate.' Tanya interrupts me.
I place my phone on the table. 'Sorry.'

'OK. Let's begin with these documents.'

I nod. Poor Tanya has the task of morphing me into a businesswoman – I wish her luck.

'Firstly, you need to sign these.' She lays out some paperwork. 'Five companies have been sold; this is just a formality for the shareholders.' She shows me where I need to sign.

I read the title on another dossier. *Rosewood Ivy Hotel, New York*. I pull it out.

'Are they buying a hotel?'

'Yes – that's one of the main reasons we're going to New York. They need a unanimous vote to purchase the hotel.'

'OK. Crap! I'm never going to get to grips with this.' My eyes fall to the amount of money at the bottom of the page. 'Bloody hell… How much?'

Tanya laughs. 'Kate, the company is worth a lot more than the cost of the hotel… This is what they do, buy and sell, similar to Luke.'

I rub my forehead.

She reaches out to me. 'It will be fine… We've got this.'

'We've got this! The only thing I've got is a splitting headache.'

Tanya continues to prep me on the various issues that will be addressed while we're in New York. Luke made the right decision suggesting I hire her.

'Do you feel OK with everything we've discussed?' Tanya asks.

I shake my head. 'Not really.'

'You'll be fine.'

'I don't have a choice.' I look at my watch. 'Is that it for now?'

'Any questions?' she asks.

'Not really, only what shall I cook for dinner?'

We stand and make our way to the door of Luke's office. I feel a tug on my arm.

'Tanya, would you excuse us?' Luke's eyes are black. So intense they have begun to peel my clothes from my sensitive body.

She shyly looks at Luke before me. 'Certainly, Mr Sutton. Kate, I will see you in a couple of days. You'll be fine,' she rambles before bolting for the door. Without doubt she has felt the tension between us.

'Luke, I have to go food shopping.'

Luke closes the door and locks it. He stands in front of my only exit.

'Fuck with my paperwork? Kate, don't push me, and don't tease me at work.'

'I was playing.'

He walks towards me as I retreat further into the room.

'I agree.' He looks down at the bulge almost bursting from his trousers.

I giggle. 'Oh.'

'You think this is funny?'

His face is within kissing distance.

'No.'

'No? Kate Harper, don't feed me bullshit.' He places his hands in my hair.

'OK – maybe a bit.'

His surprise kiss is hard-hitting, while his hands rampage all over my body. He breaks free and walks me to the sofa, where he sits and unbuttons his trousers, freeing his erection.

'Pull your tights down. I want you to sit on me,' he commands.

My hands fist on my hips. I feel slightly shocked, yet fiercely turned on.

'Only because you asked so bloody nicely.'

Luke's gaze is scorching.

'Are you still fucking with me? I know what you need… Now strip and sit on me.'

He knows my need for him is as strong as his need to control the sexual game we're playing. I remove my shoe boots, tights and knickers, complying with his demand.

He slides his hand down the full length of his erection. I'm drawn to the sight, and watch him grow harder with his touch. Fuck – I'm drooling; I need him now! I straddle him.

'Slowly,' he whispers.

Our eyes meet. Dark and commanding meets dark and compliant.

'Don't tease me at work. Do you understand?' His thumb skims my clit.

I nod.

'Good.' His free hand moves up my body to the nape of my neck. 'Ride me quick, baby – time is not on our side. I have a meeting in thirty minutes.'

Again, I nod. But he knows he has control of my orgasm. His words echo in my head: 'ride me quick.' I slam down harder on him, taking all of him inside me. He pushes my shoulders, and I lean further back, allowing his hand the space to reach my clit, ensuring I orgasm quickly. The heat between us is stifling; my body is on fire this morning. I have no control.

'Oh God, Luke.'

'Don't stop,' he demands, continuing to work my clit. 'Keep going… I'm coming hard.'

Again, my body responds until he holds my hips still and I feel his warm release.

I lean forward and gently kiss him.

Luke pulls away. 'Don't kiss me.'

'What?'

'I'm still hard for you.'

I slowly move my hips. *Christ, he is still hard!*

'Stop.'

No!

He grasp my hips. 'I have to work… No more, Kate.'

His dark eyes entice me. What he does to me… it's like nothing else I've ever encountered.

I lean to his ear. 'I'm not stopping you.'

My body begins to move. I need more. My touch becomes aggressive as I kiss him hard. His hands slide up my back, to the nape of my neck. Luke's breathing grows shallow. Round two to me: there'll be no mercy until he's offloaded in me again.

'Touch me,' I whisper.

He smiles.

'I love that you're greedy.'

His hand slips between my wet thighs, and slides across my swollen clit. Hot juices from us both lubricate me. It appears that our roles are reversed: I have become the aggressive lover and Luke my personal enabler. Again, I ride him quickly; this time it's my deadline, not his. I'm highly sensitive from my last orgasm, allowing the second to arrive quickly.

'Kate, harder, I know you're going to come. I need you harder.'

Oh Christ – my orgasm hits me. I try to maintain my speed and pressure yet the ferocious shockwaves affect my ability. Luke leaves my clit and lifts my hips, guaranteeing I take every ounce of his hardness.

'Yes... yes, Kate, keep going... OK. No more.'

I collapse to his chest. My heart beats uncontrollably, matching Luke's rhythm as our Harper–Sutton workout takes its toll on us both.

Finally, I raise my head from his chest. 'Too much for the office?' I lean up and slide myself off him, probably looking slightly dishevelled.

He stifles a smile. 'I would say so.'

He stands and strides to his en suite. I collect my clothes and follow him to the large bathroom, which is fully kitted with his usual Jo Malone masculine scent. I wash myself thoroughly – a double helping needs a little more attention than normal.

'I keep asking myself, is this going to work, the days you're here?'

My gaze meets his reflection. His smile reveals the absolute truth: he wouldn't have it any other way.

'You need some self-control, Mr S. You like to control me – maybe you need to control your dick.' I smirk.

'Is that right?'

'You told me this morning that space is not an option.' I walk out of the bathroom and retrieve my bag, then retouch my lip gloss and shake my hair, not wanting to tell all Luke's staff we've just had sex.

Luke walks to his desk. 'No, it's not, Kate, but neither is this. Christ, you know what you do to me.'

'Self-control, Luke, or you can just say no. I'm sure I

can find other ways to amuse myself.' There's no need for me to turn around; I can feel his glare burning into me… Holy shit, what did I eat this morning to make me this brave?

Within seconds Luke is at my neck, whispering in my ear: 'I like fucking you, just not where I do business.'

I turn and loop my arms around his neck.

'I love you… And I love what we just did. Is that wrong?'

He rubs his nose against mine and nips the end.

'You know it's not wrong, but this is my workplace… Please remember that.'

'I've told you before, it's not a one-way street.'

He shakes his head. 'So, your plans are… what exactly?' Luke changes the subject. Now he wants to concentrate on work.

'Food shopping, then home to prepare dinner for Mr Jones.'

'Good. I'll call Max to collect you.'

I roll my eyes. 'I can manage to find my way to the Bentley.'

'I feel you've just wasted your breath.'

Luke calls Max from his mobile, as I slip on my coat and collect my Bayswater bag, and swiftly leave Luke's office.

'Bye, Stella.' I lean over and give her a kiss.

'Bye, Kate – see you soon and congratulations.'

'Thank you.'

Luke walks me to the lift.

'Are you trying to get rid of me? Or are you shielding me from… no one?'

'Both.'

He presses the button for the lift and takes hold of my chin. 'Can I trust you to stay out of trouble?' He plants a kiss on my lips.

'Not a problem, Commander Sutton, as you won't be with me.'

'Stop fucking with me!'

'I just did – twice.'

At six thirty, the black door opens – it's Mr Jones, escorted by Max.

I join them both in the hallway, feeling particularly happy to see Mr Jones. As ever, he wears a three-piece suit, shirt and tie – definitely a Jones Tailor creation. Although he is in his sixties and slender, his presence always commands attention: old-school charm runs through his veins.

'Kate.' Mr Jones gives me a hug. 'How was your Christmas?'

'Good. Come in, let me get you a drink.'

Mr Jones and Max follow me through to the kitchen.

'Kate, what time will you need me to take Mr Jones home?' Max waits for his instructions. I hate the authority that Luke has given me.

'I'm not sure; it won't be late.'

'Call me when you're ready to leave.' He walks towards the door leading to the apartments at the far end of the kitchen.

'I'll bring your dinner to you when it's ready.'

He stops in his tracks. 'Kate!'

'Stop moaning. It's roast lamb, your favourite.'

He smiles and holds up his hands, and walks off to his apartment.

'It would seem you have Luke's staff under your spell.' Mr Jones looks at me.

'I worry about him. You know what Max went through.' I blow air through my lips. 'Here.' I pass him a glass of red wine.

'He looks remarkable, considering… Anyway, happy new year, Kate.'

'You too, Mr Jones. Dinner will be half an hour, so we can chat. Follow me.' I walk into Luke's office and guide Mr Jones to the sofa.

'How was Harry's wedding?'

'We had the best day, and the snow – it was lovely. Oh my God, she looked so beautiful. I'll show you some pictures later.'

'I can imagine.'

'What about you? I wish you could have been there.'

'And I am truly grateful you asked, but Christmas for me is always quiet – I suppose I'm getting old.'

'Never! Anyway, I wanted to see you for a couple of reasons.'

'Hmm, sounds like the good old days.' Mr Jones smiles with curiosity.

'The first reason…' I hold up my hand.

He takes my hand to examine my ring. 'Well, I never… When did Luke ask you?'

'New Year's Eve: he bought me a car with "marry me" as the number plate.' The thought still makes me smile.

'How very ingenious of him – why am I not surprised? Good news; I always wanted you to be happy.'

'I know, so you understand what that means.' I turn my head towards a framed picture Mr Jones gave me on my birthday. Not only is it my favourite picture from his archive collection, it's also a full-length strapless dress with a huge train. Essentially, it's a wedding dress.

He chuckles. 'And of course the fabric is yours.' He takes my hand.

'How do you feel about that? Honestly, I know you gave me the fabric when I left the tailor's, but…'

'I'm honoured.'

'Really? I feel bad; you might want to give it to someone else. I totally understand if you've changed your mind.'

'Kate, I gave you that fabric because I knew you would love it, like I did all those years ago in France. I repeat, I am honoured that you want to create a dress to share with Luke from my history.'

'Oh crap! You get me every time…' I swallow my emotions. 'The other thing is… we want to get married in Venice, and I want you there.'

He squeezes my hand. 'I'm not sure what to say… You have a place in my heart, Kate, always.'

'Yes, and you can't talk like that because I'll cry.' I sip my wine. 'So, I have one more question for you.' I reach for my *Eat me* pink leather book and open the front page.

Mr Jones looks at the page and then at me. 'Is that what you want – Harper Jones?'

'Yes! Let's do it, let's start Harper Jones. I feel really excited about it. I've got so many ideas, and with your drawings, too, we're ready to go – sort of. I told you when I saw you before Christmas that I needed to do something for me.'

He smiles. 'Yes, you did. I can see you have given it some thought.'

I nod. 'I said if I won the lottery this is what I would do with the money. OK, I haven't won the lottery, but I do have a large bank account.'

'Your mother's money?'

I inhale and nod.

He takes my hand. 'Kate, it must be so painful having no memory of her.'

He's right.

'What I would give just to be able to touch her face.'

'My dear Kate, without doubt life has been testing for you – and of course Luke.'

'Honestly, I hate thinking about her, which feels wrong.'

'Not at all. Perhaps putting her money to good use will give you some comfort.'

'I hope so and in that case yes is the only word I want to hear… Holy shit, I sound like a bloody Sutton. Honestly, just think about it.'

'It will be hard work.' He takes a large sip of red wine.

'I know, but it will be so much fun, seeing all your drawings come to life. Also, I want to ask my friend Maria, I'm sure I've mentioned her to you. I worked with her for a day just before…' He reaches for my hand, understanding my emotion. 'And you know Valerie, Luke's stylist.'

'Yes, of course.'

'Obviously, I haven't asked them yet – I wanted to wait until I'd spoken to you. This is you – your clothes and handiwork.'

'Harper Jones will be us, Kate. I know you will bring your own twist to my ideas.'

'Oh my God, yeah, I have so many ideas.'

'So you have a plan in mind?'

'Not really, but when I get back from New York we can have a meeting and discuss it. Is it a yes?'

He extends his hand. 'Deal.'

The following morning I open my eyes, stretch, and feel rested, although in the pit of my stomach there is a sense of trepidation about tomorrow and the dreaded trip to New York. I look at my watch – it's nine o'clock! Shit. But I have nowhere to be, so I guess the time is irrelevant.

I turn my head and see a note on Luke's pillow; that's a sure-fire way to make me smile. God, I miss the good old days when this was our only way of communicating. Anonymity was quite exciting!

> *Dear fiancée…*
>
> *You looked beautiful in our bed this morning.*
>
> *I shall miss you today, after your presence yesterday – which was fun.*
>
> *Please call me and let me know of your plans – not to control them merely to have knowledge.*
>
> *Max will take you anywhere you wish to go. Stay out of trouble.*
>
> *I love you.*
>
> *Luke, aka your fiancé, Adonis, Techno Boy, sex god and ex-boss. (How life has changed.)*

I hold the note and laugh at his list of alter egos: honestly, I would take any of them! The man drives me mad, physically and emotionally. Nevertheless, I agree yesterday was fun. This gives me an idea.

I spend the morning baking, after which I pack my sugary treats into containers. I look up as Max enters the kitchen.

'You're just the person I wanted to see. Can we go to Luke's office?'

'Is he expecting you?'

'No.' *That's the point!*

Max and I wait by the busy lifts at Sutton Global. This double-act routine is becoming pretty tedious. The doors open and we step in.

'A question for you, Max!'

He lowers his gaze.

'Aren't you bored following me? I mean, not being able to get in the lift alone is bloody ridiculous… Maybe you should have a word with Luke?' *Because he doesn't listen to me…*

'If you're asking me to agree with you, then you're barking up the wrong tree… May I remind you that I was in an explosion, and we still don't know who's responsible?'

I glare at him, hurt and pissed off.

'No, I don't need reminding. You know it still haunts me… and that was a low blow. My point is that it was nearly six months ago; don't you think they would have tried something else by now? Surely Luke would have something to go on, what with all his contacts? But they haven't found out anything more about Ivor, or any plans for me.'

'Jesus, Kate.' Max looks around the lift at the other people.

'What?'

'Keep it down – and no news is not always good news. Silence can mean a number of things.'

'Like what?'

The lift pings.

'Max! Like what?'

'Talk to Luke. But don't ask to be let loose… that's not happening.'

I exhale in frustration, as I appear to be talking to Max in a foreign language.

Max walks behind me as I approach Luke's office.

Stella looks up. 'Kate – two days in a row?'

'I know, I must love it here… Is Luke around, or is he busy?' I place the containers filled with sugary treats on her desk.

'He does have some people with him. Let me check.' She looks down at the boxes on her desk. 'I see you have been busy.'

'There's an extra fruit cake for you to take home.'

'Kate, call me when you want to leave, I'll be in my office.' Max says, heading in the opposite direction.

'OK. Give me some space, for God's sake.' I mutter under my breath.

'He loves you like his own darling, plain and simple.' Stella touches my hand and her words touch my heart. 'Let me call Luke.' She picks up her phone. 'You have a visitor – your fiancée.' She looks at me and winks. 'Yes… very well.' She replaces her handset. 'He said to go in.'

'Thanks, Stella.'

I manage to open the door with my arms full of the boxes. My heart skips a beat as it does every time I see Luke – I enjoy watching him control his empire. Placing my food parcels on his desk, I lean against it, waiting for him to finish his conversation with several members of staff seated at the boardroom table. His eyes hover in my direction, and he flashes me his Sutton smile. Fuck, I could drop to my knees for him, right here, right now. He gestures for me to join him.

'Hi.' I extend a warm welcome to his staff, who smile and nod.

'OK... change the drawings. I want costings for all the alterations. No more surprises! You have until I get back from New York; let's make use of the time. Email me with any questions. In the meantime, use your staff to research for you.'

The staff stand, collect various pieces of paperwork and leave the office. I smile as they exit.

Alone at last, Luke takes my hand and walks me towards his desk.

'I see you brought cakes.' His eyes scan the parcels as he sits down.

'Yeah.' Immediately I head for his lap. Luke moves his arms, allowing me the space. 'Thank you for my note; I really miss them.'

He smiles, knowing how much his words brighten up my day. 'You're welcome.'

'I'm here for a reason, not to tease you!'

Our dark eyes connect.

Luke rubs his jawline. 'What do you want?'

'OK, so, yesterday was fun.'

'Not today... Th—'

I place my finger over his lips. 'I'm not just talking about what we did on your sofa, but I mean getting up, having a purpose to my day. That got me thinking.'

'Where are you going with this?'

I'm babbling. 'Do you have an office, I mean a room, somewhere I can set up the Harper Jones business – hopefully? I know it's early days, but...'

'Office?'

'Yeah, here… with you.'

'You want an office here?' He laughs. 'Yesterday, you told me you wanted space and now you want to be under my feet… You hate being under my control.' Luke's brows knit together.

'That's not strictly true. I like it when I like it, but not when I don't. Besides, it's my prerogative to change my mind – daily. Anyway, this isn't a power trip.'

'Power trip!' Luke throws his head back, laughing.

'Come on – your middle name is power! Followed by control and then irrational, lastly delusional!' I laugh.

'Is this your idea of stroking my ego? If so, you need to rethink your strategy.'

'Honestly, I like it here; I feel safe.'

He takes my face in his hands and kisses me. I respond as I always do. This must be an early birthday present for him, offering him twenty-four hour surveillance on me.

He releases me.

'You know I can't kiss you… I made my point yesterday.'

'Self-control, Luke… You must be able to buy it.'

'Funny! OK, so you want an office here?' He runs his hands through his hair. 'If I agree, there will be conditions.'

'Fine.' *What conditions?*

'Firstly, this is where I work, and I command a certain amount of respect. My members of staff understand what I expect of them, so this' – his fingers gesture between us – 'has to remain under control. No fucking games, literally.'

I try to speak but Luke presses his finger to my lips.

'I'm aware that your approach to business will clash with mine, but you have to respect me. I don't want my staff thinking just because you work here I will have different expectations of them… Do you understand?'

'I do… Luke, I admire you and your empire. Your staff will have nothing to do with me.' I place my hands on his shoulders. 'Look, I just thought we could come to work together, that's all. If I'm here with you, you know I'll be safe. Besides, I can shut the door and have a boundary that we can both respect until five o'clock.'

He places his hands on my breasts, sizing up the deal that's on offer.

'Perhaps… there could be a positive side to you being here.'

'I think the boundary should be no sex at work.' Bullshit!

'Are you challenging me?' He takes my hand and kisses my sparkly ring.

'That's up to you, Mr Sutton, boss man… Shall I drop to my knees and challenge you.'

'Hmm, why do I think I'm about to regret my decision?' His chest expands. 'Right, an office… Let me show you something.'

I move from his lap. We exit his office and walk across the hall, literally ten foot from Luke's office. He opens a set of double doors to reveal a large room, not the same as Luke's, but nonetheless bloody huge.

'Will this do?' He stands, relaxed, his hands in his pockets, looking his usual fuckable self.

'Are you shitting me?'

He shakes his head. 'No! I'm not shitting you.'

'Oh my God, I wasn't expecting this.' I walk towards the floor-to-ceiling windows taking in the view: a view I will be able to look at every day.

'If you like it, then it's yours. Now I can really keep an eye on you.'

'I guess you can. Do you mind if I choose my own furniture?' I look at the dull boardroom table and ugly chairs.

'It's yours – do as you please.'

I pull him towards me. 'Thank you.' I reach up on tiptoe to kiss him gratefully.

'Jesus, how much work am I going to get done with you around?'

'Not changing your mind?'

'Not yet!'

'Get back to work then; let's start as we mean to go on.' I jump up and down with excitement. 'This is perfect; you know l love designing interiors. Lucky Max is in for a real treat – furniture shopping.'

'Don't forget Sandbanks.'

'I won't. I'll make a start when we get back from New York… Besides, I liked just having a bed there.'

After an eventful afternoon of furniture shopping, I lie in bed alone and look at my watch. It's ten o'clock. I roll onto my side and pull the duvet under my chin. I take a deep breath, praying the next few days will pass quickly. My eyes close.

Next thing I know, a cold arm grips my waist, making me stir from my sleep.

'Shh. Sleep, baby, I'm home.'

I inhale the Sutton scent. 'Love you,' I mumble and take his hand.

'Back at you… I'll meet you in your dreams.'

10

I stir and look at my watch: five thirty, far too early to face the world of business. I hear the shower stop and then Luke padding into the bedroom.

'You're awake.' He places a damp kiss on my forehead.

'Unfortunately. Why don't you come back to bed? I'll make it worth your while.'

'Are you trying to bribe me with sex?' Luke runs his hand down the side of my face.

'Yes.' I pull the duvet up under my chin.

'Get up.' He begins to move away, but not before I yank his towel from his damp body.

'Oi! Seriously, Kate, get up.'

I lean up onto my elbows. 'You're no fun.' I sigh, and get up from my security blanket.

Luke taps the glass of the shower. 'You have twenty minutes… Don't make me come in there and drag you out.'

'Fine.' I move towards a towel that he lovingly wraps around me. I look up at his face. 'Sorry… I know I'm irritating you, but honestly, I'm petrified. These people are not from my world.'

'Kate, you are one of the strongest people I know. Don't compare yourself to the Coopers! Jesus, you flew to Russia, which was stupid, yet courageous.'

I nod and move away, allowing my towel to hit the floor.

'So, your new strategy is to stand naked in front of me.' He tilts his head.

'Is it working?' I laugh.

'It will when we arrive in New York.'

Twenty-five minutes later I meet Luke in the hall. 'You're late.' He looks at me. I'm smart casual today, in a black lace skater girl dress that stops just above my knee, black opaque tights and shoe boots, with my long black riding coat over my arm.

'All part of my plan. Did we miss the plane?'

He holds his hand out to me. 'No; private jets wait for their owners! You look beautiful. Here, let me take your coat.'

Shortly, we enter Luke's stunning private jet and sit in our usual cream leather seats. This time, however, we're not alone. Tanya sits in the next row. There's a fair amount of distance between the rows, but not as huge as the distance between her and Luke – she is still awkward around him. My mission on this trip is to help them get along better, which makes the Cooper situation a walk in the park!

When we are at cruising altitude, the stewardess arrives with our breakfast.

I smile, glancing towards Luke as he eats and reads – as ever, multitasking.

'You're watching me, Harper.' His eyes flit from his paperwork to my face.

I lean towards his ear and whisper. 'Just reminding myself of Venice... you were a royal pain in the arse.'

He turns to me. 'Are you reminding me of your insubordination?' He quietly seals his words with a kiss.

Before long Luke disappears to his on-board office, which will always bring back memories of our first visit to Venice and having amazing sex in there. The time alone allows me the opportunity to chat to Tanya. I study her pretty face, framed by her dark, shoulder-length hair, offsetting her piercing blue eyes. Thirty-three and single, she comes across as highly ambitious; I guess that's why Luke wanted her to work for me. With my news of Harper Jones her face comes alive – let's hope I transmit the same excitement to Maria and Valerie when I return to London.

Eight hours later, the three of us exit JFK airport and get in a waiting limo. I wrap my black riding coat tightly around myself; the weather is just as bloody cold here as it is in London.

Having an extra person with Luke and me does feel a little odd – and they are so awkward together that it's exhausting. I try to start a conversation, which is difficult, due to Luke's unremitting need to play the role of boss and Tanya's wariness of letting her guard down in front of her ex-boss. I really need to pull him up on this, and tell Tanya to chill in his company! In the meantime, all I can do is talk – a lot – to fill in the gaps in the conversation.

I thank God when we finally arrive!

Luke steps out first. I follow, with Tanya close behind. We enter the reception area of the Four Seasons. Wow, another spectacular hotel. I'm not surprised. Luke does like the finer things in life. He releases my hand while he checks in. Soon he gives Tanya her key card and we all walk to the lift: floor fifteen for Tanya, and of course the penthouse for us.

We reach Tanya's level.

'Shall we meet at reception in half an hour?' I look at Tanya.

'Perfect, I'll see you then.'

She exits the lift. The doors close.

'OK. Am I missing something? You do like Tanya?'

He tilts his head. 'You're fishing for something – get to the point.'

'You just seem a little... arsey and cold... I don't know – hostile.'

'Arsey? Up until a few months ago, she was an employee.'

'I don't get it. I mean, your iceman attitude must work, because you're loaded.'

He arches a brow.

'Don't get me wrong; I know you need to be all commando Sutton for business, but I find it really uncomfortable.'

'I love that you feel we're close enough to say it as you see it.'

'You're missing my point.'

The lift stops and Luke holds the door open. 'Which one, arsey or cold?'

'Luke, she's trying to impress you.' I step forward, squeezing his hand, hoping he may warm to my way of thinking.

'Tanya is good at her job. If she wasn't, then I certainly wouldn't allow her to look after your schedules.'

'You don't see where I'm coming from.'

'No I don't. Kate, I like respect and distance from my staff. Familiarity breeds contempt.'

I frown. How did this conversation so rapidly go downhill? 'What about being friendly? Try it – what's the worst that could happen?'

'There's no need for me to be friendly; you provide enough warmth for us both.'

'Seriously Luke, did you just say that?'

Our arguments generally end in Luke being the conqueror. OK, Sutton, I need to up my game before we marry!

He opens a set of double doors to reveal our suite. Holy shit! My two favourite words for Mr Luke Sutton and the hotel suites he provides.

'Bloody hell, this is amazing. Look at the view.' I walk towards the window. The crystal clear sky offers a stunning backdrop to the city. 'I have a new love in my life, and his name is New York.'

Luke ignores my statement and disappears from the room.

Everywhere I turn, I'm faced with a new vista. The room has a panoramic view of the city.

'Kate?' Luke calls.

I enter the bedroom and move towards him, gazing out of the window.

'Oh my God – is that Central Park?' I place my hands on the glass, as if I am able to touch the scene.

Luke inhales. 'Go and have a look at the bathroom.'

I vanish to the next room.

'Holy shit, look at that bath! And the windows – what a view!' I run my hand along the edge of the oval bath, which is surrounded by the most beautiful marble. I'm sure it's bigger than ours at home. 'Luke, there's a TV in here!' I need a bath now!

I return to the bedroom and throw my coat on the bed.

'Thank you, this is all a bit surreal.'

His mouth closes over mine, fiercely wild, which surprises me. I run my hands up his chest and slip off his overcoat. Suddenly he pulls away.

'Jesus – I need you, but I have to leave.' He looks at his watch. 'The car is waiting.'

I don't speak. Instead my eyes communicate with his in a dance of desire. He places his hands on either side of my face.

'Don't, Kate!' His eyes gleam – displaying his sexual appetite.

'What? I'm not doing anything.' Am I? 'Go – I have to meet Tanya. Honestly.' My lips meet his, while my hand gently gropes his erection to give him something to remember me by. The vibration of a low groan is all the indication I need. I pull away.

'You should go. I know you have a long, hard and challenging day ahead of you.' I try to remain serious, but I am shit at this teasing game; it amuses me far too much.

'Hard… challenging?' His eyes are almost black. Mr Horny Sutton now stands before me in all his glory. His mobile phone rings from his trouser pocket.

'Shall I get that for you?' My hand enters his trouser pocket, feeling his hardness against my fingers while seizing his phone.

'Leave it.' Luke looks at me. Brazen Harper is in the building.

'Mr Sutton's phone, how may I help you?'

His forehead creases.

'Hold one moment.' I pass him his phone and lean to his ear. 'I've warned you before; it's rude to keep people waiting.'

He shakes his head. 'Sutton.' His voice is low and stern. Fucking sexy as hell.

Before I walk away I place tender kisses against his jaw, while my hand gropes him again. Oh, how tempting it is to drop to my knees!

I move to the lounge and stare at the Manhattan skyline.

His breath glides across my neck, starling me. 'What am I to do with you?' He spins me round.

'Fuck me.'

'Fuck you? Jesus, your mouth.'

'You want honesty…'

'I want my fiancée to stop teasing my dick.' He runs his hands through his hair. I know a frustrated Sutton when I see one. 'You know I can't take you now.'

'Is that can't… or won't?'

Suddenly he pushes me against the window and takes hold of my leg. His hand slides under my dress, disappearing in my underwear and heading for my clit. His touch is firm, yet gentle. My breathing grows shallow and my supporting leg wants to collapse. I have no strength under his spell; the continuous sensation of his warm fingers circling on my sensitive flesh is intoxicating.

'Think of me, baby, and what I am going to do to you when I get back.'

What! Bastard, I know he won't allow me to orgasm. He removes his hand and places his fingers in his mouth. I want to scream at him.

'Fuck, you taste good.' He pulls away. 'I'm now late. Stay out of trouble. You don't have Max, but I have eyes and ears everywhere.'

What? 'Eyes and ears… What's that supposed to mean?'

'It means you should be safe.'

'I'll try.'

He stops in his tracks.

'No trouble – promise me that.' His tone is stern and unforgiving.

Fifth Avenue is heaving and bloody freezing. Even so, I am in love with New York. Tanya and I try to stay together and weave through the mass of people, which is almost impossible. Having visited various shops merely to stay warm, we stumble across a champagne bar. Two words immediately jump out that sound perfect together: pink and champagne!

We sit at a cocktail table feeling warm and relaxed with the help of bubbles and fresh strawberries.

'Cheers,' I say.

'Cheers, Kate.' We sip our delicious drink. 'This feels like we're skipping school. I love it here.'

'Me too. OK, cards on the table time. I'm shitting myself about tomorrow.' I place another strawberry in my mouth.

'You'll be fine. Honestly, it'll be a breeze; there's really nothing to worry about.'

I lean on the table. 'It's not the work that bothers me; well, I am out of my depth… But Alexis hates me. Actually, we hate each other. As you know, I used to cook for Luke. I then started going to functions with him, and that's when I first met her. She told me I was no good for Luke and he needed to be with like-minded people.'

'What!' Tanya places her glass on the table. 'So this is personal?'

'If by personal you mean I want to place my right foot up her arse, then this is as personal as you can get.'

'Mr Sutton told me that you haven't gone to a boardroom meeting yet.'

'So far I've been lucky and managed to avoid them; I've just signed paperwork.'

'Look, Kate, I don't know you that well, but I have heard through the grapevine that Alexis likes Mr Sutton, or use to.'

'I worked that out within about two seconds of meeting her. Don't get me wrong, I know Luke isn't interested. Anyway, she's had it in for me the moment she said "hello, my name is super-bitch".'

'Suits her.'

'At the end of the day, my being here isn't by choice, if my mum…'

Tanya reaches for my hand.

'You'll be fine, just give yourself some time. It will all fall in to place.'

'I hope so, there's a part of me that needs to honour her, and be proud of my inheritance.' I say feeling a little overwhelmed.

'That makes sense, we can do this – together.'

'OK, lets change the subject. You said you've worked for a while with Luke, how long exactly?'

'Nearly four years; there were not that many of us back then. Stella was there long before I started.'

I take a deep breath. 'Do you remember Maddy, Luke's ex?' *Crap! I shouldn't have asked.*

'We met a few times, mainly at Sutton Global functions.'

'Oh.' *Why did I ask?*

'Kate, Mr Sutton seems really happy.' She touches my hand, sensing my hopelessness. I guess I will always feel the same – we come from such different worlds. 'Anyhow, I think it's fun seeing you at Sutton Global – shows us he's human.'

I shake my head. 'Oh, for Christ's sake! I can't stand all the formalities. Call him Luke. If he doesn't like it, tough. I'm telling you it's OK.'

'Got it. As for Maddy, she was nice – a bit stuck-up.'

'It pains me to say it, but she does seem nice.'

'Mr Sutton – sorry, Luke – has changed since you've been around.'

'Jesus, if he's changed, then what was he like before I arrived?'

'He was cold – sorry, that sounds awful – and distant.'

'Miserable mogul… I don't mean that, he's my life.'

'I remember the day you dropped off his Jones Tailor shirts.'

'Oh God, I was soaked.' Another good first impression!

We have consumed one bottle and opened the second. The champagne helps Tanya understand I may be her boss but I want us to be friends. I work differently to Luke – at least I will, when I start Harper Jones.

My phone rings and my heart skips a beat. With a bottle of champagne and an essence of bravado I retrieve the phone. Caller ID – boss.

'Hello, sex god.' Oh, shit! I look at a slightly uncomfortable Tanya. I hold my index finger to my lips.

'Where are you?'

'We're in a champagne bar somewhere.' I close my eyes, aiding my concentration skills. Not working!

'Somewhere?' Luke responds gruffly.

'Yes, somewhere on Fifth Avenue, within walking distance of the hotel. Where are you?'

'I'm returning to the hotel. I should be about half an hour.'

'OK.' I desperately try to talk coherently, but the bubbles have gone to my head. 'We'll leave shortly.' Nightfall is drawing closer, which means the temperature outside is dropping.

'How much champagne have you had?' Does he sense my fuzzy head?

'Not much – a bottle and—'

'I think a bottle is more than enough.'

'Yes, sir.' I salute the dictator on the phone, trying not to laugh.

'Don't push me, or I will come and collect you.'

'Are you joking?'

'No, I'm serious. As I recall, I instructed you to stay out of trouble. Champagne may test your ability to do so.'

'I think we can find our way back to the hotel… Or maybe you can use my watch. I know you love a bit of hide and seek.' Bubbles and bravado can only lead to trouble.

'Are you trying to fuck with me?'

'Later. Goodbye, husband-to-be… Love you.' I disconnect the call.

Tanya stifles her amusement. 'Is that how you keep him on his toes?'

'Are you kidding? Luke has his own rules.' I pour us another glass of champagne. 'I'm so sorry – sometimes I have no filter!'

'I heard the rumour at work – the loudspeaker incident not long after you started dating. So it's true?'

'Oh my God, that was so embarrassing. I called Luke to tell him about my new job, then he sent me flowers, so I called again, and that's when I called him sex god… but in my defence, he never told me I was on loudspeaker.'

'It did make us laugh.'

'I can imagine. That's my point about tomorrow.' I point at my face. 'Do you see business acumen here? No.'

The cold air bites against my cheeks as Tanya and I link arms, ploughing our way through the mass of commuters and into the strong wind. Twenty minutes later, we arrive at the hotel. The revolving doors are a pleasing sight; thankful to be in the warm. We move through the busy foyer towards the lifts.

The lift arrives at Tanya's floor.

'I'll see you in the morning. I've really enjoyed this afternoon – the start of things to come, I hope.'

'It was fun.' She flashes me a soft smile. 'Don't stress about tomorrow.'

'I won't. But I'll need some luck to deal with happy Luke!'

The doors close and I slump against the wall as I ride to the penthouse.

I open the door and stop. Luke raises his head and studies me.

'Found your way home?' He places his paperwork on his desk and downs a glass of amber liquid. Luke rarely drinks hard spirits; I'll take this as a bad sign.

I place my coat on a chair and walk towards him. 'I wasn't lost.' I perch on his desk and unzip my shoe boots, dropping them to the floor. 'How was your meeting?'

He tilts his head, looking aggravated. 'Are you bothered?'

'Of course I'm bothered,' I snap, and stand. 'If you're going to be arsey with me then I'll go and have a bath.' I move towards the bedroom, removing my tights along the way. I slide my dress over my head and strip off my underwear. As I turn, he stands in the doorway with a dark cloud over him.

His eyes lock on mine, making me feel intimidated. He moves slowly towards me, unbuttoning his shirt and dropping it to the floor. He stops and removes his handmade leather shoes and socks, then works at his trousers and boxers. No words are spoken as we stand, naked.

I reach up for his lips and kiss him softly. My hands run down his back, gripping his arse, and his erection digs in to my hip. He guides me to the bed. I scramble to the centre and lie on my back. Luke moves between my legs. Without any thought I push him to his back and straddle him. My hand instantly grips his erection, which hardens in seconds. His fiery gaze catches mine, as his breathing quickens.

'Kate.'

'Shh…' I lean towards him. 'You can't control everything, Luke, and that includes me.' I can't break away from his eyes. My body stretches and takes his thickness deep inside. His hands brush against my nipples, slide down my torso and rest on my hips. With his help, I begin to ride him. No words are spoken: our only communication is eye contact.

I have no time to scrutinise his behaviour as my orgasm arrives, quickly taking over my body and senses. My stomach contracts with the first wave.

'Luke!' is all I can gasp.

I bathe in the feeling of hedonism as my orgasm lingers. Luke holds my hips, helping me move faster, ensuring he comes quickly.

'Fuck.' He holds my body in place as I feel a faint shudder, the last of his climax.

I lean to his lips. 'I love you,' I declare before I kiss him and free myself.

He is quiet – too quiet. I tuck my body next to his, and instantly he places his arm around my waist, drawing me closer. My hands glide over the contours of his torso and the fine hairs that cover it.

'You're quiet.' Nothing. I rest my chin on his chest. 'I assume you're pissed off.'

His eyes lock to mine. 'Was.'

'Was… OK, so why are you quiet? You know I hate silence.'

'You also hate protection, and you can't be reasonable.' He's not so silent now!

'How so? Luke bloody Sutton, are you suggesting I've misbehaved? Irrational Sutton has entered the building.'

His dark eyes close. 'You and Tanya were out by yourselves. Max wasn't with you, and I worried about you. Christ, you know what buttons to push, Kate – no one else has this effect on me, personally or in business. It's hard for me to adjust.'

'You said I didn't need Max here… The trip was short and door-to-door, so to speak.'

'Every detail was last-minute, for a reason.'

'OK. Last-minute means what? You said there were eyes and ears everywhere earlier. Care to share exactly what you mean?' I know Commander Sutton when I see one.

'No…'

'Luke.'

His eyes close for a moment. 'Jesus, baby, I feel myself losing control with you.'

'Does that scare you?'

His fingers spread against my hipbone.

'Yes.'

'I know you'll never hurt me.'

'Never.'

'Then what is it? I don't understand you, Luke.'

'The explosion might still haunt you, but it's far worse for me. You need to give me this.'

I move and straddle him again. 'How's it worse for you? I saw you lying on the ground… I thought you were…' God, I hate going back to that day.

'I should be able to protect you.' He runs his hand through his hair. 'Fuck, Kate, I've been trained to protect people and then you walk into my life.'

'You say that like it's a bad thing.'

He grabs my hips and moves us both further up the bed. 'No.'

'I was drinking champagne this afternoon, that's all. I was safe. If today is why you're acting weird, then we need to sort you out.'

'Weird?'

'Yes, you're odd. At first I thought it was because you're hot and loaded, but that's not it. I went for a walk with

Tanya – that is a normal thing to do! Your behaviour is not normal.' He closes his eyes for a second. He is seriously struggling. 'Hey, I want to be your wife, but you need to change.'

He nods.

'Luke – I mean it.'

'I'm trying.'

'Bullshit! You need to trust me and give me the freedom I need to grow… Is this why you've been single for a while?' He frowns. 'Not many girls would put up with this.'

'I have never been like this with anyone else.'

'I feel so blessed.' My cheeky remark makes him smile.

'You're a head fuck, Kate Harper.'

'Sutton… very soon.'

'Sorry – very soon to be Mrs Sutton, and I'm sorry for…'

'Shh… no more.'

I move from his lap and stand. 'Let's have a bath and get room service. We can lie in bed and watch the city.' I hold my hand out to him. 'Come on, oddball.'

He laughs. 'I'll give you fucking oddball.'

It's rare, but the next morning I wake first. I turn and look at the view. The city that never sleeps is awake. I roll on my side and study the other stunning view in my life, although this one is asleep.

He pulls me towards him. Can he sense me in his sleep? Military training? I wonder.

'Good morning, wife-to-be.' Thankfully, he seems to be in better spirits today.

'Sorry I woke you.' My head turns to the view again. 'I can't help but stare. The view is amazing.'

He places his hand on my naked arse. 'I couldn't agree more.' It would seem Mr Playful is with me this morning. 'I think this T-shirt needs to go, so I can enjoy the view better.' Luke yanks at my T-shirt. 'You need a Sutton workout. Call it a de-stressing workout.'

God, I love New York.

'Are you sure?' I check my reflection again, running my hands down my fitted black faux leather pencil skirt.

'You look fine, as I told you five minutes ago.' Luke's eyes remain on his paperwork.

'I'm not sure… Does the polo neck look business-like? Maybe I should change. I mean, do people wear polo necks to meetings? Although it is winter so I guess it makes sense. But…'

'Jesus, Kate! You do realise you haven't stopped talking? Sit down and eat some breakfast.'

'I can't eat, I feel sick.' I brush my poker-straight hair again and check my makeup for the hundredth time. Too much black kohl or not enough?

The knock at the door ends my fashion dilemma – for the moment.

I open the door. 'Thank God.'

Tanya steps inside the suite.

'Fashion question for you, and Luke's not playing my game. What do you think?' I use my hand to gesture at myself from head to toe. 'I know, you don't like the polo neck, do you? I was unsure, but I thought it was smart casual.'

Tanya shuts the door and walks towards the dining table. 'It's fine, you look fine.'

'Fine? Define fine.'

'Ignore her,' Luke says.

'Cheers, Luke… I'm nervous and you're not helping.' I move towards him.

'Tanya, I have repeated myself for the last twenty minutes.' Luke stands and pours some coffee. He looks at Tanya. 'Coffee?'

'Yes please, Mr Su—'

'Oh no! Luke, I told Tanya to drop all the formal bullshit and call you Luke. Besides, I'm her boss and I'm telling her to call my fiancé by his name.'

Luke glares and Tanya bites her lip.

'Point taken. Tanya, please call me Luke.' His frown shows he would have appreciated a heads-up on this discussion.

Tanya sits awkwardly and begins to sip her coffee. I move Luke's arms, enough for me to sit on his lap.

'Is there something wrong with the other chairs?'

I link my arms around his neck and kiss his cheek. 'I need this. God, I feel sick… Look at my hands.' They are shaking.

Instantly his strong arms lock around my body. 'I've got you.'

***

Tanya and I step out of the limousine. I look up at the tall glass building, aware that I have been putting off this visit since the day I received news of Katenka's estate. *Crap, here we go.*

We step out of the lift among a sea of workers. I stop dead in my tracks. *BAGROV AND COOPER*. My mum's name in large gold script. It hits me that this was her business, my family business. I swallow hard and follow Tanya. We are escorted to a vast boardroom. We refuse a drink, and sit and wait.

One by one the chairs at the large table fill up, and various assistants come in and line the back walls. Soon, only two chairs remain empty.

Several eyes dart around the room, surreptitiously glancing at me, the woman who owns sixty per cent of their company. To say that I feel out of my depth would be a huge understatement.

The atmosphere instantly alters with the arrival of the super-bitch and her father. Philip Cooper walks in and sits directly in front of me, smartly dressed in a dark suit. He makes my skin crawl. Alexis sits in the last chair next to him. I can't help but notice her stunning black pinstripe suit: very chic. *God, I hate her, but I love her clothes.*

I keep looking forward. Breathe and don't run is my new mantra – for the next thirty minutes.

A man stands at the front of the room. He introduces himself as Mr Stewart. Apparently he's one of the board members. He then addresses the board. I look at him, not looking at the evil Cooper duo. My poker face is commendable, but internally I'm flagging. *Breathe, don't run.*

The spokesman begins to read through the items listed on the agenda. Thankfully, he needs no input from me. We reach the last two items. First, selling a company that is thriving, and has a hefty price tag. I raise my hand and agree. The hotel is the last item to be discussed. I remember the paperwork that Tanya showed me in Luke's office: the renovation of a hotel. It needs a unanimous vote.

Philip Cooper coughs, indicating he's about to speak. Unfortunately, this means I will have to look at him.

'You're fully aware we need to agree on this project in order to continue our growth within the hotel industry.' He looks at me. 'Miss Harper, I take it you understand what is going on here. I suspect your fiancé has explained the importance of this vote... I should also congratulate you on your engagement. Mr Sutton has landed on his feet, marrying into money *and* a business.' The evil smirk plastered across his face chills me, but his look of hatred when he mentions Luke's name is far more unsettling and leaves me wondering why he feels like this. I can only think he's threatened by Luke.

He has landed on his feet. Prick!

'Thinking outside the box and branching away from like-minded people has done him the world of good.' My eyes lock with Alexis's. *Yes, you bitch: that comment was a joint Cooper reply.*

'Life is full of surprises. Luke Sutton is a... let's just say, he likes business and women. You think you can tame a man like him?'

The stillness in the room is nerve-racking.

Oh my God. I clear my throat. 'I'm his new venture, Mr Cooper. Watch me tame him!'

He laughs loudly. 'I wish you luck, Miss Harper... I wish you luck.'

Luck? He's bloody lucky Luke's not here.

I lean towards Tanya's ear. 'When is the deadline for this deal?'

She skims through her paperwork. 'Tomorrow, three o'clock. Why?'

'Good.' I return my gaze to the Coopers.

The spokesman speaks to the masses. 'All those in favour?'

People raise their hands. All eyes stop at me. I search for strength. *Dig deep – you'll be a Sutton soon.*

My eyes remain on Philip Cooper. 'I'm not sure about this project.' An eerie silence fills the room like a dark cloud. *Kiss my arse, slimeball.*

'Can you repeat that, Miss Harper?' His face reddens with anger.

I lean further across the table, ensuring he can hear and see me. 'I'm not sure about this deal... You have until tomorrow. I believe three o'clock is the deadline.' I shrug my shoulders. *Fuck you, arsehole.*

He bangs so hard on the table that everyone stops breathing – including me. Clearly, he's pissed off.

'Let me make something clear! You're here because you are the beneficiary of your late mother's fortune. Do not sit there and think your input matters. All you need to do is turn up and look pretty.'

'Looks like you have a problem.' I sit back in my chair. 'I apologise for my ignorance, but I do own a majority share in this company, yes?'

I'm sure I can hear gasps from the masses watching me deal with their boss. 'Feel free to correct me at any point. As I was saying, you need my vote – and I'm not sure I want to give it to you.' I grab my bag and stand. I look at Tanya, informing her we're leaving. 'I'll let you know my answer tomorrow.'

'You're making a mistake... Just go home to your fiancé and practise playing wifey.' Philip glares at me.

I swear to God I'm going to crawl across the table and knock him out. I push my chair in. 'Oh, and when I return tomorrow I expect an office – the biggest you have, just so I can paint my fucking nails!'

The people in the room part, making way for my exit. Tanya follows. No one tries to stop us. I'm not sure if it's due to fear or utter disbelief.

We are given our coats, and make our way to the lift. Tanya looks at me, trying not to laugh. Thank goodness, the lift promptly arrives, and we step in and the door shuts.

'Fuck, fuck, fuck, crap!' I rub my forehead. 'Oh my God, what was I thinking? Shit, now I have to come back tomorrow. I need a gag! I can't help myself; I have to say whatever comes into my head. I told you this would happen. I'm not a businesswoman, and never will be. Shit, shit, shit...' I slump in the corner.

'Philip's face – I thought he was going to explode,' Tanya says, laughing.

'I know. I was amazed that Alexis just sat there and didn't say a word. Oh bloody hell, what have I done? Luke is going to go mad. All I had to do was say yes. Yes – see, it's easy; I said it.'

'He was disrespectful to you, and mentioning Luke was unethical.'

'Bloody weasel! That made me so cross. I'm guessing this is nothing like your usual meetings?'

'Far more entertaining!' She smiles.

Back at the hotel, I pace the suite, replaying the meeting in my head, feeling cross with myself for allowing the Coopers to intimidate me – and now I have to return.

Hastily, I strip off my clothes, leaving my underwear on, and slide under the duvet. I spend the next few hours watching reruns of *Friends* and the complete saga of *Keeping up with the Kardashians*, as well as eating all the overpriced M&Ms from the fridge.

'Kate!' Luke bellows from the living area.

'I'm in the bedroom.'

As he enters the room, my heart skips a beat.

'Why are you in bed?'

'Oh my God. I'm so bloody mad at myself.'

He removes his shoes and lies next to me. 'So, what happened? I can read you, Harper.' His lip curls.

'It's not funny.' I sit up slightly.

'I'm not laughing, baby.' He runs his hand down my cheek.

'Pissed off… that's what I am. It was running OK until the prick mentioned you've found yourself a catch and asked if I had the power to tame you! Apparently you like business and women – in that order… Can you believe him? I nearly crawled over the table and knocked him out. Even Tanya said he was unethical.' I fold my arms, still raging.

'Kate Harper, are you protecting me?' Luke tips up the empty packets of chocolates. 'Hungry?'

'See, this is what he's made me do, eat all the chocolate, and I bet they cost a bloody fortune… Add that to the list of reasons why I despise the man. And now I have to go back tomorrow.'

Luke looks puzzled. 'Why's that?'

'I thought you would have spoken to Tanya.'

'I tried, but her phone went to voicemail. Honestly, I thought you were in good hands.'

'Tanya was fine, if that's what you mean… They needed a unanimous vote to purchase a hotel, and I said no – well, for today. They have until tomorrow to finalise the deal.' I take a deep breath.

Luke tilts his head.

'Philip told me to stay at home and play wifey, so I asked for an office, a large one where I could paint my fucking nails.'

Luke bows his head, laughing.

'It's not funny. The weasel said they didn't need any input from me, and that I should just sit there and look pretty… How about my right foot up his arse? I'm sure that'll look pretty.'

'What am I going to do with you?' He kisses me tenderly, soothing away my anger. He pulls away and nips my nose.

'I thought you'd be pissed off.'

'No. Am I surprised something like this has happened? Not really. If Philip Cooper had kept his mouth shut, the deal would have been completed, but he spoke out of turn, and I agree with you that he can be a prick.'

I place my arms lovingly around his neck.

'As for taming me, you have.'

I scream under my breath with frustration.

Luke brushes my cheek with the back of his hand. 'There are many Philip Coopers in the world. You just need to remain calm and when the time comes you will be able to kick him up the arse.'

'Maybe… This is why I want a nine-to-five job. I'm not cut out for this world.'

'You'll get there. So, what would my headstrong fiancée like to do?'

'Let's go for a walk. I fancy a burger and a beer.'

Luke tilts his head. 'It's your choice.'

'Yep, nothing flashy, burger and then bed.'

'Bed… I like that idea.' His mouth finds mine. *Eat me, Luke.*

11

Smoke fills my lungs. I cough and call Luke's name. The grey smog begins to disperse. I watch Luke get up. He can barely stand, but he staggers to Max and begins to drag him from the flames. I try to stand, but my legs won't move. Jerry and Rosie run past me as I watch Luke collapse to the ground. No... no... no!

My eyes shoot open, my heart beating wildly. I turn to Luke and gently skim his cheek. God, I hate these nightmares. I look at my watch – four thirty. I lift the covers and head to the bathroom, where I switch on the shower, allowing the steam and hot water to get rid of the memory of the dream.

I tighten the belt of the hotel robe around my damp body and rest my head against the window. It's still dark outside but of course all the lights are on in the surrounding skyscrapers. Part of me wants Luke to wake up. It's no use; I need fresh air.

I pull my jeans on over my clammy legs, followed by Luke's hoodie and my black Converse. I scrape my hair into a ponytail. New York is not ready for Roller Girl –

come to think of it, no city should be punished with that vision. Last, I grab my black riding coat and head for the door. I stop to write Luke a note.

Dear Luke,
 I've gone for a walk.
 I love you. x

I place it on my pillow. Old habits die hard.

Pushing through the revolving door, I swiftly move to the kerb and close my eyes, allowing the cold air to wash over me.

'Excuse me, Miss Harper.'

A voice breaks my moment. I turn to see a member of staff.

'Morning.'

'Do you need anything?'

'I'm fine, thank you.'

The young man nods and begins to walk away.

'Actually, there is something. Is there a driver available, or is it too early?'

'Yes, of course. I will call him out front.'

'Thank you.'

He turns and heads back through the revolving doors.

My arms lock tightly around my body. It's bloody freezing.

'Why, if it isn't the delightful Kate Harper – or should I say soon-to-be Kate Sutton?'

I turn at the sound. A tall, lanky man beams at me. It's Charles Morley – an acquaintance of Luke's, definitely not a friend. I've only met him once before, at a ball, but for some reason I quite like him. He's odd – I guess he's slightly eccentric.

'Charles Morley… You're the last person I expected to see here.'

'Likewise.'

'You're up and out early.'

'Not out – just getting back from a night out.' He laughs.

'Long night.'

'Yes, and a long day in bed to compensate.'

'Lucky for some.'

'I live every second, Kate.' He smirks and throws his coat over his shoulder.

I'm sure he does!

A car pulls alongside me and a chauffeur steps out. 'Miss Harper.'

'Hi.'

The driver holds the door open. I turn to Charles. 'It was nice to see you – enjoy the rest of your day, sleeping.'

'I will, Kate. Oh, and tell Luke to get you down the aisle before someone steals you away from him.'

My eyes roll. 'I'm not up for grabs… But I'll tell Luke you're pleased for us.'

'Where to, Miss Harper?' The driver looks at me through the rear-view mirror.

'Oh! Rosewood Ivy Hotel, do you know it? I don't have the address: all I know is that it's old or probably rundown – sorry.'

'Yes, ma'am. It's being restored. It's only a few blocks from here.'

'Great.' I sit back and watch New York begin to wake up.

The car pulls up in front of a derelict building, which is huge and looks like a hotel, or at the very least a prominent building. The building is sectioned off from the public with a metal fence. I open the door and step out onto the pavement. The driver instantly arrives at my side.

'Is this it?'

I nod. 'It looks bigger in real life.' The picture Tanya showed me doesn't do it justice.

'It's great that some investor wants to bring it back to life.'

'That's me... Well, not literally me, but my company.' *Wow – my company!* 'Do you have a torch?'

'Yes, ma'am.' The driver returns with a reasonably large torch. 'Can I ask, are you going into the building? They probably have security?'

'Yeah, I want to look inside.' I scan for cameras or some form of security.

'That's breaking and entering in this city.'

'Not if you own it – sort of. I can go in alone.'

'No, I'd better go with you.'

I extend my hand. 'I'm Kate Harper, and you are?'

'Michael, ma'am.'

'Let's drop the ma'am; you're making me feel like I'm a hundred.'

Michael laughs. 'It's protocol...'

'Kate.' I end his statement.

'Kate.'

'See, that was a walk in the park.' I turn to look at the magnificent building; it must have been stunning in its heyday.

There is a small opening in the metal fence that is large enough to fit through. Michael is fairly short, and

233

squeezes through behind me. We walk towards the front of the building. I yank the lock on the main door, which is keeping out unwanted visitors – I guess I fall into that category. To the right I notice a small window opening, which is not boarded up. I begin to climb through.

'Are you sure about this?' Michael asks.

'It'll be fine. Besides, we won't be long.'

My leg goes through first, and I scramble in, falling to the floor, covering my coat in dust.

'You OK?'

'Yeah.' I get to my feet and pat the dust from my coat. 'Some cleaning wouldn't go amiss.'

Michael soon joins me. I switch the torch on and scan the area. We are in a rundown room, with a broken bar area in one corner and a large fireplace in the centre. We continue through to what looks like the main reception area. For the first time I'm grateful that I'm not alone. Not only is the huge building in complete darkness, but the silence is eerie.

The torch offers me a glimpse of what was once here. The décor is from the 1920s: the art nouveau designs are tired, yet evident.

I wander further into the main area, shining my torch around. As I turn around, I scream. Michael heads to my side. My torch has shone in someone's face! Their arm is over their face, shielding them from the glare.

'I don't know who you are, but remove that torch from my face.' A voice echoes through the great room.

'Crap… Sorry. You made me jump.' *Shit. I've been caught.*

I can hear the person move away. I suddenly hear a sound – perhaps some kind of generator – and then powerful lights beam from every corner of the room, making me squint. I switch my torch off.

'You want to explain why you're here before I call the cops?'

I can now see the man who has found me. He stands with his hands on his hips. Wow, he's good-looking, in jeans, a navy shirt and a tweed jacket, with streaked mousey hair falling around his face. On second thoughts, he's hot! I can feel my cheeks flush.

'I'm from Bagrov and Cooper,' I say.

He walks towards me, taking my arm, guiding me away from the lights. 'Careful of the leads.'

I look down and cautiously step over the various leads snaking around the room.

'My company may buy this hotel.'

'I know who they are.' He's arsey – and hot. 'You shouldn't really be here. There are guidelines – not to mention you don't have any safety equipment.'

My hands fist on my hips – never a good sign!

'Neither do you.' *Oh, here I go. Someone switch my filter on.* 'To be honest, your security system is crap. I wandered straight in. You love a lawsuit in this country, so I'm sure that's asking for trouble.' *Christ, this man is good-looking. Stay on your game, Harper.*

He smiles, and moves closer. 'Is that so?'

'Merely an observation. Take it or leave it.' *Is it hot in here, or is it me?*

'How did you get in?'

'A window. Actually, it wasn't boarded up; you might as well have left a welcome sign.'

His smile spreads wide. Wow, it's dazzling. 'Next time, go through the correct channels.'

I shrug and bite my lip. 'Fair enough. Anyway, who are you?'

He extends his hand. 'Bradley Taylor, architect. We could end up working together if you like what you see.'

'Like what I see?' *Shit, did I just repeat his words?*

'Yeah, do you like what you see?'

Fuck, is he talking about the hotel or him? It's far too early for flirting.

He tilts his head. 'Your name is…'

I cough, clearing my throat. 'Kate Harper – and, honestly, I've seen better and I haven't said yes yet, so this might be a waste of your time.'

The sound of a woman's voice calling Bradley's name thankfully cools the atmosphere. Still, his eyes remain on me.

We both look at where the voice came from. *Shit! It's Alexis Cooper.*

'Kate! What are you doing here?'

'I wanted to see what all the fuss was about. Besides, it's early.' I look at my watch. It's now six thirty. 'I didn't expect to see anyone here.' Least of all her! Shit. I'm completely out of my depth, not to mention underdressed for the occasion – unlike Alexis, who wears a fitted tan suit and black shirt. As usual, she epitomises a businesswoman. I, on the other hand, resemble a vagrant.

'I have back-to-back meetings. Time is money, Kate.' She walks closer to Bradley and me. 'You should have asked. I would have arranged for someone to show you the building yesterday… I take it your visit means you're going to vote for buying the hotel?'

'You were confident I'd say yes to this project, weren't you? I mean, you already have an architect working on the drawings.'

'We needed to make sure our idea was viable.'

'Do you want me to be honest with you?' I fold my arms.

'Please,' she says curtly.

'Your dad needs to keep his opinions to himself. It makes no difference to me whether this plan goes ahead or not.'

She laughs. 'You have no clue about my father.'

I take a step forward. 'Your father's a prick, and you can tell him that too.'

Bradley moves between us. 'OK, ladies, shall we stop this discussion?' He places his hand against my back and gestures with his other hand to Alexis. 'Let's take this to the table.'

We move.

'Alexis, you're here to look over the plans?'

'Yes.'

'Kate, you need to see them too. Hopefully this will help with your decision.'

'Fine,' I reply grumpily.

We all walk towards a large desk on which are laid various architectural designs of the existing building and the proposed new layout.

'So, ladies, here are the revised plans. Alexis, you will notice the modifications you requested, and the changes your father also wanted.'

I look at the plans. This man is good. The new building looks stunning. However, I can't see the magnificent staircase that is directly in front of us. Even dilapidated, it remains breath-taking.

'Can I ask a question?'

Bradley nods.

'The staircase – it's not the same. It makes no sense to remove it. Surely it can be repaired?'

Bradley smiles, flashing his perfect all-American teeth. Christ, he's handsome. Still, he's no Luke Sutton.

'Alexis and I have discussed this. However, Philip doesn't like the staircase and wants to modernise the entrance.'

I lean off the desk and stand up. 'What the hell does Philip Cooper know about interiors? Seriously, that's the worst decision. He may be a good businessman, but to remove this staircase would be criminal.'

'My father knows what he's talking about.'

Why is she defending a decision that she clearly has issues with? After her silence yesterday, I now begin to analyse her behaviour. How strong is she?

'I think that's bullshit, and you know it. To remove this structure would be like taking away the essence of the building. Bradley, do you agree?' Alexis and I stare at him.

'I agree with Kate; this staircase can be made to look contemporary. Alexis, you wanted to keep it, and we've had many debates with your father over this.' Bradley stands back and slides his hands into his jeans pockets.

'Well then, it's sorted. If he wants my vote, the staircase stays.'

'Kate, I'm warning you, do not piss off my father. He can be brutal if you get on the wrong side of him. Don't say I didn't warn you.'

'Is that a girl-to-girl warning? I think we've been here before. I don't care what your dad thinks; I'll make my own decisions.' I look across the room to see Michael shifting from side to side, looking uncomfortable. 'I think I should leave.' Before I launch at her. 'Nice to meet you, Bradley.'

'You too, Kate. I'm sure we'll be seeing a lot more of each other.' He's definitely flirting. 'Let me open the main door. Unless you like crawling through windows.'

'Very funny.'

He laughs. 'You're quite amusing.'

'That's the British for you.'

Michael and I follow him towards the main door.

'Until next time, Kate.'

The car pulls up outside the hotel, and I look at my watch. It's nearly eight o'clock – crap, where did the time go?

'Anything else I can help you with, Miss Harper – sorry, Kate?'

'No, but thanks for your help.'

'Not a problem.'

The heat from the hotel lobby is a welcome treat. I swiftly move to the lift and arrive at the top floor. I wonder if Luke is awake?

I open the door and watch Luke pace the lounge area, speaking on his phone, dressed in black trousers and white shirt, his tie hanging loose. He catches sight of me and stops.

'Tell the team to stand down; she's here.' He places his phone in his pocket, and moves towards me. 'Where the fuck have you been?' His eyes are almost black.

'What?'

'Where have you been? It's a simple question.' He runs a hand through his hair.

'I left you a note. I went for a walk.'

'I've been awake since six; it must have been a long fucking walk.' He moves to the desk and holds up a mobile phone – *my* mobile phone. 'This is your phone; you're supposed to keep it with you.' He looks ready to explode.

'OK. I forgot my phone. You do realise that you're being bloody irrational again? And you mentioned a team – who were you talking to?'

'Oh no, you don't get to ask questions.' He laughs humourlessly. 'You were missing and you want to call *me* irrational. Fuck. I should have brought Max.'

'Luke, this is ridiculous. I woke from a nightmare and needed air. I went downstairs, and instead of walking the streets in the dark, I asked a driver to show me the hotel that Bagrov and Cooper want to buy. It's no big deal.'

'A pointless exercise; you didn't need to see the hotel. As for your nightmare, you should have woken me.'

'Hang on a minute. Back up… What do you mean a pointless exercise?' I can't believe his flippant remark.

'Kate, there was no need to visit the hotel; you said yourself you wanted to let Philip sweat overnight.'

I shake my head. 'That's bullshit, and clearly not what you meant. Just tell me how it is. You have the same opinion as Philip, don't you? Just turn up and look pretty. What possible input can I bring? Well, thank you very much.' I look at the floor, feeling betrayed.

'No, you don't, Harper. This discussion is not about your ability, so don't stand there and flip it on its arse. You went AWOL.' Luke points his finger in my face. 'Someone tried to harm you and kill me, so you're fucking right I want to know where you are.' He looks at his watch. 'I don't have time for this.'

'No, but you have time to tell me I'm crap at this business bullshit.'

He glares at me. 'Tanya has the address of where you need to meet me for lunch, as I have a surprise guest turning up.' He speaks at me, not to me. He turns and collects his jacket from the desk.

I shake my head at him. 'Are you for real?'

He stops. 'You were in the wrong disappearing this morning. Whether you like it or not, this proves my point.'

'Which one, Luke?'

'Trust. I can't trust you.'

'Trust? That's rich coming from you! I found out about the real Luke Sutton when I was tied to a bloody chair! Lucky me, my boyfriend is some kind of psycho who likes his girlfriends to wear tracking devices. Oh, because that's not fucked up, is it? '

'That watch saved your life! *I* saved your life.'

'Oh, whatever, Luke! You're really getting on my tits,' I murmur and head towards the bedroom. Luke follows me.

'Don't mumble – if you have something else to add then say it. As for your safety, I will protect you at all costs.' He collects his black wool overcoat from the bed.

'Why don't you put a bloody leash around my neck? Is that clear enough for you.'

'Don't tempt me.'

'Oh my God, you're out of control. Seriously, Luke, if you don't start listening to me we won't make it to the bloody altar.'

His eyes meet mine.

'Russia was a walk in the park compared to you.' I slam the bedroom door.

For the meeting, I decide to dress to kill. The mood I'm in, the Coopers had better watch out.

I look in the mirror at my outfit. Smart black tailored shorts – actually, they are rather short – with a tightly fitted black blazer. A white shirt, a skinny black leather tie, and my most daring item, black fishnet tights and shoe boots. The look is a little quirky and very me. My hair is pulled back into a ponytail, and I wear my usual makeup. I achieve extra drama with heavier kohl and red lipstick – let's hope Luke doesn't think his luck's in. There'll be no visits to bathroom cubicles to suck his dick today!

Tanya and I stand on the pavement, and I look up to the tall building with a sense of déjà vu. As soon as we enter a new sensation washes over me. The stress of yesterday has altered; a personal crusade to take down the Coopers is motivating me today.

'Ready, Kate?' Tanya presses the button for the top floor.

'Not really. OK, if I speak, kick me – hard.'

Once again the Bagrov and Cooper sign hits me. Undeniably, my business insight is sketchy, but Ivor did say I had Katenka's passion. Perhaps that's what I need to draw on here.

We enter the boardroom and take our former seats. The room begins to fill, including the evil duo. Eyes forward is today's mantra. I can feel Philip's intense glare; his hatred for me consumes the entire room.

The spokesman from yesterday takes his place at the head of the table. He then proceeds to explain the reason for the meeting. I do have something to say. I take a deep breath and find some courage.

'May I say something?'

Silence washes over the room as all eyes fall on me.

'Yes, Miss Harper.' The spokesman gestures for me to take to the floor and speak.

'Thank you. I visited the hotel this morning.'

Philip Cooper looks at me and raises his brows – fucking prick.

'And I agree it is a magnificent building. However, I looked at the drawings as well. The bottom line is, if you want my vote, there is a condition. You can't touch the staircase.'

Philip Cooper begins to laugh, not with humour but with shock.

'Are you joking? You roll in here demanding to keep some structure you clearly know nothing about. You have some balls, Miss Harper.' Philip sits back in his chair, shaking his head.

'First, you need my vote, so don't sit there and shake your head at me. And, second, your idea was shit. The staircase adds historical value. Reception areas are the first view of any hotel, so why would you want to remove an iconic structure? Besides, Bradley Taylor agreed with me.'

I turn to Tanya. No need to kick me; it's too late.

The spokesman stands. 'Thank you, Miss Harper. OK, so we need to vote, with the additional clause, the staircase remains. All those in favour, raise their hands.' One by one the hands around the room begin to rise, including mine. Philip Cooper is the last member to vote.

He looks at me as he raises his arm – he clearly hates me. Not a problem; the man makes my skin crawl.

'The vote is unanimous, so we can now go ahead with the finance. Thank you, everyone, for attending, and to you, Miss Harper.'

I nod. It's over. I can go home. Except I have to deal with Mr Moody Bollocks Sutton first.

Ten minutes later, Tanya and I stand on the kerb. I take a deep breath and relax for the first time since we arrived.

'Thank God it's over.' I link my arm through hers as we make our way towards the car.

'You did well. I was a little surprised about the staircase, and so was Philip Cooper… But you held on to your principles, so well done.'

The car returns Tanya to the hotel and then takes me to meet Luke for lunch. He mentioned a surprise guest. I wonder who it is. Within fifteen minutes the car draws up outside a restaurant. I step out and walk through the door.

'Afternoon, ma'am,' a host instantly greets me.

'Hi, I'm meeting Mr Sutton.' I scan the room, looking for Luke. I remove my coat and pass it to the woman on reception.

'This way. Mr Sutton is already here.' I follow the waitress to a cocktail table with glasses and an open bottle of wine.

'This is Mr Sutton's table.'

'Thank you.' I smile and stand alone, waiting for Luke. The bar is filled with businessmen.

'Kate Harper.'

I turn, to see Bradley Taylor standing there. His eyes drink in my body.

'You look… different from this morning.'

'Better, I hope.'

'I like what I see.'

Crap. He's flirting again. This isn't good.

'I'm here to discuss staircases with Philip Cooper. Apparently, there have been some alterations to the plans.'

'So I hear.' I tilt my head and smile.

'Do you know anything about that? I wondered, after I received the call, did Kate Harper change Philip Cooper's mind? I doubt it; there must have been guns drawn and a bloody battle.' His hand runs down the arm of my jacket. 'I'm impressed.'

'Don't be fooled. My business skills are rubbish.'

'Expect the unexpected works for me.'

'Your luck's in; I don't do expectations. What you see is what you get.'

He tries to speak.

'No. Don't say you like what you see. Anyway, you might have worked out that the Coopers and I aren't friends. He's a weasel – with no appreciation for stunning staircases.'

Bradley's face lights up with his smile.

'I get it. I admire your tenacity.'

I nod, and accept his compliment.

The scent hits me, before I feel a gentle touch against the small of my back. I turn to see the love of my life. My eyes lock on his, as Luke leans down and places a kiss on my cheek. Is this a sign of affection or ownership?

'Hey, baby.' Ownership – he doesn't do 'baby' in public.

'Luke, this is Bradley Taylor, the architect working on the hotel for Bagrov and Cooper. Bradley, this is my fiancé, Luke Sutton.'

Bradley leans across and shakes Luke's hand. 'We have a mutual friend, Zhan Abdul. We've worked on several projects together. The last time we spoke he showed me the plans of your hotel in Dubai.'

'Small world.' Luke smiles, but I sense hostility.

'Very small. I met Kate this morning as she climbed through a window into the hotel – and now she has laid out stipulations for Philip Cooper. She's definitely strong-minded.'

'She is.' Luke spreads his hand wide across my hipbone, drawing me closer.

'Speaking of Mr Cooper, I had better go. Luke, good to meet you; tell Zhan I said hello. Kate.' He kisses my cheek.

Alone, Luke turns to face me, and runs his tongue across his lower lip. Christ, he looks hot. I must stay focused – I'm still pissed off at him.

He begins to snigger.

'Something bothering you?' I ask.

'Where do I begin? First, climbing through windows… Jesus, do you want to get arrested?'

'For your information, it wasn't boarded up, and I would have told you this morning, except you went off on one.'

'Off on one! You went missing, and not for the first time. I need to trust you.'

'You can. I'm not flying off anywhere, and I wasn't missing. Speaking of this morning, you sidestepped my question about what team you meant.'

He shakes his head. 'There are eyes and ears everywhere, a bit like this room.'

'What do you mean?'

'Do you know how many men have been watching you?'

'Might I suggest you buy some blindfolds?' I shake my head. 'There must be a doctor out there that can help you. Your irrational behaviour is getting out of control.'

Luke pulls at my chin. 'Kate Harper, very nearly Sutton, right now I want to take you back to the hotel and fuck you. You're as testing as ever. With your lips the shade they are, you know I can't kiss you. Please do not push me, not after this morning.'

My hand swiftly moves to his arse, drawing him close. 'Back at you, Luke. And for the record, I'm fuming about this morning.'

'Fuming?'

'Too bloody right I am.'

'Bradley Taylor likes my fiancée… How do I feel about that? Pissed off.'

I pull away and take a glass of wine from the table.

'You're seriously worried about an architect I don't even know… you have seen what you look like, right?'

'What the hell are you talking about?' He takes his wine.

'Just listen. You're a good-looking man – no, let's say it how it is. You're the most handsome man I've ever met. I could come just by looking at you.'

He nearly spits his wine out. 'For Christ's sake, Kate.'

'When you walk in a room, women are already sliding off their knickers for you, and they don't even know what you've got going on under the suit! Don't stand there and act like I've just revealed some breaking news… You know the effect you have on women. Apparently, business and women are your thing.'

'Irrelevant; I have no interest in anyone else.'

'That's where you're wrong. I have a bloody good point to make. You look like a bloody model, and I look like me. Not really much of a challenge, is it? My point is, I should be the one being jealous, not the other way round.'

He drinks some wine and places his glass on the table. 'Look around you. Do you see the men in this room? They have been watching you since the moment you arrived.' He looks at my legs then at my eyes. 'Fishnet tights? I'm not surprised you've caused a stir in their trousers.'

'Luke!' I hit his arm and pull him close. My arms lock around his neck. 'Your trousers are my only concern. I have agreed to become your wife – ownership goes both ways.'

'Yes… Please don't forget I possess you.'

'Possess me? That's fucked-up. Am I supposed to be impressed with that? You don't possess me, Luke. I choose whether I want to be with you… Think carefully about that: suffocate me and we're over.'

He takes his glass of wine, downs the remainder and places it on our table. His dark eyes lock to mine; this morning has unnerved him, without doubt.

'Say something.'

He takes my left hand and gently kisses me. 'You always have a choice, Kate.'

'Then don't force me to make one…' *Oh God, I would never leave him.* 'I need your help to get through this. We're a team, not at odds, and I don't want my future husband judging me.'

He tilts his head. 'Noted.'

'Good, and for the record I'm still mad with you.' This time I smile. I am mad but I hope he's listening.

'You should have taken your phone.'

'Noted!' I smirk.

'Are you taking the piss?' He laughs and kisses my neck. 'I still need to fuck you.' His eyes fix on mine.

'I want you to eat me; let's run.'

'We can't cancel, but soon I'll lick you dry.'

I've gone. He has me, hook line and sinker.

We sit and wait. Within minutes, Luke stands.

'Mrs Gold.' Luke guides the elderly lady, a friend of his family, to our table.

I stand too. 'Mrs Gold, Luke said he had invited a surprise guest.'

'Kate, my darling, I do hope I'm not a disappointment.' She offers me a double kiss and a warm smile.

'No, it's good to see you again.' We all sit down.

'Luke sent me an email informing me that you were here in New York. As luck would have it, so was I. So tell me, I believe you have some news of your own.' She reaches for my left hand and gazes at my ring. 'I was thrilled when Luke told me. I won't lie, Luke, I have been waiting for this day. Ask your mother – she'll tell you.' She looks across at him. 'What are your wedding plans?'

The Sutton boys grew up surrounded by people like the Coopers, so what a change it is for him to be in the company of an old family friend with a heart!

During our main course, I spot Philip Cooper. I shake my head. How unfortunate – he appears to be heading our way.

'Luke, congratulations on your engagement.'

Luke stands and shakes the weasel's hand. I feel he'll need a serious amount of antibacterial soap afterwards.

'Thank you, Philip. You know Mrs Gold and, of course, my beautiful fiancée.'

'Mrs Gold, you look well… Kate.'

'Hello, Mr Cooper,' Mrs Gold responds while she gazes across at me.

If he thinks I'm talking to him, then he can think again.

'I will leave you to your lunch. Perhaps we will catch up in London? Are you going to Klosters next weekend?' Philip asks.

'Yes.' Luke takes his seat.

'No doubt I will see you there.'

Not if I push you off a cliff first.

'Mrs Gold, it was a pleasure.' His eyes fall on me. I remain silent. Thankfully, he walks away and takes the chill he brought with him.

Luke laughs. 'Jesus, Kate, you need to find a way to deal with the likes of Philip Cooper. I told you to rise above him.'

'Yes, and my mum taught me that if you have nothing nice to say, then best not to say anything. Sorry, Mrs Gold, I just don't like him. He makes my skin crawl and he's bloody rude. Congratulations my—'

'Kate!' Luke squeezes my fingers.

'Sorry.'

'Truthfully, I couldn't agree with you more.' Mrs Gold laughs. 'Do one thing for me, my darling.'

I nod.

'Never lose your passion – or your morals. They will keep you safe when you least expect it.'

Over lunch, we chat about many issues. Mrs Gold seems to be very interested in my life, although I'm not sure why.

'Luke, I emailed Stella with the details of the gala for the Alzheimer's charity,' says Mrs Gold.

'Stella did mention it: we have a table.'

'Can I ask the pack to come?' It will be fun to have like-minded people with me.

Luke shoots me a look. 'OK.'

Mrs Gold looks at me. 'Pack? That sounds like fun. Tell me, what does this involve?'

'Kate's pet name for her friends; just look for the noisy table.'

Mrs Gold's face lights up. 'Oh, they should bring some life to a dreary event. I may have to sit with you.'

Finally, Luke and I say our goodbyes, having fixed a date for the gala. We swiftly leave, to see Michael waiting by the kerb.

'Hi Michael, I promise not to ask you to drive me to any more derelict hotels.'

He smiles. 'Yes, Ma— sorry, Kate. Not a usual request.'

'I guess not.' I slide inside the limousine; Luke follows me. His dark eyes rest on me. 'What now?' Christ, his moods change like the wind.

'Michael?'

'He was the driver who took me to the hotel this morning.'

His fingers tap against his leg.

'Welcome back, Mr Irrational Sutton; you must have a season pass. What's your problem?'

'The problem is, you are over-familiar with people, and that's not how business works – especially with architects who want something else from you.'

I fold my arms, as I want to slap him hard. 'Did you just say that? Jesus, Luke, we just spoke about this.'

'It gives off the wrong signals.'

'OK, so the reason you're a miserable bastard is so people won't want to fuck you?'

'Jesus! You can't help yourself; watch what comes out of your mouth.'

'You just said that I want to shag Bradley Taylor.'

'Fuck me, you're relentless. I said you're over-familiar.'

'Dress it up, Luke; the Chelsea boy is never far away. It all adds up to the same thing.'

'Adds up to what?'

'I'm not cut from the same cloth as you, familiarity breeds… what is it – contempt? Well, you're wrong. Saying hello is different to saying let's shag.'

'Stop talking shit. Christ, Kate, you need to control your mouth.'

'Is this how it's going to be when we're married? I can't help being friendly. You should try it; it can be useful at times.' Holy shit. His fists are clenched and his knuckles are almost transparent: a sure sign Luke is pissed.

We arrive at the hotel. Luke takes my hand. I try to shake him off, but his grip is too tight. Once inside the lift, he presses the button for our floor. The silence kills me.

The door of the suite opens. I shake myself free of him, and walk away in the opposite direction to Luke.

'Wait,' he bellows, stopping me in my tracks. His strides are quick. I blink and his hands are in my hair.

'I don't know what you want from me.' I bow my head in confusion.

He pulls my chin. 'You, baby, that's all I need.' His thumbs brush against my cheeks. 'You drive me crazy.'

'No shit.'

'Fuck, Kate, you scare the shit out me.'

'Why?'

'You're unpredictable, and…' He trails off and looks away.

'What?'

'You're my biggest threat – losing you would destroy me.'

'Luke, I love you. Even when you drive me mad I couldn't live without you – ever.'

'I apologise for putting you down earlier. It was wrong. And I should have taken you to the hotel yesterday.'

I nod. Wow.

'You have more business acumen than you realise.' His hand moves across to my heart. 'This is your main asset. Today, you proved your worth. Tanya called me.'

'Oh.'

'I know I was cross this morning. Please, believe that I am proud of you.'

'I'm drowning, Luke. This is way over my head. '

His lips gently skim my forehead. 'It's not.'

'It is! This Bagrov stuff it's not me – I don't have a clue. And us, when it's good, it's really good, and everything in between just seems fucked.'

'Don't say that. You say you're drowning? I was, too, and you're saving me, more than you realise, Kate.'

'I piss you off all the time – how is that saving you?'

'You question me, and I know I need that.' He takes a breath. 'It kills me that the past few months have forced me back to the military – my past.'

'What do you mean? Shit – you're not going back with Sullivan?'

'No.' He shakes his head. 'But I have to be on my guard. It's the only way I know how to save you from…' He trails off. I see fear in his eyes. 'Saving you has opened up old war wounds – not physically, but mentally it's opened up the past for me.'

'Oh God. If you need to talk about it…'

'I don't.' He runs his finger down my cheek. 'I would never put you down, baby; you are my life.'

I take his hand and walk him to the bedroom, losing my jacket along the way. Luke copies me. I begin to undo the buttons of his shirt, swiftly followed by my own leather tie and shirt.

I undo his trousers and release his erection. Our eyes lock: dark and confused meets dark and challenging.

I drop to my knees, yanking his trousers and boxers down his powerful thighs, and instantly take his full length into my mouth. My lips close securely round him, and he grows quickly. I slide one hand up and down his wet shaft while the other gently cups his balls. His breathing shows he's turned on. He pushes my shoulders.

'Stop. I want you, not your mouth.'

I release him and stand up. He removes the remainder of his clothes, then slides my fishnet tights down my legs as I lift one foot at a time. 'These, I don't like.'

'Luke, they're tights.'

'No, they're not just tights… Please, for my eyes only.'

'Got it.' I smile impishly.

'Earlier, you asked me to eat you.' He smiles.

'You said you'd lick me dry.' He removes my hair band and runs his hands through my hair.

'So I did…'

12

My alarm wakes me. I'm still struggling to regain my normal sleeping pattern after our visit to New York. I look across to Luke's pillow, knowing he left early for an appointment in Scotland. I reach for the next best thing – a note.

Dear Kate,
Please behave today at Sutton Global. May I remind you of the rules? It is not necessary to be nice to everyone…
Stay away from my staff.
I love you.
Luke

Cheeky. Stay away from his staff? Is Sutton Global ready for me? Be careful what you wish for, Luke.

Wow, this feels bizarre. I stand in the middle of my office, and glance at all my new furniture, which arrived while I was in New York. A pink sofa, two leather wing-back chairs, a set of ex-library bookcases, and an old white farm table to use as a desk. I move to the en suite and quickly change into worn-out denim shorts and Dad's old shirt.

Where to start? I decide to move the furniture where I want it. With Max on a mission to retrieve Mr Jones's books and collect some silk fabric to cover the hideous boardroom chairs, I'm a little stuck. I need muscle power.

I appear at Stella's desk. She takes in my outfit and bare feet.

'I need to borrow some muscle… Do you have any suggestions?'

She stands. 'Let me think… Yes, I know.' She dials a number. 'Hello, can you send Steven to my desk?'

'Thanks, Stella.'

'I'll send him in when he arrives.'

I plug in my docking station and attach my iPod, allowing music to fill my new room. I hear a knock at the door.

'Hi. Stella said you needed a hand.'

'I do.' He looks about eighteen. I hold my hand out. 'Kate Harper, pleased to meet you. How do you feel about helping me for a few hours? I'll clear it with your manager and Mr Sutton.'

He smiles, inspecting my appearance. Perhaps I don't resemble the fiancée of a gazillionaire.

'Yeah, sure.'

We lift a heavy sheet of glass and place it on top of my desk – perfect. With all the pictures of Luke and me that I brought from home, our short history now lies under the glass for all to see. I can stare at him all day. Steven moves the bookcase against the far back wall and unpacks various boxes, while I paint the dull boardroom table. Last, we move the sofa and armchairs directly in front of the best view of London: historical buildings among modern glass towers. How does Luke get any work done? I could look at the view all day.

I appear at Stella's desk again.

'I need some photos printed – large. I know Luke had one done for me.'

'Yes, two floors down: Sutton Global Marketing. I can take them.'

'That's fine; I can do it.'

'I'll call them and let them know you're on your way.'

'Thanks Stella – I owe you.'

'No more cakes – my waistline!' She smiles.

I slip on my Converse, grab my camera and head two floors down to Sutton Global Marketing. I walk towards the reception desk, feeling completely underdressed in my decorating clothes.

'Hi, I'm Kate Harper. Stella Trevant sent me here.'

The pretty young girl looks at me. 'Yes, follow me.'

I trail behind her. Countless eyes watch me. I try to relax. Is it my clothes, or do they know I'm shacked up with their boss?

We enter another room.

'Mark this is Kate Harper. Stella called down earlier.'

A tall middle-aged man stands to greet me.

'Hi, take a seat.'

After a few hours the office begins to take shape. Max has brought Mr Jones's books, and I have reupholstered the boardroom chairs using remnants of raw silk, and the room feels smart and feminine, not so business-like.

With the door shut I crank up the volume, allowing Rihanna to help me decide where to place the last few items. I stand back to take in the effect. Perfect – it looks stunning.

Then I hear the door open and see a familiar face.

'No, don't come in – back up!' I quickly escort Luke out of the room. 'Wait here.'

'Kate?' His forehead creases.

'I want to surprise you.'

I shut the door, turn off the music and make sure everything is in order. I reopen the door to see an aggravated Luke leaning on Stella's desk.

'OK, you can come in.' I take his hands. 'Shut your eyes.' I humorously command.

'I don't have time for this,' he says gruffly.

'Stop being grumpy.'

I place my hand over his eyes and escort him to the centre of the room. I remove my hand.

'Ta-dah.'

He scans the transformation in silence.

'So, what do you think?'

A knock at the door turns my attention from Luke.

'Come in,' I shout.

'Kate.' Mark from two floors below appears with my framed pictures. I'm not sure who is shocked the most by this chance meeting, Mark or his boss.

'Hi.' I walk towards him. 'Wow, they look amazing! Can we hang them over here?'

He helps me lift the pictures. There are three in a row, and they cover the entire back wall: black-and-white images of us at various black tie events.

'They're perfect – thank you.'

'Here are the others you asked for.' Mark props the extra-large photos against a spare wall. These are far more casual – images of Luke and me relaxed and laughing, which is why they are my favourites.

'Thank you.'

Luke watches me in disbelief. Clearly, I'm breaching one of his conditions, and abusing his staff. 'Mark, have you been properly introduced to Mr Sutton?'

'No.' Mark walks towards Luke and holds his hand out. 'Pleased to meet you, Mr Sutton.'

'You too, Mark.'

'If you need anything else, just give me a call.' Mark turns and makes a sharp exit.

Alone – now for some honesty.

'Really, what do you think?' I move closer to Luke, trying to gauge his reaction.

'Where shall I begin?'

'That bad?'

He moves slowly around the room. 'It looks… different. I would say French Boudoir.'

'I like French Boudoir.'

'Yes, but not at Sutton Global.'

'Oh.' *He hates it – shit.*

He walks towards my new desk and smiles.

'I can stare at you all day.' I join him, and run my hands over the glass top.

'Yes, you can.' He turns to the far back wall, eyeing the pictures that Mark just hung. 'I may have to take these into my office. It seems you didn't listen to my request not to involve my staff in your little makeover.'

'It was more by luck than anything else.'

'Luck!'

'Lucky for me that they could print the pictures; I don't think it was abusing your staff.'

'Your outfit is… inappropriate for here.'

I laugh. 'Of course.'

'And who is Steven? Max mentioned you had some help.'

'I bet he did! He helped me move some furniture. Luke, these are your employees; they aren't going to hit on me. Besides, Steven was about eighteen. I could eat him for dinner.'

Luke shoots me a look. *What the fuck?*

'Well, not literally. I mean, he's a child.' I close the distance between us. 'Honestly, do you hate my office?' I place my arms around his neck.

'It's very… you.'

'Result for me. As you love me, you must love this room.'

He smiles for the first time. 'Word of warning: music at work – not a good idea.'

'OK, Dad, shall I bend over so you can smack my arse?' I chuckle.

'It would be my pleasure.' Luke lowers his gaze. His expression suggests this conversation could go either way – shit.

'It was a joke.'

'Not for me.' His face lights up with a hint of playfulness.

'Luke.' I tap his arm. 'I love you. Thank you for the office… I just hope I have a business to run here.'

I reach up on tiptoes and find his soft lips and I thank him with my tongue, which he accepts. My hands move from his neck to his arse, pulling him towards me. It only takes seconds for him to fire up. His hardness grows and presses against me. My hands move to the zip of his trousers.

Luke pulls away. 'Kate!' He grabs my wrists. 'We're at work.'

'No, you're in my office, and I say yes.' I slip under his arm and lock the office door. I turn and walk towards him, unbuttoning my shirt and shorts, discarding them en route. 'Are you really going to say no?'

'Jesus, I knew you would cause me problems.'

I loosen his tie, and then undo his shirt, then his trousers. My hand slides inside his tight boxers, gripping his erection. He's hot and ready – just how I like him. Luke rolls my knickers down my thighs and one-handedly unclasps my bra.

He ushers me towards my desk, resting my arse against the glass. Luke lowers his mouth to my nipples, licking and sucking, a delicious sensation that pulls at my core. My legs lock around him and I guide his pulsating hardness to my sex.

'Now, Luke.'

'What the fuck am I going to do with you? It's four o'clock in the afternoon, and I have a meeting at five.'

'Fuck me hard and fast, then.'

His hand slides between my thighs. No need to test me; I'm dripping.

'Jesus, baby.'

'It's a two-way street. I need you just the same.'

Luke grabs my hips and thrusts into me. I was not expecting it to be so carnal, but Luke is every inch an animal when he's on fire.

'This will be quick.' He pushes me back to the desk and begins to forcefully pump me. Every thrust is determined, hitting the spot. His thumb gently skims my clit. I look at his face.

'Christ, you make me so hard.'

He continues to ride me fast. I close my eyes, losing all sense of reality; this, right now, is all that exists.

'Luke... I'm... keep going.'

My breathing grows faster and he increases the pressure against my clit.

'Argh... Luke.'

My orgasm washes over me. With every thrust Luke's balls slam against the base of my arse. I watch his chest tighten and his lips seductively part. I have him. Hot fluid spurts deep inside me.

He remains still while his breathing slows.

'Thanks for christening my office.'

He slides out of me, and helps me to sit upright.

'If you told me six months ago that I would fuck you in the office next to mine, and you would have paint in your hair, I would have laughed... But here we are.'

I giggle. 'So, dreams do come true.' I slide off the desk and head to the bathroom. 'Are you regretting your decision?'

Luke appears next to me at the sink. 'No, but it means you're fucking with my work.'

'I would say sorry, but I'm not... Besides, you can always say no.'

Luke spins me and takes my face in his hands. 'Don't test me. I need respect here, Kate, to focus on my business.'

'OK. I promise it was a one-off.' I chew the inside of my lip.

'We both know that's bullshit… Timing is what I need you to give me.'

'What? Scheduled appointments to fuck! Jesus, Luke, put some money on my desk on the way out, why don't you? Who'd have thought Sutton Global could provide me with an extra income?'

'Don't be smart, Kate.'

'I'm not, but you want me to book time to be with you? Christ, if that's the case, I'll use my hand.'

I begin to do up his buttons, knowing I'm pushing his. Without doubt he drives me to play this cat and mouse game; I need him to want me.

'That's fine by me, as long as I can watch.'

'Hmm – that may be tricky, as it might be outside my allotted time.'

'I love that you're here. I just need to balance my fiancée and meetings.'

'I suggest you get a "fucking" diary… No pun intended.'

As Luke goes to leave my office, he stops to look at his painted boardroom table.

'I see you have utilised my furniture.'

'Yeah – it didn't work, and the chairs were hideous.'

'Hideous?'

'Grim!'

Luke shakes his head. 'I need to go in my office.'

'Luke, do you like it?'

'Yes.'

'Is that it?'

'Another adjustment. Did you speak to Maria and Valerie?'

'They're coming here for lunch tomorrow, along with Mr Jones. God, I feel nervous. Oh, and Barney is coming over for dinner tonight.' Luke frowns. 'Is that a problem?'

'No. Don't forget we leave on Thursday for skiing. I spoke to Valerie and ordered you various jackets and salopettes.'

'Bloody hell, Luke! You can't organise my wardrobe.' My hands fist on my hips.

'I saved you a job. Right, I need to work. What time are you going home?'

'Soon.'

Luke walks towards me and kisses the tip of my nose. 'And for the record, I like your office, nearly as much as I like fucking you in here.'

The Sutton silver tongue warms my heart. 'Thank you.'

The roast chicken smells divine: it's one of Barney's favourites, and Luke eats anything. I hear the black door close, and Luke's sexy voice echoes through the hall. I move to the kitchen doorway and watch him stride into his office, talking on his phone. I follow and perch on the edge of his desk. Five minutes later, he becomes mine. I slide onto his lap.

'Good day at the office?' I cheekily ask, loosening his tie.

'Some parts were a little distracting, but on the whole I would say it was productive.' His hand sweeps my hair away from my face.

'Good. I want to ask you something before Barney arrives.'
'Go on!'

'Be nice.'

'Spit it out, Kate.'

'OK, it's Barney's birthday in a couple of weeks and I want to throw him a party.'

'Here?' Luke's brows shoot up.

'No, definitely not here. I thought at SGI, if that's OK. He loves your club and I thought—'

'Fine. The VIP area is all yours.'

'Really! Oh my God, Barney will love it. Also, I was thinking…'

Luke smirks.

'Seriously, I do think – sometimes. Don't take the piss. I would like to buy a lease on a dance studio for him, just for a year – what do you think?'

Luke looks a little surprised. 'That's generous of you.'

'He's never had a handout, and his family are bloody useless. I want to give him something special; he's an amazing dancer, and I know he wants to branch into choreography. Do you know an agent who could help me find one? I was thinking Covent Garden or Soho.'

'I'll make a call.' Luke pulls my face to his and kisses me with absolute control. Instantly my body responds. But he pulls away, leaving me wanting more – shit bag! 'You're too kind, Kate Harper.'

Then the front door opens again.

'Oi… Princess Harper.' I smile as Barney arrives.

After dinner, we sit around the kitchen table.

'I bloody miss your cooking – can I tempt you to leave the palace and come back home? Not as my neighbour, but as my full-time cook?' Barney asks.

'Er – I was anyway, you never stayed in your own place…
You were paying rent for nothing.'

'True!'

'Besides, Luke locks me up at night.'

'Now there's a thought! Sorry to run, but I need to work,' Luke says.

'Before Luke disappears to conquer the world…' I flash him a cheeky smile. 'We have some news. We're going to throw you a birthday party at SGI.' I clap with excitement. 'Actually, Luke said we can have the VIP area.'

'I don't know what to say.' Barney runs his hands through his hair. 'Wow… cheers, Luke.' He looks down at his glass. 'My mum called today.'

'Oh. What did she want?' Family is Barney's Achilles' heel.

'Nothing, really. My brother is having another baby. Other than that, fuck all… Except my card is in the post.' He raises his glass. 'Here's to shit families.'

Luke watches closely. It's a first for him to see Barney in a downcast mood. I move and place my arms over his shoulders.

'You have us.'

He kisses my forearms.

'Anyway, I have a surprise for your birthday.' I re-take my seat.

'She has a plan.' At last Luke might understand why Barney needs me.

'What sort of surprise?' Barney asks.

I tap my nose. 'You'll have to wait. So you need to give me a guest list.'

'Yeah – sure.'

'Before I forget, we've all been invited to a charity ball. You'll get to meet the super-bitch.'

'I love bitch-slapping on the dance floor.'

'My cue to leave.' Luke stands, and kisses my cheek.

The kitchen is tidy. I take the stool next to Barney.

'Cheer up – don't let your mum upset you.'

'It would be easier if she never called.'

'You don't mean that.'

'Don't I?' He drinks his coffee.

'You know she lives in a different world to you. That doesn't mean she doesn't love you.'

'Thanks, babe, but her voice is always full of disappointment when she speaks to me. Anyhow, I hate talking about them. I see Mr Sutton is looking hot this evening... I can't believe you're going to marry him.' He squeezes my hand. 'Actually, he's a lucky bastard getting you.'

'I'm sure he would argue that point. I have – well, *we* have decided to get married in Venice. Dust down your passport, Mr Curtis.'

'Where it all started? I love it, babe.'

The sun seeps through the shutters, highlighting Luke's chiselled face and the undeniable signs that he's just about to come.

'Jesus, baby.' I slam my body down on him for the last time.

He grabs my hips and holds me still. My head falls to his chest, and moves in time with his breathing. He strokes my hair.

'I've met with your demands this morning, so I hope this means a peaceful day at the office?' I hear the amusement behind his comment.

I slide off him and lie on my back. 'We'll see. Yesterday may have been a one-off… Besides, my period is due any day.'

He leans to kiss my lips. 'It makes no difference to me. I told you, as long as you're well, we can have sex.'

I sigh. 'You're a sex freak and you need some serious help! Besides, I'm just warning you.' He stands up from the bed in all his glory.

'Why are you warning me?'

'You know what I'm like – hormonal serial killer will be on the loose!'

Even though we live together and I have watched him get dressed a thousand times, he still takes my breath away. As always, he looks masculine and hot in his black Jones Tailor suit, white shirt and black tie; simple yet captivating.

'I have to leave for a breakfast meeting.' He checks the time as he clasps his watch. 'What time will you be at the office?'

'Soon – I'm nervous about meeting Valerie and Maria.'

'Don't be… you'll be fine.' He delivers a quick kiss on the lips. 'Stay out of trouble.'

Trouble! What trouble?

I stand in front of the large French mirror and wonder if my reflection will cause trouble. Luke's black shirt looks good on me, with a wide black leather belt. Not only that, but it's a Jones Tailor's shirt; I hope it will bring me some much-needed luck. Though a four-leaf clover may be more appropriate…

I have straightened my hair, and applied simple makeup. I decide to wear a classic shoe boot with a heel. I bend a little just to confirm that my black opaque lace-top hold-ups aren't visible.

Max and I head for the lift at Sutton Global. His arms are full of fashion editorial books and mine with cakes that I made last night. We reach Sutton Global and take our usual path towards Stella and my new office.

'Morning,' I almost sing, as Max walks past me and enters my office.

Stella meets my gaze. 'Morning, Kate.' As ever, she beams when I arrive. 'Luke said you have some visitors today.'

'To be honest, Stella, I am excited, but bloody nervous. I don't do business; this is all a bit bizarre.'

'You'll be fine, and I agree it is exciting.'

'I hope some of Luke's confidence has rubbed off on me.'

Stella's phone rings, and I wander into my lovely new office.

'Kate,' Stella calls after me. I peer from the doorway. 'Luke asked if you could go in to see him? He has some clients with him.'

'Oh, OK.' Cakes or no cakes?

I open Luke's office door. He sits at the boardroom table with two unfamiliar men. I walk towards them, armed with cakes.

'Gentlemen, I would like to introduce you to my fiancée, Kate Harper.' Luke stands, placing his hand on the small of my back. 'Kate, this is Alistair McGowan and Donald Kennedy.'

I place the boxes on the table. 'Pleased to meet you.'

'Good morning,' they respond in broad Scottish accents, as their eyes fall to my boxes.

'Would anyone like some fruit cake or scones?'

I turn to Luke, who looks pleased, but not surprised. I think I'm the pawn in his meeting.

'I apologise; my fiancée insists on feeding everyone she meets.'

'I wouldn't say no.' The larger man of the two replies. 'Cakes are a pleasant change from shipping.'

'I agree.' Although I have no idea about shipping!

Luke calls Stella, who arrives with coffee and tea plates. 'Kate, join us.'

'OK.' I walk to the sofa and remove my black riding coat. I return to the table, and watch Luke's dark eyes bore into mine as he holds a chair for me. I follow his gaze, which moves from my feet to my neck, stopping at his shirt.

I take to my chair, as the men begin to make idle chitchat. Business discussions seem to have ended, and they ask me questions regarding our upcoming wedding. They seem friendly enough; still, Luke remains fairly quiet.

He places his hand on my leg, which I move further up my thigh, allowing him to feel the lace of my hold-ups. His touch becomes firm. There is tension in his fingertips. Trouble has arrived; that's my cue to leave.

I stand.

'It's been a pleasure to meet you, but I have a meeting soon.' I collect my cake boxes and place a tender kiss on Luke's cheek.

The men stand as I collect my coat and exit Luke's office.

The remainder of the morning disappears as Tanya and I discuss additional Bagrov and Cooper mergers. I also ask her to be present for the lunch meeting. With time to kill and no more business to conduct, I think it's acceptable to paint Tanya's nails.

I hear the door open and close. I smell the Sutton scent before I turn my head.

'Hi.' I say as I paint the last of Tanya's nails. 'Let them dry. Although it says sixty seconds, I think you should allow a bit longer.' I sense Tanya's uneasiness as Luke walks towards us.

'I see you are busy.' He's tone is direct.

I look at him. 'Time to kill.'

'Tanya, would you give us a moment?' Luke says.

'Of course.' Tanya stands and makes her way to the door.

'Luke, open the door, please – wet nails and door handles don't go well together.' He opens the door and refrains from looking at her – he saves his penetrating glare for me.

'I take it your meeting has finished? The men seemed quite nice.'

'We need to talk.' He strides towards me and guides me to the pink sofa. He sits close, but there's a chill in the air.

'What's wrong?'

'Where do I begin?' He runs his hand down his shirt. 'I think here is a good place to start. There must be a reason you're wearing my shirt.'

'It's a Jones shirt, and I thought it might bring me luck.'

'My beautiful Kate, don't feed me bullshit. I deal with poker-faced businessmen on a daily basis; we both know your plan was to push my buttons – and what about these? This excuse I have to hear.' His hand glides up my leg.

'I think they look nice, and so does your shirt.' My hand reaches for his jaw. Instantly I'm met with a firm grip.

'Kate, please don't tease me at work. This won't work if you do.'

'The office or us, Luke?' I pull my hand away and stand, moving towards the large windows.

'What? The office.' He stands to join me. 'Why would you think I was referring to us?'

I shrug, gazing into the distance. Luke turns me to face him.

'Is there a problem you want to share?'

I shake my head and lower my gaze. Luke pulls my chin. 'Don't lie to me.'

I take a deep breath. 'I know I push your buttons.'

'I can't argue with that. Is this the reason for the shirt and stockings?'

'I guess.' I move away from him. 'Luke, you forget the empire you have and the control that comes with it... I know we're engaged, but you could have any woman you wanted – a powerful woman like your ex, Maddy, or Alexis the super-bitch, they have more in common with you than I do.' I look at him wistfully. 'Bloody hell, I was just painting Tanya's nails – not very entrepreneurial of me.'

He moves closer and reaches for my cheek. 'Maddy! Christ, Kate, that was a long time ago... I asked *you* to spend the rest of your life with me.'

'I know, but it's not the first time you've asked someone to be your wife – suppose she hadn't had a fling with Matthew Williams? Then you'd be hitched.' God, I feel sick just thinking about it.

'Lucky escape.'

'But...' I look away, feeling despondent.

'I only deal with the present: if I think of your past, I would be in prison. Us, right now, is my life – you're my present and my future.'

I drink in his words, which are full of sincerity.

'Kate, I don't understand where this is coming from.'

'It's never left me. You can have anyone, I've always thought that. Ever since we got together I have wondered why you want me.' I wrap my arms around my body. 'I push your buttons because it's the only part of your life that I can control. It makes me feel that you're mine; no one else can touch you.' My face glows with my confession.

'Is that what you think? Testing me is the only control you have over me.'

I nod.

'Jesus, Kate, you've literally wiped the floor with me. This,' he gestures with his hand, 'us, you have me, all of me. Christ, baby, I love you.'

He pulls me into his arms.

'There will never be anyone else for me. No one can touch what we have… what you do to me.' He kisses the top of my head. 'Explain to me: are you feeling hormonal or do your emotions have a deeper meaning?'

'Both.' I hold on to him, feeling safe and secure. 'So, you're not loving the shirt?'

Luke pulls away, flashing me his one-sided Sutton smile.

'No… I want to rip it off and fuck you. Is that what you want, because you know that's what happens when you push me?' He rubs his nose along mine. 'Please, never compare yourself to anyone. I've told you what you give to me: honesty and a reason to question myself, in life and business.'

273

'I did warn you the hormonal serial killer would be on the loose.' I smile, and at the same time there's a knock at the door. 'Come in.'

Tanya appears. 'Kate, they're here.'

I take a deep breath. 'Crap, I'm nervous. Please stay and have lunch.' I hold his hands for a dose of Sutton confidence.

'You don't need me; you can do this on your own. Besides, clothes and fabric – they're not for me. But I do want to hear all about it when you're finished – then I will fuck you and show you just how much I intend to never let you go.'

Perfect…

'So, that's pretty much it. Go away and think about it. There's no rush to give me an answer.' I try to assess the faces staring at me from across the table.

'Kate, it sounds exciting. I'm just blown away you've asked me. Mr Jones, these drawings are stunning.'

I reach out and touch Maria's hand.

'Honestly, something about this has just got my blood pumping. I'm in… I'll have to work my notice, though.'

'Look, go home and really give it some thought… Obviously, I would love to steal you from your jobs, but I know it's a big decision.'

I look at Valerie, who remains reflective.

'I agree with Maria – it is incredibly exciting, but I have worked really hard to get a good client list – with your help, Kate.' I appreciate her honesty.

'I totally understand. Look, I'll take you part-time, whatever suits you. Just so we're clear, the outcome has no bearing on our friendship. But I want Harper Jones to run as a family, a team I can count on.'

Mr Jones places his hand over mine. I know I have said as much as I can.

The women continue to look at the design books and chat, weighing up their options.

A few hours later, I approach Stella's desk. 'Is Luke alone?'

She checks her watch. 'He does have an appointment shortly.'

'I won't keep him.'

I open the door, to see the love of my life at his desk. He looks up, flashing the smile that stops my world from rotating.

Without conscious thought, my legs carry me to his chair and I plant myself on his lap.

'How did it go?'

I rest my head against his chest, listening to his heartbeat.

'I'm hopeful. I'll just have to wait until next week.' My fingers glide up and down his silk tie.

'How are you feeling?'

'Guilty that I pushed your buttons.' I sit up to look at his face. 'I'm sorry, and I understand there's a time and a place, just not here.'

'It's early days; we'll find a way to make it work.'

'It's your fault – you've made me need you this way.'

He laughs. 'And your period?'

'It arrived this afternoon, what a treat… Especially with skiing in a few days, although I should be nearly finished by then.'

He tightens his hold. God, I feel safe.

'Go home, have a hot bath, and I'll bring some dinner back with me.'

'No hard sex?' His previous request races through my head.

'No hard sex.' He laughs. 'However, I will take you, and when I do you'll remember never to wear my shirt again, only at home, over your delectable naked body. Now, tell me your plans for the rest of the day.'

'Stella said you had another meeting. I thought I'd catch up with Harry – she's just got back. Will you be late?'

'No.' He tenderly kisses me, but there's always passion lurking under the tenderness. 'Kate, please don't question me about us – ever.'

I tap on the door of Harry and Raymond's rooftop apartment. It's in a converted warehouse, very arty and very Raymond. The door opens to reveal a happy Harry.

'Hello, Mrs Leclair.'

'Kate.' She pulls me into her arms, crushing the lilies I bought for the newlyweds.

She pulls away, and takes my hand. 'Coffee?'

'Yeah. I want to hear all about the honeymoon – well, most of it – not the naked painting by numbers.' Harry turns to look at me as we walk through to the open-plan kitchen.

'Very funny! Have you told anyone?' She fills the kettle as I sit on a stool at the breakfast bar.

'No, only Luke, and he said you're married to an artist.' I shrug. I guess Mr Know-It-All Sutton has a point.

'Forget about my honeymoon; let me see the ring.'

I hold it up. 'I'm still in shock. Shit, how the bloody hell did this happen? You're married to a French bloke and now I'm engaged to a controlling gazillionaire.'

'I know… It's mad. So, tell me, did he go down on his knees?' Harry raises her brows at her ambiguous comment.

'Harry Harper, you cheeky cow. Always, babe.' We both laugh. 'Actually, he proposed on the beach.'

'The beach? Oh my God, your surprise – the house you texted me about.'

'It's stunning. Apparently Luke bought the plot when we first met.'

'I can't wait to see it.' She passes me my cup of coffee. 'So…. on the beach and on his knees, Mr Romantic.'

'Midnight, pissing down with rain, we were both soaked. Anyway, he asked me to press a button… The car's headlights lit up and I could see the car's number plate: it said "marry me".'

Harry's eyes begin to haze with tears as she takes my hand.

'I'm so pleased! All I've ever wanted is for someone to love you, and Luke does… He's crazy in love with you.'

I hear a noise and turn to see Raymond heading our way. 'Kate.' He walks towards me and delivers his usual double kiss. 'I thought I heard your voice. Congratulations.'

'Thanks. You look well – so you had a good honeymoon?' I look at Harry and her face answers my question.

'Yes, it was relaxing. Harry is doing well with her French.' He places his arms around Harry's shoulders and gives her a kiss. 'I will let you talk. I have phone calls to make. We will catch up soon.'

'Definitely.'

He smiles and walks off to his art studio.

'Well, married life seems to agree with you both.'

'I know. I love him… I'm truly pathetic. Anyway, how's the pack?'

'OK. I haven't spoken to Molly for a few days, although Barney saw her and said she looks well. As for Kiki… she worries me.'

'Declan.'

'Yeah. I haven't really spoken to her because of flying to New York. She's going skiing so I'll see her in a few days. That's my point – she's going skiing with Declan.'

'Are they seeing each other?'

I drink some coffee and shake my head. 'I don't think they're dating, more like shagging. She won't admit it, but I know she likes him. Luke hasn't got a clue what his brother thinks, and isn't bothered either way.'

'Shit, I hope she doesn't get hurt.'

'I warned her and Declan about this… Two shag monsters together are not a good combination. Before I forget Barney's birthday, Luke said we could have the VIP area at SGI.'

'Barney will love being the centre of attention – that's perfect.'

'He was really excited when I told him. Also, I want you to come to a charity ball – well, the whole pack.' I drink the remainder of my coffee.

'Sounds like fun. Will the super-bitch be there?'

'Yes, so you need to come in guns blazing.'

'Absolutely,' Harry laughs. Hell has no fury like a pack of scorned women.

'You look tired, babe.'

'I'm fine. Back to reality is hard.'

'Yes, Mrs Leclair… I'll leave you to it.'

'Before you go, how was New York?'

I sigh. 'OK, sort of. Let's save that conversation for another day.'

Within half an hour I am inputting the security entry code. The large black door opens. I notice the office doors are closed. Feeling exhausted, I head straight upstairs in need of a bath. As I walk into the bedroom, Luke appears in front of me, making me jump and scream.

'Holy shit, Luke.' My hand rests against my erratic heart.

He pulls me to his arms. 'I wanted to surprise you.'

I pull away. 'Jesus, you did!'

'Sorry, baby. Your bath is run, and Chinese takeaway should be here in thirty minutes.'

I reach for his face and tenderly kiss his delicious lips. 'Thank you. I would love to have sex, but my stomach hurts like hell.'

'Christ, Kate, I'm not trying to woo you. Yes, I love fucking you, but our relationship is not based on sex.' He tilts his head to one side. 'OK, so most of the time it is – however, not tonight.' He smiles and kisses my cheek.

'Sorry. My head is all over the place.'

He takes my face in his hands. 'Baby, never doubt my need for you… Plain and simple, you are my world.'

13

Our flight from Heathrow to Zurich was relatively smooth, and we now have a two-hour drive to Klosters. Having passed through various towns, we're on the last leg of our journey. The four-by-four climbs a small hill to a chalet Livy and Edward have rented. I've switched off from Luke and Declan talking, as I can't tear my eyes from the jagged snow-capped mountains.

Then the car turns a corner and enters a cleared driveway. Livy and Edward's car is parked ahead. They drove all the way from London, as they do each year, apparently.

'Chalet' is a poor description of the house. It's huge, and most of what I can see is made of glass. As ever, I am amazed by the Suttons – we are worlds apart!

'Kate.' Luke squeezes my hand.

I turn to him. 'Bloody hell, this place is amazing.'

'Wait until you see inside.'

'I know you like a view, Mr S.' His eyes gleam. 'Oi, I wasn't referring to my arse.' I tap his arm.

'I was, soon-to-be Mrs Sutton.'

I plant a sassy kiss on his delicious lips. 'Is that right? Threatening talk from Mr Frustrated Sutton.' The tail end of my period is here, thank God.

'All right you two, at least wait until you get in your room,' Declan says.

I step out of the car and shiver.

'Edward, they're here!' Livy emerges from the front door and runs to us. 'How was the journey?'

'Good.' Declan wraps his arms around his mum. 'I'm starving.'

'There's plenty to eat inside.' She moves towards me. 'Hello, my darling.' She gives me a motherly hug.

'Hi, Livy. I can't get over this place, it's stunning.'

She pulls away and links her arm through mine. 'We love it here. Let's get you inside, Kate. The boys can get the luggage.'

Luke smiles as he watches us walk away.

We enter the chalet. It is awe-inspiring, modern and elegant. The rear of the property is made entirely of glass; the view is out of this world. I'm truly speechless. We enter the kitchen, where a chef and waitress are busy preparing breakfast. Bloody hell, this is some set-up.

'Kate, let me take your coat,' Livy says, clearly enjoying the prospect of mothering her family for the next few days.

'Thanks Livy.' I remove my coat and hand it to her.

'Now then, you must be hungry?'

'Whatever they're cooking smells good.'

'Kate, how are you?' Edward locks his arms around me, squeezing the air out of me. 'Have you lost weight? You look thinner.'

'Err… no, still the same old me.'

'Oh, Edward, leave her alone.' Livy taps her husband's arm.

'I'm sure Kate and Luke will give us our first grandchild, and I believe weight loss can affect fertility. I read an article in the paper.'

What! Is he kidding? 'Me, pregnant?' That's the last thing I need right now.

'Pregnant… who's pregnant?' Declan enters the room. 'Luke, have you knocked up your fiancée?' He laughs.

'No!' I scowl at him.

Luke arrives at my side. 'Have I missed something?'

'Apparently, Kate's pregnant.' Declan finds this highly amusing, watching me squirm.

'Thanks, Declan, but I can assure you I'm definitely not pregnant.'

'For goodness' sake, let's not discuss this any further. Luke, your father started the conversation. Sit, everyone.' Livy points to the chairs.

'I was merely saying I think Kate could do with putting on some weight, especially if they want children.' Edward takes his seat.

Oh my God, do I look like I'm ready to have children? I have problems taking care of myself.

'Thanks, Edward, I'll bear that in mind in a few years.' I sit down, Luke at my side.

'A few years?' Luke looks at me.

'Sorry?' I turn to face him.

'Is that how long you want to wait?'

'I don't know. I can't say I've given it much thought.'

'OK. I think that's enough discussion regarding children, and Kate is right, you have plenty of time to think about it. Now, the omelettes are delicious; I would highly recommend them.' I am grateful that Livy has changed the subject. At least one Sutton can see sense.

After breakfast, Luke takes me through to our bedroom. Since we're on a hill, the town in the distance looks fairly small. Everything is covered in a dusting of snow that was delivered during the night – it's stunning.

'What do you think?' Luke places his hands around my waist and lowers his lips to the top of my head.

'I love it.' I feel him smile.

He turns me, placing his lips over mine. Instantly, our tongues begin their mating dance, twining against each other, and my hands automatically cup the base of his arse, drawing close.

He pulls away. 'I need you… how do you feel about a hot shower? You said your period had stopped.'

'Just.'

'How do you feel?'

'Ready for you.' I laugh.

'Good.'

'You have no self-control, Luke.'

'Not when you're around.'

A knock at the door stops us.

'Luke, ten minutes and then I'm off.' Declan shouts a challenge through the door.

'OK.' He looks down at me.

'Go. I'll join you later.'

Eventually I make it out to the snow, wearing my newly acquired ski attire. Valerie and I decided to bring the black fitted salopettes and a black fitted jacket with a fur-trimmed hood.

We reach the top of the mountain and begin our descent. I follow Edward, as Livy skis parallel to me. It's high season so the slopes are rammed, and yet I weave through the crowds with some degree of elegance. We continue down the next run. I reach the base of the mountain before Edward and Livy. I turn and can see them approaching me, but then from nowhere I am hit by another skier and sent flying. The other skier ends up lying flat on top of me. Judging by their weight, they're male.

Within seconds someone has lifted the skier off me, and I'm pulled to standing.

'Are you OK? Kate, look at me.' Luke moves my glasses.

'I'm fine.' I brush snow from my jacket.

The skier stands up and holds a hand out to me. I wave my arm. *I'm fine and in one piece – no harm done.*

Luke removes his glasses. 'Fucking prick – next time look where you're going.' The skier clearly understands English, as he glares at Luke and moves towards him.

'Luke!' Livy reprimands her first-born.

Declan tries to calm things. 'Chill… Everyone's fine, let's move on.' He looks at the skier, encouraging him to move before Luke 'helps' him.

'He needs to watch out; she could have been hurt,' Luke says.

'Yes, but she's fine. In future, watch your language.' I admire Livy's no-nonsense approach towards her son.

Luke turns to me. 'Baby, are you sure you're OK?'

'I'm fine; it was an accident.'

'I think we could all do with a coffee break,' Edward says.

'Actually, I thought Kate and I could go into town.' Livy says with a look at Luke.

'OK, that sounds like a good idea. Go and have fun with Declan, but please be safe.'

'Back at you, baby.'

Livy drives for about twenty minutes before we arrive in Davos. She parks the car and we amble through the snow-covered streets that are lined with designer shops, clearly aimed at tourists with deep pockets. However, browsing is free.

'Edward and I found this wonderful café the other day; let's stop there and have some cake.'

'Sounds great – calorie-free, I hope.'

'Of course, my darling.'

I find a table while she orders coffee and some cake. I remove my jacket and sit back in my chair to people-watch. I glance across the room, then do a double take. You have to be kidding! A cold wind from the north obscures my view of tranquillity.

It's obvious that Alexis Cooper is aware of my presence. She glances in my direction, then quickly looks away when she sees I've noticed her.

Livy returns, armed with sugary treats.

I feel at ease with Livy; she has welcomed me into the Sutton family, for which I am really grateful.

'Any more wedding plans?' Her eyes light up as she mentions the word 'wedding'.

'No, not yet. We've only agreed on the location, but you know that… Oh, and Mr Jones has made the pattern for my dress. When it's ready, I want you and Mum to come with me for my fitting.'

'Really? I'd love to.' She reaches for my hand.

'Of course. I don't want you to feel I've stolen your son… You're a massive part of Luke's life.' She nods. 'So, you know Mr Jones will be using vintage lace for my dress.'

After a couple of hours we decide to head back to the chalet. I glance at Alexis. She is still seated in the corner of the café, studiously ignoring me.

I follow Livy to the door, which opens before we get there. What the hell?

'Maddy.' Livy greets Luke's ex-fiancée with kindness.

'Hi, Livy – you look well.' They exchange double kisses.

'Kate, nice to see you again,' says Maddy.

'Hi.' I manage a smile.

'Congratulations. I was thrilled when my dad told me about your engagement. I texted Luke congratulating you both.'

'Thank you.' Text – what bloody text? He didn't mention it to me.

'Well, we must go. Take care, Maddy, and give my love to your parents.' Livy places another kiss on her cheek.

'I will, Livy.'

'Bye,' I quietly respond, seething inside.

We return to the warmth of the chalet. Edward is the only one there, sitting in front of the crackling fire. I take refuge in my room, stripping off my clothes, leaving my underwear on, and slipping under the duvet. The super-efficient staff have lit a fire and also left me a tray of tea… I may need to take these people home as a souvenir.

Even though I'm tired, Maddy is all I can think about: she has Luke's mobile number, and can contact Luke at any time. God, the thought makes my blood boil.

I hear the door open and close, and I turn my head to see Luke. I must have fallen asleep. He walks towards the bed.

'Hi, baby.' His cheeks are rosy.

'Did you have fun?' I ask.

He looks totally relaxed.

'Kicked Declan's arse – no surprise really.'

I shake my head. His eyes follow my trail of clothes. 'I know that look, Harper.' He dives on the bed next to me. 'What's on your mind?'

'Nothing, really. I had a lovely time with your mum… But the super-bitch was at the café. I know she saw me, and she didn't even say hello to your mum.'

Luke takes a deep breath. 'It's probably best that you stay away from each other.'

'Not a problem for me. Actually, when we left the café, it was a bit awkward – Maddy was there. So your poor mum had me on one side and your ex-fiancée on the other.'

Luke's eyebrows shoot up.

'Did you know she would be here?'

'Kate, most of my parents' friends come here every year. But no, I wasn't aware that Maddy was going to be here – why would I?'

'I don't know – maybe she told you when she sent you a text?'

'I assume you are trying to make a point?'

'Too bloody right I am. It's so comforting to know your ex is just fingertips away.'

Luke leans onto his elbow. 'She did text me to congratulate us both. Other than that, I haven't heard from her.' He takes a deep breath. 'I'm tired of these pointless discussions.' His voice becomes hard.

'Pointless? Are you shitting me? You need to get a new phone number! I'm serious; I won't play second fiddle to any of your exes.'

He runs his tongue along his lower lip. 'You're jealous.'

'Well done, Sherlock! I'm cross you never told me she texted... And it pisses me off that she seems quite nice.'

'What can I say? I have good taste in fiancées.' His eyes lock to mine as he begins to laugh.

'I can't believe you just said that.'

His hand brushes against my cheek. 'It was a joke.'

'Well, I'm not laughing... I'm bloody cross.' I sit up slightly and fold my arms.

'Maybe you need to wear some red lipstick; confirm your ownership.' Luke places his head on my lap, trying to hide his laughter.

'I don't bloody think so, Sutton – the mood I'm in, I will bite your dick off, never mind suck it.' Luke is calm and laughing – how can I stay mad with him?

He raises his head.

'Step away from the red lipstick... Can we remove all red lipstick from the house?' he bellows.

'Oh, you think you're so bloody funny.' He is; I can't help but laugh. No Harper–Sutton battle today.

'Come on, let's get in the shower.' He stands and pulls me up to join him.

We stand, side by side, in the wet room, the shower running. As soon as I meet his gaze, his lips are on me: brutal kisses that leave me horny and breathless, a sexual combination I can't live without. Luke pulls away and rapidly removes his clothes.

'I need to use the toilet.' My face glows.

'Go for it.'

'Turn around.'

He smiles.

'This isn't a turn-on, now turn around.'

He obliges. Once I'm ready, I slip past him and move directly into the hot shower. He follows close behind and slides his hands around my wet torso, heading for my breasts. He turns me to face him. My hands skim his defined stomach and take hold of his erection. I manipulate him, and he grows within my firm grip. He lowers his lips to my nipples, circling his tongue round each before sucking them, hard. He is driving me crazy… just touch me.

'Luke.' My voice is low, but my body is screaming: *I need you inside me.*

His eyes show me how much he needs me. 'I know, baby.'

He moves me to the wall, lifting my leg. His fingers delve inside my sex.

I gasp.

Luke holds his fingers still.

'Too much? I need honesty.'

'I'm fine.' I kiss him hard.

He slips his fingers between my wet lips and begins to torment my pulsating clit. His free hand grasps his erection. My eyes fall to Luke's hand sliding up and down his thick shaft.

He grins. 'Talk to me.'

What? I swallow.

'I know you like me doing this. Tell me.'

I nod.

'Tell me you like it when I work my dick. You want me hard for you.'

'Yes.' My response is a whisper. I look away. He leaves my clit and lifts my head.

'You can't hide from me. I want you to do the same.'

'What?'

'You heard me. I will fuck you, but I don't think you're ready yet. I want to watch you touch your clit, and I'll do the same.'

'Luke... I...'

He kisses me passionately, his tongue moving against mine, using the tip of his erection against my sensitive clit. I feel my body begin the climb to orgasm: my breathing becomes shallow and my legs go weak.

He pulls away from my mouth. 'Use your hand – I know you want to come.'

My eyes lock on his as my hand slides between my wet lips. The circular motion of my fingers against my sensitive clit is almost too much.

'Don't come.'

I nod.

'I'm not ready – Kate, watch me.'

He works himself, pumping his erection hard. *Holy shit, I love this far too much.*

'I can't hold off much longer,' I confess.

'OK... put your leg around me.' I do as he asks, and he guides the head of his erection to the entrance to my sex. 'I'm going to lift your other leg. This will be quick, so don't stop touching yourself.'

I nod.

'Good.'

The next minute, he impales me, making me slide up the wall. His powerful body delivers hard, fast thrusts, while my hand mirrors his speed and passion on my clit. After what feels like seconds, I feel the rush of my orgasm.

Luke leans to my ear, brushing his stubbly cheek against me. 'I'm coming.' His voice – oh God.

'Luke.'

In seconds, I feel the last of his hot fluid inside me.

'Christ, I needed that.' Gently, he kisses the nape of my neck.

He slides out of me and lowers my legs to the floor.

Pushing the wet hair from my face, Luke kisses my mouth, not savagely but with tenderness. He pulls away.

'You know how much I love you, soon-to-be Mrs Sutton?'

I nod.

'Good.'

His words are music to my ears.

After our shower, I slip on black leggings and a long black T-shirt. Luke wears jeans and a black polo shirt, obviously comfortable in the company of his family.

'Kate, you look fine – everyone will be waiting, especially Kiki.'

I glare at his reflection. 'You didn't tell me she was here.'

'There was no point. They headed straight to Declan's room when we got back.'

'It would seem all the Sutton boys are getting fucked tonight.' I giggle.

Luke scowls. 'My articulate wife-to-be and her filthy mouth… Now move your delectable arse or you will be sorry.'

After dinner, the super-efficient members of staff remove our plates. The meal was divine. The atmosphere is relaxed. Declan stands to retrieve a bottle of cognac. I lean close to Kiki's ear.

'So, how are things with you and Declan?' My finger circles the top of my wine glass.

'OK.'

'OK? Is that it?'

'What do you want me to say?'

I link my arm through hers. 'I don't want you to get hurt. Declan's not ready to settle down.'

'I know what he wants, and more importantly what he doesn't want.' She takes hold of my hand with my engagement ring. 'This, I'm not ready for, and neither is Declan, so don't worry, babe.'

I lean my head on her shoulder. 'Fine. But, I'm watching you, Kiki Marlow. I know when you're bullshitting me.'

It has snowed overnight, and Luke's younger brother Ollie and his girlfriend Scarlett have arrived. The entire Sutton family will be skiing today.

'Luke, don't you dare throw that snowball at me… I'll tell your mum.' We stop, waiting for the others to catch up. What a delight to have Mr Playful Sutton at my side.

'Are you threatening me, Harper?' Luke gives me his best sexually charged grin, which hits every erogenous zone in my body.

'Two words for you, Sutton: wedding dress… I have your mum on my side.' Luke drops the icy weapon and moves closer, taking his skis around mine, stopping me from moving.

His breath glides across my lips. 'You'll need stronger bribery material than my mum and your wedding dress.' He goes in for the kill. His cool lips take my breath away. Even though we're standing outside a crowded café, Luke takes what he wants.

I pull away from him. 'Do you want me to bribe you with sex?'

'You can try, baby.' His hands run down my salopettes, cupping my arse, while his mouth returns with a vengeance.

'Jesus, Luke, put her down.' Declan arrives at speed, sending a small snowstorm across our skis.

Slowly Luke pulls away. I look into his eyes. 'Have you finished?'

'Never.' *Shit, I need him!*

Scarlett and I decide to have a coffee break. Ollie offers to come with us, which pleases my controlling fiancé. Edward and Livy return to the chalet for lunch and the remaining competitive skiers decide to test their skills further. Kiki, who is one of the lads when it comes to extreme sports, opts for black runs, not black coffee. Once again, they are welcome to it.

The three of us sit chatting about life, Ollie's job as a teacher, and my plans for Harper Jones. Ollie is the polar opposite to Luke and Declan. Luke strives for world domination, Declan is always partying when he isn't working for Luke, and Ollie wants to help disadvantaged children. Luke and Ollie's bond is beyond brotherly. How can Luke forget about Ollie trying to commit suicide when he was only sixteen? Ollie was at a difficult point in his life and Luke was off saving the world, not his brother. Living your life to the full is the only way to deal with past demons, and Ollie is proof of what doesn't break you, makes you stronger. Luke must see that.

Scarlett leaves for the bathroom, leaving Ollie and me alone.

'While we're alone there's something I want to say.' Ollie looks at his coffee. 'Declan told me that you've spoken about… when I was younger.' He lifts his eyes to mine as my mind drifts back to the afternoon in Livy's garden: an afternoon of revelations. Firstly, Ollie's attempted suicide, and then finding out that Luke was once engaged to Maddy, who Luke hadn't told me about.

'Oh!'

'Have you told Luke about… Alexis?'

I frown and shake my head.

'No. I promised Declan I wouldn't. But I think you should speak to him. If he found out, he'd be really upset. He thinks the world of you.' Playing games with Ollie's heart, and taunting him that they had slept together was the last straw for him – and the final nail in Alexis's coffin for me.

Ollie sighs. 'I know – he's cool and wants to show me the world.'

'He would give you the world, Ollie, there's no doubt about that.'

'I accept what you're saying. Christ, their paths cross all the time. The last thing I need is Luke losing it with her – you know more than anyone that his temper is unpredictable.'

'No shit! But he would calm down, eventually. He went mad the day he found out about your job, which is crazy, I know.'

'Declan told me. Look, Luke thinks I can't handle myself with out-of-control teenagers.' Ollie's anxiousness begins to fade.

'I have no reason to doubt you – you're calm, and that's one of your best assets, Ollie.'

'And you must have a talent for defusing bombs – my brother.'

'Once he saw reason! That's when he told me about your past. I tried to tell him to give you guidance and advice, not so he could control you. Did he listen? Well, that remains to be seen. You know he thinks differently to us.'

'He always has. Listen, I don't want you to feel awkward. It was a long time ago. I will talk to him, but there never seems to be a good time.'

'There's never a good time to talk about the super-bitch either – sorry, that's my nickname for her. Christ, Ollie, what the hell did you see in her? I know that's not a great comment to make, but bloody hell.'

He laughs. 'Don't hold back, Kate! I was young, and she was older than me.'

'Sorry!'

'Don't be. I know what she's like. Although we avoid each other at functions now – saves embarrassment for us both.'

'She's vicious, Ollie – she just wants to destroy things.'

Ollie laughs. 'Kate, it was a long time ago, and I am over it.'

'She makes my blood boil. Besides, we're almost family: you think Luke is your protector, you haven't seen me go yet!'

'Should I be worried?'

'Not really.'

Ollie laughs again, and then Scarlett appears from the bathroom.

'Another round?'

I head to the bar and patiently wait, in a world of my own.

'Good afternoon, Kate Harper, are you stalking me?'

I turn when I hear the familiar voice.

'Charles Morley – in your dreams. Besides, I think you're stalking me. Must be all that free time you have.'

He laughs. 'Perhaps. Having fun with the Sutton boys?'

'Yep. I take it you're here with your family? I know you hate to work, so I assume this is playtime for you.'

'Every day is playtime for me.' He sits on the stool next to me. 'A little birdie told me you caused some trouble in New York. It would seem Bagrov and Cooper may have trouble on their hands.'

'Looks like the super-bitch has been spoon-feeding you information.'

Charles can't hide his amusement. 'I knew you would mix it up. I like you, Kate Harper, a lot... But I didn't see the Bagrov estate landing in your lap.'

'That makes two of us.' My gaze falls to the bar.

'I assume the news of your late mother is a blow to you too.'

I nod, not wanting to have this conversation with him.

He reaches for my hand. 'I'm sorry for your loss.'

'Don't be. I didn't know her, and she died some time ago. Apparently, she committed suicide.' My mood takes a nosedive. 'Sorry… I have a tendency to ramble.'

Charles leans on the bar, a hint of sadness in his eyes; maybe he isn't such a dickhead after all.

'Apparently? Why would you say that?'

'Just a feeling. Ignore me.' *Why am I telling him personal information?*

'A gut instinct, perhaps.' He watches me closely.

'A delusional feeling, more likely. Honestly, I babble all the time.'

'Let me think, what year did she die?'

'Eighty-eight.'

'In London?'

'Yeah.' I look down as my emotions begin to rise. I don't want to share them with a stranger. 'Sorry, I wasn't expecting to get all deep and meaningful with you.' I try to lighten the mood.

'You can go deep on me any time, Kate.' His crude humour makes me laugh. 'Are you aware my father is a judge? Well, the eighties was his era.'

'Oh. I don't know anything about your family.'

'My father and I have a fucking awful relationship.'

'No love lost between you?'

'None. I suspect you want to know why I am telling you this?'

'Do you think I'm some kind of therapist?'

'A hot therapist! It could be a new vocation for you, if you continue to piss off Philip Cooper. My reason for mentioning his name is that my father has a secret cupboard containing various documents.'

'OK, and you're telling me this because?' This has to be the most bizarre conversation I've ever had.

'First, I like you. And, second, I will take a look inside his safe.'

'Thanks, I think. Honestly, why would your father have information on my birth mother?' I am confused.

'Your mother was wealthy, and I suspect your instinct may be spot-on.'

'You think so?' I wish Luke would show this much interest.

'It could be fun – well, not that your mother is dead, obviously. Truthfully, it's been a while since I rummaged through his private paperwork.'

'Your life must be really dull,' I say.

'So this is why we've met – you're here to brighten up my life.'

'Like I said – dull.'

'I probably won't find anything, so we have nothing to lose.'

'OK. This is still bloody odd, but thanks for the offer.'

'Odd is my middle name – besides, you can pay me in other ways. That is, if I find anything worthy of a debt.' He offers a cheeky smile.

My tray of coffees arrives. 'Never going to happen. Can I ask you, are you gay?'

He runs his hand through his hair. 'I would take you and Luke at the same time. My fucking choice swings like my mood… Speaking of fucking Luke Sutton, he is heading our way. Until we speak again.' Charles moves off rapidly, leaving me wondering what the hell our conversation was about.

Luke and Declan arrive at my side, as Kiki joins Ollie and Scarlett at the table.

'Hi. Declan, be a love, take the tray to the table and I'll order some more coffees.'

'Sure. I want food too.' He heads off to the Sutton table.

'I'll bring the menus over.' I turn to face Luke. 'Did you win?'

'What the fuck did Charles Morley want?'

OK, straight to the point. 'Chill, Luke.'

'Chill?'

'Yes, breathe, Luke. Nothing, really; he asked me about Katenka and I told him that I thought her death was suspicious.'

'You did what?'

'He's friends with Alexis; he knows about Katenka. You know his dad is a judge, right? Anyway, he has a safe containing documents from cases he worked on.'

Luke scowls at me. It's safe to say he's pissed off.

'Charles is going to take a look for me, just in case there's something about Katenka's death.'

Luke's eyes darken. 'Are you joking?'

'No! He may find something.'

'Yeah, my fist meeting his face. I told you not to go near him; you can't trust a single word that comes out of his fucking mouth. Do you understand me?' He moves closer, trying to intimidate me.

I fold my arms. 'No, I don't bloody understand, and don't tell me what to do. You haven't tried to help me, have you?'

'You bet your arse I'll tell you what to do! If Charles Morley is involved, you don't have a fucking choice.'

'Yes, I do. I know it's bloody odd, but my entire life is odd now. Anyhow, I have nothing else to go on.' My anger builds at Luke's attitude.

He pulls me behind a pillar, so people can't see us, placing his hands on either side of my head, pinning me to the spot.

'Don't push me, Kate. I won't let Charles Morley feed you bullshit. He's a fucking idiot, and why would Joseph Morley have information on Katenka?'

I place my arms around Luke's neck.

'I have no idea and, for your information, I'm not pushing you, but telling you about a conversation. I know that look in your eyes, Sutton: dark and pissed off. You want to fuck me, don't you?' I forcefully kiss him, pulling on his hair, ensuring he succumbs to my touch.

He pulls away from my mouth.

'Jesus, Kate.' He looks away. 'I don't want you to get fucked over by that prick. I told you we would look into Katenka's death – together. He would love for you to owe him a fucking favour.'

'I'm not stupid; the chances of him finding anything is zero.'

'Well, I don't give a shit about him. What I need is to get you back to the chalet – now.'

'What, no lunch? And what about skiing?'

Luke looks at me, a vision of frustration.

'So how badly do you want me?' I smile impishly, working him with my hand.

'We're leaving. I told you – don't tease me; I will win.'

Always, Luke!

Back at the chalet, Luke runs us a deep bath. With the bath full of bubbles, Luke holds my hand as I step in. The heat hits me as I lie there, watching Luke sink in at the opposite end. His erection stands to attention above the waterline.

'Horny as ever.'

'Trouble as ever.'

'Frustrated Luke?'

'How can being angry make you horny? You're quite bizarre.' I laugh.

'I'll take that as a compliment.' He takes one of my feet and begins to massage it.

'Is it only me that you lose it with, and then want to fuck?'

'What do you think?'

'You need anger management, is what I think,' I say.

'I believe there is some divine retribution heading your way.'

'I bloody hope so, Mr S. And, for future reference, don't bully me into not talking to people.'

Luke stops and frowns.

'Bully you? Stay clear of him, Kate. I know the prick a lot better than you.'

'Maybe you do. The way I see it, you can either stand with me or walk away.'

'Are you telling me what to do?'

I laugh at his bemused face. 'Novelty for you, but yes I am. As this is a new experience for you, I want you to lie there and let me suck you off.'

Silence.

I move up the bath towards Luke's erection.

'You have eight weeks.'

'What! Eight weeks' worth of blowjobs?'

Luke pulls me towards him. 'The wedding – I need a date. I want everyone to know you belong to me.'

'*Belong to you?* Can you hear yourself? Only because you asked me so lovingly. Besides, what's the urgency?' My hands slide across his pectorals as I straddle him.

'Why wait?'

I kiss his lips. 'Does this have something to do with Maddy or my conversation with Charles?'

'Neither. I just want people to know that you're Mrs Luke Sutton.'

With these words, I am his.

'OK, we'll set a date. In the meantime, would you like me to thank you with my mouth, sucking you hard and fast until—'

His hands slide into my hair, guiding his lips to mine. He makes me want him so much.

'I want to come in your mouth, and later, if you can wait that long, I will take you.'

Later, I check my dress for this evening's gathering. I'm wearing a black skater-style dress with gold and green embroidery running down the front and across the shoulders. I join the partygoers in the lounge area, my faux-fur coat resting over my arm. Luke's eyes rake over me. Have I passed the test? He smiles. Bloody good job, as it's either this or underwear!

We arrive at the restaurant, which is incredibly busy. Not only is the super-bitch there, with her slimeball father, but so is Luke's ex-fiancée and Charles Morley. *Great.*

The food and atmosphere are perfect, and watching Luke so relaxed with his brothers is a rare treat. After our meal, and after emptying numerous bottles of wine, the Sutton men retreat to the bar. The restaurant now feels like a wine bar, with people moving to other tables, hooking up with friends.

Kiki leaves my side to be with Declan, making the most of her time with him, as she leaves tomorrow to holiday with her dad.

'Kate, may I join you?' I turn my head. *It's Maddy – what the hell?*

'Hmm… yeah, sure.' Maybe I could take her phone and erase Luke's number.

'I would like to clear the air; I don't want there to be any awkwardness between us. Maybe it would help if I introduced myself as Maddy – try and forget my relationship with Luke.' She smiles. I can tell she's anxious, and I admire her courage for making the first move.

'Fair enough. ' I laugh. 'Honestly, I have tried to dislike you but, as Luke pointed out, he has good taste in fiancées.'

She looks surprised. 'Did he really say that?' We laugh, which begins to thaw the ice between us. 'Look, Kate, I know we will never be the best of friends, but in situations like this, it would be easier not having an atmosphere.'

'Agreed.'

'It's obvious Luke adores you, and you make him happy.'

'Thank you.' I look across to Luke, who is laughing. Perhaps he hasn't seen the guest of honour at our table.

She passes me a shot glass. 'I took the liberty of bringing you a drink; I did wonder if I would be wearing it.'

'I don't normally have bar brawls.'

'No. The gossip is that you have balls and speak your mind.'

'I wonder where you got your intel from. Let's just say I'll never be friends with Alexis Cooper. She hates me and has done since the moment we were introduced.'

'I've known her for years, so has Luke – we all grew up together. She is well known for her fiery behaviour.'

I tilt my head. Really? 'I can't argue with that.'

'Kate, you're not alone; we've all been on the receiving end of Alexis and her sharp tongue.' Maddy raises her glass. 'Here's to new acquaintances, and good riddance to bad feelings.'

We clink glasses.

'Cheers.' The fluid hits the roof of my mouth, burning through layers of skin. 'Christ, what the hell have you given me?'

'Poison! That's what we call it. My advice? Don't have too many.'

'Safe to say, this will be my first and last.'

She looks across at the bar. 'Well, it has been a pleasure to get to know you, but I can see Luke watching you. I'll leave you to it.'

I stand with Maddy. 'I appreciate you clearing the air. Thank you.'

'Take care, Kate.'

Luke watches me closely as I manoeuvre around people to reach him. My arms instantly slide around him.

'What was that all about?' He looks curiously at me.

'You know, comparing notes. Maddy agrees that you have good taste in fiancées!'

'You told her?'

'Yes. Kiss me.' His face comes alive as the smile that knocks me senseless creeps across it. My tongue swirls against his. With no hesitation, he meets my heat with desire.

'Mr S – please take me home and fuck me as you promised.'

14

I scan the pictures scattered across the countertop, feeling as confused as I did last night. We're back from skiing, which means reality is knocking at my door, and the first thing I have to deal with is the kitchen in Sandbanks. Luke has asked me to design the kitchen, and it's a massive room with a huge budget.

Luke enters the kitchen, on his phone. I gesture that I need a word. He's fully aware I'm staring at him, and he flashes the Sutton smile that filters through my core and reaches my clit. Sexual desire will drive me wild all day.

He finishes his call. 'You wanted me?' He tilts his head, knowing I literally want him. What the hell has he done to me?

'Always!' I smirk. 'OK – look at these kitchen pictures?'

'You showed them to me last night.'

'Yes, but you were distracted last night.'

'By you.'

'That's irrelevant. I need your opinion – the kitchen company wants my final choice today.'

He leans over my shoulder.

'As I said, they all look the same.' He plants a tender kiss on the top of my head.

'Not really. Yes, they're all white, but they are different.'

Luke moves his hand over the images. 'Where did you get these pictures from?'

'Magazines I bought while we were in New York. The Hamptons reminds me of Sandbanks, and I bought some stunning lamps and starfish…' I look up to a silent Luke. 'You're not loving the idea? I thought, as the house is so close to the beach, a beach theme would be good… and grey weatherboarding in the kitchen.' I wait for a response.

'You'll make the right decision – you always do.'

'Luke, this is serious. The kitchen company charges a lot of bloody money. To be honest, I think we could get it cheaper elsewhere.'

'No. I used them here; they're efficient and produce good-quality products. Kate, I have no reason to doubt your taste: your office at Sutton Global is a perfect example.'

'Oh! You've never really said much about it. Considering you have an opinion on most things, sometimes you don't say enough.' Should I be careful what I wish for?

He pulls me to standing and straight into his arms.

'I don't have time to tell you every thought I have.' He gently kisses me. 'As for your office, I told you I liked it.'

He kisses the tip of my nose and then pulls away.

'OK, so you want my opinion?'

I nod.

He points to his choice. 'This stands out more than the others.'

I give a girly clap. 'Fab, that's my favourite too.'

'Looks like we're on the same page for once, baby.'

I begin to gather the magazines. 'For once.'

'Before I forget, these are for you, and I need an answer ASAP.' He hands me a couple of brochures. 'I would go with the Covent Garden studio; however, the rent price matches the trendy area.'

I look at the pictures. 'You need to know now?'

'The agent has held both studios, but I know he has potential buyers showing interest.'

'Shit… the pressure.' I rub my temples. 'There's not much difference in the size, so maybe the location. I think you're right: Covent Garden will be better for Barney. OK, that's my decision: Covent Garden. Oh my God, Barney will burst when he finds out.'

Luke looks at his watch. 'What time is your appointment?'

'Ten. Do you want me to call you when I've finished?' I continue to clear away the breakfast crockery.

'Yes.' He walks towards me and gives me a kiss. 'Stay out of trouble.'

'Are you sure?' the kitchen designer asks, for the hundredth time.

'Yes. Can you print me a picture to take home?'

'Certainly. You just need to check and sign the paperwork, and return it as soon as possible.'

I stand up from my chair and allow the blood to flow to my numb arse. *Don't give a girl too many choices!*

'I'll drop it off in the next couple of days.'

'Very well.' The patient kitchen designer hands me a folder containing my 3D image of a potential design layout.

I make my way towards Max, who is in the corner of the kitchen showroom, overdosing on caffeine.

He looks up. 'Ready?'

'Sorry, it took a lot longer than I thought it would. No wonder Luke gave me the job.'

'Where to now?'

'I want to stop at the deli and I need some currants; I promised Jerry a cake.'

'OK.'

We head to the car park. Once again, Max drives my new car, and now it feels normal to sit next to him. I've given up trying to drive alone.

I sit admiring my kitchen choice, excited about decorating our first home, together. I only wish Sandbanks was on my doorstep. I find my mobile and search for Luke in my contacts. Suddenly the car comes to a sudden stop. Giving me no time to understand what's going on, Max unfastens his seatbelt and opens his door.

'Max!' I call.

'Stay in the car.' He says without looking at me, and slams the door shut.

All I can see is a man walking down the street. My stomach instantly churns and a wave of panic washes through me.

Max closes the space between himself and the stranger, and punches him. His first punch was a surprise, but the stranger was expecting the second one.

Holy shit! I open the door and run towards them.

'Max, stop!' I scream, but he continues to pound the man.

What the hell is going on? I'm no match to stop them.

Max takes another blow to his face, and he falls. While he is on the ground, the other man kicks him hard in the stomach. Somehow Max manages to stagger to his feet. The stranger clenches his fist, ready to deliver a hard blow to Max's face. I can't take any more; I stand in front of Max. The stranger punches me instead. Jesus, that hurt! I manage to get up, and face the stranger as he raises his arm again.

'Go on, hit me.' I push at his chest. 'You fucking arsehole, are you going to hit me again? Because you're not hitting him.'

'Fuck off, you bitch.' The man wipes his face with the sleeve of his shirt.

'I suggest you leave. As I saw it, you started it!' I look around, wondering if there's any CCTV to catch me out.

'You fucking cunt, don't lie to protect this piece of shit,' the man spits.

'We're going to leave. I advise you to walk in the other direction.'

Amazingly, he turns and begins to walk away. My eyes fall to Max, who is doubled up on the ground. Fuck! What did he do that for? The taste of iron swirls in my mouth. I wipe the blood off my lip, and touch my tender cheekbone.

'Shit, Max, look at the state of you.' I bend to help him stand. 'Lean on me; let's get to the car.' My fear is that the man might return, this time not alone. 'Max, please, we need to get to the car.'

I shuffle along, almost dragging Max with me. He is over six foot. My five-foot-five frame is no match for his. We reach the car. I lean Max against the passenger side and open the door. He falls into the seat. Christ, what just happened? I reach for his seatbelt and buckle it around him, although I'm too late to protect him. I race round to the driver's door.

With the door shut and locked, I move the seat forward and push the start button. Shit, I don't know where I am. My hands begin to shake as tears begin to fall. I search for Luke's number from the car, thanking God for Bluetooth, having dropped my phone somewhere in the car. His mobile goes straight to voicemail. I call Stella.

'Stella Trevant speaking.'

'Stella…' I try to speak but my emotions are all over the place.

'Kate, what's wrong?'

Within seconds Luke's voice echoes through the car. 'Baby, what's wrong?'

'Max is covered in blood and I don't know where I am.'

'Kate, slow down. Take a deep breath. What's happened?'

I begin to inhale and exhale slowly, calming my voice.

'Max just had a fight. I didn't know what to do. Luke, he has blood everywhere. I think he needs the hospital.'

'No. I'll take care of him. Are you hurt?'

'Just a cut lip.'

Heavy breathing is his response. *Hurt me and you will die!*

'You said you don't know where you are. Look around you.'

Max always drives through the rat runs in London; he never sticks to recognisable main routes. I look up and notice a street sign on a house.

'Drayton Gardens.'

'Good – that's ten minutes from Sutton Global. Press your sat-nav button and hit memory. I have already stored the address. Press it now, and start driving. I'll meet you out the front.'

I nod and press the buttons on the sat-nav.

'Kate?'

'Yeah, I'm moving.'

'I'll be waiting.'

I nod as tears flow down my cheeks. I look across at Max. My instinct tells me there's more to his silence than physical pain.

Luke was right. Ten minutes later, the car draws up along Sutton Global. I see him running towards the road in black trousers and white shirt. I stop the car and jump out, falling into his arms, sobbing.

'Luke, I'm sorry. I tried to get them to stop… they kept hitting each other… I tried.'

He holds me close, and lowers his face into my hair.

'Shh, it's OK.' He pulls away and looks at me. 'Fuck, look at your lip.' He rubs his hand across my cheekbone.

'Ow!' I wince. His chest rises. Once again he was unable to protect me.

'Get in the car.' Luke moves the car seat forward, allowing me to climb in the back. He gets in the driver's seat. Max turns his head for the first time and looks at Luke. Their eyes communicate silently.

'Anderson?'

Max nods. Luke shakes his head and rubs his jaw.

Anderson… Who the hell is Anderson? I'm guessing the man with a good right hook. I'm also guessing I shouldn't ask.

We arrive at the palace relatively quickly, given the traffic. Luke steps out of the car and moves the seat forward, allowing me to exit. I enter my number in the black door and watch Luke help Max out of the car. How can a man who feels the need to protect me crumble before my eyes?

Luke half-carries Max inside. I feel completely helpless as Luke continues through to the kitchen, and gently lowers Max to a chair. At the same moment Rosie walks through.

Her hands cover her mouth as she rushes over to us. 'Oh my God… What's happened?'

'I need you to get Max a clean shirt and pack him a bag for a few days,' Luke says.

Rosie silently nods and walks off to Max's apartment.

'Luke, what do you want me to do?' I look at him. He is in complete control.

'Help me undo his shirt.'

'OK.' I reach forward and begin to undo the buttons of his shirt as Luke checks his wounds. I notice a large cut on his shoulder, maybe from when he fell to the ground. 'There's a lot of blood coming out of this cut.'

'Use his shirt to compress the wound. I'll get my medical kit.'

Luke disappears into his office. Max raises his eyes in my direction. It kills me to see the hurt in his eyes. I reach forward and give his blood-soaked cheek a kiss.

'You'll be fine. Luke will sort you out.' I place my arm around his shoulder and then hear the familiar sound of Jerry whistling. He stops dead in his tracks.

'Jesus! What the hell happened?' His words fire out so quickly that his Northern Irish accent thickens.

'Max had an… accident.'

Jerry frowns, definitely not swallowing my bullshit, and moves towards us. Luke returns to Max, bag in hand.

'Kate, get me some warm water. Jerry, pour Max something strong to drink, and get an ice pack for Kate's cheek.' We all carry out our tasks set by Commander Sutton.

Within ten minutes, Rosie returns with a shirt and an overnight bag. All three of us watch Luke clean and attend to Max's wounds, using steri-strips to close his lacerations. Luke helps Max into a clean shirt.

'Kate – a word.'

I follow Luke to his office, holding the ice pack against my cheek.

He pushes the door slightly closed.

'Let me look at you.' He gently touches my cheek. 'It feels fine – I think it's just bruised, and your lip.' He touches it with his thumb and then tenderly kisses me. He pulls me into his arms. 'I'm sorry, this should never have happened. I know you have questions, but I need to take Max away for a few days.'

I look up to his face, panicked. 'You too?'

He shakes his head. 'Just Max, but I don't know what time I'll be home. Please don't leave the house. Thomas is here with extra security staff.'

'Luke, you're scaring me.'

He smiles, trying to ease my mind. 'Precaution, nothing more. I will answer any questions you have when I return.' He gently kisses me.

Cut lip again! My hand runs against my bruised cheek. My reflection confirms I look a little battered, but nothing compared to Max. The thought sends a shiver through my body. I brush my wet hair and slip on my usual grey slouchy clothes.

The sound of Jerry and Rosie echoes through the hall as I make my way to the kitchen.

'Kate, darling, sit down. I'll make some tea.' Rosie stands.

'Thanks. What a bloody nightmare.' I sit next to Jerry and take his hand. 'Sorry about earlier, feeding you bullshit. I still can't believe what happened.'

Jerry squeezes my fingers. 'You looked dreadful, flower, but not as bad as Max.'

'I don't know what came over him. He stopped the car, got out and started attacking a man.'

'Did you recognise him?' Jerry asks.

I shake my head. 'No.'

'Here – drink this.' Rosie places a mug of tea in front of me. 'Luke will sort him out. Those two are as thick as thieves, have been since the day we arrived.'

'I've always thought that.' History! That's what binds you with someone.

'Bloody madness… That's not like Max. Something must have driven him to it.' Jerry says.

'God knows. Anyway, I'm starving. Anyone fancy beans on toast?'

'Not for me, Kate.' Rosie stands and washes her cup in the sink.

'I've got to get on, flower.' Jerry heads towards the garden.

'Do you want me to sit with you until Luke gets back?' Rosie walks to my side, rubbing her hand across my back.

'No, I'm going to lose myself in some bad TV.'

Midnight arrives, but there's no sign of Luke. I lie on the sofa in his office, channel hopping and clock watching. My eyes begin to close.

A tender kiss on my good cheek wakes me. My eyes instantly open. 'Hi.'

'How are you feeling?' Luke crouches by the sofa.

I sit up, yawning. 'Fine… Max – is he OK?'

'Bearing up. I took him to his sister's for a few days.'

'Oh! I didn't even know he had a sister. Obviously I don't really know that much about him.'

He kisses my forehead. 'You know the best bits. You should be in bed.'

'Not until I knew you were OK. Have you eaten?'

'I'm not hungry.'

'You need to eat – French toast?'

A smile appears on his weary face. God, it warms my heart to see his face light up. 'Is that for you or me?'

'Both. You look exhausted.'

'It's been a long day. Let me shower. I'll be down in ten minutes.'

'OK.'

The first batch of toast sits on a plate ready for Luke to dip in the saucepan of warm raspberries. This has to be the best form of world peace on a plate.

'Smells good.' Luke enters the kitchen in his comfy jogger shorts and T-shirt.

'Sit down.' I pass him his plate, and watch him devour the treat.

'I was hungrier than I thought.'

'Here.' I pile his plate high with more.

I take the stool next to Luke and watch him eat while I drink my tea.

'So, ask what you need to ask.' Luke turns to me with honesty in his eyes. However, I also see another emotion – sadness.

'Let me be clear, I'm not expecting you to divulge information that's between you and Max. He's your friend and you have history.'

'A kind gesture, Kate, but after today I feel you are owed an explanation.' Luke stands and holds his hand out. 'I have something to show you.'

We descend to the basement and head for the wine cellar, a place I seldom visit. Luke releases my hand and presses a button at the side of the floor-to-ceiling wine rack. It moves slightly, revealing a keypad. What's he doing?

He looks at my shocked expression.

'Nothing scary – I promise.'

He inputs a code. The door unlocks and Luke steps forward. I take a deep breath, feeling apprehensive; today has truly unnerved me. A fluorescent light illuminates a fairly large room.

I move in and slowly scan the room. 'What is this, a secret den?'

'You could call it that – a store room, a panic room.'

There are racks filled with books and tons of paperwork, and – shockingly – piles of cash.

'It's more than a store room!' I stop dead in my tracks. Holy shit – guns. 'Should I ask?'

'I had it built when I first moved in. I needed more than a safe to keep important documents and weapons.

Kate, you have seen the work I was involved in; this is evidence.'

'What the hell were you involved in?' I hold my hand up. 'Actually, don't tell me... Are you allowed to keep guns in your home?'

'I am.'

I walk around the room, stopping at a box that looks a little bizarre. I look inside, to reveal handcuffs and several other toys. Luke rolls his eyes and swiftly moves to my side.

'I forgot these were here. I haven't been in here for a long time, since we got together.'

'Six months, nearly seven – not that I'm counting.' Clearly, all girls count – it's what we do. 'I take it this box is for recreational use.' I pull out a large bar with handcuffs attached.

Luke removes it from my hands and returns it the box.

'Let's just say I had a sexual partner who liked to be manhandled.'

'What, whipped and shit like that?' I've always wondered, and now there's evidence.

'Yes.'

'Oh my God. I don't know what to say.'

'I didn't bring you down here to discuss my past... whipping experience.' He smiles and pushes the box further back.

'I'm telling you now, if you come near me with a whip I'll knock you out.' My arms automatically fold at the thought of Luke doing that – not to me, but to another woman.

'I have no intention of ever whipping you... unless...' He trails off, a delectable smirk forms across his face.

'Let me stop you there. That's never going to happen, or you can find yourself a new Mrs S.'

He pulls me into his arms.

'I would never hurt you.' He kisses my forehead. 'Sit down. There's something I want to show you that doesn't involve bondage – although tying you up...' He raises his brows.

'Ha, very bloody funny.'

I sit down. Shit, I'm having a day of revelations. I can't believe Luke whipped a previous partner. Maddy? No, she doesn't look the type. What is the type? I have no bloody idea!

'Kate!'

'What?'

'Are you with me?'

'Yeah, sorry. Actually, was it Maddy?'

His brows shoot up.

'Miss Whiplash: was it Maddy?'

He chuckles. 'Max always said you were like a dog with a bone.'

'You just threw me one to chew.'

'No.'

'What, no it wasn't Maddy or no, you're not going to tell me?'

'Both. So don't ask, you'll never meet her – I can guarantee that.'

My hand covers my mouth. 'Did you kill her?'

'Jesus, Kate, do you really think I kill random people? Is that what you think of me. It was a while ago. She briefly worked in London before she headed back to...'

'Yes? To where?' The Outer Hebrides, I hope!

He takes a deep breath. 'Sweden.'

'You like a blonde.'

'I like you. So please stop talking.'

He turns and collects what appears to be a scrapbook from a rack and places it on the table.

'As you know, Max and I go way back.'

I nod.

'I met Max via his son, Paul Maxwell.'

I frown.

'Max's name is Anthony Maxwell, but I've only ever known him as Max.'

'Oh! I just assumed that was his name.'

'Most people do.'

Luke opens the book and skips a few pages, leaving it open at a page containing various newspaper articles. One headline reads: *Teenager dies outside London nightclub.* I begin to read as Luke sits back in his chair, running his hands through his hair.

'Shit, Luke, were you there when this happened?' I continue to read. 'Bloody hell. Poor Max... and you, was he your best friend?'

Luke nods silently. My eyes brim with tears. I reach across for his hand and turn the page. A name in an article jumps out at me – Anderson. It must have something to do with today; it can't be a coincidence.

I carry on reading. 'It went to court... Jesus, Luke.'

He inhales deeply, trying to find the words to explain. God, no. Watching him crumble kills me.

'Luke, please, baby, don't say any more. I can't bear to see you hurt.'

'I need to. One night Paul and I went out clubbing, we had a few drinks, and some trouble broke out.' Luke takes a deep breath. 'The bouncers attacked us, even though we had done nothing. They threw us out – we tried to defend ourselves, but there were too many to fight off. All I remember was Paul lying face down.'

'Oh shit! Luke, I'm so sorry. Poor Max.'

'He died in my arms, Kate. By the time the paramedics arrived, it was too late. I couldn't do anything to help him except hold him until he stopped breathing.' He lowers his head in his hands, hiding what lies in his eyes.

I go to him, wrapping my arms around him. 'I'm so sorry – to go through that at seventeen… I love you so much. I hate seeing you in pain.' Tonight is my turn to be strong.

He pulls away slightly, his head held low, not in the usual manner of Luke Sutton. I lift his chin and use my thumbs to wipe away the dampness on his cheeks.

'Kate, I'm sorry about today.'

'You just told me your best friend died in your arms. Bloody hell, that's a huge thing to get over.' I move back to my chair, bringing it closer so our knees are touching.

'I met Paul through being at the wrong place at the wrong time; we immediately hit it off. We had totally different backgrounds: I was wealthy, and he was from a council estate, but it made no difference. He was clever and funny. The way he died really fucked me up. It killed me that I couldn't help him.'

'No shit. I can't imagine what you went through – and Max, of course. What about your parents? Did they know?'

'Not really. I'm the first to admit I was rebellious. I was sharp enough to never bring trouble to my doorstep; my school results were always good, so they never had any real cause to worry.'

'Luke Sutton was a bright boy? Why am I not surprised? But how did you cope afterwards? I mean, it must have been bloody lonely.'

'I managed to get through the funeral and then there was a court case. You've just read that the bastards got off.'

I nod, my eyes remaining fixed to his. I don't want him to stop talking.

'Kate…' He breathes out and sits back in his chair. 'That's when I lost it and went after Derrick Anderson. I wanted to kill him – and still do, for what he did to Paul. Thankfully, Max came after me just as I was about to kick the shit out of the prick. Max threw me in his car and took me away before I did something I'd regret.'

'So, that's why you owe Max – he rescued you.'

'Max was in the military when he was young, and got out when Paul was born. He never married Paul's mum, but they remained close for his sake. He also kept in contact with his old military friends. He drove me to Hereford – that's where I started my training – and the rest is history.'

What the hell? I wasn't wrong about a night of revelations.

'Anderson was the guy today?'

'He played a part in what happened to Paul. He denied touching him, but I saw him with my own eyes. When I got out of the SAS and started Sutton Global, I went after Anderson. I wanted to destroy him. Look at the picture again – do you recognise it?'

I consider the black-and-white newspaper images. 'Oh my God, it's SGI; I could barely recognise it.'

'I managed to dig deep into Anderson's business and found out he was a rogue operator. After some investigation,

322

he got put away for dealing in drugs and money laundering. Nothing too hardcore, but enough to see him behind bars. He got out some time ago.'

'That's why you own the club.'

'He had to sell it in order to pay his legal bill. I was there to pick it up for next to nothing, and now it's a thriving business. It belongs to Max: I signed it over to him a long time ago, in honour of Paul. Although Max never visits the club, and I just keep an eye on it. I had no idea Anderson had returned to London; he's been off my radar for some time.'

'Bloody hell, so today was a massive shock for Max? No wonder he went mad. Luke, I don't know what to say. I can't believe Max lost his child.'

This time Luke pulls me into his lap.

'Max told me you tried to stop the fight; standing in front of two men fighting is not clever.'

'I couldn't watch that man hit him.'

Luke gently kisses my lips.

'Max thinks the world of you. This should never have happened with you there, Kate.'

'You can't say that. Max protects me, but how he must have felt, seeing the man who killed his child… Luke, you just said you wanted to kill him – just imagine if that was your son.'

'You shouldn't have been caught in the crossfire.'

'Wrong time and place, that's all. I would do it again. Actually, I lied to that Anderson man. I said I saw him throw the first punch… I did look for CCTV but couldn't see any.'

'So now you lie for your friends.' He runs his hands through my hair.

'Absolutely, honour among friends – shit! Luke, I didn't mean it like that.'

'I know. Max appreciates you were defending him. Kate, he's never got over how much time you spent with him after the explosion. Well, between my room and his.'

'Yes, and if I remember rightly, your room was a little more challenging.'

Luke laughs for the first time. 'What can I say? Rehabilitation.'

'Rehabilitation, bullshit. I would describe it as the most embarrassing day of my life. That poor nurse – caught us having sex!'

'As I said, rehabilitation.'

'Yes, well, thank God I didn't see her again.'

He gently kisses me again then looks at his watch.

'Three o'clock – you should be asleep.'

'Thank you for sharing your life. You very rarely tell me anything. I'm here for you always – you know that.'

'I know, baby. Now, bed. You look exhausted and bruised.'

We stand as Luke puts the book away and I look at the Swedish pleasure box.

'This needs to go in the bin.'

I run to Luke and Max, who are lying on the ground, unconscious. I check their pulses – they're faint. I try to breathe, but my chest hurts. I gasp for air. Please, God, help them…

I wake, alarmed that I've had a nightmare – my first since New York. I look at my watch: eight thirty. Luke remains spread-eagled across the bed.

I slide out from the covers, needing some air. The house is quiet; maybe Rosie and Jerry heard what time

Luke arrived home. I grab a blanket from the sofa and go out into the garden.

There, my eyes close, and I allow the morning chill to coat my skin.

I feel a kiss on the top of my head. 'Nightmare?'

'Yeah.' I turn to face Luke. 'You were asleep, I wanted you to rest. I was going to call Stella.'

'I emailed her last night. I'm not going to work today.'

'Oh.'

'You and I have a date in the gym.'

'What?' I know the gym is at the back of the house, but it's not a room I visit. Does he think otherwise?

'Driving back last night, I had time to think. Yes, you know where the panic button is…'

'In our bedroom.'

'Right. But you're poorly armed for these situations.'

'Poorly armed.' Where's this heading? 'Luke, this won't happen again.'

'We both know trouble follows you, so I'm going to teach you self-defence… and this afternoon you have an appointment at my gun club.'

'Are you shitting me? Gun club! Luke, I will never go near your guns – ever. You say I'm not to be trusted with technology, but you want me to handle a gun? You're either brave or bloody stupid.'

'I see it as a challenge. I need to know you can handle yourself. I'll sort out the license and—'

'And I think you need some breakfast; clearly you're not thinking straight!'

After breakfast, Luke tries to explain what happened yesterday to Jerry and Rosie. Seeing Luke in pain last night hit me hard. I can't watch their reaction to Max's loss, and wander off to the office. Once I have checked my emails, I collect some drawings ready for my meeting with Tanya and Maria – where hopefully they will offer me a 'yes' to Harper Jones. Last, I write Luke's Valentine card for tomorrow. Our first!

Luke pads, barefoot, in to the office.

'Everything OK?'

'Yes.'

'Good. Have you heard from Max?'

'His sister called. He slept well and he's talking.' He sounds stressed.

Lighten the mood, Harper.

'So you want me to kick your arse, do you, Sutton?'

'In your dreams, baby, but I'll teach you to defend yourself.'

We stand in the well-equipped house gym.

'Kate!'

I look at Luke, who's standing in front of me. 'You need to concentrate.'

'Yeah, but I was just thinking I should exercise. Well, not today, and tomorrow, as I'm busy, then I have Barney's party to sort out, and a couple of dress fittings with Mr Jones…'

'Jesus. Were you this easily distracted at school?'

I place my hands on my hips, slightly offended.

'No!' Of course I was easily distracted!

'So tell me what you know about self-defence.' Luke stands in front of me, arms folded, looking all Commander Sutton.

'Kneeing whoever in the balls and then run, and of course scream. And always make sure I have my phone with me.'

'Fuck all, then.' Suddenly Luke grabs me and holds me tightly, my arms locked around me. 'Can you reach my balls, or your phone?'

'Obviously not – you're holding me too tight.' He releases me. 'I wasn't ready.'

'That's my point, baby – an attacker doesn't warn you so you can call for help. You do know that, having been on the receiving end.'

'Fine.' I roll my eyes.

'Hit me.'

What? 'I'm not going to hit you; I might hurt you.'

Luke laughs.

'That's unlikely. Now hit me.'

'No!'

Luke pushes my shoulder.

'Ow! What was that for?'

'Hit me.'

'No, I don't want to.'

'Kate, you need to hit me so I can show you how to defend yourself.'

This game is shit. I have no intention of hitting him. However, if he pushes me again I'll knock him out.

'Fine, if you want me to hit you, then close your eyes.'

'Shut my eyes?' He smirks.

'Yes, is there something wrong with your hearing? Besides, with all your stealth 007 wannabe training, I'm sure your super-senses will detect where I am going to attack you.'

'Is that so?'

'Eyes shut.'

To my amazement, he closes them. My first attack is directed at his lips as I lock my arms around his neck. Obliging Commander Sutton allows my tongue to probe in his mouth, inviting him to enjoy the assault.

Finally Luke pulls away. 'That's how you defend yourself?'

'Only from you.' I kiss his jaw, as my hand moves to the waistband of his joggers, heading for his erection.

'Do you need to defend yourself from me?' Luke's voice is low and sexy. I can hear that Commander Sutton has left the building and now my sex god is standing in front of me.

'No. But you may want to defend yourself from me,' I say.

My mouth finds his again as my hand works on his thick erection. He scoops me up in his arms and walks to the bench press, pulling me to him. I rid myself of my grey leggings and his joggers, allowing his hardness to spring free. It's a bonus we're both commando this morning!

Silently, I straddle him and lower myself onto him. Slowly he sinks further inside me.

'Christ…' He takes a deep breath and reaches for my T-shirt, pulling it over my head. Then he grabs my breasts, using his thumb and index fingers to play with my nipples. As my feet are able to touch the floor I have the power to ride him fast, sliding up and down his shaft, taking him deeper with every thrust. His hand leaves my nipples and slides between my wet lips, brushing against my clit.

My thrusting becomes quicker, as Luke's fingers mirror the pace set on my clit. I am desperate to come. The world around me dissolves, until only we exist; it happens every time my body surrenders to Luke.

Minutes later, I've gone.

'Luke.'

Shit, why does each orgasm still take me by surprise?

'Give it to me, baby. Kate, look at me.'

My eyes rest on his as the last wave washes over me. He has me; this is me, stripped naked. Luke's hands move to my hips. He takes a low breath and I know he's coming.

'Fuck...'

Seconds later he holds me still. I lean forward and tenderly kiss him.

'I think my idea of self-defence has actually knocked you on your arse.'

'Touché, baby.' He laughs at my evaluation as I slide myself off him and stand.

'I quite like this form of self-defence. What's it called – fuck and run?'

Later that day we leave for my next Sutton training, one that I have absolutely zero interest in. After last night, I can't help but wonder if this made Luke the way he is today: watching your best friend die in your arms must alter you in some way.

'What happened after Max took you to Hereford? Sorry, shouldn't I ask? I mean, you don't have to tell me.'

He reaches over and squeezes my thigh.

'Basic army training. They definitely kicked the arrogant arsehole out of me.'

'Really?' I reply sarcastically.

Luke laughs. I'm sure he's reminiscing about my initial thoughts of him, which I did share more than once.

'Kate Harper, tell me your opinion has changed.' He tries to act wounded.

'Well, all I can say is they obviously didn't kick you hard enough.'

'Maybe.' He offers me a sideways smile. 'After my induction I then went through rigorous army training. I was a quick learner. As you know, I speak fluent French, Italian, and I can get by in German, plus a few additional languages – it came easy to me.'

I turn to him, full of admiration.

'Bloody hell, Luke.' My attempt at ordering a drink in French seems somewhat pathetic!

'A few years down the line I was picked out and deployed to the SAS. We trained hard at Hereford; the Brecon Beacons were tough, and – the rest is history that I won't disclose.'

'You leave me speechless. How the hell have you packed so much into your life? Christ, this time last year I was working with Mr Jones – and now you're engaged to me.' I laugh; he must have drawn the short straw.

'Why is that funny?'

'Christ, Luke, you're a hot gazillionaire who can shoot and speak in God knows how many languages, and yet you're with someone who thinks French toast is the answer to any world problems.'

'It did help last night.' He squeezes my leg again. 'Kate, you keep me grounded, and you keep me thinking the best of people.'

'Your business – did you start it as soon as you left Sullivan and Parker?'

'I've always had a love affair with stocks and shares. I began to use my grandfather's inheritance to make enough money to start Sutton Global.'

'You said your family don't know about your 007 life.'

He turns to me.

'007! And, no, they think I was working abroad in a bank.'

I laugh. 'Really, not out assassinating people? I can't imagine you in a bank. More to the point, how on earth did they believe that? They must have asked questions.'

'The day I signed up, I knew I had found my calling. Max was right – I needed to channel my anger into something.'

'But you left home – surely your mum was worried?'

'I took my passport, packed some clothes and told her I was travelling and working. The bank job – so to speak – came slightly later. I had no intention of them finding out what I was involved in, so I invented a career to stop my parents asking questions. I went home when I could, trained hard, and took up a hobby of investing in stocks and shares.'

'You give a whole new meaning to the word hobby.' I say.

'Kate, I knew that at some point I wanted to start Sutton Global. So, in between various... jobs—'

I laugh. 'Jobs? Is that code for assassinations?'

'I've never unlawfully killed anyone. However, taking one man out with a bomb to save a school bus full of innocent children – that's a no-brainer.'

331

'I'm teasing you. Luke, you have to remember my life has been so sheltered compared to yours. Not just our backgrounds, but every part of you. We're so different. I mean, you planned Sutton Global in between missions, you can hear how mad that is – but not for you. You think so differently to me.'

Luke pulls up in a parking space.

'I don't think we're that different, Kate. I need you as much as you need me. Surely that's enough.'

I lean over and kiss his lips. 'It is for me.'

I stand in a cubicle, Luke at my side. He leans forward to whisper in my ear.

'Why do you always look so hot?'

'I don't – it's you and your addiction to sex,' I say cheekily. His statement has me in his hands.

Within ten minutes a gun specialist who Luke seems to know well joins us. He is carrying a handgun.

'Luke, is this what you want?'

Luke takes the weapon and points it forward. Then he slides something up and down. I'm already lost in the world of military Sutton.

'Kate, put your ear defenders on – I'm going to shoot.'

I nod, feeling a little anxious. I know I heard gunfire in Russia but this feels different, maybe because we're in a controlled environment. Luke holds the gun forward and points it towards a long-range target. There is a loud noise that causes me to scream. Luke and his friend turn to look at me.

'Sorry!' My face glows. Clearly, I'm out of my comfort zone.

'It's perfect for Kate'

Sorry – did I hear right? 'Luke, I don't think any gun is perfect for me.'

'I'll leave you to it. You have a box of ammo underneath. Do you want me to put it on your account?' the gun specialist says.

'Yes,' Luke says, inspecting the gun and removing the cartridge.

We're alone. My training session is about to begin. Luke hands me the gun.

'Here, take hold of it. I want you to feel it in your hands.'

'Really?' I look at the love of my life, who is wearing his stern face.

'Kate, this is an introduction – you won't be leaving here with a gun; I just want you to know how the mechanics work.'

'What's the point?'

'Peace of mind for me… I hate that you were surrounded by weapons in Russia and clueless about how they worked.'

'Luke, I wouldn't have picked up a gun anyway. Besides, I have you with me 24/7 – personal Sutton security!'

'Funny. This is for your protection, that's all.' He touches my cheek. 'Just let me show you.'

'Fine.'

'Here.' He hands me the gun again, and I hold it at arm's length, letting it swing from my fingers. 'Kate, you need to have more contact with it. Hold it the same way I did.'

I mirror Luke's action. It does feel bizarre. I bring it closer.

'Well, what do you think?'

'Hmm… Do they make it in pink?'

Luke's face drops.

'I'm joking! But I could stick some diamantes on it.'

'No! Now be serious.'

'OK, chill, Commander Sutton.'

15

The annoying sound of my alarm wakes me. My eyes closed, I switch it off. *Crap!* Today is D-day: do or die for Harper Jones. I'm mentally prepared for a 'no'.

I roll to my side, knowing Luke left in the early hours of the morning. Instead of him, there is a note and a single red rose. I sit up and take hold of both gifts, smelling the rose first.

Dear Kate,

Happy Valentine's Day.

Sorry I'm not with you this morning – our first.

I have planned a romantic evening, but I will have to meet you there. All I'm going to tell you is that for some part we will be outside.

I love you.

Luke x

My heart skips a beat with excitement. What the bloody hell shall I wear? Sensible or daring? I'll think about it today.

Within an hour Thomas is walking me to my office.

Stella looks up. 'Kate, how are you? I spoke to Luke last night.' She makes her way round the desk to join me. 'Poor Max – and you too.'

'I'm fine, Stella, just worried about Max and Luke.'

She follows me through to my office. 'I can't believe it – how do you get over losing a son?'

'I don't know. Burying your only child – dear God… That poor man.' Stella places her hand over her mouth.

'Luke was only seventeen.'

'I can't bear it, Kate.'

I place my arm around her shoulder, pulling her towards me.

'I just hope Max can cope with us all knowing about it – he's pretty guarded, and rarely talks about personal stuff.'

'We need to behave normally around him, and if he needs us then of course we will help. Let me get you a coffee. Tanya is here, and I believe your Harper Jones recruits will be here shortly.'

'Don't remind me. I hope they want to be recruited.' My hand slides across my stomach, which is cramping with nerves.

'Of course they will – who wouldn't want to be a part of your project?'

'You should join us. I love having you around, but I know Luke would never let you go.'

'I would never leave him, my darling.' She smiles for the first time this morning, then leaves the room as Tanya enters.

'Morning, Kate.'

'Hi – are you ready for today?' I ask. 'God, I feel nervous.'

'I've got a good feeling about this.' She makes her way towards the board table.

A knock at the door halts my thoughts, which I'm grateful for.

'Come in.'

A delivery boy from the post room walks towards me, carrying a bouquet of red roses.

'Miss Harper, these were delivered for you.' He hands me the flowers.

'Oh, thank you.'

Tanya smiles. We all know who's sent the bouquet of love.

I place the bouquet, which is already in water and tied with a stunning red silk bow, on my desk, and read the note.

Dear Cook,
   I will always remain in your hands, today and every day.
   Yours always,
   Boss x

I smile at the message, which reminds me of how I met Luke, when I was his cook, and he was my elusive boss. I take my mobile out of my bag – I need to thank him.

Dear love of my life,
Thank you for the bouquet and the message. Yes, you will be in my hands tonight. However, food will not be the reason!
Love you forever x

'Sorry, Luke's gone all mushy. Shall we go over the Bagrov paperwork before the others arrive?'

'Yes, sure.' We sit at the board table as Tanya tells me in great detail about mergers and contracts. I struggle to take it all in. When will this all make sense?

I check my watch. It's time for my guests to arrive. There is a knock at my door.

'Come in.' The same delivery boy enters, holding a duplicate bouquet of flowers. I move towards him. 'Thank you again. It looks like I might get to know you pretty well.'

He smiles awkwardly. 'Maybe.'

'You're popular.' Tanya laughs.

I remove the card.

Dear Kate,
I hope your day is long and hard, waiting for me to live up to the title that you have given me.
Yours always, Sex God x

Holy shit. A burning crimson tide creeps up my neck. I clear my throat. 'I swear to God someone has possessed Luke.'

Again, I retrieve my mobile.

'You give me hope that romance is still alive,' Tanya says.

Now what shall I text him?

Dear Sex God,

I believe it was you who said that distance makes the heart and groin grow harder.

Think of me while you are at work today, with my hair all over your lap and my mouth sucking you dry.

338

Love you from the moment you got me wet…

PS: love the roses. Thank you – again x

Will he be able to continue his day of self-discipline? I hope not!

There is another knock at the door – not more flowers?

'Come in.'

The door opens. 'Hi.' It's Maria.

She joins us at the boardroom table, and is shortly followed by Valerie and Mr Jones.

'I can't believe it… Honestly, I'm so bloody excited, you've made the best decision. I promise I won't let you down.' I raise my glass. 'Here's to Harper Jones – and lots of fabulous clothes.'

We raise our glasses, but yet another knock on the door interrupts the celebrations.

'Come in.' My new friend returns with yet another identical bouquet of roses. 'You have to be kidding.' I laugh as I make my way to the post boy. 'I was joking earlier, but you may as well tell me your name.'

'Toby Miller.'

I hold my hand out. 'Pleased to meet you, Toby, and call me Kate.' I take the new bouquet. 'Now, am I likely to see you again, Toby?'

'I don't know.' He suppresses a smile. Thank God he can't read the notes with the flowers.

I place the new flowers on the coffee table and take the note.

Dear Kate… aka the techno-phobic female in my life: how can someone with a fear of buttons push mine daily?

Tonight – let's push boundaries!
Yours always, Techno Boy x

Oh my God, I want to cry and combust at the same time. Shit, he's planned this flawlessly. His delivery and timing are in perfect sync: he is matching all of his alter egos from our past notes, reminding me of our history from the beginning. I stand and collect my phone.

Dear Techno Boy,
You know I love pushing your buttons; I feel pushing them later is a must.
Maybe I am at the moment! You know how fond I am of your black shirt.
Yours always, the techno-phobic woman in your life.
PS: thank you for more roses x

I return to the table. I wish he were here so I could thank him in person.

Our first decision as Harper Jones is to take it one step at a time, allowing Maria and Valerie to continue working – for the time being. This gives us time to source fabrics and decide on our target market, and research the styles we want to sell – although we all prefer classic styles. Our secret weapon is Mr Jones and his fabulous design books.

After we have discussed various issues, lunch arrives. Stella is happy to join us. There's a knock at the door.

'Come in,' I call. *God, not again!* I smile as my new friend Toby tries to hide his amusement, 'Toby, really? Again?'

'Yep, another has just arrived.'

'Trust Luke. Kate, you know he probably planned this weeks in advance.' Stella knows Luke far too well.

'You're probably right.' I make my way to Toby and the abundance of red roses. 'Thank you again.' Toby smiles and walks away.

Quickly I read the words on the card.

Dear Voyeur,

I see you watching me all the time… are your eyes commanding me? Wanting me to take you as only I can?

My plan is to watch you – let me see what you can do to yourself.

Yours always, Adonis x

Holy fuck, is it hot in here? I'm seriously overheating. Bastard, he's fully aware of the effect that note would have on me. Thankfully, everyone is engrossed in food and conversation. I take a deep breath and text Luke.

Dear Adonis,

You want to watch me touch myself the same way you touch me? What a shame I'm alone. I feel my wandering hand may need to start a little sooner than tonight.

I have to go, as my needs have not been dealt with today.

Love from your sexually deprived lover

PS: thank you for all the roses x

I take my seat. I can feel my body aching for him, the result of his sexual word association game.

Finally, Mr Jones and I are alone. I stand on the boardroom table, allowing him to pin the lining of my wedding dress. The pattern is taking shape, even though it is a rough outline. It's a full-length sleeveless dress with a small sweetheart neckline, which is incredibly fitted.

Another knock at the door stops the pinning process. 'Come in,' I call.

'Hi.' Toby appears – again.

'Hi. Can you put the flowers on my desk and pass me the note and my mobile, please?'

Toby passes me both and quickly leaves. I'm sure I will be the subject of office gossip, not only due to the number of bouquets, but also because I'm standing on a table covered in calico!

Dear fiancée,

Where do I begin to tell you how much you have altered my life? You have changed the course I was on, taking me to a better place and making me a complete person. To think of you not being in my life hurts like no other pain. I will love you for eternity.

The best day of my life was when you said yes.

Your fiancé x

Tears roll down my cheeks.

'Kate, what on earth's wrong?' Mr Jones asks. I pass him the card.

'He is certainly open about his feelings for you.'

'I know.'

'Let me help you to the chair.' Mr Jones helps me off the table. 'Tears of joy, Kate? It looks as though Prince Charming is in love with you.'

I place my arms around Mr Jones and laugh through my tears.

'Do you remember the first time I met him, and the tie we made? So much has happened since them.'

'Good things, Kate.'

'I'm useless – look what a simple note can do to me. Bloody hell.' Mr Jones passes me a handkerchief. 'Thank you.'

'Never underestimate simple; it will keep you grounded.'

I take a deep breath. 'I guess. But Luke is anything but simple, that's why… this note has…'

'Listen to me – you make Luke happy. You give him what has been missing in his world – not the other way round.'

I frown.

'Money makes the world go round – but not your heart.'

'I know.' I sniff.

'And so does he… Even if he had no money, you would still love him.'

'Yes.'

'I rest my case.' He takes his hanky and wipes my cheeks. 'Now then, young lady, we have had a day full of great surprises, and I suggest you go home. I'm sure Luke has something planned for this evening.'

I nod.

'Of course he has. So, the wedding dress pattern fits, and I will cut the fabric.' He also collects another drawing from the table, a dress I drew for Mrs Gold's upcoming charity gala. 'Now, this may be a little difficult – it's achievable, but tricky. Kate, I think you have talent – not so much for drawing, but an eye for design.'

'Really? That means a lot coming from you.'

Alone, I need to text Luke.

> I love you xxxxxxxxxxxxxxxxxxxxxxxxxxxxxxxxxxxxxxxxx
> xxxxxxxxxxxxxxxxxxxxxxxxxxxxxxxxxxxxxxxxxxxxxx
> xxxxxxxxxxxxxxxxxxxxxxxxxxxxxxxxxxxxxxxxxx
> Worlds apart – souls together – always x

I hit send. There is nothing else to say. My phone vibrates in my hand. Caller ID – boss.

> Back at you, baby x

At home, I try to find the best possible outfit. I scan my wardrobe, but nothing jumps out at me, other than my fur coat! I open a drawer and pull out a black lingerie set with garter belt and stockings. Why not? I decide to go for daring, not safe. Luke did say we would be outside, so I guess the coat is practical!

I blow-dry my hair poker-straight and apply smoky eye makeup. I stand in front of the French mirror examining my underwear. Last, I slip my coat on and grab my black Hunter wellington boots – and Luke's gift bag.

Thomas drives me to the surprise destination. After a while I realise he is taking me to a familiar spot, Luke's private view of London – Primrose Hill.

The car stops and a waiter opens the car door. The pathway is lit with lanterns, leading me to a candlelit table – and, most importantly, to the love of my life.

As I begin to walk, a string quartet wearing long black coats begins to play. I can't help but laugh.

'We found love.' I walk towards Luke's open arms, linking my hands around his neck. 'Rhianna! A string quartet playing Rhianna – I'm impressed.'

'The first time I saw you, you were in my kitchen, dancing to this song.' Luke lowers his lips and kisses me gently. 'Happy Valentine's Day, baby. God, I've missed you.'

'Not as much as I've missed you.' I return his kiss with passion, and maybe a hint of frustration from the various notes he's sent. The music makes me laugh. 'How did you get them to play classical Rhianna?'

'They were up for the challenge. Allow me.' Luke pulls out my chair, as a waiter pours champagne.

'Thank you.'

I look around to see we are alone except for the usual burger van, waiters, string quartet and the security team!

'Are you warm enough?'

I nod, grateful Luke has provided patio heaters. He thinks of everything!

'So, are you wondering why we're here?' His captivating smile hits me.

'Yeah. I am surprised.' I take a sip of champagne.

He takes my hand across the table.

'Today is a first for us. We've had lots of ups and downs.'

'You could say that.'

'It reminded me of all the firsts we have had together. Do you remember the first time I brought you here?'

I nod. 'After the jazz club – Toulouse? You brought me here for coffee.'

'The night you were spying on me.' He gives his one-sided Sutton smile. My body has been on fire since this afternoon.

'I wasn't spying; we just happened to be in the same place.' I can't help but laugh. Honestly, we're both telling the truth. 'I was shocked it was you, I needed to make sure.'

'OK, so you were looking at me?'

'I was.' My poker face is broken!

'Seeing you backed into the corner trying to avoid punches – I saw red.' His eyes lock with mine. There is no humour in his, just unadulterated passion. 'I knew then you had to be mine; the thought of anyone touching you made my blood boil. When we danced that night I could see in your eyes you felt the same way; it was just a matter of time.' He sits back in his chair. 'Kate, I've never brought anyone here. I used to come up here with Paul – we'd play football, do teenage stuff – so when I brought you here I guess I was letting you in my life.'

My eyes fill with tears.

Two waiters arrive, breaking the emotional moment, placing a silver cloche in front of us and removing the dome lids to reveal lasagne.

'The first meal I cooked for you!'

'You got it, baby. I didn't cook this one, but I did show your recipe to the chef.'

'Did you show them the cookbook? Our notes?'

He laughs. 'No, I would never share that with anyone. I gave him a copy of your recipe.'

'Good.' I begin to eat, and another song begins to play. I can't help but laugh. '"Beautiful People" – I love Chris Brown.'

'At SGI – you were dancing with Barney.'

I laugh. 'I can't believe you remembered, and you never told me it was your club. You gave me tickets like you were being a thoughtful boss.'

'I was. I wanted you at a place I could keep you safe.'

'You actually believe yourself? Oh my God, it seems like a lifetime ago. Do you remember Barney kissed you that night?'

'You set me up.' He raises his brows.

'As I recall, you asked me to be a prostitute that night.'

Luke's throws his head back, laughing. 'That's not what I said.' He takes hold of his champagne glass.

'No, you said that you couldn't fuck me, not that you wouldn't!' I squirm in my seat. 'Are you pleased we got disturbed that night? Do you think we would have had sex?'

'Yes.' Wow, he looks so hot. 'You knew how hard I was for you. Do I think waiting was the better option? I think it probably was, at least until we got to know each other.'

'I agree. But, I was shocked, and secretly happy you wanted me.' I feel my face flush; thankfully the darkness is helping.

'Not as surprised as I was when you revealed your lack of underwear.'

I place my hands over my face and laugh.

'I can't believe I said that.' I remove my hands to look at Luke. 'Why does that always happen to me?'

'Speaking before you think? You have no filter.' He eats another mouthful of lasagne.

'You wanted to enter my world; I told you we were different.' I shake my head, as Usher's 'Scream' begins to play. The classical version makes me want to cry. 'This is our song.'

'I do like to make you scream.'

I've lost my appetite. I want to go home.

'Yes, you do – mainly with frustration, and not just sexual frustration.' The waiters take our plates, and I pass Luke his gift bag. 'I wanted to get you something, but as usual you're the hardest person to buy for.'

'You didn't need to buy me anything, but thank you.' He removes two cards.

He opens the first one, and some tickets fall out.

'The game is this Saturday. Now, you know I love rugby – well, the hot men, but I have Barney's party and I'm giving him the keys for the studio so I can't come with you.'

'I wouldn't take you anyway.'

'Thanks! OK, so I wasn't sure what countries you wanted to see England play against, so I went for France.'

'Good choice, baby.' He opens the other card. 'I haven't seen this picture.'

'I called your mum; she emailed me some photos from skiing. I know it's a bit childish to make a card, but I loved it so…'

'It's beautiful.' He reaches for my hand.

The waiter returns with two plates, which he places in front of us.

I laugh. 'Really? These are significant to you?'

'I've got a thing for flapjacks since my cook started making them for me... That day, it hit me: you're just a homely girl.' He holds up his handmade card. 'This is exactly what I mean.'

'I don't know what to say. Luke, you're a hopeless romantic. You've knocked me on my arse all day.'

'I've had various awkward moments myself. Do you know how difficult it is to talk money with a hard dick?'

'You should have... handled yourself.'

'I came close. But then I know how much you like to watch me make myself come.'

I swallow hard. 'Luke!' I look around us.

'I love it when your eyes are on fire, baby.'

Luke's phone rings. He takes it out and looks at caller ID.

'It's Dad. I'd better get this.'

'Hello?' His expression alters. 'When will the doctor arrive?' His eyes flit from mine to the table. 'OK. I'll call Dr Jacob and ask her to check her out.' Silence again. 'She's the best. I want her to see Mum. OK... Bye.'

'What's happened?'

'Mum's collapsed.'

'Shit... Is she OK?'

'They're waiting for the doctor.'

I immediately stand. 'Let's go.' I hold my hand for Luke.

He joins me. 'Sorry – this was not part of my plan.'

Within twenty minutes Luke is driving his Bentley down the sweeping driveway of his parents' home. Luke opens the door. We head through the hallway and come face to face with Edward.

'You didn't have to come.' He hugs Luke. 'Your doctor friend called; she's on her way. Honestly, two doctors? Your mother will go mad.'

'She's the best… and I trust her.'

'Hi Edward, how is she?'

'Not too bad, just a bit shocked. Come through – she's lying on the sofa.'

Luke moves ahead of us, removing his coat as he goes.

'Kate, let me take your coat.' Edward holds his hand out. But it's my only item of clothing. Fuck!

'No, that's fine… I feel a bit cold.' Oh, shit – another plan that's gone tits up. I do remove my Hunters, and join Luke and his dad in the lounge.

Luke crouches by his mum and takes her pulse. 'It feels slow; have you had any dizzy spells?' He looks in her eyes. 'Your pupils appear to be normal.'

'No, darling, I just felt woozy earlier and then I was out cold. Your poor father… Anyhow, I am cross you're here – it's Valentine's Day.' She reaches for Luke's hand.

I join him. 'We wanted to make sure that you were OK.'

'Edward, take Kate's coat; it's awfully warm in here.'

Not again! What is it with his family and their need to remove people's coats?

'I'm fine, actually I'm a bit chilly.' But I'm actually getting a bit warm. At this rate, I'll bloody pass out. 'Let me make some tea.'

I relieve myself from the potential coat-removing offers and lay a tray out with cups and saucers. I shortly return to the lounge to see two doctors tending to Livy: her own doctor and Luke's private physician.

Feeling helpless, I move towards the closed back doors, hoping to feel a draught from somewhere to cool my body. Trust the Sutton family home to have the best double-glazing possible; there's not a bloody draught in sight.

'Kate, do you want more tea?' Edwards asks.

I walk back towards Luke. 'No, thank you, I'm fine.' Except, I am going to pass out very soon.

Luke looks at me.

'Are you OK?'

I nod and turn away. He pulls at my chin. 'You look flushed; take your coat off.'

'I'm fine.'

Luke frowns. 'Kate!'

I lean closer to his ear. 'I need to speak to you – alone.'

I follow Luke into the kitchen.

'What's wrong?'

'I'm going to pass out!.'

He looks confused.

I undo my coat, but at the same time Declan walks in. Crap! I wrap up my overheated body once more.

'Wow… sexy, Kate.'

Luke glares at his brother. 'Go!'

We're alone once more.

'This was not part of my plan; you told me we'd be outside.'

He pulls me to his arms. 'You do amuse me.'

'Good. But in the meantime, this coat is like a bloody furnace.'

He takes my hand and guides me to the downstairs bathroom. He removes his jacket, then his shirt, which he passes to me.

'Put this on.'

I remove my coat and lean my hot back against the cold tiles.

'Oh God, that feels good.' I chuckle. I pull him towards me and his lips meet mine. My need to kiss him has been building all day.

'Let me look at you.' His eyes scan my lingerie-clad body. 'I can see what your plan was; sorry for the slight diversion. You look hot, and now I'm hard.'

I button up Luke's shirt and he slips on his black suit jacket, causing me to laugh.

'This looks bloody obvious – you've lost a shirt and I've gained one.'

'My mum is used to us having our girlfriends over.'

'Really! You brought girls home to shag them?'

We return to the lounge. Ollie has arrived, so Livy now has all her boys at her side. I blush, realising everyone will clock my attire – or the very noticeable lack of Luke's shirt.

'Tea, everyone?' I ask and disappear.

I turn to see Declan entering the kitchen, smirking at me.

'You can wipe that smile of your face, Declan Sutton.'

'Sexy Kate… Now I know you're worthy of the title.' He flashes a smile.

'Ha, ha, very bloody funny. I didn't expect to come here tonight.'

'No, I bet you didn't.' He laughs.

'Anyway, have you seen Kiki? Since it's Valentine's Day?' I watch his expression alter.

'No, I already had plans.' He collects some biscuits from the larder.

'What do you mean, plans? With another girl or your friends.'

'Kiki and I have an open friendship.'

I spin on my heels.

'You mean you're fuck buddies.'

He remains silent – a guilty silence.

'Is that all you are?' I blurt.

Luke enters the kitchen.

'I told you to be careful – actually, I told you both. So if you want a fuck buddy relationship, then she needs to know this.'

'Kate!' Luke scowls at me.

'I'm not happy about this. I'll call her tomorrow to make sure you're both on the same page, and if you're not then you'd better hide your sorry arse from me, Declan.' I pass the tray to Luke. 'Can you carry this for me, please?'

'Don't overreact,' Declan says sulkily.

'Declan, enough. Move, Kate,' Luke commands.

'I'm warning you, Declan.'

After the doctors have checked Luke's mum and she's given the all clear, we return to the palace. In the car, Luke places his hand on my thigh. 'Not quite the romantic evening I had planned.'

I look at his silhouette as we drive through London.

'She's OK, that's the most important thing. Besides, she was thrilled to see you – all of you.'

'Speaking of my brothers, you can't tell Declan who he can and can't date.' Luke turns to me.

I fold my arms. 'Actually, I can. Luke, I warned him.'

He begins to laugh. 'Kiki is as much to blame.'

'Maybe, but I won't let either of them hurt one another.'

I feel helpless to resolve Kiki and Declan's situation. My fingers skim Luke's bare chest.

'Are you admiring my outfit?'

'Yes.' My hand moves from his chest towards his groin.

'Can I help you?' He lifts my hand and gently kisses my fingers.

'Actually, you promised me a night of romance.' I move my hand from Luke's firm grip and brush against his growing hardness

'Insatiable Kate is with me.'

I lean across and kiss his neck, then bite his ear.

'I'm greedy for you.'

Music to his ears. 'Good.'

We pull into the driveway. I get out of the car and input my code, my coat and Hunter boots in my arms.

I walk towards the stairs, Luke directly behind me. His hands link around my waist as I place my foot on the first step. He moves my hair aside, allowing him the space to place small tender kisses on my neck.

'Sorry tonight's plan went slightly off course. Now we're home, I'm going to fuck you.'

I turn to face him. 'Good. I've needed you all day.'

Luke scoops me into his arms and begins to climb the stairs.

In our room, he puts me on the floor, and our dark eyes lock.

Luke places his hand inside his jacket and removes a small box.

'Your gift.'

I take the box. 'You've given me so many flowers today – I'm well acquainted with the post boy. Honestly, you've done so much.'

'Open it.'

'OK.' I open the box to reveal a black velvet pouch. I pull apart the drawstring and empty the contents into my hand. It's a distressed platinum bangle with two hearts. I look closely: each heart has an initial – a K and an L.

'Do you like it?' Luke asks.

I nod as my eyes fill with tears.

'Thank you. I love it.' I slip it on my wrist, the same wrist I wear my watch.

Luke places his hands on the buttons of my shirt. 'I'm beginning to wonder if your present was to tease me this evening.'

'It was never my intention, but I would say it was a bonus. I know you love a challenge, Mr S, and your challenge this evening was to keep your self-control.'

He slips his shirt off my shoulders.

'A Harper challenge – always a bonus, baby. Now I intend to take what's mine.'

16

'Quick, Luke, he's here.' I collect Barney's cake and balloons from the island and head to the larder, a room I've adopted as my birthday surprise hideaway.

Luke reluctantly follows me. 'Jesus, Kate, he's not a child.'

'FYI, Luke, Barney is the biggest kid ever. You know his family don't give a shit about him. Now, take the balloons for me.' I pass him the balloons and reach for his lips, feeling how soft his freshly shaven face is. 'You smell fuckable, Mr Sutton.'

'Is that right? You have a lot to say.'

'I suggest you silence me, then.' I tilt my head. 'And, yes, that was a challenge.'

My eyes lock on Luke's. Holy shit. Matches may not be necessary; the heat between us could spark a fire.

'Kate? Kate!' Barney yells.

'Ready?' I whisper.

Luke smiles at me. We exit the larder belting out a Harper–Sutton rendition of happy birthday. Luke sees this means the world to Barney, as he shows his emotions.

'Happy birthday to the light in my life.' I place the cake on the island and head to Barney's open arms.

'Thanks, babe. Shit, I wasn't expecting cake and balloons.'

'I always get you cake and balloons.'

'I know, but I thought now you're living with lover boy, you might not bother.'

'Never.'

'Happy birthday, Barney.' Luke embraces Barney, his head turned away – there'll be no kissing today, not from Luke.

'Cheers, Luke.'

I pass a glass of bubbly to the men in my life. 'Here's to the birthday boy.'

All three of us salute his milestone of twenty-nine.

'Kate, you know I love you, babe – but that singing was bad. Jesus Christ, girl, don't give up your day job.'

'You cheeky git.'

I turn to a bemused Luke. 'He has a point.'

'Luke, you're into that kinky shit – you must have a gag for Kate?'

Luke's eyes widen. Is he wondering how much information I've divulged to Barney?

I look at him. 'Handcuffs – kinky eighty-year-old codger – when I didn't know who you were?'

'OK – it's present time.' I pass Barney two boxes.

'I bloody love presents – thanks, babe.'

I jump up and sit on the island, pulling the man of my dreams between my legs.

Barney chooses to open the large present first. He unties the red bow and removes the shiny red paper to reveal another box.

'Bloody hell – Jones Tailor.' Barney looks at me with delight and excitement as he removes the lid and takes out the black shirt. 'I love it, Kate – Christ, they're bloody expensive.'

'You're worth it.' I wrap my arms firmly around Luke's shoulders, drawing him closer.

Now for the smaller box – this will confuse him. Paper and ribbon discarded, Barney removes a set of keys.

'You've lost me. What are these for? I already live in your house, and I know Luke has issues with keys... Harper, what are you hiding?'

I tap my nose. 'We'll leave in ten minutes.'

'Where to?' Barney asks.

'You'll see.'

Luke turns himself between my legs, planting a kiss on my forehead as I run my hands through his damp hair.

'What time are you meeting Declan?'

'I'll pick him up in a couple of hours. The game doesn't start until two thirty.'

'OK, and then SGI – what time will you be there tonight? I thought Barney and I would go early. I want to make sure everything is set up.'

'I'll drop Declan home, change, and then I'll join you.'

I scowl. No Declan means a stroppy Kiki Marlow.

Luke reads my thoughts. 'Kate, Kiki and Declan are free to date whoever they want... Get over it.'

'I know, but she's nuts about your brother, and he behaves like he doesn't care... Barney, how was Kiki yesterday?'

'Miserable. Poor Henry, she nearly bit his head off. I asked her about Declan and she said it was over. Bullshit, it's not over for her. Sorry, Luke, but Declan has taken the piss out of her. I've seen him out with loads of birds.'

Luke raises his hands. 'They both went into this with matching reputations. Besides, Declan is far from ready to settle down. End of conversation.'

Barney's eyes widen. 'I'm not arguing, Luke, but he played Kiki.'

I kiss his lips before he can respond. I pull away as our eyes meet, feeling mixed loyalties. 'Listen, I think the world of Declan, but I think he's behaved really badly here.'

Luke's dark eyes lock on mine. 'Thomas is waiting for you.'

'I was going to drive, as I have Barney with me.'

'No,' Luke says gruffly and moves towards his office.

'Luke, don't walk away.' I look at Barney. 'He drives me mad. For Christ's sake, all I want to do is drive my car – you would have thought I asked if I could go out naked.'

'Babe, I'm sure he's just… being careful.'

'Careful, my arse. Allow me to introduce you to Mr Moody Bollocks Sutton.' I shake my head and jump off the island. 'Give me a minute and then we can go.'

Luke registers my arrival with a sigh. 'I'm not changing my mind,' he responds without looking up.

'Luke, you're being unfair and irrational. Let's just throw in suffocating while I'm at it.'

He looks at me. 'Suffocating? I suffocate you? Since when?'

'Since now.'

'You feel I'm suffocating you, even though I'm trying to keep you safe? Driving alone falls into the category of unsafe.'

'I have Barney with me. What's your problem?' I move to the side of his desk.

'Do I think Barney is a good person? Yes. Do I think he could protect you from any threats? No.'

I sigh. What's the point of arguing? He never listens. Silence is what I'll leave him with.

'Kate.'

I stop and turn. 'What?'

'I love you, have fun.'

'Whatever.' I turn.

'Baby.' Oh God. My heart skips a beat with the one word that liquefies me. I turn. ' I love you.'

'I love you too. You just – oh, never mind. I love you.'

Barney and I sit in the back of the Range Rover.

'He can flip,' Barney says.

I nod, continuing to look forward. Barney takes my hand and run his fingers over my knuckles.

'He would never hurt me.'

'I know, babe; he just likes to control everything and everyone, and that includes you.'

I turn to face him. 'I'll never lose who I am. I'm still the same girl who lived next door to you.'

He places his arm around my shoulder. 'Yeah, except you have a few million quid in the bank and a shit-hot fiancé. But other than that, everything is still the same.'

We drive for another fifteen minutes. I reach into my bag and pull out a black silk blindfold. 'Slip this over your eyes; we're nearly there.'

'I love a bit of skulduggery… You aren't taking me to a kinky sex club, are you?'

'Of course! I'll let them tie you up and do rude things to you.' I laugh, feeling my surprise may not seem as exciting now.

'Tell me, babe, do you wear this mask for lover boy?'

'No! Luke used it on me when he wanted to surprise me with Sandbanks. Actually, don't tell anyone, but Luke used to whip one of his girlfriends – apparently she liked it rough.'

Barney moves the mask, revealing one extremely shocked eye. 'No fucking way.'

'Mask down now.' I instruct. 'Yes, way. It came up in conversation.' I swallow. 'I told Luke to forget it; we'll never go down that road.'

'You never know, babe, once you whip a path to your arse there's no turning back. Don't knock what you haven't had flogged, that's what I say. I remember this one bloke I was with, and he—'

'No, thanks, Barney, keep that story to yourself… Anyway, we're here.'

I take his hands and guide him to the door.

'Slow steps, lean on me. Do you still have the keys?'

'Yeah.'

'OK. Stop.' I remove the blindfold. 'Go for it, use your keys.' I can't conceal my excitement.

'Christ, why am I so bloody nervous?'

He unlocks the door and we enter a small room. Directly in front of us is a set of double doors, which we push open at the same time.

'Surprise.'

'What the shitting hell have you done?'

'It's yours, your very own studio – well, I've bought the

lease for a year, just to see how you get on.' I look at him. 'Barney?'

He has no words, which is rare, and looks completely stunned. He grabs me, holding me as though his life depends on it.

'Do you like it?'

'I don't know what to say.' He loosens his grip and places his hands on either side of my face. 'It's the best bloody present I've ever had.'

'I know you want to branch out into choreography, and this seems the perfect place for you to start.'

'Bloody hell, babe, I'm lost for words. What did Luke say?' Barney leaves my side and begins to look around.

'His agent found me the studio.'

'It's amazing. I need a sign: *Barney Curtis, dance choreographer* – what do you think?'

'Sounds perfect.'

He swoops me into his arms and swings me round. He feels alive: this is more than a gift, this is a step in the right direction for his career.

'Before I forget, Luke had a new Bose sound system fitted.' I move towards a unit in the far corner of the room. 'He said there would be paperwork and instructions, apparently you can attach your iPhone to it.' I look at Barney. 'Are you OK?'

'What do you think? I can't believe you've done this for me.'

'You deserve it – besides, you're a good investment. Now plug some music in and wiggle your butt, birthday boy.'

Barney, who is a little more techno-minded than I am (which is not difficult), connects his phone to the sound system and searches for a song. I sit on the floor and lean against the full-length mirror.

An instrumental track begins to echo around the room. Not Barney's usual club beat, this sound is graceful. His tall athletic body spins and leaps: even wearing jeans and a T-shirt, he is breath-taking to watch. But my eyes are drawn to his face. This is more than contemporary dance; this is Barney's life, and each movement tells a story. I lose myself in his dance.

The routine comes to an end, leaving him breathless and emotionally exhausted. I clap and cheer, realising what I have given him.

'Amazing, bloody brilliant.' Christ, he's so emotive.

He takes a bow. 'Thank you, thank you, and thank you.'

'Tell me the story you just told.'

'I don't know.' He pats his chest. 'It comes from here.' He walks towards a water cooler. Shit, he always hurts on his birthday. It's an annual reminder that his family has rejected him for no reason other than his sexuality.

The main door opens and Thomas appears.

Perfect timing. 'Lunch.' I stand, and almost skip to the double doors.

I collect the brown paper bags from Thomas and move towards Barney.

'You know me too well, babe.'

'I thought about booking an uber-posh restaurant, but then I know how much you love quarter pounders with cheese.'

'Still the same Harper.'

Later that afternoon we curl up on the sofa in Luke's office with a glass of wine.

'Are you excited? I know that being the centre of attention is a tall order for a shy, retiring person like you.' I reach over and touch his hand.

'Can't bloody wait. Today has been the best! You have some serious work ahead for you to outdo this next year, so you'd better get started, party planner extraordinaire.'

'One-off, babe.'

He pulls my feet into his lap and begins to massage them, ensuring they're ready for painful shoes and far too much dancing.

'Why do we always sit in this room? Don't you use the other lounge?'

'Not really. Luke's always in here, and I follow him like a bad penny.'

'I wonder what Luke use to do before you arrived on the scene. Not too much shagging, I hope.' Barney laughs.

'When Luke asked me to move in, he told me I was the first woman he had brought here. Apparently, he finds his home too personal to share with people for a quick shag.'

'Shocker! The sex god has a heart.'

'I know, I was surprised too. He once told me he has fucked a lot of woman but only had a few relationships.'

'How many?'

'God knows. Just the thought kills me.' I take a large sip of wine. 'Luke knows I'm not sure why he's with me – he could have anyone.'

'What are you talking about? He's nuts about you.'

'I guess. But let's be honest: he's handsome, loaded and lives a dream life.' I meet Barney's confused expression.

'And then there's me: the girl next door who cooks bloody fruitcakes, has no business brain, and no worldly experience.'

'Is that how you really feel?'

'Barney, I love Luke more than life, but let's face it he could have any woman.'

'Stop wallowing! He's lucky to have you. I see the way he looks at you... More than that, babe, I've watched him when men are around you – he's scared.'

'Scared!' I laugh. 'Luke's never scared.'

'Flip this convo: Luke knows you could have any man; you just chose him – the shit-hot fucking model, with a large bulge in his pocket.'

I tap his leg playfully. 'Barney!'

'His wallet, babe – that's your dirty little mind twisting my words.'

Barney stands next to me, ready to party, wearing skinny fitted black-waxed jeans and his beautiful new black Jones Tailor shirt. As ever, he makes women melt, and other gay men are desperate for him.

'What do you think?' I hold up two possible dresses.

He takes the first from my hand and throws it to the floor.

'Hey!'

'Bloody hell, babe, that dress is fine if you're going to a Bagrov meeting, but not for tonight. Now let me look at the next victim.'

I hold up the other black dress, which is not as dull as its predecessor.

Barney rubs his chin. 'It's not yanking my chain... What else have you got?'

'Really – I thought it would look nice.'

Barney's right. Going out with my plus-one normally unleashes the exotic dancer in me; I need an appropriate outfit to match my alter ego.

I walk to the far side of the closet, remembering a faux leather bandeau skater girl dress I have. Perhaps it's a little eighties, and if my memory serves me correctly, it's a little short. I slip it on over my black strapless bra and silk French knickers.

I twirl. 'Well, does this meet your expectations?'

I open a drawer, which I have renamed the sex god drawer, and take out a pair of sheer lace-top hold-ups, with a black seam running down the back. I slip them on, ensuring the line is straight.

Barney returns just as I finish. 'Bloody hell, babe.'

'You like?' I raise my brows.

'You're a saucy bitch. I take it that's a personal invite for some nookie.'

'I bloody hope so.'

Eight o'clock arrives and Thomas drives us safely to SGI. It's far too early for hardcore clubbers. We are greeted by the super-efficient manager and escorted to the VIP area. The entire zone has been allocated to Barney's private party. Everyone who enters the zone will be given a black wristband.

The area looks perfect for a Barney party. Cocktail tables are draped with silver cloths with ice buckets and chilled champagne. The DJ begins his sound check, pumping volume through the entire building.

'Kate.'

I turn to see Kiki, which surprises me, as she's usually fashionably late.

'Hiya.' I pull her towards me. 'You OK?'

'Fine. I see Barney's already performing.' She smiles with pride at our dearest friend, lapping up the attention he's receiving.

'He's been excited all day.'

'I can imagine. Did he like the studio?' Kiki pours some champagne and passes me a glass.

'He loved it. Cheers – here's to Barney, may he be happy in life.'

'Barney.' Kiki salutes the birthday boy, scanning the room. 'I take it I'm the first to arrive.'

'Yes, weirdly, I know how much you love to be on time.'

'Only when it matters. So, who else is coming?' She downs her first glass of bubbly and pours another. Is she numbing her sadness?

I reach across for her hand. 'Don't bullshit me, Marlow. As far as I know, Declan's not coming.'

'Kate, I'm not bothered.' Her eyes meet mine. 'Sure, I liked him, and clearly he liked fucking me – but nothing else.' She downs her second glass.

Oh, crap. 'I knew you bloody liked him. Look, I think he's not ready for a relationship. Even so, I hate seeing you like this – it pisses me off that Declan hurt you, and I told Luke that.'

'What? That's the last thing I want; he thinks he's God's gift to women. Luke had better not bloody say anything.'

This is the first time I've seen Kiki need and want to be with someone for the right reason – her heart.

Within the next half an hour the entire pack arrives. Molly is the first, with her expanding stomach, swollen ankles – and, of course, Danny. Worryingly, she still has quite a few weeks to go – how large is she going to get? Harry and Raymond join our cocktail table, completing our circle. The only one missing is Luke.

By nine thirty the music is pumping and the dance floor is full to capacity. A tug on my arm informs me Barney wants to go downstairs and dance. My night of inflicting pain on my feet is about to commence. Barney drags me to the dance floor, where we find a small space in the centre, surrounded by hot, clammy bodies. Instantly, the music pumps through my veins, encouraging me to gyrate provocatively with Barney. Here comes my alter ego for the evening.

Soon I am overheating and dehydrated. A Barney dance workout is not for the faint-hearted. He asks if I'd like a drink, and I nod eagerly. He takes my hand and leads us to the bar directly in front of the dance floor.

Barney catches the eye of the bartender; I can just about hear him order two bottles of sparkling water. Thank God. I down my drink and instantly feel the coldness enter my body.

'Hey, what's your opinion of the staircase here?' I feel someone breathing on my neck as his words filter through my ear.

I turn to see an unexpected face. 'Mr Bradley Taylor… Are you stalking me?'

'If I said yes, would you run?' He flashes his all-American smile.

'Maybe. What are you doing here? This is not your neck of the woods.'

'My what?' he shouts over the music.

'Sorry, what are you doing here?'

He points to the far corner. 'I went to university with that guy – he now lives in London, not far from here.' His eyes lock on mine. 'And you.'

'My best friend's birthday party is upstairs.' I pull Barney's arm – he's engrossed in conversation with someone to his right. 'Barney, this is Bradley Taylor, the architect working on the hotel in New York for Bagrov and Cooper. Bradley, this is my best friend and the guest of honour, Barney.'

As ever, Barney doesn't disappoint me. Bradley wasn't expecting a kiss on the cheek from the birthday boy. I can't help but snigger. Barney looks at me, noticing how dashing the American is.

'No, he isn't gay!' I laugh, leaving Bradley looking a little confused. He can't be gay. If he's gay, I need a new gaydar…

Bradley shakes his head. 'No, I'm not.'

I lean towards him, as the noise is incredible. 'Just checking. I didn't think you were.'

Barney tugs at my arm. 'I'm going in, babe. You joining me or staying put with Mr Ivy League?'

'You go and I'll join you in a minute.'

Barney disappears into the sea of bodies.

I turn to face Bradley.

'So, Kate Harper, I have another question for you.' This time he is serious. There is sexual tension in the air. Fuck, have I unwittingly caused this?

'Go ahead, Mr Taylor, I'm all yours.' *Shit, don't speak, Kate, for Christ's sake; let's hope that was lost in translation.*

'I like the sound of that.'

Crap!

'If my timing was better, would you have considered going on a date with me?' He moves a stray strand of hair away from my eyes, skimming my cheek with his finger. *Holy shit, please don't touch me.*

'I can't answer that; you know I'm engaged.'

'Kate, hypothetically speaking, if you were single, on the market and available, what would your answer be?'

'Maybe – I don't know. You're a really nice guy, and—'

'Nice!' He looks away.

'Nice is good. I could have called you an arsehole or self-assured.'

'Nice hurts my ego.'

'OK. You're good-looking and you seem like one of the good guys. But you know I'm engaged, so it's irrelevant what I think. Why don't you come upstairs and meet my friends? Luke should be here soon.' I know I can't avoid him because of Bagrov and Cooper, I decide to be polite. Perhaps if he sees me with Luke again he will back off. Besides, Kiki is single and available!

'Deflection. Are you treating this like a business meeting?'

'Oh God, no! I don't do business jargon. Honesty, that's all I know. Follow me.' I turn to leave the tension between us, but he tugs my arm.

I stop. He's directly behind me, and his rough cheek brushes against my face as he leans to my ear.

'Kate, I don't want to make you feel awkward, but there's something about you that I would love to get to know. If timing were on my side, I would sweep you up in my arms and take you to my bed. Honesty – is that what you want to hear?'

No!

'Yes, you are handsome and charismatic, but—'

He places a finger over my lips.

'Timing, Kate, that is all I'm talking about, if things were different. I know you feel the same.'

I fold my arms so he can't touch me. Only one person has the right to do so – although he is missing from the party.

We head towards the VIP area and Bradley gets a wristband. I see the pack standing where I left them.

'Hi, everyone, I would like to introduce you to Bradley Taylor: he's the architect working for Bagrov and Cooper in New York.'

'Hey,' he raises his hand in greeting and leans to my ear. 'I thought perhaps we could call ourselves friends.'

Playfully, I nudge his arm. 'Of course we are. Let me introduce you to Kiki – she's single.' I wave my arm at Kiki, gesturing for her to meet Bradley.

'I'm not really interested in anyone else right now, but thanks for the offer.' Great! Surely Kiki is attractive? I'm engaged.

'Kiki, this is Bradley Taylor – you remember the good-looking architect I was telling you about from New York?' I turn to Bradley. 'This is Kiki, another best friend.'

'Hi,' she says. Is that it? The only time I need rescuing from a male predator and she's off-colour... Bloody peachy.

'Maybe you two should go and get a drink.' I smile, pulling Kiki's arm towards Bradley.

371

'Only if you join us, Kate.' Bradley smirks, clearly playing me.

'Fine.' I head towards the bar with the two singletons who are refusing to play ball. 'What do you want to drink?' I look at both of them.

'Tequila – actually, a bottle and a shot glass. Do you feel like getting pissed, Mr American?' Kiki snaps. Apparently rude and abrupt is on the menu this evening. I can't wait until I catch up with Declan.

'Something's rattled you?' Bradley says to Kiki.

'Men! I think you're all the same.' *Really? Since when do you hate men?*

Jesus, Kiki. 'OK. Tequila it is.' Within minutes the glasses are lined up on the bar. 'Ready, shall we down them in one?'

'Whatever,' Kiki says and downs hers.

Three empty glasses are lined up on the bar. There is an awkward silence.

Kiki takes the bottle and her glass. 'Don't mind me; I'll leave you both to it.' She disappears and returns to the pack. Are you kidding me?

'She's not herself tonight.'

'She's not you, Kate.' He looks at me. I swallow hard.

'Let's get back to the others.' I walk quickly to the table.

I introduce Bradley to Danny, hoping they may have a common interest as Kiki has let me down. Shit, what the hell has Declan done to her?

Silently, I people-watch, until I smell a familiar smell. No need to turn, I shut my eyes and inhale.

'Took you long enough. I was getting worried.'

He moves to my ear. 'You were?'

I turn to see the love of my life, looking shit-hot in black jeans and a slate-grey shirt. I link my arms around his neck. His eyes are almost black; even in the dim lighting of the club I can see how dark they are. Dark and seriously pissed off meets dark and very confused.

'I would like to talk to you in private.'

I nod. 'OK.'

Luke kisses me ferociously, piercing me with his wild passion. As ever I respond; my body would never allow me to question its need for him. He releases me and looks across to the table and the audience we have gained. 'Good evening. I hope you're all enjoying yourselves.' His mouth moves to my ear. 'I see a new face at your table.'

'Bradley – yeah, I bumped into him at the bar downstairs. He's here with some friends who live in London.' Was that convincing?

'Interesting.' Interesting! One very small word leaves a doubt in my mind.

With my hand in his firm grip Luke begins to walk – actually, Luke drags me.

I stop and pull at his arm. 'I can't walk that quickly.' He looks at me, his eyes black. 'What's wrong?'

He pulls me into his arms as though his life depends on it. 'I need you now,' he says in my ear, his words ricocheting to my core.

I take the lead, striding in front of him.

We reach the door to his office, and the keypad. I turn to him.

'Venice,' he says.

The word means so much to us both, but his face remains solemn.

'Really? OK.' I input the date, the very special date that seems to be inscribed in our memories: the date our lives changed forever.

The door opens and I step forward. Within seconds I hear it close and the lock secured. Luke immediately bands his arms around my waist, and his lips head towards my neck, caressing my skin. I tilt my head, enticing him to do more of the same. Luke turns me to face him, sliding his hand up my thigh. I wait for his approval of my stockings. Bingo – he takes a deep breath and closes his eyes.

He lifts me and places me firmly on the edge of his desk. Rough and unwavering is his chosen mode tonight. I'm not complaining, but I am confused.

'Explain yourself, Sutton.'

His eyes meet my mine, while his hands travel up my legs, reaching the apex of my thighs.

'I need you is that not enough?'

'Bullshit. You always need me, but you don't always need me like this.'

His mouth fixes on mine as he links his fingers round my knickers and slides them off. I reach out for his belt and the zip of his jeans, and release his erection.

The touch of his fingers against my clit takes my breath away. I have wanted him since this morning.

'Unzip your dress – I want to suck your tits and make you come.'

'Romantic this evening?'

'Don't push me, Kate, not tonight.'

Not tonight? Why not? I have no time to think, as the sensation of his fingers against my clit triggers a rush of sensation through my core.

I pull my dress above my head, leaving myself almost naked. He slides my strapless bra to my waist and lowers his soft lips to my nipples, moving from one to the other, painfully and deliciously arousing me. His heavy erection lies thick and ready in my hands.

'I need to fuck you.' Tonight is about ownership, pure and simple.

He gently lowers me to the desk, aligning the tip of his hardness to my sex. I turn my head to the computer screen. *What the hell?* Luke impales me at the very same time I see various black-and-white images of Bradley Taylor talking to me, at the bar.

'Luke!' I cry out, shocked at the images and his hardness, which is like a steel rod.

Luke bends over me. Using a mouse he enlarges an image – shit, it's an image of Bradley touching my cheek. I can see how this must appear to Luke.

He's played me. He's fucking me on his desk in direct view of Bradley. I try to regain normality – not an easy task with Luke hitting the spot deep inside and my clit lost in the sensation of a Sutton hand-job.

'Luke, talk to me.' Miraculously, I manage to speak!

'Baby, I have eyes and ears everywhere.'

Wow, he is in full control of the situation. How can he hold off needing to come? My orgasm is building, and I know I can't withstand the sensation for much longer.

'You know I love you.' I pull him towards me, needing his mouth on mine.

'I know.' His free hand moves the mouse again, enlarging an image of my eyes. 'I told you, I can read you. You're mine, baby.'

'Yes – kiss me, I want to come.'

His mouth hits my lips as he continues to work me hard.

I turn my head to breathe. 'Luke…'

My entire body contracts in a wave of orgasm. I lose myself in the sensation. My pulsating clit throbs, with Luke's hand delivering the very last drop of euphoric pleasure. He pumps me with strength and vigour, releasing his anger in the form of hot fluid deep within me. He needed to possess me.

His hips stop moving, but his erection remains hard and deep-rooted inside me. Will there be round two?

I catch my breath. 'How long have you been here? More importantly, how long have you been watching me?'

'Two questions you should not be asking me, Harper.'

'Luke, how long have you been watching me?'

He lowers his head, layering tender kisses across my ribcage.

'I'm serious – you can't secretly watch me. That's messed-up shit, even for you.'

He slides out of me and stands up. Taking my hands, he pulls me upright.

'It's irrelevant how long I have been watching you.'

My hands rest against my hips.

'No, it's not. Don't patronise me, Luke.' He offers me a tissue. I snatch it from his hand.

I move my bra to its original position and collect my knickers from the floor. Luke fixes himself, looking shit-hot.

'I had to deal with some business before I joined you. The security cameras continuously record. I saw you dancing with Barney – very erotically. I assume you know how the remainder of the evening played out.' His unforgiving expression cuts me.

'Erotically? Luke, I was having fun with Barney. Maybe you should try it some time.'

His dark eyes lock to mine – it would seem I have just kicked the hornet's nest.

'Do you think of Bradley Taylor when you think of fun?'

'What! I can't believe you just said that! For Christ's sake, Luke, you know how much I love you. I'll tell you what – why don't I get it tattooed on my forehead, then everyone will know.'

'Don't be petulant.'

'Petulant?' Great, I sound like a bloody parrot. 'Oh my God, you make me want to scream, Luke Sutton.'

'Don't let me stop you, baby.' He smirks, watching me slip my knickers on. 'Seems a shame that you're getting dressed.'

'It's not my fault Bradley's here… And besides I can't change the fact he works for Bagrov and Cooper.' I grab my dress from the floor.

'Kate, the man wants to fuck you. I do know what I'm talking about.' He walks towards the corner of his office and pours two drinks, adding some ice.

'Well, I don't want to shag him. And in future, don't bloody watch me.'

He offers me a tumbler. 'Drink this.'

'I don't want a drink!'

Luke shakes his head, downs his drink, and places both glasses on the desk.

'I can see the way he looks at you. How do I feel about

him touching your face?' He turns away, rubbing his jaw. 'Fucking mad.' He perches on the edge of the desk and pulls me towards him.

'How many times do I need to tell you I love you? Us, this is it.' I look away. 'I'm bloody cross that you sat up here watching me – it's wrong. Besides, he wasn't touching me; he moved my hair.'

Luke's hand travels up my dress, while the other moves to my hair. I sigh and look at the ground.

'I have the means to protect you, and I will.' He places his hand under my chin. 'What did he say to you?' What the hell?

I swallow the truth. 'Nothing, really.'

'Shall I ask him?' His expression makes me believe he will do as he threatens.

I roll my eyes and look away. 'For God's sake, Luke.'

'It's a simple question, Kate.'

'Fine.' My head lowers slightly. 'He asked me, if I wasn't engaged, would I go on a date with him.'

Once again Luke lifts my chin. 'You're mumbling. Did you say date?'

'No, not really. Well, sort of. He asked if I would go out with him if I was single.'

Luke takes my glass and downs the calming, rational thought-provoking fluid – I hope!

'And your answer was?' He places the empty glass on the table next to his. 'Kate, what did you say to him?'

I fold my arms, feeling incredibly exposed through no fault of my own.

'I said he shouldn't ask me questions like that as I'm engaged to you. He wasn't trying to upset me; he did laugh.'

'Laugh – yes, I imagine he would laugh. It was a highly inappropriate question. You might have noticed that I don't find this amusing. I'm fucking pissed off.'

'You know I don't have feelings for him.'

'I know.' He turns the monitor and taps the images. 'You can't lie to me.'

'Or hide, it would seem. You've seriously lost the plot.'

'He will never touch you again – do you understand me?'

'Christ, Luke, he didn't really touch me.'

'Shall I call Maddy to touch me?'

'That was shitty, and you know it. I'm not Maddy, and you can kiss my arse if you think I'm going to stand here and let you fire bullshit at me.'

I move away from him and head towards the door. Agile Luke reaches the door before me.

He moves the hair from my neck and brushes his lips against my skin. 'I was making a point, not a comparison.'

'Don't compare me to her. Or maybe you do. Am I not living up to your expectations?' I shut my eyes and lean my forehead on the door.

'This has nothing to do with expectations. Kate, turn around.'

'No.'

'Kate, turn around… Baby, please.'

Baby. God. He turns me. My eyes are compelled to speak the truth as one tear falls down my cheek.

'Jesus, Kate, you know I love you.' He wipes away my tear.

'Not Maddy,' I whisper.

He bows his head. 'No. I fucked up! I wanted you to know how it feels when someone invades your space.'

'Invades your space? It takes two, Luke, why don't you understand I'm not interested? Bloody hell, we're going to be married soon.'

'That will make me feel secure.'

'Really? I don't think either of us believe that a change of name and a ring on my finger will stop you being irrational – or invading my privacy.'

Luke laughs.

'Yes – that's what you're doing. You have no right to do this.'

'It's for your own protection, baby.'

'Stop treating me like a bloody child.' The atmosphere between us alters.

'I don't want to argue, Kate, but whether you like it or not, Bradley Taylor wants to fuck you. I need to protect what's mine. You will never change my mind on this.'

'Then you need to trust me. I'm not Maddy.' I reach out to touch his face. 'I would die for you but, Luke, you will kill me if you can't control your temper.'

His face softens slightly. Is he listening? 'Jesus, Kate, I would never hurt you.'

'Not physically, but this tonight… Watching me, that hurts. I will never leave you. Christ, you have all of me – never have I felt like this… never. The way you touch me – I can't explain it. Each kiss feels like the first time we touched.'

He rests his forehead on mine and takes my hand, placing it over his heart. The pounding ricochets against my palm. I'm the one thing that scares him.

Tenderly, I kiss his jaw. 'Us, Luke, no one else.'

His breathing hitches. I know the sound and what this

means. My hand slides across his zip. As predicted, he's hard as steel again. I take his hand and guide him to the black leather sofa.

'Sit down.'

Without questioning me, he sits. I unzip my dress and roll my knickers down my thighs. I fall to my knees and undo his trousers, freeing his hot erection. I lower my mouth and take him in.

'Christ, Kate.'

He tastes of sex. My warm mouth works quickly, pumping him hard. He needs no time tonight, as pre-cum hits my tongue quickly.

He pulls my shoulders. 'Kate, sit on me.'

I stand and begin to straddle his lap.

'No baby, turn around.'

I look at him, slightly confused.

He moves to the edge of the sofa, and I straddle him again, this time with my back to his chest. Luke guides my body to the head of his hardness.

'Slowly, baby.'

I gently sink onto Luke's erection. He unclasps my bra and fingers my hardened nipples, which scream for his dexterous touch. The delicious pull in my core sparks the launch of my next orgasm.

'Look forward.'

Bloody hell. There's a huge mirror directly in front of us – answering my question as to why the change of position. Releasing one hand from my nipples, he moves it directly to my clit, rubbing it in circular actions that make me gasp for air.

'This image, baby, this is us.' His voice is low and raspy.

Slowly, I look away. I have never seen us so together and so raw.

'Kate, look at yourself.' His voice is stern.

'Luke, I...'

One hand still rubbing my clit, his free hand moves gently to my face.

'Watch yourself ride me, taking all of me: baby, you own me too.'

I have no words. I just feel confusion and desire.

'No one will ever have you except me.'

Once again I nod. Jesus Christ, how can he speak coherently when all I can do is perform like a bloody nodding dog?

He takes my hand and places it on my clit.

'Touch yourself, baby, I need two hands to take you harder.'

'OK.' Wow – I've managed to say a word...

My hand is as demanding as Luke's hold on my hips. Instantly, my body responds.

'Luke, I'm coming...'

'Look in the mirror – I need to see your face.'

My vision locks on Luke's reflection.

God, I'm on fire. My orgasm explodes and my entire body shakes. My eyes remain fixed on the sight of Luke climaxing: his jaw tightens and his lips slightly part. I'm addicted to sex with him.

He loosens his grip on my hips and leans forward, gently kissing each vertebra.

My body is spent. I lean on Luke's firm thighs and free myself. I slump next to him, feeling emotionally exhausted. He moves the loose hair from my face.

'Only me, baby, please.' There's a vulnerability in his tone.

'I would never leave you. Christ, I need you too much, you're under my skin.'

He takes a large breath and gives a relaxed smile. 'Shall we return to the party?'

I stand up, in desperate need of the bathroom.

'I need to know you're OK – I mean, with Bradley. Please, Luke, no blood-shed.'

'No blood, I promise. However, I do have a proposition for him.'

'Proposition?'

'Dubai. I want to ensure he stays the fuck away from you.'

'What? You've lost me.' I fold my arms.

'Zhan has another project in Colorado. I need a good architect to take over my hotel.'

'So, you thought of Bradley? You have officially gone mad.'

He kisses the tip of my nose. 'Kate, keep your friends close and your enemies closer. By giving him a large pay rise and a challenging project… I hate that he likes you, but I respect his solid reputation.'

'You're basically paying him to stay away from me.'

'Yes.'

We arrive at the VIP area. Luke slips away as I watch him closely. Within ten minutes of circulating he goes in for the kill, selling Bradley a ticket to Dubai. Smiles and handshakes confirm that Bradley accepted the deal; a deal that pleases his new employer more than he realises. I pour myself some champagne, as Bradley and Luke head in my direction.

'Kate, I have to leave – my friends want to head off.'

'It was lovely to see you.' I smile.

He plants a kiss on my cheek.

'You too, Kate. I'll drop by Sutton Global and update you on the Rosewood Ivy.'

'OK. Just call the office and speak to Tanya. I have a couple of wedding dress fittings this week.' Dropping the word 'wedding' is a threat and a promise to both men.

'I have your cell number. I'll call you.' *Great – more ammo for Luke.*

Bradley turns to Luke. 'I'll look forward to receiving the contracts.' He holds his hand out to Luke.

Peace on earth!

17

A tantalising touch wakes me. The warm sensation increases, then slows to a gentle stroke. My eyes open fully. I am in our darkened bedroom. I lift my head.

'If you carry on, I'll come.' I smile at my words and the feeling of Luke's mouth delivering pleasure to my clit far too early.

He lifts his head. 'All part of my plan – I thought I would wake you before I leave in approximately twenty minutes.'

'Shh, please, no more words. Use your mouth wisely, Mr S…' I chuckle.

Luke laughs before he resumes his toe-curling touch with his tongue. I try to hold off, which is pointless. Luke's mouth controls how and when I come.

'Oh God!' I grip the sheet and try to move my legs, but they are pinned to the bed by Luke's strong arms.

His tongue slows with tenderness as the last of my orgasm lingers. He kisses my thighs and moves towards my hipbone, sliding my short silk nightdress up my body. His mouth makes contact with my erect nipples, drawing the peaks between his lips. He continues his journey of discovery until he reaches my face.

'Morning, baby – I couldn't resist.' Tenderly, he kisses my lips, allowing me to taste a very early morning orgasm on his mouth. He pulls away, smiling, before he gets ready to embark on a day of global domination.

'What's the time?'

'Nearly five o'clock – more importantly, it's time for me to have you.' He moves his body between my legs.

'Five o'clock!' I link my hands around his neck.

'We've barely seen each other this week, and I will be home late again.' He runs his nose along mine. 'I apologise for the early morning call. What can I say? I need you.'

'Well, stop talking and take me.'

The head of his hardness makes contact with the edge of my sex. I cup his arse to encourage him. He smiles lovingly, pleased that I'm greedy for him. One thrust from his perfectly toned hips and he is inside me. Our eyes lock: dark and deprived meets dark and fully awake. Our lips meet and at the same time he begins to slowly ride me. He knows I'm a hard and fast girl, early morning or not. I lock my legs around him.

'Luke, harder.'

'I want it to last – any harder and I'll come. This has got to see me through a long day.'

'I want more.'

'Jesus, you're killing me.'

'Well, you woke me. Harder, Luke.'

One hand takes hold of my hip, tilting me, and he thrusts faster, working me into the mattress, hard and fast. My body adjusts to the quickness. I try to muster enough self-control to withstand my climax, but fail.

'Luke…'

'Go, baby, I'm with you.'

Luke gives me my second orgasm at approximately five fifteen. I'm exhausted by the arrival of two orgasms at a ridiculous hour of the day. Luke continues to thrust until he delivers every last drop inside me.

'I'm sorry to fuck and run.' He cheekily kisses me on the lips and releases himself.

'That's fine; I'm fully aware that was a booty call.'

He gets up and laughs. 'Booty call! Point taken. Now go back to sleep.'

My eyes are already closing. Two orgasms is a sedative in itself.

My phone wakes me. I hit snooze again, then roll onto my back and allow my eyes to adjust to the light in the room. I turn my head to Luke's side of the bed. There's a note.

Dear Kate,

The booty call was needed more than you know. It will keep me going – all day.

As I said at five o'clock, sorry – I'll be home late – again.

May your day be trouble-free; I suggest you stay in bed and dream of me.

Yours always,

Luke x

I chuckle at his words. I place the note in the drawer next to my bed, adding it to my growing collection.

Now what to wear for a day in the office? Smart casual, I think. I select black crepe boyfriend trousers rolled up to reveal my ankles, and my black shoe boots, a black lace fitted turtleneck (although a little transparent, it steers away from slutty and remains sophisticated). I pull my hair into a ponytail, and apply my usual makeup, with extra black kohl for added drama.

I grab a thermos mug and fill it with hot coffee.

'Morning, Kate.'

I turn. 'Hiya. Did you get the latest email from Adam? I left it in the usual place.'

'I did…' Rosie touches her lip nervously. 'Do you think he'll definitely come?'

I look across at her. 'What's wrong? Are you worried about Jerry finding out – I mean, not just the emails but about Adam coming over?'

'Yeah. Oh Kate, to have contact with my son again is… I can't tell you how grateful I am for what've you done.'

'Hey, you're his mum, it's the right thing to do. OK, so Jerry is—' Jerry is stubborn and scared, scared that he will have to accept his son is gay. 'Look, for what it's worth, I would do the same.'

She sits on a stool, locking her fingers together.

'He'll go bloody mad. Besides, where will Adam stay? I'll want to see him.' She runs her hand through her unruly strawberry blonde hair.

I sit next to her and take her hand. 'Firstly, we don't know that he's definitely coming, and secondly Adam can stay at my old house with Barney.' I raise my brows at a disconcerting thought: Barney the man slut and a handsome gay houseguest! 'You'll have lots of errands that week, which means you will have to "disappear" a lot.'

'You're right. I just keep thinking, what if Jerry finds out? He'll be so angry.'

'Let's cross that bridge when and if we come to it.' I kiss her cheek. 'I need to go, or Thomas will be in here searching for me. See you later.'

My new office at Sutton Global feels safe: even though Luke can watch my every move, I know it was the right decision. I kick off my shoe boots and slip in my ear buds – playing music in the office breaches the Sutton code of conduct. The coffee table is scattered with gel pens and glitter: is this work? It feels slightly reminiscent of my childhood. I lie on the sofa holding up some completed drawings: Mr Jones's simple designs with the added twist of leather, studs and fabulous fabrics.

I'm lost in the world of fashion and glitter when someone touching my bare foot causes me to scream. I turn to see the culprit, and remove my ear buds.

'Sorry, I did knock.'

Holy shit – what the hell is Bradley Taylor doing in my office?

I give him a friendly smile, and sit up.

'Hi, what are you doing here?'

'Pleased to see you too,' he responds drolly.

I reach across and tap his arm. 'That's not what I meant. I didn't know you were coming here today.'

'Luke needed my contracts before I head back to New York this evening, and I've just had a meeting with the Coopers. I thought I'd bring you up to speed.'

'That's nice for you – feel free to use antibacterial wash.'

'Cat fighting at such an early hour. I agree, Philip Cooper is an acquired taste.' He moves towards the leather wing-back chair.

'Acquired taste!' I shift in my seat and sit cross-legged. 'What can I say? He makes my skin crawl.'

Bradley laughs. 'Don't hold back, Kate.'

'I told you, I'm always honest.' His eyes fix on mine. Shit, I've now given him a reason to return to the evening in question, and his declaration of his feelings for me. I need a diversion. 'Do you like homemade cakes?'

He smirks. 'Actually, I wanted to take you and Luke out to lunch.'

'Oh. Luke isn't here – he has another meeting somewhere, I can't remember where.' Once again he begins to laugh. 'Something I said?'

He sits back in the chair, resting his leg on his knee, running his hand through his mid-length wavy hair. 'The more I'm in your company, the more I understand you.'

'There really isn't a great deal to understand – what you see is what you get.' I gesture from my head to my toes.

'And that's what's so enchanting about you.'

I laugh. 'Enchanting?'

'What I want to say, I can't.' He sighs and rubs his jaw. 'Luke is a lucky man. Jesus, my timing is crap.'

Fuck! I look away.

'Hey. I like what I see, even though I can't touch.' He holds his hands up. 'What are you working on?' He leans towards the coffee table and picks up a drawing.

I breathe a sigh of relief that the subject has changed. 'The Harper Jones fashion line for next year.'

'I don't know a huge amount about fashion, but these look good.'

'Thank you. I'm not sure you can call it work – working with pens.'

'I buy clay in bulk: when I design buildings, I like to sculpt them too.' He places the drawings on the table. 'So, it's just us for lunch.'

'That's fine; I'm sure you have a million things to do.' I begin to clear away my art and crafts.

'No, I just have to be at Heathrow for six o'clock. Kate, I don't bite; we can sit and eat lunch together.'

I look up from the table – you don't bite? Every word he says feels slightly ambiguous. Am I looking for his words to confuse me?

'So that's settled.' He looks at his watch. 'I took the liberty of reserving a table at Gasto's – do you know it?'

I shake my head. Crap, I need to explain this to Luke. *Hey babe, I went to lunch with the man who wants to take me to his bed...*

'If you like Italian food, then you'll love it.'

'OK – my driver can take us.' I stand up and Bradley joins me, almost within kissing distance. The air seems to shimmer with sex – from him. 'I'll just tell Thomas that we need to go.'

Thankfully we arrive at Gasto's relatively quickly. The journey was uncomfortable, as I felt the need to gabble so much that even Thomas looked at me in his rear-view mirror. However, my chattering did keep Bradley silent, and the conversation remained decent.

Having never been to Gasto's before, I had no expectations of it. It's incredibly modern, almost odd. It has small alcoves with bizarre paintings and handmade ceiling lights made from reclaimed metal, making it feel more like an art gallery. Thankfully, we are sitting in the main part, in full view of everyone. On the plus side, the menu choices are divine; the seafood pasta has me drooling.

'What do you think?' Bradley says, dipping bread in oil.

'Different!' I look around the room as Bradley laughs. 'Truthfully? It's a little too weird for me.'

'My friend designed the layout – he's a bit eccentric.'

'That explains quite a lot.' I join him, dipping bread in oil.

'So you like to design?'

'Harper Jones has come about through fate: I worked with Mr Jones, who is responsible for the drawings and an amazing tailor – actually he's the best.' I take a sip of wine, washing away the breadcrumbs and oil from my mouth. 'I came into some money; the rest is history. We've got a long road ahead of us.'

'Determination and believing in your brand is key to success in any business – clothes, buildings, whatever.'

'Maybe. Time will tell. What about you? Are you excited about the job in Dubai?' Are you excited that my future husband wants to exile you to another part of the world? More to the point, has Bradley worked out Luke's devious plan?

'It's an amazing opportunity and I welcome the challenge.'

I nod. I bet he does!

'I did want to see Luke as I have a few ideas – small alterations that may save his wallet.'

'I can call him for you.' Luke will love that I called him, only to hear Bradley's voice, but to mention his name in conversation would seem I'm honouring him.

'No, I'll call him when I get back to New York. Besides, I'm here with a beautiful woman, why would I want to talk to anyone else?'

I roll my eyes. 'Bradley Taylor, you're the biggest flirt.'

'Flirting! Not something I'm normally interested in, but you stir something in me Kate. I told you – in my arms and in my bed… exactly in that order.'

My phone vibrates in my bag. I reach in to find it, only to have missed the call. Caller ID: boss. Has Thomas told him about my lunch date – correction, meeting? I slip my phone in my bag.

After the meal Bradley scrolls through his laptop showing me the developments at the Rosewood Ivy. The transformation from when I saw it all those weeks ago is amazing.

'The staircase looks incredible.' I laugh. The first Harper–Cooper stand-off, and I can imagine that it won't be the last.

'That was a good call, Kate.' Bradley catches the eye of a waiter. 'Can I get the check, please?'

'So this is it – you're going home and then on to a new challenge.'

'I'm sure I'll see you in Dubai; there's a new hotel opening there soon. It won't be long before I get my next Kate Harper fix.' He laughs.

'I'll send you a picture.' He opens his mouth to speak but I place my index finger over his lips. 'I think you've incriminated yourself enough today.'

We head towards the exit. I can see Thomas standing alongside the Bentley. I reach for the door handle, only to feel a yank on my arm; Bradley pulls me into a secluded corner. His hand skims my cheek. Oh, fuck!

'If you ever need anything…'

I frown. What will I need from him? I sense he wants me to need him – period.

'You know I'm getting married, and I love Luke.'

His face drops.

'Please… I feel bad. You're an incredible man, and the woman who captures your heart will be bloody lucky. Maybe, a different time and place we could have had something, but…' I look down. This lunch date – which is clearly not a bloody meeting – is rapidly going tits up.

He pulls me into his arms. I inhale his scent – he doesn't smell like Luke, yet he is just as intoxicating.

He releases me from his hold, and gently kisses my lips. Not with passion, just tenderness.

'Be happy.'

'I'm sorry if I led you on,' I say

'You didn't.' He exhales. 'You're enchanting, Kate Harper.'

He opens the door. To feel the fresh air on my face and the sight of Thomas is a relief.

Bradley walks me to the car.

'I can get Thomas to drop you off at Heathrow.'

'No. I'll get the Tube.' He reaches into his leather satchel and pulls out a manila envelope. 'Contracts for Luke – and my excuse for a visit.' He flashes a cheeky smile. I take the envelope and place it in my bag.

'Until next time.' I reach towards him and plant a kiss

on his cheek – a sign of affection, definitely not an act of transgression.

Bradley opens the car door for me. 'I'll see you soon.'

I slump into my seat. A feeling of self-reproach washes over me. Two men who want something from me, but Luke has me and always will…

Thomas drives the car in the opposite direction to Bradley. I am exhausted after today's mind-blowing events, which began at approximately five o'clock this morning. I take a deep breath and dial Luke's number – thank God it goes to voicemail. A text is the next best thing.

To the love of my life,
I hope your day has been OK, and not too hard.
Should I fear another early morning booty call?
Love you forever, soon-to-be Mrs Luke Sutton ;-)
XX

I hit send, and relax. I feel exonerated by my attempt to make contact. Within seconds my phone vibrates.

Dear Mrs Luke Sutton-to-be,
I have booked a tattooist; I feel the need to exploit your impertinent suggestion you made at Sutton Global – my name on your forehead. Did you enjoy your lunch? I have eyes and ears everywhere, but my hands will be everywhere very soon.
Your not-soon-enough husband-to-be X

Thanks, Thomas. I guess Luke does pay his wages. Crap – double crap – actually, fuck it. I knew he would be pissed off. Maybe his suggestion of lying in bed waiting for him was not such a bad idea!

I decide to return to Sutton Global, as it's only three o'clock. Rather than go home and wait for Mr Moody Bollocks Sutton, I can work on some more designs.

My phone vibrates again. What does he want now? But no – caller ID: Harry.

SOS – PETE'S ASAP XOXO

I stop mid-walk. 'Thomas, there's been a change of plan.'

Within fifteen minutes we draw up outside Pete's. I walk through the door and see Pete at the bar.

'Hello, stranger.' I immediately hug him.

'How are you?' He releases me, wearing the biggest grin on his unshaven face.

'Not bad – I miss you and Fiona like crazy.'

'You can always come back; the stockroom hasn't been the same since you left.'

'I can't tell you how tempting that is.'

'I take it you're here to see the girls.'

'Yeah,' I look across to our usual spot and there they are – my three besties with glum faces. 'First, I need a coffee.'

'I wouldn't bother; Kiki is already downing shots and swearing – a lot.'

'Thanks for the heads-up.' I stroke his arm and walk over to the girls.

'Hi girls.' You could cut the atmosphere with a knife. 'Right,' I sit on an empty stool, 'which one of you is going first?'

'I've had a fucking shit day, Molly's got some pre-thing – I can't remember what it's called – and Harry, well she can tell you.' Kiki passes me a shot glass filled to the rim.

'Molly, are you OK, and the baby?'

'I feel fine, but the midwife was a bit concerned I've got protein in my urine and my blood pressure is higher than normal.'

'So, what does that mean exactly?'

'She's worried about pre-eclampsia.'

'Bloody hell, that can be really dangerous, can't it?' I'm out of my depth.

'Yeah, but…' Molly says.

'No, there is no but, you should be resting. Actually, I'll take you home right now. Have you told Danny?'

'Kate, I'm fine. Besides, I got the SOS text when I left the doctor, and came straight here.'

I reach across for her hand. 'I think you should be at home.'

'I do too.' Harry speaks for the first time.

'Thomas can take you; I'm not arguing with you about this. Please.'

'Honestly, I'm fine,' she protests.

'Molly, she won't give up.' Kiki downs another shot.

'Kate's right, I'll text you later.' Harry places her hand on Molly's back.

'Fine. Make sure you call me.'

'I will,' Harry says.

I help her off the stool and head to the car. I tap on the window, making Thomas jump.

He steps out. 'Is everything all right?'

'Yeah fine, but can you take Molly home please?'

His forehead creases. 'I really can't leave you here.'

'I'll be fine. Besides, I'm not planning on going anywhere.'

'I'll need to check with Mr Sutton.'

'Oh, for Christ's sake, Mr Sutton won't find out! I wouldn't ask if it wasn't serious. Honestly, she needs to rest – please.'

He holds his hands up. 'Fine.'

'Thank you.'

'I don't want to cause trouble in paradise,' Molly says.

My hands move to Molly's hair. 'You know me, trouble finds me like flies to shit… Anyway, Luke's already pissed off with me, so how much worse can it get?'

A thought races through my head – crap, Bradley's contract. 'Thomas, wait here! I have an envelope that Stella needs urgently; you'll have to drop it off after taking Molly home.'

Two special deliveries, and time away from me: I can only imagine the distress this is causing him.

A shot glass sits in front of me; I try to decide which way this afternoon is heading. Down it, or walk away?

'OK, let me have it.' I look at Kiki. 'No prizes for guessing Declan's pissed you off.'

'Fucking arsehole.'

'So what's he done now, other than break your heart?' Kiki glares, but her eyes are transparent; she's hurting.

'Break my heart? I'll break his fucking neck.' She downs another shot. 'I saw him today at the new office block we've just purchased – you know, the one in Shoreditch.'

'Near the bar we like,' I say.

'Yeah. I saw him leaving with his arm around a slut; he was all over her like a fucking rash.'

Harry reaches for Kiki's hand. 'I know it's hard when something is over, but you need to move on. You can't want to kill him every time you see him.'

'Harry's right. I'm the first to admit he's been a real shit-bag towards you – but you have to get over it.'

'It wasn't over two nights ago when he was fucking me,' she spits. She looks away; she hates showing emotion or appearing weak.

'What the hell is wrong with you? For Christ's sake, Kiki, why would you let him back in your bed?' My anger overflows. 'Did you honestly think this would help?' The tequila is at my lips before my mind rejects the notion – down in one.

'Kate, she obviously really likes him; you can't tell her to stay away,' Harry says.

'I can and I will. Now he's just used her again, the bastard. When I get my hands on him, I'll knock him out.'

'I'll tell you what I don't need, and that's your sanctimonious bullshit. Good for you that you've found your controlling soul mate, but I can fuck Declan if I want to… it has fuck all to do with you.' This time there is no need for a shot glass; she tips up the bottle and drinks from it.

'Kiki, stop drinking like that,' Harry says with conviction, and not with her usual tone of empathy.

I stand and move towards Kiki, placing my arm around her shoulders, still feeling a little shocked that she just ripped into me.

'Sleeping with him will just confuse you… I love you so much it kills me to see you lost.'

She is silent. Then, 'Sorry. Fuck this shit, I hate feeling like this.'

Harry reaches across and touches Kiki's arm. 'That's what love does to you; it takes you to places even if you don't want to go.'

I move to the stool, and slide my glass towards my heartbroken BFF.

'OK, it's your turn, Harriet Harper – oops, Leclair. What's wrong?' My glass is replenished with more burning liquid.

'This morning… I decided it was time to ask Dad.'

'Bloody hell.' I down my second shot and slide the glass back to Kiki. 'Why didn't you call me? I would have gone with you for moral support.'

'I needed to speak to him on my own.'

'I get it.' My hand reaches for hers. 'So what's wrong?'

'He's not my dad.' A solitary tear rolls down her cheek.

Not her dad? I don't understand. Ivor was in prison – so who?

I take her in my arms. 'I'm so sorry.'

'Kate, I feel lost,' she sniffles, trying to speak. 'And Dad was really hurt.'

I pull away. 'Hurt?'

'That we thought he'd slept with Katenka behind Mum's back.'

'Oh, crap. I guess he would. I only assumed it was Dad because of Ivor; it made sense.'

'It did to me too. So now I have no parents.'

'What a bloody mess… Did Dad have any ideas?'

'No, he was just in shock that you and I had both assumed it was him – well, since last year.' She downs her shot, as her tears fall again.

'Harry, please don't cry,' I say.

'Susan and Malcolm worship you both,' Kiki says.

'I just feel empty.'

'Look, my dad doesn't want to know me – let's not forget he probably left me for dead, and may have planted a bomb at my house... I think knowing who your biological father is is a little overrated.' Harry releases a very emotional giggle.

Kiki and I both return to our stools.

'Harry, I don't know how to make this better.' I squeeze her fingers, feeling helpless.

'I do; my friend has just started working the door at Vista. Let's get pissed.' Before we have agreed, Kiki's already texting – I'm assuming the friend at the door.

Harry sighs and runs her fingers through her hair. 'What a shit day! I keep thinking this morning I was none the wiser and now my world has been shattered – again... And to think I really hurt Dad.'

'He'll understand. Thank God we never told Mum – Christ, the shit would have hit the fan then. What about Raymond? What did he say?'

Harry looks at her hands, twiddling her fingers. 'I haven't told him; he's super-busy getting a collection ready and he's already up against the clock.'

'Do you want to go home and talk to him?' I ask.

'He's at the studio. I may as well stay with you two, and wallow with a glass of wine in my hand.'

'That's my girl! None of this self-deprecating bullshit; we're made of strong stuff. Now let's go, my driver is outside,' Kiki commands her pack in full Kiki style – she is in princess warrior mode this evening.

As soon as we arrive at the top floor of Vista the noise hits us. Kiki, being the driving force, leads us to an empty table. Harry and I hang back as she pushes her way through the crowds of people. I send a quick text to Thomas: *I'm breathing, and take the night off!* Almost being married to the boss must give me the power!

Kiki weaves her way through the sea of punters with her arms full: one ice bucket, two bottles, and three glasses.

'Looks like we're here for the night.' I remove the ice bucket from her arms and place it on the table.

'That's right: I'm here for one reason only – or maybe two if the mood takes me,' says Kiki.

I look across to her. 'I think you should abstain from shagging... try it.'

She takes a bottle and begins to pour. 'Or I could just get back on the horse.'

'Kiki, I'm serious – a dry spell might do you good.'

Harry takes her glass. 'Cheers, girls, here's to lost parents, shit men, and...' She looks at me, waiting for a reason that I can join their club.

I raise my glass. 'Controlling fiancés and strangers who want to get in your knickers!' The girls stare in disbelief.

'Strangers in your knickers? Kate bloody Harper, you need to explain yourself.' Harry demands.

'Nothing to tell, other than Bradley Taylor has the hots for me. He said he'd "like to carry me to his bed".'

'No bloody way... and when were you going to tell me?' Harry asks.

'He's the guy from Barney's party... Good-looking, if I remember? That night feels a bit sketchy,' says Kiki.

'You were a grumpy bitch that night – so much for my shag monster saving me.'

Kiki pours more bubbles. 'So I can shag blokes when it helps you out, but other than that I'm to keep my chastity belt locked? I suppose you want the bloody key.'

'Too bloody right.' I laugh.

'I take it Luke doesn't know, and I guess the man is still breathing?' Harry says.

'Actually, he does – at SGI he was watching me from his office, that's where all the security cameras record. He saw me dancing with Barney and then talking to Bradley.' I raise my brows, waiting for their response.

'He's seriously fucked up! He can't watch you like that.' Kiki tells me how it is – and I agree.

'Oh, he can, and clearly he does. To be fair, I think he happened to be in his office the moment I started talking to Bradley, so right place, right time, or in my case wrong place, wrong time.' I drink the remainder of my second glass.

'That doesn't explain how Luke knows – shit, did you kiss him?'

'Harry! No I bloody didn't. I told Luke – well, not the part about him wanting to carry me to his bed – I assume Bradley wants to see his next birthday. Anyway, Luke's offered him a job in Dubai finishing off his hotel.' I raise my glass again. 'As I said, here's to a controlling fiancé who will pay huge amounts of money to get other men away from me.'

'Cheers, here's to the fucked-up Sutton boys.' Kiki needs no excuse to feel angry with Declan. Her relationship with Luke is fragile; I must monitor the amount of ammunition I give her.

'Did I mention I had lunch with Bradley today?' I look at my watch. 'He's in the air as we speak, heading back to New York.'

'Do you have a death wish? I assume Luke doesn't know,' Harry says.

'Thomas, the mole, informed Mr Control Freak Sutton – not that he's admitted he knows, merely hinted that payback will be a bitch.'

Kiki tilts her head. 'I can't deny pissing Declan off always ended with a good shag. Come to think of it, I'm sure I did it on purpose.'

Two bottles of Prosecco take us an hour to consume. I barge my way through the crowds to the bar for a refill with Kiki's help, who takes shit from no one. Within fifteen minutes we return to Harry with ice bucket number two, and another two bottles of bubbly.

'You all right, babe?' I plant a tender kiss on her cheek, nearly falling in the process. I can't be drunk!

'I just texted Raymond, warning him I'm getting pissed.'

'I was thinking, let's go shopping tomorrow – Oxford Street, like the good old days, fifty pounds in our pocket and share a lunch? We can stop at Mum and Dad's for a coffee on the way home.'

'Yeah. It would be good to do something, like we used to,' says Harry.

'Definitely.'

My thoughts stop as I hear my phone ringing. I pull it out of my bag. Caller ID: boss. Crap!

'Wish me luck – controlling fiancé on the loose.'

The girls fall about laughing. I try to compose myself. 'Hi.' I shut my eyes to focus.

'Kate.'

'Luke.' I mimic his tone perfectly, which makes me laugh.

'Are you drinking?' Oh, here goes with the unrelenting questioning.

'Just a couple; the girls have had a shit day… How are you?'

'How am I?'

'Is there something wrong with the reception where you are?'

'As ever, the love of my life wants to be the pain in my arse.'

'How so?'

'Explain to me why Thomas is not with you, and I would love to know why you gave him the night off.'

'I asked him to run some errands for me – anyway, we have Kiki's driver.'

'Errands!'

'Yes – e-r-r-a-n-d-s… shall I speak slower for you?'

'Don't fucking push me, Kate.'

I look at the girls; their eyes are glued to me.

'Push you, and how exactly am I pushing you? I am out with my sister and Kiki.'

'That spells trouble.'

'What?' Oh my God, I want to slap him.

'So you're pissed off because I gave Thomas the night off?'

He laughs, with no humour. 'You can add that to the list if you wish.'

'So I have a list for pissing you off? You're unbelievable, do you know that?'

'How was your lunch?'

'Well, I didn't fuck anyone, if that's what you're asking.' There is a stony silence at the end of the phone. I push the receiver closer to my ear – heavy breathing is all I can hear. 'I bet you love having spies watching me. I couldn't get out of it. He wanted to take both of us to lunch – but you weren't there.'

'I'm on my way to get you.'

'For Christ's sake, Luke, I'm not a bloody child.'

'Clearly you like to behave like one.'

'That's because you treat me like one… Loosen the reins, Luke.' A nibbling suspicion causes alarm bells to ring in my head. 'Back up, 007 wannabe, how the hell do you know where I am?'

'I'm on my way – stay where you are.'

'You used my watch.' I begin to pace the area surrounding our table. The girls look on, intrigued.

'I did find you with the help of my security team. This proves that if I could trust you to stay out of trouble, I wouldn't need to search for you.'

'You know that irrational behaviour we've spoken about? It's back like the fucking plague… How about you call me and ask, "Hey, honey, where are you?" That's what normal people do… But I forgot you're not bloody normal.'

I slam the phone on the table.

Harry reaches for my hand. 'Babe, are you OK?'

'Oh my God, I want to murder him! He used my watch to find me. That's some seriously fucked-up behaviour, and now he's coming to get me.'

'He gets worried; the past haunts him.'

'Haunts him! Jesus, Harry, I can't live with him

monitoring my every move.' My blood is boiling hotter than ever. 'I need the toilet.'

'I'll come with you,' Kiki says.

My reflection looks beat; maybe I should be at home, not here, in my fuzzy, inebriated state of mind. I know the backlash will commence the moment Luke arrives – how tempting it is to move to a different location. A Harper–Sutton hide and seek challenge.

Kiki joins me at the sink. 'I guess you love him; there's no way I would put up with his fucked-up behaviour.'

'He drives me insane.'

She holds up my watch. 'So what's this all about?'

I look around the bathroom, checking that we're alone. 'It has a tracking device; that's how Luke found me in Russia. Tied to a chair.'

'Holy fuck!'

I shake my head.

'You've never really spoken about Russia. I didn't want to push you… But tied to a chair – Christ, Kate, who did it?'

'Luke thinks Ivor, but…' I shake my head.

'Is that why he behaves like a controlling lunatic?'

'I would love to say yes, but honestly, Russian ancestors or not, he would be the bloody same.' I sigh, and pull my ponytail tight. 'Not a word to anyone about the watch, not even Declan… Promise me?'

'Not a problem, as I don't want to talk to that fucking loser… I have your back.' She links her arm through mine. Solidarity always wins.

We re-enter the noisy bar and weave our way back. A pull at my arm stops us.

'Kate Harper?'

It's Matthew Williams.

'What a treat, two hot girls, and who are you?' His eyes scan my sexy friend.

'Never mind that – who are you?' Kiki asks.

'A twat.' I lean to Kiki's ear. 'This is the moron who shagged Luke's ex, Maddy, behind his back.'

'Best friends, then!' she says.

'Come on, let's go.' I push Kiki to move, but Matthew is still holding my arm.

'Like I said, I'm still hunting,' Matthew says.

'Don't touch me.' I look at Kiki. 'Move.'

'Kate Harper, you know it's mandatory for me to fuck Luke's fiancées.'

I stop and turn. 'What did you say?'

'Kate, ignore him, come on.'

'No! What did you just say?'

'You know I test out his potential candidates.'

Time seems to slow down. My fist clenches into a tight ball. Without hesitation it shoots out from my body and hits the very surprised Matthew Williams.

'What the fuck?' His words ring in my head, as I begin to return to the here and now.

'Bloody hell, Kate.' Kiki bellows.

I hear the lift ping. My head turns as my eyes meet the glare of a very pissed-off Luke. He heads straight towards me.

'Oh, bollocks! Kiki, we need to get Luke out of here… now!'

'What?'

Too late. Luke is at my side.

Matthew smirks, while rubbing his cheek. 'I hope you're here to control your fiancée; she's just fucking punched me.'

'Luke, let's go.' I place my hands on his chest and try to push him.

'Did he touch you?' His sexy tone is raw.

'No.' I look at his eyes, allowing him to see that I'm fine – pissed off with him, yes, but physically OK.

'Not yet,' Matthew says.

Oh, for Christ's sake. I glare at Matthew. 'You're pathetic. Luke, let's go.' I try to push him again; this time Kiki reads the potential Code Red situation and joins me.

'What did you say?' Holy fuck, how to ruffle Sutton feathers.

'I guess she's not Maddy, but I'll try anything. If it's good enough for you...' Matthew turns to his friends, laughing.

Quickly Luke closes the distance between them. They stand nose to nose. 'If you fucking touch her, I will kill you, make no mistake.'

Bloody hell, this is getting out of control. 'Kiki, grab Harry and our bags – we need to leave.' I turn to Luke and try to pull him away. 'He's not worth it. Don't play into his hands, Luke, please.'

Matthew sniggers. 'The sound of a begging Sutton fiancée.'

Luke grabs Matthew's shirt collar, forcefully backing him to the bar. At least it stops the man from speaking.

'Luke, leave it... Luke.'

From the corner of my eye I watch one of Matthew's friends try to rescue his friend. Agile Luke frees one hand, gripping the other man's wrist and twisting it until I hear something snap, followed by a whimper.

His face returns to Matthew's. 'I repeat, if you touch her, I will kill you with my bare hands.'

Harry and Kiki are at my side. 'I'll get the lift.' Harry feels the need to help. With this display of testosterone, there is nothing we can do to defuse the situation.

I hear the lift ping, and turn to Harry. It's Declan and his friends. What on earth are they doing here? Christ, could today get any more bloody bizarre?

'Luke, let go of him.' Declan pulls at his arms. 'Luke, drop it.'

I turn to Kiki. She looks like a lovesick teenager. She immediately heads towards the lift, fearful that Declan will see how much she needs him.

Luke releases his grip, but not before he taps the side of Matthew's face. 'Remember what I told you – I am a man of my word.'

'Fuck off, Sutton,' Matthew responds hesitantly.

I pull Luke's arm again, and this time his hand slides into mine. Finally he moves towards the lift as Declan follows us.

'Kate, are you OK?' Declan looks at me. 'What happened?'

'Nothing, really. Matthew was talking crap, so I punched him.'

'You did what? Jesus, Kate.' Declan laughs.

'Don't encourage her.' Luke glares at me.

'What! He was bloody rude to me, to us…' I release my hand from his grip and place it on my hips.

'I'm pissed off at you. Do not mistake my tolerance for weakness.'

'You tolerate me? Un-fucking-believable.' I glare at Luke, mainly in shock. 'Thanks for rescuing your brother, Declan. I'm going home.'

I turn to the girls who clearly don't know what to say or where to look.

Declan moves towards us all. 'See you later – oh, and Kate, try not to piss off my brother… Harry, Kiki.'

I follow Harry and a silent Kiki to the lift. Luke presses the button for the ground floor.

'Bye.' I give a small wave to Declan.

I look at Kiki. As the doors close she offers Declan her inner thoughts – using her finger!

The four of us make it out in one piece, although I lost my sanity somewhere today – any number of places could be housing it.

Luke hands over a card for his car.

'Girls, I'll take you home.'

'I'm going out to get hammered.' Kiki leans to me. 'Take care. If you need me give me a call.' She looks at Luke, once again allowing him to see her princess warrior persona.

'Kiki, I think you've had enough alcohol. I'll take you home,' Luke says.

'That bullshit may work with Kate, but not on me, Sutton. So you can take your need for control and shove it up your fucking arse.'

'Kiki!' I move towards her. 'Don't be like this… It's my war, not yours. But Luke is right; I think you should go home.'

'I'm exhausted; I need my husband and my bed.' Harry looks like a deflated child.

'I can party on my own,' Kiki says.

411

Luke's Range Rover pulls up beside us.

'Kiki, please get in,' I plead.

'No.' She begins to walk off down the street.

'Crap. I hate leaving her out alone – maybe I should go with her.'

Luke glares at me. 'Don't even think about it.'

'I'll be safe; you can find me at any time. You can only imagine how comforting that is.' My cutting tone fuels Luke's rage.

Luke holds the door open for me. 'Get in the fucking car, or I will put you in there myself.'

Luke draws the car up at Harry's courtyard, then jumps out and heads for her door. She leans forward and plants a kiss on my cheek.

'See you tomorrow. I'll come to yours around eleven.'

'OK. Love you.'

'You too.' She's gone. I watch Harry open her front door. Raymond has come to meet her. Thank God he's home, I know she's hurting.

After a fairly short drive, Luke and I arrive home. We both remained silent for the entire journey; I have no words for him, or none that he would like to hear. I place my foot on the first step.

'I'm going to bed – alone.' I announce, needing some time alone – maybe we both do.

'As you wish,' he says, not turning his head as he enters his office.

'As you wish,' I childishly mimic.

'Kate, are you mumbling? Please share any delightful thoughts you may have,' he calls from his office.

Delightful thoughts? How about 'shove it up your arse, you controlling lunatic'? I copy Kiki and flip him my middle finger too.

I step in the hot shower and smell Luke's scent. For the first time ever, I can't use it.

After a long shower I feel a bit better, and put on comfy grey leggings and T-shirt. My eyes fall to my tracking device. It feels much later than ten o'clock. I unclasp the watch and leave it on the centre unit in the dressing room – something else to piss off Luke!

My head feels heavy – stress, I think. In need of a drink and some painkillers, I head downstairs. I hear Luke in his office. There's no way I'm speaking to him tonight.

Returning to our room, I sit on the bed, wide awake, my mind going over today's events. Feeling agitated, I head to the second floor – and the spare room.

Making myself comfortable on the bed, I unpack a couple of Ivor's sealed boxes. My phone bleeps. It's Kiki – thank God.

Hi,
I'm home, so you can tell that control freak I can look after myself.
Love you, babe.
XOXO

Clearly, I won't relay the exact message to Luke.

I have laid the box's contents out on the bed. It's mainly photos. This box seems to be more about Ivor and Katenka than me. I have evidence of a happy couple: they look so young, even younger than Luke and me. I touch the photo, skimming my fingers over Katenka's face, knowing I will never touch her skin, or smell her. I flop to the bed as I crumple into an emotional heap, crying for someone I can't have – and another person who wishes to remain absent from my life. The man I do want is downstairs trying to keep me safe. I know he is the love of my life and always will be.

My head turns slightly. I feel myself being lowered onto a pillow, and the security of an arm wrapped around my body. I return to a place of peacefulness as I hear, 'Love you, baby.'

18

I open my eyes and move my tousled hair off my face. Shit! My hand hurts like hell. The events of yesterday come flooding back. I just hope Matthew Williams face is suffering the same pain. My other hand touches my bare wrist. What a night!

I venture downstairs. I jump down the two remaining steps and hear a familiar voice coming from the kitchen. I pick up speed.

'You're a sight for sore eyes.' I run to Max's open arms. 'Kate.'

'I'm glad you're back.' He releases his hold. I recognise the look in his eyes – guilt.

'Kate, I'm—'

'Shh. I get it… Jesus, Max. You can talk to me any time; I'm here for you.' My hands brush against the roughness of his face. 'Maybe warn me next time you want to kick the crap out of someone, though?'

His face softens. 'There won't be a next time, and thanks for the offer.' He returns to the stool. 'Luke tells me that you had your own battle last night.'

I hold my hand out. It does look a little swollen. 'Yes, well, the idiot deserved it – besides, Luke suggested that I learn self-defence.' I walk towards the kettle.

'Not to use without reason.' Luke stands and refills his coffee cup.

I give him a sideways glance. 'OK, so Matthew asking if he could test me out wasn't a good enough motive? Oh yes, I forgot Luke Sutton has his own rules that I'm not privy to.'

'Kate, don't start, I'm not in the mood for it.'

'That makes two of us.'

Max sits awkwardly, caught in the centre of another Harper–Sutton stand-off.

'Luke, I'm going to the larder to get some bread. Feel free to call the security team if I don't resurface within the next five minutes.'

'You're walking on thin ice, Kate.'

I skirt past him. 'Actually, I'm running… keep up.'

Beyond Luke, Rosie appears in the far corner of the kitchen, waving to get my attention. Something's amiss: it's Saturday, and I never see her or Jerry over the weekend.

I walk past Luke and Max, and I can feel Luke's eyes burn into my back.

'What's wrong?'

'Jerry found the emails.'

'Crap!'

'I was reading them yesterday and… Oh, Kate, he's so mad at me. I knew this would happen.'

I pull her into my arms. 'Don't worry, I'll sort it.' I release her shoulders. 'Trust me.'

She nods.

'Where is he?'

'He stormed off into the garden, probably the shed. He always goes there when he's stressed.'

'OK. I'll take some cake for back-up.'

'I don't think either of us can win him over – he knows you helped me because of the email address. Sorry, darling, but I've landed you right in the middle.'

I plant a quick kiss on her cheek. 'Don't be silly. Besides, I would do it again. Maybe something good will come of it, at least he knows now.'

I head to the larder dressed in my garden coat and Hunters. Fruitcake is my weapon to sweeten his pain, and I have a super-strong tea for Jerry in his mug.

'Going somewhere?' Luke asks.

'You could call your security team; they'll be able to tell you.'

'Christ, you two, is this what I've come back to?' Max says.

'For your information, Jerry is pissed off – seems to be a generic feeling in this house today. He found the emails Rosie and I have been sending to Adam.'

Max whistles and raises his brows. Crap – now I'm worried. Perhaps I'll need more than fruitcake.

'Feel free to say "I told you so".' My eyes lock on Luke's, free from fear; bring it on, Sutton.

He raises his hands in the air. Of course he knows he's right; his body language blatantly displays it.

Rosie's prediction was spot-on. I open the door of the shed; Jerry sits slumped in a chair. I place all items on the potting table, while Jerry looks down at his Sudoku book.

'I thought you might be hungry.'

'No,' he answers.

I scrape the spare metal-framed chair across the wooden floor.

Jerry looks up from his book and removes his reading glasses. 'I'm not in the mood, Kate.'

I make myself as comfortable as I can on a chair that looks as though it will collapse with any sudden movement.

'I know you're pissed off, but…'

'You've upset me, flower.' His rich Northern Irish accent cuts me to the core, and tears prick at my eyes. He's heartbroken and I know I'm partly to blame.

'I would never hurt you; you mean the world to me.'

I reach across and take hold of his cold weathered hand.

'You lied to me, flower; you both did.'

'It wasn't really a lie; we just withheld information.' *Jesus H Christ, I sound like a Sutton.* I wonder if Jerry will buy in to my Suttonism.

He raises his brows; clearly I need some practice.

'Honestly, Jerry, this was hard for Rosie and me…'

'Lying comes easy to the both of you. Now, if you don't mind, I would rather be alone.' His eyes remain low, as does his mood.

I swallow my bitter saliva. 'Please, Jerry, don't be like this.'

'Kate, leave me alone.'

Standing from the rickety chair, I move towards the door. I stop and take a deep breath. This was a just cause – pure and simple. I turn.

'Honestly, I'm cross with you.'

His jaw almost hits the floor. 'Kate, I'm warning you.'

'No, you don't get to be the victim here. The day we sent the first email was on Adam's birthday – yes, your son. The word "son" should mean something to you, Jerry. Rosie was devastated that she couldn't speak to Adam on his birthday because of you, her husband, the father of her child. Who gave you the right to dictate to her that she must end all ties with her baby? Not the Jerry I know and love, because he would never be so nasty.'

'You don't understand.'

I move closer to him. 'That's where you're wrong. I've seen what happens when you abandon a child because he's gay.' Jerry glares at me. 'Yes, I said the word gay and you haven't blown up. Your son is gay.'

'Enough.' He stands up directly in front of me.

'Jerry, your son is also caring, handsome and incredibly intelligent. Working in a developing country performing surgery on children – it's a noble thing to do. Being gay is just another word; there's so much more to your baby.'

He rubs his jaw and looks away. 'You don't know how I feel.'

'Of course I don't, but I tell you what I do understand and that's abandonment. My dad has left me, so I know how Adam feels, and I can tell you it hurts like hell.'

'It's not the same, flower.'

My emotions reach my eyes, conveying my most inner thoughts to Jerry.

'Maybe not, but I can only imagine that Adam must be hurting. Being gay is not a choice! Barney has always said that being straight would be far easier than dealing with prejudice.' I turn and move towards the door, having spoken from my heart.

419

'Kate, wait!'

I turn to look at him, my eyes filled with emotion.

'I can't eat all this cake on my own.' He tries to smile; I sense it's forced for my benefit.

I take his hand. 'Small steps, Jerry, that's all. There's not an ounce of hate in your soul.' His thumb rubs against my knuckles.

The garden was bloody cold; luckily, the heat from the kitchen instantly thaws me. Luke is nowhere to be seen. As soon as I walk past the office door, I hear him working. He may drive me mad, but I love him.

The sound of the black door unlocking interrupts my thoughts.

'Hi.' Harry looks at my confused face. 'It's eleven o'clock... and you're not dressed.'

'Crap!'

'You forgot.' Harry moves towards me.

'Sort of... I've had a manic morning.'

Harry smirks.

'Definitely no action... Jerry found out about the emails.'

'Oh, shit.'

'Oh shit, indeed.'

Luke steps out from the office. 'Morning, Harry.'

'Hi Luke, how are you?' She moves towards him and plants a kiss on his cheek, which will be the only Harper affection he'll be receiving.

'How's your head?'

'A mild hangover... Raymond nursed me most of the night.'

'We're going shopping.' I announce, linking my arm through Harry's. 'Come upstairs while I get ready.'

My eyes move away from Luke, not giving him a sideways glance or the time to question me.

I push the bedroom door shut.

'Jesus, Kate! You can cut the tension with a bloody knife. What went down last night?'

'Nothing. That's the problem. Of course I've been dropping hints that his irrational behaviour is out of control, but he's said nothing.'

'He struggles with you. Babe, he has loads of people who hang off his every word, and you don't.'

We move to the bed.

'Harry, you can't defend him, he's lost the plot.'

'That's not what I mean. Look, he's been single for a while and from what you've said, other than one-night stands he wasn't interested. Then comes along the girl next door with shitloads of baggage.'

'That's not my fault.'

'No. But you've shacked up with a guy whose hobby, for want of a better word, was to hunt people and protect people. You've become his hobby! Do you get me?'

I fall back on the bed. 'Not really.'

'He didn't know what he was taking on, but luckily his military background can protect you. Whether you want to accept it or not, his past has saved your future.'

'Ready?' I look at Harry, lying on my bed reading this month's *Vogue*.

'Yeah.' She laughs and assesses my appearance. 'You're as bad as Luke.'

'Never.'

'OK. Don't say I didn't warn you.'

I grab my mobile. 'Let me call Max – I hope he's with me, not the mole.'

'Thomas works for Luke – what did you expect?' Harry chuckles.

'Loyalty to me.'

Max answers instantly. 'Kate.'

'Hi, Harry and I are going shopping – are you working with me now?'

'Yeah. Luke didn't say you were going out.'

'That's because he's only just found out.'

'I'll meet you both out the front.'

'Thank you.'

'Ready, Mrs Leclair?'

We check our reflections in the large French mirror. Harry is smart casual in dark jeans and blazer. I, on the other hand, look fairly smart, in a short black-and-grey shift dress and a black leather biker jacket. Dress to impress, Harper!

Harry and I head to the front door. There's no sign of Luke. I should hunt him down to say goodbye, but I don't want to. I'm still too angry with him.

Outside, the fresh air hits me – and so does the sight of Luke, in jeans and a white T-shirt, leaning casually against my Bentley. God, I hate that he's so bloody good-looking; my heart aches and my clit screams. This is such an unfair battle.

Max holds the car door open. 'Harry,' he says, ensuring she gets in. Max then slides into the driver's seat. Luke and I face each other.

'I believe you have forgotten something.'

'Is that so?' I fold my arms.

He holds up his fingers, allowing my watch to swing from side to side. 'I would hate for you to get lost.'

He takes my wrist. At first I resist, but then crumble with the gentleness of his fingers brushing against my knuckles – he wins.

With my watch returned to its rightful place, his hand moves to my neck, pulling me closer until our lips are within kissing distance. His breath mixes with mine, and we are at one, if for only a few seconds.

'Don't push me, baby. You're my world, do you understand?'

Silently, I nod.

His mouth locks on mine. I pull away. 'I'm so mad at you,' I confess.

'I know.'

His hand moves to my arse, pulling me close as his soft lips claim me again.

'You look far too hot to be leaving this house. Have fun shopping and be safe – what time will you be home?'

'I don't know. We're going to see Mum and Dad. After yesterday, I think we need to show Dad we love him.'

Luke frowns.

'Of course – you don't know what happened. Harry confronted Dad. Apparently he never slept with Katenka; in fact, he was horrified we thought he did.'

'That's why Harry was drunk last night.'

I place my hands on his chest. 'If you'd have let me explain why I was out with the girls, I would have told you, but no, instead you played search and rescue.' He smiles.

'OK, I'll see you later. Wish me luck with Harry – we have fifty pounds each to spend, just like the good old days.' I chuckle; how life has changed.

'The good old days – do you mean before you met me?' Luke opens the car door for me.

'No, the days when we had no money.' I hold my wrist up. 'And of course no tracking devices.'

Our day, which we spent shopping for bargains, proved to be quite fruitful. It was refreshing to be queuing in Primark with several accessories, which cost twenty pounds, but I paid for them using Luke's black credit card with unlimited credit! After Harry's emotional breakdown yesterday I assumed she would be fragile, but she surprised me with her positive outlook. I suppose she can't change her past, so moving forward is her only option.

Later, we arrive at Mum and Dad's. Our timing is perfect as Mum is out shopping. So the three of us sit around the kitchen table. You could cut the tension with a knife. I reach across for Dad's hand, but he sighs and looks away. Clearly, he's hurting from our assumptions.

'Let's make a fresh start.' I break the ice.

Harry looks across at me. 'Good idea.'

'Dad?'

He says nothing.

'We have to start somewhere. Blame me – I told Harry that I thought you slept with Katenka.'

He holds his hands up. 'Kate, I don't want to talk about it.'

'You're hurt, I get it, and I said sorry,' Harry says.

'Girls.' His voice is stern.

'You're mad at us, but what were we to think? The timing added up and Ivor—' Dad's gaze meets mine, shocked at hearing Ivor's name.

'It's not our fault you kept us in the dark about our adoption.'

'Bloody hell, Kate!' Harry says.

'It's true! Christ, Mum dances round the situation like it's never happened, and Dad is… Dad, you look at us like you – hate us.' I have no filter today.

'Jesus, Kate!' Harry moans again.

'I'm fed up with it, Harry. Dad, you lied to us, not the other way round! We're willing to forgive and forget, but you're acting like someone died.'

'That's unfair, Kate! You girls are our world, you know that. I don't like the fact that *he* contacted you.'

'Ivor!' *Say his name, Dad. Christ, you brought up his child.* 'Yes, he did, and now he's gone. Look, the way I see it, we either move on or this will break up our family. '

'Kate is right, Dad.'

He reaches for our hands. 'We let you down.'

'How? You took us in, Dad – you and Mum saved us from God knows what.' I take a breath. 'We need to be able to talk about it, but you walk out of the room when we enter.'

'You do, Dad,' Harry agrees.

He sits back in his chair. 'OK, I hear you.' He sighs deeply. 'Let's start again. Ask me anything about Katenka and I'll answer.'

Harry meets my gaze. I shrug.

'Honestly, I don't know what to ask.' Knowing she may not have committed suicide makes the subject taboo for me. I can't share my thoughts – I don't want to hurt them. I remain silent.

'Me neither; I can't think straight right now.'

He looks at us. 'I see her in both of you.'

'Dad,' Harry whispers. He wipes the single tear rolling down her cheek.

The sound of the door opening and Mum's voice instantly alters the atmosphere in the kitchen. Although our conversation was short, this is the most we have spoken about Ivor and Katenka. It's a start!

At home, I open the black door, Harry close behind me. After yesterday we're both totally drained.

I place my bags on the bottom step and look at Harry. 'Tea?'

'Yeah.' She removes her jacket and discards her shopping bags next to mine.

Walking past the office door I hear Luke's raspy voice, and another I can't place. Harry and I enter the office.

'You have to be kidding me! What the bloody hell are you doing here?'

'Kate, Harry.' Aunt Christina stands awkwardly.

'You haven't answered my question.' I fist my hands on my hips, pissed off that she is here.

'I'll leave.' She looks at Luke. 'Thank you for the tea.'

Behind his desk, Luke stands up. 'No, wait.' He moves towards me. 'Kate, a word in private.'

He pulls my arm and marches me to the kitchen.

'Why did you let her in?'

'Firstly, she rang the gate and wanted to speak to you.' He runs his hand through his hair. 'Secondly, don't behave like this – the one thing you're not is intolerant of others. You, more than anyone, have forgiveness seeping from your pores, a rare quality today. Christ, Kate, you're always telling me to be more friendly with my staff.'

'This is different.' I look down. 'Luke, I can't forgive her. She knew so much about us – and she took money from my father all those years.'

'This isn't like you, Kate.' He moves closer.

'Well, maybe I've changed, grown hardened to people shitting on me.' I close my eyes for a second, feeling confused. 'I want her to leave.'

'No.'

'What do you mean, no? This is my home too, and I want her gone.' My eyes lock to Luke's. 'Fine, I'll tell her myself.'

Luke grabs my arm. 'Don't do this. You're not a bitch and never will be – please don't behave like this. I don't want to see you change into someone you're not.'

I try to shake him off, but his grip prevents me from running. He pulls me to his chest, locking his arms around me.

'Baby, I know she betrayed you.' He lifts my chin to look at him, gently skimming my cheek with his thumb. 'Kate, it's been six months with no contact, and she wants to put right her wrongs. Whether you accept her apology is up to you, but at least give her the chance to explain.' He places his lips tenderly over mine. Just his warm touch seems to thaw the ice covering my heart.

I take in his words. 'I feel so hurt. She knew about Ivor and said nothing.'

'So did your parents.'

'Not like this; they never had any contact with him.'

'Fair point.'

'The photos at his house.' I shut my eyes and place my head on his chest. 'It's bloody crappy, that's what it is. I don't want to deal with this shit any more.' I look at his eyes, needing to absorb his strength.

'Take one day at a time. Today Christina's here, and she needs your forgiveness.'

'Are you trying to make me feel guilty?'

'No – perhaps.' He smiles. 'But I don't want you to regret not making amends. Against my better judgement, I have also given some thought to tracking Ivor.'

My lips instantly find his. 'I love you, Luke Sutton. Even when you drive me mad, I couldn't live without you.'

'Good – I love you too, baby. Ready to make amends?'

'As I'll ever be.'

We return to the office, where Aunt Christina remains in front of Luke's desk. She looks tired and gaunt.

'Ladies, shall we sit?' Luke takes charge of the proceedings. Perhaps he wants to make sure I'll listen to Aunt Christina.

Thankfully Luke sits next to me, and Harry and Christina sit in the two leather armchairs.

'Kate, could I explain?' Christina says.

'OK.' I bite my lower lip – to stop me telling her some home truths.

'I have no excuse, and I would feel the same as you.'

'Good.'

Luke looks at me. I bite harder.

'You're absolutely right, and I wasn't expecting any other response. At first I thought I was helping. But I got worried when Ivor contacted me – he knew about the adoption. He never threatened anyone directly, but I didn't want him to contact either of you girls or, worse, your mum and dad. Part of Katenka's condition was secrecy, but at the time I didn't know why. When Ivor turned up I wondered if she wanted to keep the adoption secret from *him*.'

Harry and I remain mute. Luke takes my hand, encouraging me to listen.

'This is so raw for us both.' I look at Harry and take a deep breath. 'I don't hate *you*. I hate what you did. To see my life on his wall was shocking… it was just wrong.'

'And I'm truly sorry.'

Her sadness is evident. I can only imagine that this day has been hanging over her like a dark cloud. She slips her hand inside her bag and passes me an envelope.

'I managed to gather enough money; the cheque is for the same amount that Ivor paid me over the years. Kate, it was never about the money. I know it's an ugly truth, but when my company was struggling I used it to keep my business going.'

My eyes fall to the envelope. I have no interest in his money and never will. I rip the envelope in half.

'I don't want your money. It was the betrayal of Dad that hurt.'

She reaches across and touches my hand. 'For that I'm sincerely regretful; that's why I didn't come to your wedding, Harry.' She looks across to Harry. 'I know Malcolm was upset with me, but I would never have ruined your day.'

'I told Kate that's what I thought; Dad said you had work commitments.'

'There was some truth in it; I did have a big case.' She stands, looking a little overwhelmed. 'I'd better go. It's getting dark and I have a fair drive ahead of me.'

Crap! The outcome of this reunion falls to me. I stand directly in front of Christina.

'It'll take time for me to accept all that's happened, and I guess you thought you were doing the right thing.'

'Maybe we could all have a family meal here.' Luke offers an idea.

'That would be lovely.' Christina looks at Harry and me. 'When you're both ready.'

Maybe that time will never come.

★★★

My fingers skim the bubbles. I close my eyes to shut out the outside world, exhausted.

'Do you mind if I join you?' My eyes open to the most glorious view – my naked sex god.

I watch Luke step into the bath. He settles himself then takes hold of my feet, massaging them gently. 'Feeling better?'

'Bubbles and you – a winning combination.' My hands rest on Luke's calves.

'I'm pleased to be of service. You've been quiet all evening.'

'Yeah, my head is all over the place, what with you and then that prick Matthew and now today, and bloody Aunt Christina. I'm destined for an early grave! Oh, and let's not forget Jerry, who I betrayed.'

Luke stops. 'You never betrayed him. I get why you did it.'

'Time will tell. It'll kill me if he hates me.'

Luke smirks.

'Don't look like that; it's not the same situation as Aunt Christina. I may as well drown…'

'Share the load, we're in this together.'

'You're the only person I can count on.' My eyes lock to his. 'I need you.'

'You have me.' He smiles, savouring my words.

'No, you misunderstand me. I need you! I wasn't referring to Luke the control freak; I was calling for my sex god.'

He laughs. 'You prefer the sex god to me, your protective boyfriend?'

'Hell, yes!' I giggle.

Within seconds Luke has a towel ready for me. He wraps me in it and carries me to the bed. Strong and seductive is what I need tonight.

Laying me on the mattress, his mouth begins to travel south, where it makes contact with my clit. Sensing my need, he doesn't tease me, and I lose myself to him. My orgasm crashes through me like a tornado. Lost in our private world, I lie and relish my feelings of euphoria, but he's not finished. He's kneeling in front of me, his erection prominent.

'I want you to sit on me, baby.'

I nod. I have no need to speak; too many words have been used over the last twenty-four hours. For once, silence, and Luke telling me what to do, is very welcome.

I straddle him and link my arms around his neck. I slide down on him with ease; after my first orgasm I'm wet and ready for the next one. Instantly my body begins to expand.

'Slowly, baby.'

'OK.' One word whispers from my lips.

Luke guides the rhythm, gripping my hips firmly. Without him asking me to, my hand moves to my clit and my fingers move gently, giving me the last touch of sensation I need to tip me over the edge. His eyes fall to my hand: he's always pleased to watch me masturbate.

'I'm trying not to come.'

'Just go, baby.'

'I can't hold off, Luke – now.' My hips work double time. 'Oh God.' The last wave of my orgasm smashes through my body.

'Harder, baby – fuck, I need you harder.'

I'm spent and have nothing left to give. Luke lowers me to the bed, entering me again, pumping me hard into the mattress. His breathing quickens and he gives me everything he has, leaving every drop of his possession in me.

Afterwards, our bodies become slack. Luke runs his nose along mine and finds my lips, placing gentle kisses on my soft skin. My hands reach for his hair, pulling him to me to deepen our embrace; not sexually, but I need to be close to him. He lies next to me, running his fingers up and down my body.

'I love you,' I say.

'I love you too, baby.'

'We've barely spoken about yesterday.' I roll to my side and meet his eyes.

'You can't go AWOL and expect me to be happy about it, Kate.'

My fingers skim the roughness of his cheeks.

'You should have called me to ask where I was. I would never lie to you... Anyway, I don't want to argue about it. I'm too exhausted.'

'You having lunch with Bradley Taylor made me fucking mad.'

I look at the mattress. Luke pulls my face to look at him.

'But you knew it would, and that's my point – why antagonise me, Kate? I don't play games.'

'I wasn't trying to upset you. I didn't know how to get out of it.' God, he confuses me. I need him to want me like no one else.

'That's bullshit – you say no often enough to me. Does he have an exemption card?'

I frown, knowing he's right. 'I would never hurt you.'

'But you did yesterday.'

'I didn't mean to. Christ, I wouldn't.'

'Bradley Taylor is your Maddy – do you get it now?'

'That's totally different – you were engaged.'

'Relationship aside, we both feel insecure when these names are mentioned.'

Fuck!

'It was just lunch; I have absolutely no feelings for him. Remember, all or nothing.'

'Don't push me again.'

'Luke, you can't tell me who to have lunch with. Besides, he showed me what progress has been made on the hotel in New York, so theoretically it was a working lunch.'

'I told you yesterday, don't mistake my tolerance for weakness. The man wants to fuck you. Baby, you shouldn't lead him on.'

'Luke!'

He arches a brow. Bloody hell, he knows me better than I know myself.

'This is what you do to me.'

He lowers his gaze towards his erection. I giggle at his need for sex, for me, for possession.

'I hope you're ready for round two, baby.'

19

'I don't know what to say.' My eyes meets Mr Jones's eyes in the mirror.

'You look breath-taking, but I knew you would.' His hand rests against my back as we take in the dress. It is made from the most exquisite vintage lace from France. 'Shall we show your family?'

This is the dress I'll wear to say 'I do'. Holy shit, I'm getting married to Luke. For the first time since Sandbanks, it really hits me.

'Let's wait a couple of minutes.' I take hold of Mr Jones' hand. 'I'm lost for words.'

'There's a first time for everything, Miss Harper.' He nudges my arm, trying to lighten the mood.

'Honestly, I love it. OK, I'm ready.'

Mr Jones pulls back the curtain from the large changing area, and I take a step forward. As predicted, Mum squeals when she sees me, but most surprising is Livy's reaction: she shrieks then claps her hands. I look across at Mr Jones; we had predicted a happy reaction, but maybe not one that was quite so loud.

'You look beautiful. Dad's going to crumble – I know he will.' Mum walks round me, admiring every small detail of the dress.

'My darling girl, your mum is right. You look… you look like an angel.' Livy takes my hand. 'Absolutely stunning.'

'How clever is Mr Jones?' I gesture in the direction of the man in question.

'Very clever,' Livy says, swept away by the idea of our wedding and her son taking the role of Prince Charming.

'My pleasure, ladies – she is worth all the hard work. Now, I think a cup of tea is in order.'

Mr Jones disappears, allowing Mum and Livy to examine the dress. The vintage lace is what makes the dress unique, although the design is simple and elegant. It's a strapless dress with a very discreet sweetheart neckline, and extremely fitted, clinging to every curve of my body. From the knee the dress flares into a swirling fishtail design, with a long train.

'I love it – it was just what I wanted. Livy, look at the picture on the cutting table.'

She walks to the table and picks up the picture, comparing it to the real dress.

'It's identical.'

'Do you remember the picture in Luke's office – the charcoal drawing in the silver frame?'

She nods.

'This is the picture – well, a photocopy. It was my favourite from all of Mr Jones's books.'

She takes my hand. 'Thank you for today – I will treasure this moment forever. I can't wait to tell Edward, but I won't tell him what the dress looks like, just that you looked like an angel.'

'Actually, I wanted to ask you a question.' I clear my throat. 'In your wedding picture you were wearing a short lace veil. I asked Luke about it and he said he thought it belonged to his grandmother.' I watch her eyes begin to fill with emotion.

'It did belong to my mother, and hers before that. I believe it was handmade somewhere in Europe.'

'Would I be able to borrow it?'

She takes my hand. 'I would be honoured. My mother adored Luke – she loved all the boys, but I have to admit he was her favourite. I thought it was because he was the first-born, but it was more than that; they had the same independent souls. She would have adored you, and loved how happy you make Luke.'

'Are you trying to make me cry?' I desperately try to hold back my tears. How can fabric evoke such strong emotions?

Later that afternoon Mr Jones and I are alone in the tailor's and return to discussing the serious business of Harper Jones. I'm zipped into another dress that is the polar opposite to my beautiful wedding dress. To say it's a little revealing would be an understatement. It's a floor-length silk black strapless dress, but my arms and neck are covered in fine black chiffon. I turn in the mirror to reveal the back of the dress. Black chiffon covers my exposed back, and stops at the base of my spine. From there, the black silk continues to the floor.

'Do you think it needs a split?'

'It is already rather risqué, Kate.'

'Maybe not; less is more. I love it. It's definitely got the wow factor. What do you think?'

Mr Jones looks at me over his glasses. 'I admit you look incredibly… suggestive!'

I giggle. 'Suggestive? Mr Jones, this dress is a sexy number – say it how it is.'

'Yes, perhaps, but in my day, wearing such an outfit would make you look suggestive – not always a good thing.' He tilts his head. 'However, you look stunning, that we can both agree on.'

With all my dresses hanging in the fitting area, I return to the cutting table.

'What do you think?' I watch his reaction to yet another drawing I have done of an evening dress.

'Hmm. I think you take pleasure in presenting me with challenges. When do you need it?'

'This Saturday. Apparently we're off to Dubai for some new hotel opening; we have to be seen at these functions before Luke's hotel is ready. He told me last night – as usual, last-minute.com. So, I thought it would be another opportunity for a Harper Jones dress.'

He stifles a smile. 'Advertising our brand before we launch our ready-to-wear collection?'

'Exactly! Look, don't worry if it's too much.'

'My wonderful business partner, I would never let you down. Besides, I won't need much fabric!'

'OK, but if the pressure heats up, I have other dresses I can wear, or Valerie can get me something.'

'Leave it with me.'

'Have you thought about Friday – Mrs Gold's ball? I know you said you don't want to go, but you can change your mind…'

Mr Jones reaches across the table and takes my hand.

'Honestly, I do have a prior engagement. Thank you for asking – again.'

'Not a date, I hope?'

'Most certainly not; I'm far too old.'

'You're never too old.' I giggle, not wanting to make him feel awkward. 'Can I ask you about the fabric for my wedding dress – who did you buy it for?'

'No one in particular.'

'Oh... I just assumed it was for a lost love.'

'No lost love, my dear.'

'I suppose I thought you bought it for someone special – a girlfriend.'

He takes a sip of tea.

'As you know I went to France, where I visited many fabric suppliers. In a room full of wool and silks, the vintage lace shone like a star. I haggled for the best price, which happened to be all that remained in my pocket.' He smiles and removes his glasses, rubbing his eyes. 'The memory stayed with me: maybe that makes the fabric special. It reminds me of my youth, and a trip that is close to my heart.'

He looks sad. *Change the subject, Harper!*

'I had a thought about my wedding dress – can you attach a small ribbon at the waist? It may give the dress a better silhouette. What do you think?'

'Hmm, yes, that could work. I'll source some silk ribbons, and let you know.'

'Fab. You know, the super-bitch will be at Mrs Gold's ball? That black dress will put her in her bloody place.'

'Kate Harper – language! Remember, refinement and quality should run through your veins.'

'She hates me.'

'That may be so, but never lower your morals and manners to suit others – one day you may need each other.'

'If hell freezes over.'

'My point is, treat people how you wish to be treated. Never allow someone to alter your mindset by their own immoral behaviour. You have more strength than you realise, so I suggest you call upon it when you are in her company.'

Wow!

Max pulls up alongside Sutton Global, but I remain seated in the back of the Bentley, waiting for Luke. My mind is full of my two dresses, and how excited I feel about the first dress designed and created by Harper Jones. I guess it's a start.

The sound of Luke opening the car door brings me back to the here and now, and makes me smile – for various reasons. He's looking shit-hot, and I love my wedding dress.

He leans forward to kiss me – my thoughts exactly. I lock my arms around his neck, maintaining our connection for as long as possible.

Luke pulls away; his eyes gleam with gratitude. Dark and possessive meets dark and possessed.

'Pleased to see me?'

'Always. I had a fab afternoon. Luke, my dress is so dreamy.'

'Apparently so.'

I look across at him.

'My mum called – actually, she was crying. Apparently you looked like an angel.' He tilts his head. I'm guessing the words 'angel' and 'Kate Harper' do not mix – in his head.

'Yep, that's exactly how your mum described me – an angel.'

Luke takes hold of my hand and kisses my fingers. 'I didn't want to burst her bubble and tell her that you're anything but angelic.'

I tap his arm. 'Harsh words, Sutton.'

He pulls me to his side. 'The truth, Harper. And you asked to borrow my grandmother's veil?'

'It's beautiful, and I wanted to involve your mum as much as mine.'

'Thank you.'

'So, where are we going for dinner.'

'A hotel.'

'OK, so what's the meeting and dinner about?' My hands run up and down his shirt, allowing my fingers to investigate between the buttons. A hint of flesh touches my fingertips. I wish we were going home.

'You met these two men the day you wore my black shirt to work, remember? I'm buying their shipping company.'

I giggle. 'The two Scottish men? They liked my scones.'

'Nearly as much as I appreciated you wearing my shirt.'

'I haven't worn it for a while; it probably needs dusting down.'

His lips rest on my head again. 'Do I have my impertinent fiancée with me, or are you going to behave yourself?'

I look up at him.

'Luke, I'm always good, just don't mess with my halo!'

Within twenty minutes we arrive at the hotel. I step out on to the pavement, and place my hand in Luke's.

He leans to my ear. 'You look hotter than you did this morning.'

'That's because you're hornier than you were this morning! I suspect you've had a long hard day of self-discipline.' I free my hand to give his arse a cheeky squeeze. 'If I may make a suggestion, don't sit too close; you know how bored I get with business jargon.'

We walk through the open doors to the hotel.

'Not tonight – this meeting is far too important for you to tease me.'

'Like I said – boring.'

He stops mid-stride. 'Kate, I'm serious. Don't test me tonight, do you understand?'

I salute Mr Businessman Sutton, and long for Mr Playful Sutton to return.

He frowns at my immaturity. 'Kate.' He takes the lead again and walks on.

'Fine, I'll behave. But I'm no use to you, and clearly may hinder your ability to perform to your usual high standards.'

'I want you here! They're a family-run business and—'

'That's why you want me here – to make yourself look good by showing them your family?'

'Partly.'

'Oh well, in that case I'll try my best.'

'Even you can behave for a few hours.'

'Really? Care to take a wager on that?'

'Yeah – your arse is mine if you fuck with me tonight.'

'OK. Bring it on.'

His smile takes my breath away.

The hotel is incredibly grand. We are escorted by the maître d' to our table, where the two Scottish men are already waiting. They stand.

'Luke, good to see you.' The first man reaches across the table and shakes Luke's hand, followed by the second man.

'Gentlemen, I'm sure you remember my fiancée, Kate Harper.'

'Hello again.' I shake their hands.

'I see you've not brought any cakes with you,' Alistair says in a broad Scottish accent.

'No, sorry! Next time I promise a fruitcake for each of you.' They both seem as I remember, friendly and warm.

We sit and chat. Luke orders wine for the table, and a waiter places menus in front of us.

'We're waiting for Declan,' Luke whispers. 'He'll be running the majority of the business for me.'

I nod. But why is he warning me? I do have a few words to deliver to the Sutton boy in question, but not tonight.

My eyes scan the menu, which has far too many tantalising temptations. The men chat casually about work.

From the corner of my eye, I see Declan appear – and he's not alone! You have to be shitting me! He's turned up with a new woman on his arm – but she's clearly not that new if their body language is anything to go by.

I'm forced to stand as the remainder of the table welcome the new arrivals.

'Good evening, gentlemen, Kate – let me introduce you to Sophie,' Declan says.

Sophie, who the fuck is Sophie? Oh my God, Declan Sutton, I'm going to crawl across the table and knock you on your not-so-sorry arse.

I muster a girlie wave and a hello. My scowling eyes meet his. I hope his eye-reading skills are on point.

Unfortunately, poor innocent Sophie is seated directly opposite me. I call on my inner strength, but it seems to have left the building. Maybe Luke should have taken me home after all.

The waiter takes our order, leaving me some free time to chat.

'So, Sophie tell me about yourself.' My smile is fake and so is my question.

'I live in Chelsea and I'm a model – actually, I've just got back from a shoot in France.' *Of course you're a model, all five foot ten of you!*

'How lovely for you.' I take a sip of wine as Luke squeezes my leg. I'm fully aware of his warning. I will, however, remain obtuse.

'How long have you and Declan been an item?' This I need to hear.

Declan places his arm around Sophie, knowing my question is primarily directed at him.

'You don't have to answer Kate's questions.' He laughs and places a kiss on her cheek. Bastard!

'That's what families do, Declan, we look out for each other.' I offer yet another fake smile.

'I couldn't agree more,' Alistair pipes up.

'I think it's sweet that you have people wanting you to be happy.' Sophie kisses him. Oh my God!

'So how long?' I ask.

'I guess it's been about a month, right, Dec?' Sophie says.

A month! Not a day or an hour, a bloody month! I may be shit at maths, but last week was definitely not a month ago. Dec, what the hell is that all about? I take a deep breath, feeling my pulse quicken and my temper gain some momentum.

'Hmm, Declan has kept you a secret from us, hasn't he, Luke?' I nudge his arm.

'Yes, he has.' Luke leans towards me. 'Play nicely.'

I look at him. 'I always do.' I lean closer. 'Thanks for the heads up, Luke. Tell me, is Sophie another selling ploy?' I fix him with a stare, although it has little power as I try to remain the best fiancée any man could ask for.

My eyes rest on Sophie once again. 'Let me think. I saw you at the end of last week with Kiki, and you never mentioned your little surprise.'

Luke takes my hand and squeezes my fingers, delivering another warning. 'Oh, by the way, Dec! Kiki thanked you for oiling her door last week. It was so good of you to shoot over there and give her a hand.' I look across at Sophie. *He was working her body, not her bloody door. Wake up and run!*

'Declan told me that you and Luke will be getting married soon.'

'Yeah, we are – in Venice. We wanted a small wedding, with just family and close friends. My best friends will be there, Kiki and Molly.'

Declan glares at me at the mention of Kiki's name, yet again. Glare away, Mr Sutton. I may need to remind him that he was in her bed last week, keeping her warm!

'You would love Kiki – she's the life and soul of the party, isn't she, Dec?'

'She sounds great.' Sophie appears to be clueless.

The arrival of our food momentarily defuses my mood.

Starters consumed, my temper back on track, and so too is my need to kick Declan up his sorry arse.

'How long were you in France?' I ask, even though I have no interest in the answer; it's merely my way of causing Declan to squirm – the little shit.

'Only a week. It was a great experience. I had the most amazing photographer.'

'Sounds like a wonderful job. I went to France a couple of times last year – my friend Kiki's dad has a villa there, and of course Luke took me to Paris for my birthday.'

'The City of Love; I told Dec that we should go.'

Shortly the main course arrives, but my appetite has disappeared. However, my alcohol consumption is increasing – the wine is going down well.

Alistair McGowan stands to take a call, and Donald Kennedy moves to the bar. Luke excuses himself too. Perfect timing for me to attack Declan. I stand. 'Declan, can I have a word in private?' I smile sweetly, but I am seriously pissed off.

'We can speak later.' His eyes bore into me.

I don't think so, you little shit.

'It's important that we talk. Sorry, Sophie, we'll only be five minutes; it's a business discussion.'

'Go for it, Dec, but pour me some wine first.' She smiles at me and then gives Declan a kiss. Poor girl, he will dump her by next week – if she's lucky.

He stands and follows me to the entrance of the restaurant. I stop and turn to face him.

'Don't start with me, Kate. Do you know how fucking uncomfortable this meal has been?'

I look around, ensuring we can't be heard or seen. 'You should have thought about that before you brought your new woman with you – sitting her opposite me. For Christ's sake, what is wrong with you?' I point my finger aggressively at him.

'You can't tell me who to shag – you're not my mum. Jesus.'

'But why shag Kiki again last week? You know how she feels about you.' I shake my head at him. 'You don't have a bloody clue, do you? For some stupid reason, she loves you – not that she's told me, but I know she does. Honestly, I can't think why.'

'I'm irresistible… you should know all about the Sutton charm.' He tries to smile, hoping to defuse my mood, but fails.

'It's not funny! She's at home, trying to mend her broken heart. What the hell is wrong with you?'

'I never promised her the world. We had fun, I lost my mojo and moved on.'

'Lost your bloody mojo? You'll lose more than that. I don't understand how you can work your way through women like you do shirts.'

'Kate, I'm not Luke. I don't want to settle down. What can I say? I love women.'

I fold my arms. A precautionary act, as my hands are itching to slap him. 'Too bloody right you're not Luke.'

Declan laughs cynically. 'Kate, you're naive with regards to my brother. Christ, he fucked half of Chelsea before you arrived.'

My face falls. 'What did you say?'

'It's what us Sutton boys do; we like women.'

At that point Luke appears, looking ready to explode.

'What the hell is going on?' His voice is low. 'For Christ's sake, get over your differences and sit at the bloody table. I'm warning you both, do not fuck with this deal. Declan, I don't need to point out to you how important this is.'

'Actually, Declan has just informed me that you've fucked half of Chelsea! What do you say to that? Your brother is a selfish, narcissistic arsehole.'

Luke's stern expression shows his rage. 'Declan… go before I lose it with you.'

'Jesus, Luke, you need to rein your girl in.'

'Watch it! Go – now,' Luke fires.

Declan turns to go, and I shove him. He spins round to look at me.

Luke glares. 'How fucking mature of you. I've had enough of this. You can't control who Declan dates – and let's face it, one-night stands are Kiki's hobby.'

'Looks like you have something in common, then – and for the record your brother is an arse, and so are you, letting him bring someone with him to this bloody meal.'

'For Christ's sake, get over it, Kate, and stop this witch-hunt for Declan. Sophie turning up was a surprise for me too.'

'Ooh, poor little Declan.' I mimic him, backing up Luke's belief that I'm juvenile.

'Enough.' His eyes meet mine.

'Whatever! You always side with Declan, and I'm really impressed to be adding to the notches on your bed post – that really pleases me.'

Without allowing Luke the chance to touch me, I push past him and regain my seat at the table. Refusing to make eye contact with him, I move my chair away from his. Distance is my best form of defence – all three inches.

The four men continue to discuss the McGowan and Kennedy shipping business. From what I can work out, the company is based in Glasgow, but once Luke takes over he wants to expand further south, with a view to going global and adding more branches. I sit in silence and watch Luke work his magic, with Declan as his assistant. They are good; it kills me to say, but Declan does have some of Luke's skill.

We have dessert and coffee with no more arguments. Thankfully, the two businessmen are completely unaware of the battle that has played out.

'So how many daughters do you have?' I make small talk with Donald Kennedy.

'Three, which means three sets of hormones, plus my wife.' He laughs and swirls his glass of brandy.

'How old are they?' I sip my coffee, trying to appear interested, if only for the sake of Luke's business deal.

'Sixteen, nineteen and twenty-one.' He whistles. 'They're good kids, but now we have boyfriends knocking at the door, is it wrong to lock them up?'

'They'll be fine. Besides, there are good men out there – look at Luke and Declan.'

Luke tries to smile.

'I hope your daughters find kind, caring boys like the Sutton brothers; family is so important to us.' I look across to Declan; he makes eye contact with Luke. 'I feel so blessed to be part of their lives, wouldn't you agree, Sophie? I tell you, Donald, I don't think it will be long before Dec settles down, and has a troop of Sutton boys running around.'

Luke places his hand on mine, telling me to shut the fuck up. He should have thought about that earlier. I simply return his hand to his thigh. *Screw you!*

Thankfully the meal is soon over. Luke speaks to McGowan and Kennedy, and I begin to make my way to the foyer. Declan and Sophie walk on ahead, and she stops to face me.

'Kate, it was lovely to meet you – perhaps we can do this again?' She kisses both my cheeks.

'Perhaps.'

'Kate.' Declan leans to me for a kiss.

Kiss my arse, Declan Sutton. I move away.

I notice Max waiting at the revolving door. I head straight towards him, linking my arm through his.

'What's up?' For a man who doesn't like to chat, he can read me well.

'Let's get out of here.'

'Where's Luke?'

'Talking.'

I see Luke walking towards me. Christ, he looks handsome.

I pull Max's arm, encouraging him to move out to the cold air, and straight to the Bentley. I sit in my usual position and wait for Luke's wrath.

He enters the car. My head turns to stare blindly at the darkness outside. I'm exhausted after another evening of unnecessary stress, I close my eyes for a moment of peace.

'Have you got over your tantrum?'

I turn to see Luke.

'No, I haven't.' I return my gaze to the window.

'For some reason, McGowan and Kennedy think you're adorable and honest, with a huge passion for family.'

I stare once again. 'Are you taking the piss?'

He rubs his jaw. 'No; they think I have found myself a strong woman.'

'It took you long enough to work your way round Chelsea to find me.' Again my eyes return to the darkness outside. 'Maybe I should have posted you the bloody shirts.' Oh, how I love to push a Sutton button.

'Clearly you're infuriated with my brother.'

'Well done, Sherlock!'

'Kate, please look at me when I'm speaking to you.'

'Actually, I don't want to. Maybe you should have hung out with your brother tonight – you know, like-minded people together. Oh no, you can't, he's too busy shagging your leftovers.'

'We both have pasts, Kate, and I refuse to indulge you.'

My eyes meet his. 'Indulge me? Sometimes your spoiled Chelsea roots gleam like a bloody shining star. I must pinch myself that I'm so blessed to be with you. You're lucky I haven't fucked half of Chelsea.'

'Watch your mouth.'

'It's OK for Declan to say it, but I can't? There's a surprise!'

'You're impossible when you can't see reason.'

'Then don't talk to me.'

Thankfully the car soon pulls up at the palace. I get out of the car, feeling sick and cross. Needing a drink, I head straight to the kitchen and down a glass of water. I hear Luke but don't turn to look at him. Instead I move swiftly from the kitchen and head towards the staircase.

At the first step I look back. He leans against the kitchen door, watching me. *Crap – don't look at me.* I instantly weaken.

'You've upset me – again. And I mean really upset me.'

He moves slowly towards me. 'You have brought some of this on yourself.'

'No, I haven't, that's unfair. You know I would be the same if it was Declan hurting. I wouldn't let Kiki treat him like shit.'

He reaches out to me. 'It was wrong of Declan to bring Sophie and to use my past to upset you.'

'You didn't stop him – that's what hurts.'

'It won't happen again, that I can promise.'

'So how many women have you fucked? I want a number.'

His lips make contact with my neck. 'No.' The smoothness of his mouth arouses me.

'Shall I give you a number? Shall I tell you how many men have touched me?' My fingers are burning; I'm taking a risk, placing them near the flames of Luke's temper.

'No numbers – do you understand? I can't think about someone touching you where I touch you, someone placing their lips on your naked body.' With one hand at the nape of my neck, his other hand snakes around my waist.

'I hate arguing with you.' I spin around. 'Shitty comments about your past kill me.'

'It's in the past.'

'Luke, it may as well have been yesterday. Just the thought of you with someone else…' I trail off.

He sighs.

'Luke, do you understand what you've done to me?

452

You're under my skin and I can't breathe, which makes me sound like a bloody lunatic.'

'It's the same for me too.'

'This can't be healthy for either of us.'

He takes my face between his hands. 'I can't stop it, Kate, even if I wanted to.'

My lips give him the answer he wants.

20

The sun beams through the cracks in the shutters, making me stir. Luke left early for a meeting in Glasgow with McGowan and Kennedy – who would have thought you could discuss shipping for so long? I roll onto my side and smile when I see a note resting on his pillow.

To the love of my life, Kate,
Leaving you alone and naked in our bed leaves me feeling frustrated. I know today will be a busy day for you and the Harper Jones crew. I have faith in you and your designs. Chase your dreams, baby.
Yours always,
Under your skin, Luke

I spend the entire morning at Jones Tailors. Although Harper Jones will be run from Sutton Global, keeping Mr Jones's business premises, with all his machinery there, is the best temporary option. The first two Harper Jones designs are completed: one dress for this evening and the other for the hotel opening in Dubai tomorrow. With the first two creations under our belt, our dream is rapidly becoming a reality.

Shortly after lunch, Max arrives to take me to Sutton Global, as I plan to spend the remainder of my day designing more dresses.

Stella appears at my door. 'Kate.'

I glance at her friendly face. 'Hi.'

'You have a call on line one. Bagrov and Cooper.'

I swallow. 'OK.'

'They have requested you attend an emergency meeting in their London office – today. I have put them on hold.'

'Why?' I place my scissors and leatherette fabric on the table and move towards her.

'It's Mary on the phone, Philip's PA. She was unsure why, but the meeting is in an hour and you have to attend.'

'Crap!' My stomach flips. Not only do I have to leave my office, but now I have to meet the super-bitch and her slimeball father.

'I know Tanya is on leave today, so do you want me to come with you? I'm sure Luke would rather you didn't go alone.'

'This is ridiculous; I have to stand on my own two feet.' *I call on my inner strength – come on, Katenka, fire me up.* 'I'll be fine; besides, I'll take Max with me.'

'OK.'

Stella disappears, leaving me feeling wretched. I need to conquer my fear of dealing with these two despicable human beings; more importantly, I need to get to grips with Katenka's business.

The hour passed slowly, nearly as slowly as the journey to Bagrov and Cooper's London offices. I think of Luke and how forthright he would be in my position. However, I'm not Luke, and would rather stay here working on Harper Jones designs!

Max and I step out of the lift and come face to face with the large gold B&C sign. My stomach begins to feel as if I'm on a rollercoaster.

I yank Max's arm. 'Give me a minute.' I head towards the bathroom.

Washing my hands, I persuade myself that within half an hour I'll be leaving and returning home to the palace – my safe haven. Thankfully, I dressed well this morning, in navy fitted trousers and a jacket to match, with a tan silk blouse and tan ankle boots.

Max and I are escorted to Philip Cooper's office, not the boardroom. This feels odd.

'Do you want me to come in with you?' Max looks at me.

'No.' I take a deep breath. 'I have to do this.'

He brushes his hand against my cheek. 'I'll be here.'

A woman arrives at my side. 'They're ready for you, Miss Harper.'

'Thank you.' She must be Mary – today I will refer to her as bloody unlucky Mary. She opens the door. I swallow hard and move into the room.

Philip Cooper is seated at his desk, with Alexis in front of the desk, an empty chair next to her, presumably for me.

They watch me walk towards them. Alexis scans me from head to toe.

'Kate, take a seat.' She gestures towards the empty chair.

Nervously I sit.

Philip leans his elbows on the desk, allowing his eyes to bore into me. This heightens my hatred of this evil man.

'I'll cut to the chase.' He glances at me. 'We have the opportunity to purchase a company that will float on the market within,' he looks at his watch, 'an hour.'

'Kate, we need your signature to release additional finance,' Alexis says softly.

'OK.'

Philip passes a dossier to me. Alexis reaches across and opens the file. I feel subdued and out of my depth. I look at the paperwork.

'You need to sign here.' Alexis points to the X.

'What's the money for?' I ask.

'Does it matter?' Philip snaps, clearly loathing my presence and question.

Don't worry, you prick, I'll look for myself. I scan the documents, then turn the page. Holy shit! In bold print, it says: *MCGOWAN & KENNEDY...*

What the hell? Luke is in Scotland sealing a deal with these men. Are they double-crossing him?

Luckily, I work ignorance well. I will have to act obtuse for the next half an hour.

'Who are McGowan and Kennedy?' I look at Alexis, knowing Philip will keep his cards close to his chest.

'A shipping company,' she responds calmly.

'Sign the paperwork, Kate.' Philip leers at me. For a small man, his presence is hugely intimidating.

'No.' I close the dossier and slide it back to him.

'What? You can't say no.' His voice remains calm but the tone he uses shows he's pissed off.

457

'I can, and I have. I just don't feel comfortable releasing that amount of money.'

'Kate, this is how we do business. If you want to be part of the team, you need to listen to us. Do you honestly believe my father and I would make a bad business decision? We never tolerate losing money at Bagrov and Cooper.'

I stand up. 'I'm not signing the paperwork.'

Philip stands and moves towards me.

'I'm not asking you, Kate, I'm *telling* you to sign the paperwork. Do you understand me?'

I fold my arms. For the first time I fear this man. Not only does he make my skin crawl, but I fear him.

'Don't tell me what to do, and you can't make me.'

He moves, closing the icy space between us. 'You will not come in here and refuse what I want. Now sign the fucking paperwork.'

'Daddy!' Alexis stands. 'Let's all calm down.'

I swallow my fear. 'I'm leaving.' My heart beats rapidly against my chest.

'No! Sign it – now.' He takes my wrist and pulls me to the desk.

'Get off me!' His hateful eyes fix on mine.

'Do what I fucking say.' His free arm rises.

Holy shit – what is going on? I freeze.

'Daddy!'

He looks to Alexis and lowers his hand to the nape of my neck, pulling me towards him.

'I don't like to ask twice – now sign the fucking paperwork.'

'Max!' I shout, trying to shake Philip from me. 'Let go of me!'

A second later, the door flies open. Philip releases my wrist the moment he sees Max.

'Kate!' Max looks at me, and then at Philip. He points at him. 'If you ever touch her again, I'll break your fucking legs.'

I walk to Max, and tuck myself behind him.

'Get out of my fucking office before I call security.' Philip glares at us both, small droplets of sweat covering his reddened forehead.

'Kate, you're making a big mistake.' Alexis warns, but for the first time she seems weak. Two revelations from the Coopers today.

'Max, let's go.' I pull at his arm, but he remains stuck to the spot.

'This is not over, Kate! Go, and take your fucking puppet with you!' Philip shouts.

Max shakes his head. 'You don't have a fucking clue.' He grips my hand. 'It's not me you need to fear; when Luke finds out, you'd better watch your back.'

Finally we exit the building. Max stops. 'Look at me – are you OK?'

'No, not really.' I hold out my hand, which is trembling. 'He scared the shit out of me. I think he was going to hit me.' Without hesitation I lean into Max's chest, and his strong arms hold me close. 'I need to call Luke. The money they wanted has something to do with the Scottish company Luke's buying today.' I look up to him. 'I haven't got a bloody clue what's going on.'

'I'll call him.'

We head for the car while Max calls Luke, relaying what just went down.

'He wants to speak to you.' Max hands me his phone.

'Baby, are you OK?'

'I'm fine, a bit shell-shocked but OK. Luke, they wanted me to sign some forms, but Philip wouldn't tell me what they were for, and then I saw the names McGowan and Kennedy – Philip did say he only had an hour until the company was going to float on the market.'

'How dare he fucking touch you!' His tone is raw – matching his temper, no doubt.

'I'm fine, honestly. Max was with me – thank God. What about the company? How can they sell to you and the Coopers?'

Max opens the car door for me to get in.

'Don't worry about it. Where are you?'

'In the car.'

'Go straight home – no arguing, please.'

'He's rattled my cage, Luke. I told you there was something about him I didn't like… God, he makes my skin crawl.'

'I know, baby. Go home and get ready for tonight. I'll make sure Max stays with you.'

'Not in the bath, I hope.' I try to disperse my anxiety with humour.

'Absolutely not!' I can hear him smile.

'What about the shipping company? Just leave it and come home.'

'I will leave soon, but first I need to kick some arse. Give my tux to Thomas; I'll meet you at the ball.'

'OK. I need to pack for Dubai.'

'Good – now let me speak to Max.'

'I love you, Mr S.'

'Back at you, baby.' His words make me smile as I pass the phone to Max.

Max barely speaks, merely listens to whatever request Luke is making. When the call has ended, he begins to drive.

'Kate.' He knows I'm not comfortable with silence.

I turn to look at him, as a solitary tear rolls down my cheek. 'Christ, Max, thank God you were with me.'

'You and Tanya are never to see him alone, do I make myself clear?'

'Crystal.' I reach over and take his hand.

Pulling my robe tightly around my body, I zip the last case and move it to the bedroom, ready for an early departure to Dubai tomorrow.

I need tea and biscuits. Dipping my first biscuit in my tea, my body freezes as I hear the black door open. I slowly move to the hallway.

'Christ, Barney, you scared me.' He walks towards me dressed in his tux and plants a cold kiss on my cheek.

'Sorry, babe.'

'Why are you here?'

'I'm pleased to see you too.'

'I'm all for good time-keeping, but…'

He follows me through to the kitchen. 'Sutton called me; he didn't want you to be on your own. He said something about the Coopers upsetting you.' He walks towards the kettle and begins to make himself a tea. 'To be honest, I'm amazed he asked me – flattered, but shocked.'

That makes two of us.

'So what happened? Luke didn't give me the low-down; he sounded crazy busy.'

'Philip wanted me to sign some paperwork and I wouldn't, so he…' I take a breath. 'If Alexis hadn't stopped him, he would have hit me.'

'Jesus, Kate!'

'Thank God Max was there, and he came rushing in.'

'Cheeky fucker! Did Max lay him out?'

'No. But Luke is pissed off, and the company they wanted the money for is double-crossing Luke.'

Barney whistles. 'Wow, play with fire and you get your fingers burned. You don't want to piss off Sutton.'

'Hurry up, Harper, you're taking forever.'

'Alright – I want you to be surprised. Give me a minute.'

'Yeah, I'll be surprised alright – when you're bloody ready.'

Moving away from the mirror in the dressing room, I finally appear in front of Barney, who's lying on my bed.

'Bloody hell, you look amazing.' He stands up, taking in my appearance. 'Hot to bloody trot… Sutton's going to come in his pants.'

'Barney!' I slap his arm playfully. 'Do you really like it?'

'You know bullshit is not my thing. You look fan-bloody-tastic. I can't believe you designed it.'

'Mr Jones is so clever; he made it from the drawing I gave him.'

'Talented, babe, super-talented.' He pulls me into his arms. 'I'm proud of you, girl.'

I pull away from his grip and hold my hand out. 'Fancy taking me to a ball?'

Of course Max delivers us safely to the door – actually, he even escorts us to the bar. Before leaving he scans the room. I can only assume Russians are not his point of interest this evening; maybe he's looking for short, balding men who make your skin crawl!

With a glass of champagne, the bubbles entering our bloodstream, tonight is now starting to look promising.

'Kate.' I turn to see the super-bitch in all her glory – she looks as stunning as ever.

'Barney, this is Alexis.' I coldly introduce the light in my life to the chill.

'I would say I'm pleased to meet you, but that would be a lie, so I won't,' Barney refuses to be courteous.

'I have nothing to say to you. Your dad is... where shall I start?'

'He shouldn't have touched you, but as a shareholder you have a responsibility to the company. You can't come to meetings and disrupt our plans.' Her eyes look different tonight; I can't explain how or why.

I desperately want to give her a piece of my mind but for Luke's sake my mouth remains shut.

'Kate, I have warned you before not to piss my father off. Getting on the wrong side of him is... lethal.'

'And I've told you I won't be bullied.'

'We run a tight business that involves a lot of money for a considerable amount of people. If you wish to continue at Bagrov and Cooper, then you need to be a team player.' The old Alexis is returning, 'Kate, there is no "I" in team.' She stands strong, defending her slimeball dad – poor deluded woman.

Barney laughs. 'Un-fucking-believable. I tell you what, sweetheart, there is a "U" in fuck you – now I suggest you jog on.' He takes my hand. 'Come on, babe, there's a bad smell under my fucking nose.'

Alexis's face falls. Did she think Barney had perfect etiquette and decorum? Big mistake!

'Kate… Kate, my lovely.'

I turn to see Mrs Gold approaching us, wearing a full-length silver lamé dress.

'Wow, Mrs Gold, you look fab.'

'I have to keep up with you young people.' She pulls me towards her for a double kiss. 'Likewise, you look beautiful.'

'Thank you – this is the first dress made by my new business.'

'How exciting, you must tell me more – but first, who is this handsome chap?'

'Mrs Gold, this is Barney Curtis, my best friend. Barney, this is Mrs Gold, the lady who organised this event.'

Barney takes her hand in a firm grip and gives her a double smacker.

'Pleasure to meet you, Mrs G. Kate is right – you look fan-bloody-tastic.'

Laughter is her only option. Barney evokes the same response from most.

'Kate, I already love him. Mr Curtis, I assume you will be seated with Kate at the noisy table?' She offers me a wink.

'He *is* the noise at the table.'

'There's no point denying it, Mrs G.' Barney holds his hands up in defeat. 'I hope you weren't expecting a quiet night.'

Mrs Gold links her arm through Barney's. 'On the contrary, these events normally bore me to tears. So I am looking forward to an evening of noise and raucous behaviour.'

'You're in luck – the party bus is here, climb aboard.'

Hook, line and sinker, I've sold Barney to the highest bidder.

'Kate, would you mind if I steal Mr Curtis and introduce him to my friends, to inject some life into the proceedings? Are you up for the challenge, Barney?'

'Mrs G, are you asking me to misbehave?'

'Yes.' She reaches across and takes my hand. 'And where's my handsome Luke?'

'He should be here soon. Take Barney, have fun.'

'I'm not leaving you alone. I promised Luke I would stay with you.'

My eyes scan beyond Barney. 'No need – I can see him.'

Barney and Mrs Gold disappear, and my eyes remain locked to Luke. I watch as he scans the sea of guests. Bingo! Dark and protective meets dark and anxious.

His strides are long; I count in my head to ten until he reaches me. I link my arms around his neck. His lips reach mine first. After the day I've had, this is what I need.

He pulls away, searching my eyes.

'I'm fine… In one piece. He only grabbed my arm, and…'

Luke is furious. 'What else?'

'Nothing. Max came in.'

'Never again.'

I place my hands on his cheeks. 'He didn't hurt me, just took me by surprise.'

'He tried to – that's the same in my book. In all my years of business I have never resorted to any form of bodily harm. If you lose, then you lose – a lesson learned. You don't fucking hurt people.'

My hands slip into his. 'Luke, what happened in Scotland?'

'Nothing.'

'Did it get physical?'

'I threatened them, that's all.'

'And Philip Cooper?'

'He is AWOL. And of course he's now not attending tonight.'

'Please don't go after him. I know he's a creep, but this could blow up in our faces… He might call the police, or worse.'

'Worse! He threatened you – it doesn't get any fucking worse.' He kisses me again. 'I've made a decision to buy your share of Bagrov and Cooper. You will never go near him again.'

'Can you do that?'

'My lawyers are already looking into it.'

'Good. I never want to see him again.' I smile. 'You know what this means – you owe me twenty pounds. That was how much I asked for the company at the beginning.'

'I owe you?' One side of his lip curls.

I nod. 'Don't worry if you don't have the money; you can work it off.'

'I'm always happy to work it off, but we do have one small issue to discuss first.'

'Go on.'

'Your dress – well, what there is of it. Stand back and let me look.'

I hold my breath – this could go either way. I hope he likes it.

'I'm impressed. Is this your design?'

'Yep, all mine… and of course Mr Jones brought it to life.'

'You look stunning – well done.'

'You really like it?'

'I do… But I'd like it to be on the floor of our bedroom. Now I have to sit and watch you all evening.'

We are interrupted by one of the organisers, who is taking photos and interviewing people. With his empire, Luke is high on the list. Most surprisingly, the organiser wants to speak to me about Harper Jones and the kind of designs people should expect from us. I am a little overwhelmed and speechless, so Luke entices her with more information on the brand – bloody hell, he's good at this. Words fall from his mouth. God, he could sell ice to Eskimos…

Tonight the entire pack is seated together. Poor Molly looks ready to burst, but Kiki seems to be finally getting over Declan – I hope. Harry chats to Tanya and Maria, and Barney is deep in conversation with Valerie. As everyone is engrossed in table chitchat, I get to chat to my delicious sex god.

Tonight I am grateful that Luke's arm rests against the back of my chair, as I still feel unnerved by Philip's actions.

'Will we get to see your hotel tomorrow?' I lean towards him, inhaling his scent, which is intoxicating and far too exhilarating.

'A brief visit.' His lips work their way from my jaw to my ear, and the roughness of his cheek makes the hairs on the back of my neck stand on end.

I turn to face him. 'So tell me, do you have a plan to work off your debt?'

He frowns mischievously. 'Debt?'

'Yes – twenty pounds.'

'Argh – yes, to be paid in kind.'

'To be paid in full. I warn you, don't go in arrears.' I laugh and run my hand up his thigh. I believe a small amount of teasing is on the menu – who needs dessert with this edible man seated next to me?

Luke takes hold of my wandering hand and gently kisses my fingers, stopping at my engagement ring. His eyes lock to mine. 'I've made an appointment with Asprey for our wedding rings.'

'You did? When?'

'Today.'

'Today? You didn't say you we were going to book an appointment.'

'That's because I only made the decision today.'

'Before or after my visit to Bagrov and Cooper?'

'After.'

'OK. It has nothing to do with you buying my share of the company; being Mrs Sutton would make life easier.'

'I could buy Bagrov and Cooper in a second; this is just about my need to make you my wife.'

'You're my kind of crazy, Luke.'

'Good.' His eyes begin to darken. God, I love it when Mr Frustrated Sutton is with me – welcome!

'Oi, get a room, you two,' Barney says.

I nudge his arm. 'Leave us alone, we haven't seen each other since last night.' I giggle at my incessant need to be with Luke, any way I can get him.

Luke stands up from the table. 'I'll be back in a moment.'

'Where are you going?'

He taps his nose.

Silence falls when dessert is presented – lemon soufflé.

'Where's lover boy?' Barney asks.

'I have no idea. You don't think he's gone to find Alexis, do you? He's pissed off with the Coopers.'

'They deserve it,' Barney says.

'Maybe.'

I smell the Sutton scent before I even get a chance to turn around. Luke is at my side, holding his hand out.

'You've lost me… are we going somewhere?' I place my hand in his palm, feeling slightly confused.

'You may need your bag.'

'Why?' I collect my simple black Chanel bag from the table.

'Do I need to give you a reason?' He smiles.

'Yes.' I giggle, reading his eyes. 'Mr S, you're up to no good. What's going on?'

He looks at his watch. 'We have fifty minutes – actually, make it forty-nine and ticking before people will notice – so move your delectable arse.'

Barney stands to join us, stretching after the generous meal. He's eaten half of mine too.

'Off somewhere?'

'I don't know – are we going somewhere?' I look at Luke, still searching for an answer.

'Yes. Apparently you can book rooms by the hour.' His eyes are scorching, a personal invite for my libido to cartwheel.

'Oh my God, have you booked a room for a booty call? Luke!' What the hell!

'Bloody hell, Sutton, you're on form tonight.' Barney almost gives Luke a high five.

469

'Luke, I can't believe you would book a room for an hour – no, sorry, fifty minutes. Actually, it's probably forty-eight minutes.'

'We have a suite that cost three thousand pounds – that was all they had. Speeches start promptly in forty-eight minutes, now move.'

'Jesus H Christ, three grand? Bloody hell, Sutton, I normally get a toilet cubicle – they're free, mate... Not very stylish, but free.'

Luke almost drags me across the ballroom. I spot Alexis seated in the far corner. Luke also turns his head in her direction.

'Luke.' We stop – no, that's not strictly true. Someone stops us, giving no thought or consideration to our needs.

'Jack, how are you?' Luke shakes the man's hand.

'Very well, and yourself?'

'Good, thanks Jack. This is my fiancée, Kate Harper.'

'Pleased to meet you,' I say.

He leans to my cheek. 'Edward speaks very highly of you, Kate.'

'Oh, thank you. I don't mean to be rude, but we have...' I look at my watch, 'to be somewhere urgently.'

'Of course, don't let me stop you.'

'Jack, I will catch up with you shortly,' Luke says over his shoulder as I yank his arm to move.

'Do you know where we're going?'

'Top floor.' He gives me his best 'fuck me now' smile.

'A room with a view.' Of course it is. Mr 'I Only Buy The Best View' Sutton would book the top floor for a booty call.

The lift doors slide open and we race to the door of the suite. Luke opens the door with urgency. I walk in ahead of him. As expected, the room is stunning. Shame we won't enjoy it for long. I follow him towards the bedroom. He removes his jacket and sits in a large armchair, his eyes focused on me: not undressing me, merely watching me.

'Strip… slowly.'

'What? Are you feeling frustrated?'

'Yes, turned on and fucking horny. Now strip – slowly.'

'Yes, sir.'

First I undo the button at my neck and then the delicate buttons at each cuff, then the zip is all that remains. I slide it down my arms and the dress falls directly to the floor.

'Fuck… You've been naked all this time.'

I nod suggestively and move towards him. My eyes lock to his and then move slowly towards his bulge, which has ripened beautifully.

'Stop. Touch yourself.'

Anything for you. My confidence has risen to another level, as my hand wanders effortlessly between my legs. Taking a deep breath I absorb the sensation.

'Does it feel good?'

I nod.

'Tell me.'

'Yes,' I whisper.

'You look so fucking sexy, I could come right now.'

He undoes his zip and releases his erection. Oh God, this alone will tip me over the edge.

'Jesus, baby, I'm so hard. Are you wet yet?'

I nod. *Fuck this, I need him.*

I drop to my knees in front of him and watch his hand slide up and down his thick, heavy erection.

'Let me take over.' I lick my lips and gently take him into my mouth, holding him firmly between my lips.

'Argh… Jesus, Kate.'

His hands move to the side of my head, holding me there, while his hips move in time with my rhythm. After just a few minutes of intense pressure from my mouth, his breathing alters: he breathes more shallowly, and makes small noises in his throat.

'Baby, slow down.'

Gradually, I reduce the speed and pressure, leisurely licking the full length of his shaft and paying special attention to his crown, only to resume sucking him faster again.

'Kate, no. I want to fuck you, not your mouth,' he hisses. Whatever! I can taste pre-cum, and I know he's ready. 'Keep going, baby, harder.' His hips rise to my touch, pushing his erection further into my mouth, almost gagging me.

He comes hard and fast. I swallow quickly and then release him. From my position on my knees, I look up at his face and move towards him. He grabs my breasts.

'I wanted to fuck you, not your mouth.'

'You must have left your self-control downstairs.' I can't help but chuckle.

'You know we don't have time for round two.'

'Please tell me that's the first time you've paid three thousand pounds for a blow-job.'

'Yes.' He suppresses a smile and stands up, adjusting himself. 'Lie on the bed and spread your legs.'

I look at my watch. 'We don't have time… you can pay me back later.'

'Lie on the bed. I'm not asking you, Kate; I'm telling you.'

Giving me no time to think, Luke guides me to the edge of the bed, and lies me on the mattress.

He sinks to his knees and begins to devour my clit in firm circular movements. My body is already climbing, and he knows it.

'Luke, keep going – I'm coming.' My hands move to his hair as my hips begin to sway. My orgasm slowly begins to subside, but as I open my eyes I see Luke has begun to undo his trousers.

'We'll be late.'

'Jesus, Kate, this is what you do to me.' He looks down at his erection. 'Don't worry; this will be quick.'

I nod. He pushes me further up the bed and rests between my thighs; his entry is quick. I lock my legs tightly around him as he begins to work me.

'Fuck it.' He pulls out. 'On your knees.'

'Luke!'

'Now.'

I move to my knees and rest my elbows on the mattress.

'I want to touch you everywhere.'

'Everywhere?'

'Yes.' His fingers slip inside my sex before sliding to the entrance of my arse.

Giving me no time to question him, he thrusts hard into me, burying himself deep inside me. *Oh God, I have him again.*

'Jesus, you are so fucking wet. This gets me every time.'

One hand moves to my clit as the other glides across the entrance of my arse.

'I love you,' he says as his thumb slides into my arse. This is enough to make me come. 'Give it to me, Kate. Fuck, your body is on fire tonight.'

True to his word, he is touching me everywhere. He works me hard, too hard for me to hold off my orgasm.

'Luke… Fuck!'

'I know, baby… I'm coming with you.'

A few minutes later, we stand in the lift wearing identical 'just fucked' expressions. We enter the ballroom, which is silent except for one person speaking on behalf of the charity for Alzheimer's. Luke grips my hand and confidently guides us to our table.

He remains close to me, his arm resting against the back of my chair. I refrain from looking around the auditorium in case people are watching us, knowing why we're late.

Barney leans to my ear. 'You might need to switch to digital, babe. I think you'll find you were fifty-five minutes.'

I look at him, trying to stifle a giggle.

'Not that I was timing you!'

We laugh quietly.

21

Luke! Please let him be alive. I gasp for air and bang my fist against his chest. I look across to Jerry, who is trying to help Max. Panic-stricken tears fall from my eyes. God help them…

My eyes open wide. I wipe my tears away. I've just had another nightmare. My hand moves to Luke's side of the bed, but feels only an empty space. I panic. Scrambling free of the sheets, I head for the stairs.

'Luke! Luke!'

As my foot reaches the last step, he appears from the office.

'Kate!'

'Thank God.' I run to his arms. This is what I need: him, safe and alive. Within a couple of seconds my breathing is calming.

'Shh, it's OK.' He pulls away and looks at my face. 'Nightmare?'

'Yeah… It took me by surprise.'

He lowers his lips and tenderly kisses me. 'Yesterday

probably triggered it. Being afraid can sometimes reignite old memories.'

'Maybe. I don't want to think about the Coopers or the explosion.' I look at my watch – it's four o'clock in the morning. 'What time are we leaving?'

'In half an hour. I was going to wake you.'

I yawn. I didn't get to bed until one.

'Did you actually sleep?'

Luke begins to return to his office. 'A little.'

'That means no. You worry me; you'll burn yourself out.' I walk towards his desk. 'What are you working on?'

'Contracts.' A one-word response means he's concealing information.

'Contracts – what sort of contracts?'

He looks up to me. 'Your contract with Bagrov and Cooper. I told you I don't want you returning there. I need to research the clauses.'

'Good. I never want to go back. I thought you said your lawyers are looking into it.'

'They are, but I never go into a situation blind.' He sits back in his chair, rubbing his jaw. 'Before Max saved me from beating the crap out of Anderson, I had just sat my A levels, one of which was law. I was considering becoming a lawyer.'

'Christ. Luke, is there anything you don't bloody know?'

'Many things – that's why I need you.' He catches my eyes.

I'll never be able to compete with him. 'Tea?'

'Please.'

'Would you like anything to eat?'

'No, we can eat at Heathrow airport.'

'Heathrow?'

'Yes.'

'No private jet?'

'Virgin Airlines today.'

'I bet it's first class,' I mutter under my breath as I walk away.

'Yes, it is,' Luke bellows.

Having slept for most of the flight to Dubai, I feel a little more awake when we land. The moment we step out of the airport the heat hits me. Wow – it's intense. Luke guides us towards a waiting limousine, and our luggage follows. The minute I slide in the car I am grateful for the air con. All around us is a concrete landscape.

'What do you think of Dubai?' he asks.

'Everywhere looks so new. Christ, Luke, did you just wake up one day and think, "Hey, I'm bored, I'll build a hotel"?'

'Why not? The world is too big to stick with one project.'

'I know, but you were buying a shipping company yesterday and now we're visiting your hotel.'

'I still want a shipping company – just not them. Kate, how I look at business is simple. If I have a hotel, perhaps I will need to ship things here. I will also need the very best in advertising, security, etc.—'

'SGI Security? You're a shrewd operator, Mr Sutton.'

'Essentially, they all belong to me, so one business can help sustain the others.'

'I guess. So, the hotel we're staying at belongs to who?' Luke hasn't mentioned any names, or perhaps I don't remember.

'A man called Tim Reynolds; he owns a chain of hotels around the world.'

'So, is this Tim guy a friend of yours?'

'Acquaintance.' Luke looks ahead. 'We're here.'

The hotel, Aurora Sands, is stunning. To think that Luke is building a hotel not far from here… is madness. I have never given it much thought until now. My fiancé is building a bloody hotel!

Luke heads for reception, while I soak up the stunning entrance. The floor-to-ceiling windows overlook beautiful botanical gardens and a tropical pool area, which has a waterfall. I am acclimatising to the heat, which feels wonderful: what a way to beat a cold dreary day in London!

I feel him behind me. 'They've done a good job here.'

'It looks amazing.' I turn to face him. 'But I think yours will impress me more. Come to think of it, what are you going to call it?'

'What do you think we should call it?'

'Hmm… Sutton Global or SGI.'

'Maybe. Let's go, the car is waiting to take us to our hotel.'

'Our hotel? Your hotel.'

'Ours very soon – which reminds me: I want to discuss our wedding.'

'OK. Are we really going to book it?'

He takes my hand as we begin to walk towards the car.

'You said Venice, I assume that's what you want?'

'As long as it's doable. I want everyone there – family, friends, Stella, Jerry, even Fiona and Pete.'

'Hotel Cipriani should be doable,' he smiles. 'Where it started.'

We arrive at the new Sutton venture, which is currently an expanse of waste ground surrounded by wire fencing. Two large gates open as we enter the site, and I can see that the main building is complete, and various large stone buildings on either side are half-built. It looks as though it will be huge.

I turn to watch Luke's face as we drive towards one of his dreams. God, he just looks alive, I can almost hear his brain whirring, making notes and planning.

The car stops outside the largest building. Presumably it will be the entrance: it has huge stone pillars linked by intricate stonework. It looks like a Roman atrium, smart and simple.

Luke steps out of the car, holding out his hand for me. I join him.

'What do you think?' He turns to look at me.

'I don't know what to say. It's going to be amazing. I'm lost for words.'

Then my thoughts freeze as I spot Bradley Taylor moving towards us carrying two yellow hard hats.

'Welcome to Sutton Global Palace.'

I gaze at Luke. 'Palace!' I laugh.

'I stole your word, baby.'

'Kate, how are you?' Bradley places a kiss on my cheek.

I look across to Luke; he seems unruffled. I guess it was a friendly 'hello', not 'hello, here is the key to my room'.

'I'm good, thanks. Are you settling in?'

'It's been a busy first week.'

'I can imagine. It looks amazing – honestly, I'm so impressed.'

'The stonework fits well, better than we thought.' Luke examines the entrance more closely.

'I won't lie, it was a hell of a day…' Bradley moves towards Luke, concentrating on talking business. 'The extra steel has made a huge difference: now we've decided to go up, we had no choice.'

'Good. I researched what we spoke about; you were right to act now.'

'It'll cost more, but the extra space you gain will be worth it. OK – you'll both need one of these.' He passes us hard hats. 'Shall we get a cold drink before we start the tour? It's definitely hotter than yesterday – at least forty degrees.' Bradley removes his hat, wiping the perspiration from his forehead.

We move from the intense heat and enter the building. My eyes soak up every detail; although no interior work has been carried out yet, I can picture what the end result may look like. Staircases and ceiling structures are in place, with numerous glaziers working on fixing huge glass panels. We stand in what will be the reception area, which is already taking shape. Scaffolding surrounds the domed roof, and men are working on a mosaic ceiling. The backdrop is purely glass, with what looks like platforms leading to other areas. I assume a garden and swimming area will be designed later. It's my first view of Sutton Global Palace and, from what I can see, the hotel will be worth the wait.

After two hours of touring the site, the heat is almost unbearable. I have blisters on my feet thanks to my bad choice of footwear. I'm rapidly wilting. Bradley leaves us alone.

'I wanted to show you this area myself.'

'OK.' We stand at another entrance. Beyond this point is wasteland.

Luke points to a diagram stuck to the wall. 'This is ours.'

'What do you mean?'

He guides me closer to the drawing. 'This will be our apartment.'

'What?'

'Look closely.' He points to the blueprint. 'Four bedrooms, a couple of living areas and a kitchen.' Luke gives his captivating Sutton smile. 'We can come and go as we please. It will be attached to the hotel, so we can use the facilities, but sealed off from the hotel guests.'

'It looks incredible.' I scan the drawing. 'You've given this some serious thought.' He looks at me. 'As you do everything.'

He plants a kiss on my lips. 'Bet your arse I do.' He looks at his watch. 'We need to leave.'

I lock my arms around his neck. 'Luke Sutton, you bowl me over.' I kiss the man of my dreams – who is standing inside his dream.

Out on the terrace I lie on a sunbed, a slice of pizza in one hand, a glass of bubbly in the other, looking at the best view in the world – my sex god. I close my eyes. Does life get much better than this?

'What are you working on?' I look across to Luke, seated at the table under a parasol.

'Steel work for Bradley.'

'Are you going back there?'

'Tomorrow morning.'

'Oh.' I lick my fingers clean of tomato sauce. 'What time do we need to head downstairs?'

'Eight o'clock.' Luke's eyes remain on the drawings scattered across the table.

I gaze at my watch. Five o'clock – hmm, I need to be ready for eight. This gives me enough time to entertain myself – and Luke is my chosen toy.

I stand up from the sunbed, placing my empty plate and glass on the tray.

'I think you've worked long enough.'

No response.

'Luke!'

Blankly, he glances at me.

'I think you've worked long enough.'

He tilts his head. 'Is that right?'

'Yes.' Triangle bikini tops and tied bottoms are great for taking off quickly, and also a clear winner for attracting my sex god. As both items meet the ground, I move slowly towards him.

'Are you bored?' He smiles provocatively.

'Have you finished working yet?' I kiss him fiercely, allowing my tongue to invite him to join me in playtime.

He pulls away. 'What do you have in mind?'

'What do you want? Of course, if you're busy I can please myself.'

How to evoke the best Sutton smile in the world – just a few words, and he delivers.

'You now have my undivided attention, baby.'

★★★

482

'What?' I ask, leaning against the wall of the lift.

Luke's eyes continue to drink in my new Harper Jones dress.

'You look beautiful. Jesus, Kate!' He takes my hand to press against the bulge pushing against his zip. 'This is what your dress has done to me.'

Thank God the lift is empty.

My hands slide down the lapels of his black jacket. 'Good. I love that you want me.' I move towards him and kiss his lips erotically slowly.

The lift doors open to a room that is filled to capacity. Luke takes my hand and begins to weave us through the crowds.

We make our way to the ballroom. After several glasses of champagne, I need to find the bathroom. I leave Luke chatting.

Drying my hands, I move towards the full-length mirror to check my dress is holding up to this prestigious occasion: it's our first invite to a hotel opening, and I assume it will be the first of many. Originally I designed the dress in black, but changed my mind and went for white. It's a stunning white silk full-length gown with a floor-to-thigh split at each leg. The dress rests straight across the tops of my breasts and is held up with spaghetti straps that cross over and sit neatly at the base of my spine.

I return to the ballroom, which is full of businesspeople. I scan around for Luke. He's nowhere to be seen. Oh well, the bar looks lonely! I lean against the counter and sip champagne.

'I was hoping to find you here.' I hear a familiar voice and turn around. 'And you're alone – that's a bonus.'

'How are you, Charles?'

'Bearing up under the strain; I had to cut short my trip to St Bart's. But I guess it's warm here too.' He catches the barman's eye.

'My heart bleeds for you.' I chuckle. 'I didn't know you were into this line of work.'

He laughs. 'Kate, as you know I'm not into any line of work.'

'Oh yes, lazy bastard syndrome. You might want to take something for that – it's called a job.'

He takes my hand and squeezes it. 'How bizarre, I do believe I have missed you.'

'Bloody bizarre!' For some reason, I like him.

'I heard you were attending, so where is Luke?'

My eyes move around the room. 'I have no idea. He's here somewhere. I'm sure he'll find me – he usually does.'

'He seems to be in control of you – or he thinks he is.' He taps his temple. 'You are quite cunning. Luke thinks he controls you.' He shakes his head and laughs. 'It's you with your finger on the pulse – his pulse.'

'You think?'

'The woman on a man's arm speaks volumes about his choices in life, in business and otherwise.'

'You think I make Luke look good? Come on, you've seen him. I know you swing both ways – you must fancy the pants off him.'

'Well, I wouldn't say no. Although I like them younger! As I was saying, he should count his lucky stars.'

I can't help but laugh. 'How much have you had to drink?'

'Not nearly enough to deal with this room.' He looks at the bartender. 'Scotch, neat, with some ice.'

'Manners, Charles, they're free.'

'You and I would never work. But we could have fun together.'

'Dream on.'

'Always, Kate.' He reaches into his jacket pocket. 'This is for you.' He slides a folded piece of paper towards me.

'What is it?'

'Read it and you'll find out.'

I look at him and then at the paper, lying flat on the bar. I scan the document but my mind feels hazy.

He takes his drink and downs it, placing the empty glass on the countertop. 'Another, please!' he requests the bartender. 'As promised, I searched my father's not-so-secret safe. As you can see, it's a post-mortem report for a woman. Cause of death – suicide.'

I read it. 'I don't understand. It doesn't say Katenka's name. OK, the date looks the same, but it could be about anyone.'

'Do you really believe that two women of the same age and in the same city took their lives on the same day?'

'Perhaps. I mean, it's possible. A bit odd – but possible.'

'Odd! Yes, I agree. Nearly as odd as this half-written report. Look at the bottom, Kate.' He points.

'Chief coroner?' I say.

'The name – read the name.'

'George Williams.' I look at Charles, totally clueless.

'Williams.' Charles raises his brows. 'My dear Kate, if we do a quiz, you are most definitely not on my team. Williams as in Matthew Williams – George is his father.'

'Oh! Why would I have known that?'

'Anyway, this leads you to one or two avenues. First, my father has only half the report: where is the rest? You must understand: my father is a cantankerous old fool, but a methodical old fool who has always run a tight ship. But I smell a rat. Second, George deals with criminal cases, or second opinions. There was no inquest on this suicide, so why has my father kept a copy of his report?'

'Maybe it was… I don't know! Because he likes to keep copies?' I don't have a bloody clue. 'That's if it is her; you can't tell from this alone. Besides, why would their names be associated with Katenka? It doesn't make sense.'

'Exactly – why would two high-profile men at the peak of their careers be involved, if only on paper, with the suicide of a supposedly Russian nobody? No offence to Katenka.'

'None taken. It can't have been coincidental.'

'No, I don't believe in coincidence.'

'Shit… Do you think I've uncovered something?'

'It would be safe to say that if you dig deep enough you may ruffle a few feathers. This information leaves us – well, nowhere. Except…' He smiles.

'Except what? Spill.'

'Perhaps George Williams has secret information which Matthew may be able to help you find.'

'That sounds possible. Can you ask him?' I say.

'No!'

'What do you mean, no? I thought you Chelsea people lived in each other's pockets.'

'Us Chelsea people do fall out, frequently. Let's just say we don't see eye to eye. You'll have to ask him yourself.' He drinks the remainder of his second whisky.

'Is that all? I thought you were going to ask me to run around this ballroom stark bloody naked.'

Charles tries desperately to not choke on his drink.

'As you know, he's Luke's arch-rival – plus, my fist had a run in with his face last week. Also, I'm quite keen on breathing… talking to him may have an impact on my ability to do that.'

Charles can't hide his amusement. 'Well, then, Kate Harper, we seem to be in a quandary. But there was something else; I found an address attached to the paperwork. In Wales.'

'Wales.' I shake my head. 'Doesn't ring any bells.'

'Hmm, I just thought I would ask. As I said, you need to speak to Matthew – he may be able to help. But I agree, this isn't coincidental. I will continue to dig around for you, but really there's not an awful lot to go on.'

'I guess not.'

'It would seem your gut instinct was spot on.'

'This doesn't look good.'

'No I agree.'

I take his hand. 'I really appreciate your help… If there's anything you ever need just ask. But not for sexual favours!'

'What a shame.' He retrieves his wallet and passes me a business card. 'Take this, in case you need it.'

I lean towards him and plant a kiss on his cheek. 'Thanks, Charles.'

'You're welcome. I'll leave you to find Luke. By the way, fucking awesome dress, but you already know that.' His eyes almost smile. Charles, the brash individual, seems almost self-effacing!

He disappears into the crowds, leaving me to think. My hands tremble as I place the business card and paper in my clutch bag. This is madness!

'You look lost.'

I recognise the voice and turn. 'Bradley, you scrub up well.'

'Thanks, I guess! That was a compliment, right?'

'It was – you look dashing this evening.'

'Dashing? That's a new one. And you look – well, what I want to say and what I am allowed to say.' He whistles. 'My boss is a very lucky man. Speaking of Luke, where is he?'

'You're the second person to ask me. He's gone AWOL. Actually let's mingle – you can help me find him.'

'My pleasure.' He holds his hand out. I look at it. Am I reading too much into it? He looks over his shoulder at me and winks. 'Remember, I don't bite.' I place my hand in his and he holds it firmly. 'Unless you want me to?'

I tap his shoulder. 'Move, pest.'

Bradley manoeuvres his way through the masses of people. 'I see him.' He says into my ear. We move towards Luke and stop. My eyes fix on Luke – talking to Alexis! Actually, he's smiling. What the hell is he doing? But then I see Alexis lean in to kiss Luke.

'Kate, are you OK?' Bradley asks me.

I move to Alexis. 'What the fuck is going on?' My voice is louder than I expected. Some people turn and stare.

'Kate – Kate, look at me,' Luke says, but I can't look at him. My eyes fix on Alexis. Deliberately, my hand rises, and I give her the most powerful slap I can muster. Given the state of my temper, this almost knocks her flying.

'Jesus, Kate!'

Luke's voice echoes in my ears. 'What? Don't Jesus me.'

He helps Alexis regain her balance. Note to self, I must slap harder when Alexis is the fucking target.

'Are you kidding me? Why would you help her?' My hands fist on my hips. 'This is unbelievable. You know what? You're welcome to each other.'

I turn and storm away.

I easily lose myself among the sea of bodies. The sound of Luke's voice grows fainter until I can no longer hear anything except people chatting. I find the lift we used earlier. Thankfully, the attendant holds the door for me before it closes. The lift begins to rise. I want to crumble to the floor, but grimly I hold onto the small amount of sanity I can muster and close my eyes, holding back my tears.

The sound of the lift door opening brings me back to reality. Seconds later, I come face to face with the door to our suite.

'Fuck!' I mutter. I don't have a bloody key card. There's no point searching my bag; Luke never gave me one.

My back makes contact with the wall, and I slide down to the floor. I'm mortified at how the evening has played out, cross that I don't have a bloody key, and furious with Alexis. She kissed Luke!

I hear the lift. I raise my head to see a very cross Luke marching towards me.

I pull myself to standing. *Can I face a battle tonight? If Alexis is the driving force, bet your arse I can.*

'I called after you.' His dark eyes blaze.

'Can you open the door… please.' My politeness is cutting.

He finally opens the door.

I move past him into the room.

'Are you enjoying yourself, Luke? I guess that was a bonus tonight.' I start to pace, needing to get rid of my pent-up energy.

'Do not fucking go there! You know she kissed me.'

'Whatever! It makes no difference.'

'What is that supposed to mean?'

'She wants you, and always has.'

'She was apologising for Philip's behaviour.'

'Yeah, of course she was. There is no "get out of jail" card for him, Luke; he scares the crap out of me.'

'I never said there was. No one fucking touches you. I know you don't like Alexis, bu—'

'You're not bloody wrong. Let's add kissing my fiancé to the growing list of reasons I don't like her.'

'She was drunk. I have known her for years. Yes, she is confident and brash.'

'How about rude and obnoxious? Let me think what else I can add.'

'But you can't hit people when you feel like it! We had this discussion only a week ago.' He moves away from the door and heads towards the drinks cabinet.

'May I remind you that you taught me how to hit people?'

He turns to face me. 'In self-defence, Kate, not to attack innocent people.'

'Innocent? Are you shitting me? She's one of the nastiest people I've ever met – along with her slimeball dad.'

His eyes scan me. 'I just told you I will deal with him. I know she's direct and tough.'

'You mean a bitch.'

His eyes dance with mine.

'She has been awful to me, Luke.'

'She was fairly remorseful.'

'Remorseful, my arse.' I stop and stare in disbelief. 'Have you forgiven her? Please don't tell me you've patched things up.'

'Kate, this is not a fucking playground. I merely listened to her.'

'I'm surprised you heard her with her tongue down your fucking throat.'

He downs his brandy and flashes me his dark eyes.

'Enough of this shit. I need to be able to work with her when I take over your shares.'

'How fucking peachy for you both.' I walk away. 'You're welcome to her, but I wouldn't tell your brothers.' With no filter, words leave my lips to wound him. Shit!

'What did you say?' Luke walks towards me.

'Nothing.' Poker-face Harper is hopefully with me.

'Nothing? No, you said not to tell Declan and Ollie. Why is that?'

I fold my arms. 'I know they don't like her.' I swallow hard, hoping that my words are enough to stall Luke.

Luke takes my arm and turns me to face him. 'Don't bullshit me, Kate.'

'I'm not.'

'OK.' He retrieves his mobile from his pocket.

'What are you doing?' Panic sets in; I know he's playing me.

'Calling Declan. I know you're lying, so either you tell me or he will.'

491

Fuck, fuck, fuck. My stupid mouth has landed me in a situation that is going to erupt like a bloody volcano.

I grab his phone from his hand. 'Fine.'

'I'm waiting.' He towers over me.

I take a deep breath and pray that Ollie will want to remain my friend after this.

My head lowers. 'Ollie slept with Alexis.'

Luke lifts my chin. 'Stop mumbling.'

'I'm not.' I said it. Do I have to repeat it?

'Kate, I am fucking warning you.'

'Ollie slept with Alexis. Well, Alexis took advantage of Ollie a long time ago.'

'I don't understand.'

'Declan told me that Alexis tried it on with him, but he wasn't interested. Ultimately she wanted you – there's a fucking surprise – so she had Ollie instead. She took his virginity. It was just before—' My mouth freezes.

'His attempted suicide.'

I nod. 'Declan said that Ollie found out she'd done it for a dare or a joke, then losing his friend and the bullying… It tipped him over the edge. That's why Declan has no time for Alexis, he blames her for some of what happened.'

Luke's face drains of colour, and his eyes become strangely dark.

'Move.'

'What?' *Holy fuck, he is going to find Alexis.* 'No.' My back hits the door. *Crap, I need to keep him here. God only knows what he will do.*

'Move!'

'Let's talk about it… Ollie is OK with what happened; he told me himself.'

492

'This just keeps getting better. Am I the only one still in the dark?'

I shake my head. 'Your parents don't know. Ollie wanted to tell you, but he knew you would go mad.'

He points his finger in my face. 'How could you keep this from me? You know how I feel about Ollie. This is low, even for you.' He shakes his head. 'It makes me wonder why I asked you to marry me. Where's your honesty? Move away from the fucking door, or I will move you.'

'No. I don't trust you… I know you wouldn't hurt Alexis, but—'

I raise my hand to his face. He takes my wrist. I do the same with the other hand. He now has both my wrists.

'Luke, I'm sorry. I should have told you. But I promised Ollie, and he wanted to tell you himself.'

'How can I trust you?' His voice pierces my heart.

'This isn't my fault. Declan asked me not say anything, and it wasn't my secret to tell.'

'Bullshit.' He releases my hands.

'Luke please, stay here… Please.'

'I'm so angry with you. Do you understand? This is more than keeping your word. I have to deal with Alexis… Christ, Kate, I can't look at you.'

'Fine, hate me. But don't go and find her. You need to speak to Ollie – you owe him that much.'

'Don't fucking stand there and tell me what to do.'

'I'm not. You just need to calm down.'

'Fucking calm down? You've got a nerve after your performance tonight… such ladylike behaviour at a fucking function.'

'Are you kidding me? Do you know what, Luke, I'm sick to death with your holier-than-thou bullshit. I forgot just how perfect you are.'

His eyes glint with a dark rage. I move away from the door. 'Go. As I repulse you so much, I would hate for you to stay.'

I move away and head towards the bar, desperate for a drink.

'Stop being so fucking dramatic.'

'Dramatic? Oh my God, you make me so mad. Go on, go and do whatever it is you so desperately need to do. I'm sure Alexis will oblige you, now you know she wants to fuck all the Sutton boys.'

He moves towards me. 'As ever, you stoop low to get a reaction from me.'

'Low, that wasn't low? This is low.' I remove my engagement ring and place it on the desk. 'I've had enough.'

As I walk away, Luke grabs my arm and pulls me towards him.

'If you remove that ring, you remove me from your life… Think very carefully about it.'

'Luke, you can't treat me like this. I'm not perfect, but neither are you. Do what you bloody want – I've had enough.'

'Is this what you want?'

'You think everything is my fault. Your brother got seduced by the super-bitch while you were off saving the world, but, hey, of course it's my fault. Even though I didn't bloody know you then! What do you want me to say?'

'You make me so fucking mad.' His face reflects his words: deep-set lines score across his forehead and his features are hard.

'Tell me something I don't know. Just fuck me hard and let's get this over with.'

My hand reaches for his groin. As I thought, he's hard. Giving me no time to think, his lips are on mine. Reluctantly, I return his kiss. His body seems to have been taken over by another force: he needs to eradicate his anger and I'm the tool for him to use. I am probably the only person who knows how he works. Even though I could say no, I know what he needs.

He turns me to face the desk. My body folds forward as his hand slides up my thigh and snatches at my knickers.

My body yearns for his touch, and I think it always will, but my mind is full of anguish. One thrust and he enters me, full and hard. He remains stationary, allowing my body time to accept him, but no amount of time will relax me tonight. My eyes close as tears begin to roll down my cheeks.

The spaghetti straps keeping my dress together are not strong enough to withstand Luke's manhandling. They break, exposing my breasts. Luke works hard to find his release. He is just thinking of himself; there is no satisfaction for me, no orgasm waiting. Each thrust feels harder, and as his breathing grows shallow I know his climax is almost with him. Two more thrusts, and then he stops. He lowers his face to my back.

'Fuck! Kate, I didn't... Jesus, what have I done?' He pulls out of me. 'Christ, you're bleeding.'

'My period is due; it wasn't you.' I wipe my tears and look down to see what was once a beautiful dress and is now pieces of ripped fabric.

Luke scoops me into his arms. I have no energy to argue, and rest my face in the crook of his neck as he carries me towards the bathroom. He lowers me and turns on the bath taps. Then he locks his strong arms around my shivering torso, while I continue to sob.

'Forgive me, baby, please.'

'For what?'

He places his hands on either side of my face. 'The way I took you. I never meant to – Jesus, I'm sorry.'

His lips seal his words with a gentle kiss.

'It was either me or someone else.'

His hands run through his hair. 'I would never hurt you.'

I look away.

'Kate.'

I meet his eyes. 'You just did, Luke.'

'Fuck.' He face is consumed with fear. He pulls me close again and kisses the top of my head. 'I need you more than you'll ever understand… I can't lose you.'

I nod against his chest.

'I will never forgive myself for what I just did. Please believe me. Don't walk away from me.'

'I won't.' I lift my head to show him I'm telling the truth.

He briefly closes his eyes. 'Christ, I have never fucked up something in my life so badly. Your ring, Kate, please put your ring back on.'

'Luke, I can't take much more.'

'I would give up everything tomorrow, but I could never give up on you – on us.'

'You said I wasn't who you thought I was,' I say, sniffling through the last of my tears.

'I can't lie and tell you that keeping something like this from me doesn't hurt.'

'I told Ollie to speak to you! He's going to hate me; it will crush him that you know.'

'I'll deal with Ollie, but not yet. I need to think this through.'

He slips the remains of my dress from my hips, and I stand before him, naked. He helps me into the warm water and turns the taps off.

My initial reaction is to draw my knees up to my chest. I feel physically and emotionally exposed. Luke disappears from the bathroom and returns with two glasses and my ring.

First he takes my hand and gently slides my ring to its rightful place.

'Please, never remove this again – that's all I ask of you. I know I don't deserve it, but please, Kate.'

I nod.

He passes me the glass. I down it. It does have some effect: a calming sensation washes through my core.

He lowers himself down and sweeps his hand against my cheek. 'Can I join you, unless—'

I nod.

Luke strips and steps in the bath behind me. He pulls my back to his chest, encouraging me to uncurl from my foetal position. My head relaxes against his chest. I start to cry again. Will I ever stop? My tears fall to my cheeks and overflow onto Luke's damp chest.

'Shh, Kate, please…'

I cling to Luke as though my life depends on him. God I feel hurt. I turn slightly and see his anguish.

'I'm sorry about Ollie.'

'No more.' His arms tighten around me.

'Luke, I could have said no. I know how you work.' I look at his face. 'You needed me.'

'I'll never need you like that again… I attacked you; it wasn't sex.'

I bolt upright, sloshing the water over the edge of the bath.

'You didn't attack me, never say that… I knew what you were doing.'

'I did attack you. You can't hide the truth, Kate.' His chest rises and his eyes close, tormented by what he's done.

'You see red. I know what that means; I've seen it for myself.' I link his fingers in mine.

'That's no excuse.'

'I'm not saying it is.'

'And the blood?'

'I told you – my period is due, earlier than I thought. Luke, look at me. We've had rough sex before – sometimes rougher than tonight. I'm not lying; you didn't hurt me.'

His hand slides across my breast and rests against my heart. 'But here is where I hurt you, baby.'

22

In the middle of the night I bolt to the bathroom, clasping my hand over my mouth. The contents of my stomach make it to the toilet just in time.

'Baby, are you OK?' Luke joins me, gently touching my back.

I nod. 'I am now.' I stand and make my way to the sink, where I wash my face and brush my teeth. I look at him in the mirror, and then at my watch. It's two o'clock in the morning.

'Have you been working?' I ask. I was alone when I woke.

'Do you feel ill?' He sidesteps my question.

'No – it must be my period.'

'What do you need? Water, tea…?'

I shake my head. 'Just you – please hold me in bed so I can sleep.'

He smiles, but his smile doesn't reach his eyes.

We lie in our usual position, my back resting against his chest. Safety has arrived – him.

'Love you,' I murmur as my eyes close.

Feeling the sun's warmth seeping through the windows is relaxing. I look at my watch. Seven thirty, and where is Luke? I tie the hotel bathrobe tightly around my body.

From the large French doors of the lounge area, I watch him, sitting out on the veranda. I walk over to him and place my arms around his shoulders.

'Working already?'

'Yes.' OK – one-word answers. I guess the wounds of last night are still raw.

I take the chair next to him.

'How are you feeling?' he asks.

'OK.'

'Good. I ordered a light breakfast – just breads and fruit.'

I reach for a croissant. 'I'm starving.' I pour myself some coffee and top up Luke's cup. 'What are you working on?'

'Us.'

I look at him. 'Sorry? Us... we need work.'

I raise my brows; this is absolutely bloody true.

'Actually I was talking about our wedding.'

'Oh.' I drink some coffee, feeling pleased and a little confused.

His gaze fixes on me. 'Saturday – we're getting married on Saturday.'

Luke nearly receives my mouthful of coffee.

'Are you shitting me? Saturday?'

He tilts his head. 'I'm not shitting you, and yes Saturday.'

'As in... today is Sunday, so less than a week?'

'Yes.' Luke begins to gather his paperwork together.

'Can I ask why the sudden change of plan? And why you didn't think to speak to me first? This does affect both of us. And how the hell have you managed to book a wedding in less than a week?'

'I have my ways.'

'How?'

'Does it matter?'

'Er – yes it does. Luke, you've just informed me that we are getting married in less than a week. Where was I in this decision?'

He sits back in his chair. 'You do want to get married in Venice?'

'Yes.'

'And, I assume, the Hotel Cipriani, as discussed?' He passes me various printouts and taps a sheet. 'Is there anyone I have missed out? Other than Molly, who said she would rather not fly?'

I scan the names. 'No.'

Grrr – I want to scream at him. 'OK. So you've listed everyone, but what about all the details? A wedding day is every girl's dream, and I want it to be perfect.'

'The city hall and venue are booked, and the jets will be ready and waiting for everyone on Friday. You told me your dress is finished, and we already have an appointment to choose our rings. You will need to speak to the hotel manager, who speaks perfectly good English. He wants to know about flowers, cakes, etc.'

I sigh and draw my legs up to my chest.

'Luke, you're missing the bigger picture – I wanted to do it *with* you.'

He takes my hand. 'I like control. Last night I lost control and went to a place… a place I don't want to go back to. Please allow me to do this for you, to make us

501

permanent, I want to give you the day you deserve.' He leans to my lips and gently kisses me. 'I will never hurt you again, please let me do this for you.'

I run my hands through my matted hair. 'Talk to me, don't just book our wedding without me! Sometimes, Luke, I don't understand you.' *Only sometimes?*

He watches me closely. 'There's no point waiting.'

'Maybe not… But can we arrange everything in six days? Will everyone be free? '

'I've spoken to everyone on the list. We depart Friday morning, and our wedding is on Saturday at two o'clock, at the city hall and then afterwards at the hotel.'

'I'm sure you need permission or paperwork, don't you? There's a lot more to it than you think.'

'I think about everything, Kate. Trust me: I have it sorted.'

'Clearly.'

He stands and places a kiss on my forehead. 'I have a meeting with Bradley.' He waves his hotel plans at me. 'I should be no more than a couple of hours; you can come with me if you want.'

'No, I'll stay here… and think about *our* wedding.'

At eleven o'clock, feeling exhausted, not only from our flight home but our entire stay at Dubai, I climb into bed. My mind is spinning. Bloody hell, I'm getting married in six days! Holy shit.

The following day Luke and I sit at his boardroom table, several rings laid out in front of us. They are all platinum and bloody expensive – I feel as though I am in the most self-indulgent sweet shop in the world.

'Which shall I try first?' I look at Luke, then at the man from the jewellery shop, then at his security guard, and then at Max.

'May I make a suggestion?' the jeweller says.

'Yes, please.'

He selects a band, which is a little too large for my liking.

'Hmm, I'm not sure. Luke, what do you think?'

'It's up to you.'

I look at Max, and he shakes his head. I scan the box and catch sight of a thin band, covered in the most beautiful, delicate square-cut diamonds. It's simple and elegant.

'This one.'

'Try it on,' Luke commands.

I try it with my engagement ring, and hold my hand up to the light.

'I love it – what do you think?'

Luke takes my hand. 'Perfect.'

My eyes meet Max's look of approval. Now Luke has to choose. This takes all of thirty seconds: he goes for a simple platinum band.

Another day passes in which I have barely any contact with Luke, verbally or physically. Apparently he's super-busy at work, with early mornings and late-night meetings. *Bullshit*. Once again, I lie in bed alone.

This week is filled with dress fittings; Mr Jones the perfectionist wants every detail to be flawless. As for the wedding, there really isn't much planning needed, as the day will be held under one roof and the hotel will organise everything. Luke and I had decided a while ago not to have bridesmaids and a best man; we didn't see the point in having a small number of guests and turning them into puppets for the day.

On Thursday afternoon, I check the cases, ensuring every detail is in order. Mr Jones has made a new white shirt for Luke, with *Mr & Mrs Sutton* written on the inside of his cuff as a surprise for him, and I have bought him some socks from Primark (a pack of six for five pounds). Each pair carries a different message: *Mr Perfect, Mr Right, 100% Man, I'm Always Right, I'm The Best,* and *You and Me = Right.* He can decide which to wear on the day! I pack the black tie I made with Mr Jones the day after we met, and then his *eat me* cufflinks. All will be worn with his classic black Jones Tailors suit.

On Thursday evening, Fiona seals the last foil in my hair: this is the last thing on my to-do list before we leave tomorrow.

'Forty-five minutes, and then you need to rinse, OK?'

'Fine. Is Pete looking forward to tomorrow?'

'We both are. I've always wanted to go to Venice. Kate, I'm so excited.'

She sits next to me, finishing her tea.

'You seem nervous.'

I sigh. 'I am.' I look at my mug. 'To be honest, I think Luke is avoiding me. That sounds great, considering we're getting married in just over forty-eight hours.'

She reaches across for my hand. 'Men get nervous too. He thinks the world of you. I have to admit, when I spoke to him on Sunday I was shocked – shocked he called, but also that you were unaware of his plans. He told me that you were asleep and he needed to know numbers instantly for the hotel booking.'

'Ah, so you have been introduced to Mr Control Freak Sutton. We had a... heated discussion... on Saturday, and I know he is festering over it. Let's hope he gets over it sooner rather than later.'

She stands and places her cup in the sink. 'Why don't you take him by surprise – I mean, *make* him see you?'

'Maybe! It does feel like he's avoiding me, and he hasn't had dinner yet...'

'He'll have to see you tomorrow.'

'I guess, unless we travel in separate jets!'

My hair washed and straightened, my body cleansed in the best scent in the world, I stand in the walk-in closet rummaging through my underwear drawer. Bra, French knickers, garter and stockings – all that remains is Luke's black Jones Tailor shirt. Perfect attire in which to call my sex god. I also pack a hamper filled with his favourite foods.

The lift doors slide open and I'm faced with the large silver lettering saying *SUTTON GLOBAL INDUSTRIES*.

I hold Max's arm before he walks forward. 'I can make it the rest of the way.' I feel a battle brewing, and there's no need for Max to witness it.

'What's going on with Luke?' he asks.

I thought it was just me, but maybe other people have noticed that Luke is behaving oddly.

'Nothing, really.'

'Let Luke tell me you're leaving with him.'

'Look, he lost his temper on Saturday – and I mean he lost it big-time with me. That's why he booked the wedding – he actually planned the entire day while I was asleep. He said that when he was so angry he went to a place he didn't want to revisit. I don't know if he meant something to do with his previous work or... Paul.' Max closes his eyes. This is the first time I have mentioned his son's name. I grip his hand. 'Sorry.'

'Don't be.'

'Max, I hate that he's distant from me. I need him to talk to me, get it out of his system. Christ, we're leaving for Venice in the morning.' He couldn't protect me from his temper, the one thing he strives for, and yet he didn't save me – like he couldn't save Paul.

'OK.'

'Max – I didn't mean to...' I tail off.

'Shh – it's fine. Paul was a big part of his life. If he's back there, then he'll need you.' He smiles and brushes his thumb against my cheek. 'Paul would have liked you, Kate.'

'Are you trying to make me cry?' I give a pathetic smile, hoping it will delay my tears.

'Go and rescue him, but don't leave this floor without Luke – promise?'

'Promise.'

I nervously fiddle with the door handle to Luke's office. He looks up from his desk.

'Kate.' He checks the time.

I move towards his desk. 'Hi. I thought you might be hungry, and you've barely been home all week.'

'I'm busy.' *Busy? Here we go: the battle has commenced.*

'You still need to eat.' Despite his words, I walk towards the boardroom table and set the hamper down.

506

He remains buried in his paperwork. This mission may be more challenging than I thought.

'Kate, I said I'm busy. Go home – I shouldn't be much longer.'

I sit. 'I'll wait.'

He tilts his head. 'We leave tomorrow; I have a lot of work to complete before then. Where's Max?'

'I told him to leave; he's waiting in the car.' I check my nails, killing time.

'Kate, I don't have time for this... Go home.'

I stand and move towards him. 'You don't have time to eat – or time for me.'

'No. I have work.' His head remains low.

'I'm not leaving until you talk to me. As you just said, we leave for our wedding tomorrow. Yes, us – me and you... But there hasn't been an "us" since Saturday.' His dark eyes meet my hurt eyes. 'You've left early every day and worked stupidly late... Why?'

'I really don't have time for a sermon. You can eat and then leave.'

'No, I want to sort this out. Why haven't you touched me since Dubai?'

'You have your period, and...'

'And you've been busy... Bullshit, Luke.' I move to his side of the desk. 'We had a heated debate, it's done. Get over it. Besides, my period finished a few days ago.'

He runs a hand through his hair and groans in frustration. 'Have you finished?'

'That depends on your next words... And as for my period, it's never stopped you before. You always ask me if I'm feeling OK before we have sex.'

'Christ, you drive me mad.'

'Good – I would hate for you to get bored.'

I take his pen from his hand and kiss him gently, but his response is cold.

He stands up from his chair. 'Jesus, Kate, not now.'

He has never refused me before. This is what we do, how we complete us.

'You're saying no to me?'

'I'm saying not now.'

'Luke, we had sex on Saturday and, yes, you were rougher than usual, but it's over with.'

He shuts his eyes, taking long slow breaths. 'Fuck, Kate, I can't do this. Stop it.'

'Stop what? Luke, talk to me.' *God, I want to punch him, he frustrates me so much.*

'I won't take you. It's not the right time.'

'What do you mean it's not the right time? What the hell are you saying?'

'Go home, Kate.'

'Fine: you leave me no choice.'

Changing tactics, I undo the buttons of his shirt and slip it off. All I'm wearing underneath is my sexy lingerie.

'Jesus, Kate… I said I can't, not now!' he shouts.

'Can't or won't?' *Come on, Sutton.* I move towards the door of his office. 'OK, have it your own way. I'll leave.'

'Aren't you missing something? Your coat?'

'No! What difference does it make who sees me? Clearly you have an issue with me.'

'Don't you dare set foot outside this office.'

I turn to him. 'Or what?'

He glares. 'Don't push me.'

'I wouldn't do that; it may tip you over the edge. Oh no, it already has.'

I reach the door and turn the handle. I can already hear him moving towards me. I make it to Stella's desk. I'm sure no one is working late; I don't remember seeing anyone, only the cleaners!

Luke scoops me up in his arms and marches back to his office, slamming the door behind us.

'What the fuck is wrong with you?' he rages at me.

'You – you're my problem. Where is my Luke? It's not this person standing in front of me.' I push his shoulder, hoping for a reaction.

His fists clench, allowing me to read the tell-tale signs of his frustration. Bollocks to this! With no warning, I launch myself at him. Locking my arms around his neck, I pull him towards me, allowing my lips to make contact with his. At last he responds, his tongue violently swirling in my mouth. My hands move to his hair, encouraging him to deepen the kiss.

Finally I pull away. 'Fuck me now.' *I sound like a Sutton in training.*

My hands move to his shirt and I rip the buttons – please let it be an inexpensive shirt!

'I need you, Luke.'

He pushes me back against the wall, grabbing my breasts, freeing them of my bra. His mouth takes hold of my nipples, sucking and nipping.

'Shit, Luke.'

He repeats the act again, this time wilder. Sensations erupt inside me. 'I want you inside me.'

My hands move to his button and zip, freeing his erection into my hand.

'I love you, always,' I announce.

His eyes lock to mine: dark and remorseful meets dark and forgiving.

Luke slides my knickers off me; I wriggle to help him. I hook one leg around him and take hold of his erection.

'I need more space.' At last he speaks.

He picks me up. I lock my legs around him as he carries me to the boardroom table. My arse meets the cold wood as he positions me at the edge of the table. Holding his erection, he enters me with force.

We remain immobile, absorbing each other.

'Baby, I'm sorry.'

'Shhh, Luke. Hard and fast, just as I like it. Please.'

My back makes contact with the table as Luke begins to drive deep inside me, hitting the spot that sparks my body into a frenzy. This is what I need: him taking me. The climb is almost too much, as my body begins to shudder with the first wave of my orgasm.

'I'm coming...' My back arches as I ride the wave of my orgasm.

'Fuck. Yes.' His eyes remain shut as he comes. A residue of his guilt and basic need lies deep within me.

He holds himself in place, ensuring I have all of him – body and soul – tonight. He leans towards me, planting a kiss on my lips, and I tug his hair, begging for his touch. He slides out of me. Taking my hand, he pulls me to face him.

'Don't ever leave me out in the cold again, Luke. Never.'

He bows his head. 'I can't get the memory of Saturday out of my head.'

'It's gone. This, right here, is the only memory you need.' I pull his face to meet mine. 'Luke, I don't fear you – I fear losing you.'

23

'Ready?' Luke looks at me. Holy crap, this is it: the start of us becoming husband and wife. God, I'm nervous, but my excitement is overwhelming. I love him with all my heart.

'I guess.' My stomach turns cartwheels as the car door opens. 'Thanks, Thomas.' I step out and a take a breath.

'You're welcome, Miss Harper.'

'I won't be Miss Harper for much longer!'

We enter City Airport to cheers and whistles. We are both equally shocked by the unexpected attention. We separate to greet our friends. My first stop is Barney.

'Here comes the bride, all fa—'

I tap his shoulder. 'Oi – watch it.'

'Jesus, Kate – tomorrow you'll be Mrs Sutton. Christ, that makes you sound prehistoric.'

'Any other compliments you want to share? I'm likely to throw you in the bloody canal at Venice.'

He nudges my arm. 'Chill. How's Mr Three-Grand-an-Hour Sutton?'

'OK.' I think! 'Where's Kiki?'

'You have three guesses – oh, and she isn't late.'

'You're joking! Please don't tell me she's jumped back into Declan's bed.'

'Bloody hell, babe, hold your horses; they're only talking. We're not all like you and lover boy; some of us have willpower.'

'I assume "us" does not include you.'

'Point taken! As soon as we got here, Declan came over and wanted a word – apparently to clear the air. Oh Christ, don't look now.'

'What?' I turn to see Declan and Kiki locked in an embrace, with full-on lip contact. 'Not again! Give me strength.'

Luke holds my hand during take-off. I rest my head on his shoulder, feeling relaxed for the first time since last week.

'Are you OK?' Luke kisses the top of my head.

'More than OK. I'm excited – what about you?' I tilt my head to read his eyes. Thankfully, the dark cloud has lifted.

'I'll be happier once tomorrow is over.'

'Oh – that's not quite what I was expecting to hear.'

He gives me a smile, the one that makes me melt. 'Not for your perfect day to be over, but you'll be mine forever, Mrs Sutton.'

'Now I get you. I feel nervous. I just hope everything runs smoothly.'

'It will, baby.'

'What time will James and Scott arrive?'

'Sullivan should already be there, and Parker will arrive at the same time as us.'

'The story you've told everyone – you said they're your old colleagues from the bank?'

He laughs. 'Yes, the bank.'

'You must have had some serious paper cuts.'

'The worst.' He looks above us to see the seatbelt sign has turned green. 'Come to the office.'

'What!' I look at him with curiosity.

'There's something we need to discuss in private, we won't get time when we land.'

He stands from his seat and holds out his hand, without hesitation I join him.

'Where are you two going? Mile-high club – whoop whoop.'

I hit Barney's arm.

'Oi, Sutton, I bet this baby costs more than three grand an hour.'

I turn and glare at Barney, who finds himself highly amusing.

In his office, Luke sits at his desk, and pulls me to his lap.

'Go on, I know it's about money… a pre-nup thing.'

'What?' He runs his hand up my back to the nape of my neck.

'It's what you do if you're loaded… Safeguard your money.'

Luke tries to hide his amusement. 'Thanks, baby, I do know what it is, I'm just confused about why you said it.'

'I don't know. It's just hit me that you're loaded an—'

'We both have healthy bank accounts. Kate, if you left me tomorrow, take all the money with you. It's worth fuck all to me without you.'

'Oh, I wasn't trying to hurt you, it just came to me. Actually, I watched a film the other night and the man in the film got one. I don't want one, not that I know anything about them. I told you from the get-go I want you, not your money, and nothing's changed.'

'Good.' He takes my hand and rests it against his chest. 'You own *this*. I've never given it to anyone else – trust what I'm saying.'

'OK. I think I'm going to cry.'

'Not today.'

'Sorry… I hate what money does to people.'

'I know; that's what makes you special.' He reaches for a book on his desk and opens it. 'Right, choose anywhere you'd like to go.'

I glance at the page; it's a map of the world.

'You've lost me.'

'Choose where you'd like to go on honeymoon – anywhere in the world. All I need is time to arrange my diary, and then I'm all yours for two weeks.

'Bloody hell, two weeks? I've never had you for that long before.' I squeal and clap. 'God, I have no idea, where shall we go? There are too many places to choose from. You choose.'

'No, I want it to be your dream destination.'

'I feel the pressure… I don't know.'

'Close your eyes and put your finger on the map.'

'I love playing games. OK, here goes.' I close my eyes and rotate my finger before placing it firmly on the map. I open my eyes and look. 'What? Where the hell is Novosibirsk?'

Luke looks at me. 'What is it with you and Russia?'

'I'm drawn to it, must be in the blood… You choose.'

'How about the Four Seasons in Bora Bora?'

'That was my next choice. Sounds fabulous!'

Our taxi boat draws up to the side entrance of the Hotel Cipriani. It does feel different this time – not only because of the number of people we are with, but also the weather. The end of March feels a lot cooler than August.

Within a couple of hours the Harper–Sutton wedding party has hijacked the entire bar at the hotel. Sullivan and Parker have arrived. What we lack in numbers we make up for in the level of noise, which grows as we empty more and more bottles of champagne.

Luke stands and taps the side of his glass for attention.

'While we are all together, I would like to go over a few details.' Commander Sutton is with us. 'Kate and I are very pleased that you could join us to celebrate our wedding. You will all have your room key cards. If you need food, drinks, or a boat to take you across to the square, please charge it to your room. This weekend is our wedding, and it is also a chance for us to give something back to you all, to thank you for all your support.' He raises his glass. 'I'd like to propose a toast to our family and friends.'

Everyone joins him in the first of many toasts.

'The plan for tomorrow – as you know, the wedding will take place at the Palazzo Cavallis at two o'clock. Transportation is arranged, so if everyone can meet here at one; after our wedding we will return here for our meal in the Antique Garden.' Luke points across the room. 'Tonight, yo—'

'Hold on, Luke.' Kiki stands and moves towards us both. 'Livy and I have been chatting, and we want a girls' night. You and the boys can eat out somewhere tonight, and us ladies will do the same. This is Kate's last night as a single woman, and I want her to spend it with us.' She reaches across and takes my hand.

I turn to Luke; this was not part of his plan.

'I agree.' Livy also stands, perhaps reading the wilful look in her son's eyes. She moves towards Luke. 'You go out with Dad and the boys. I would love to spend time with the girls. I think it's a wonderful idea.'

'OK, so the ladies are out alone—'

'Luke, I'm going to get you rat-arsed,' Declan shouts, much to Luke's dismay – God forbid he loses control.

'You'd better not, Declan,' I call.

I look at Barney. 'You're with me.'

He holds his glass up. 'I wouldn't have it any other way.'

'So, girls, we'll meet here at…' Kiki looks at her watch. 'Six o'clock. Declan, do you want to go for a walk with me?'

I grab her arm. 'Oi, Marlow, what's going on?'

'I don't really know.'

'Please don't let him shag and run; you deserve more than that. I told him so too.'

'I know. He told me that you're pissed off at him.'

'Oh.'

'He also told me about Sophie and the meal you all had.'

My face drains of colour. I have held out on her.

'It's fine; don't worry. I know why you didn't tell me about it.'

'I can't bear to see you hurt.'

517

'I know, and I love you for it. We're going for a walk, not to my bed. We'll talk. I'll see you at six.'

We spend the afternoon with the wedding planners, checking everything is organised for tomorrow. Luke sits next to me, his hand on my leg. I'm guessing this is not his idea of fun, discussing minor things like the location of lanterns. I want the theme to be modern and contemporary, and I don't want the venue to be overrun with wedding paraphernalia. Each table will have a large vase filled with lily of the valley and candles, plus white table linen. Elegant and simple – perfect.

Finally, Luke and I return to our suite. I collapse onto the bed and give a small scream.

'Kate!'

I drag myself to my knees. 'It feels like Christmas Eve.' I hold my hands out for him to join me.

'Good.' He smiles.

His lips reach out for mine, and a wave of desire washes over me. I need him. He pushes me to the bed, still kissing me. I manage to roll him and straddle his lap, clasping our hands together above his head. I feel his erection through his tightly fitting jeans. He loosens his grip and slides his hands under my flowing cream blouse. A simple flick against my nipples causes my groin to pulsate. Every time!

He sits up on the bed, holding me close, allowing his lips to make contact with my breasts, sucking, licking and giving me small tantalising nips.

I slide my blouse over my head before returning my gaze to meet his. 'I need you now.'

'I know.'

But then there is a banging on our door.

'Shh – pretend we're not here.' My mouth returns to his.

The unrelenting banging continues, this time harder.

'Kate, we know you're in there.' Barney's voice filters through the gaps of the door.

'Bloody hell, go away,' I whisper.

The tapping continues.

'Kate, we've got a bottle of bubbly,' Harry calls.

'Bang harder.' That's Kiki.

Luke smiles. 'Baby, as much as I want them to leave, we both know they won't.'

'Bloody nuisance.' The pack has the most dreadful timing.

I scramble off the bed, readjusting my bra and collecting my blouse from the floor.

'I'm coming,' I shout.

Luke joins me. I can't help but give him a quick grope; he remains incredibly firm. 'You may need a cold shower.'

He spins me around quickly and claims my mouth, then pulls away, leaving me panting for more.

'Cold shower? No, I need you,' he says and walks away.

I can just about breathe. 'God, I hate my friends right now.'

Reluctantly, I open the door.

'Hi.' I fake a smile.

'Took you long enough.' Barney winks and enters the suite. 'Bloody hell, Kate, this place is huge.'

Kiki and Harry follow him, armed with a bottle of bubbly.

'Oh my God, this room is stunning,' Harry says as Luke enters the lounge area. 'Hi Luke.'

'Hi.' He walks towards me, placing his arms around my shoulders. 'You three look as though you have a plan.' He looks at his watch. 'I thought you weren't meeting for another hour.'

'Best friend's prerogative; I can steal her any time.' Kiki looks steadily at Luke. I sense her words are a warning.

'In that case, I will leave you to it. I assume Declan is at the bar?'

'Raymond is. I'm sure he'll be pleased to see you.'

'Right then, wife-to-be, you have roughly twenty hours of being a Harper, and then you're mine, Mrs Sutton. Have fun.'

We all sit in the lounge, drinking our second glass of bubbly. My hand interlocks with Harry's, as my mind returns to the night before her wedding and the snow angels we made.

'You OK?' She looks at me. I nod. 'Tomorrow will be the best day of your life – I promise.'

'I hope so. This is it; there's no going back. Luke is the man I'm going to grow old with. Harry, this is madness! This time last year I was single and jobless.'

'I know! It's crazy how life has changed. You deserve it. Besides, Luke is smitten with you.'

'Who isn't?' Barney raises his glass in honour of me.

Later – much later – my eyes flit from Harry to Fiona and then to Valerie in desperation.

'How the hell am I going to explain to Luke that his mum is dancing on the bar with Italian men – lots of Italian men?' We break into hysterical giggles.

The restaurant we stumbled across was a small bistro that only comes alive after ten o'clock at night. After a traditional meal of pasta and far too much vino, Livy ordered a couple of bottles of grappa. I would have never put the two together: Livy plus grappa equals dancing seductively on the bar!

Mum pulls my arm to encourage me to join the partygoers. I refuse to leave without the remaining girls. My heart could burst. It has been a perfect impromptu evening for my last night as a Harper.

After another hour, Kiki and I support a very drunk Livy through the hotel foyer.

'I'll take her to her room.' Kiki takes Livy's bag and retrieves her key card.

'Are you sure? I don't mind.'

'It's fine. Her room is two doors away from mine.'

'OK – and thanks for tonight. It was perfect.' I deliver a kiss to my forever girl.

'It's been fun. Now go and find your fiancé and finish what you started earlier.'

I frown.

'I'm the shag monster, remember? I sense sex a mile off. Now go.'

I slide my key card in the door – and come face to face with Ollie.

'She's back.' Ollie smirks at me.

'What's going on? Where's Luke?'

'My brother is pissed – and I mean completely off his face.'

'What? Never! Mr Control Freak Sutton drunk? This I have to see.'

'I've only ever seen him like this once before.' Ollie laughs.

We walk towards the bedroom. Holy shit, Luke is passed out on the bed. I giggle.

'Declan, did you do this?'

'Fucking hell, yeah,' he bellows.

'James, I thought you would take care of him.'

'Declan gave him a few extra vodka shots. Before we knew it, he was almost on his back.'

'Well, he is now. I never thought I would see the day.' I look at Declan, who is a vile shade of green. 'No you don't, Declan Sutton: don't you dare throw up in here. Ollie, take him to his room – actually, take him to Kiki. She'll look after him.'

'See you tomorrow, sis-in-law.' Declan laughs at his slurred speech.

'Goodbye, boys.'

I turn to see Scott and James walking towards us. Scott carries a needle. He moves towards Luke, yanks his jeans down, and injects his arse.

'Urgh, what's going on? Drunk I can cope with; drugged is not good!'

Scott stands next to me. 'This will help him: it's a mixture of various ingredients – sugar, salt, et cetera. It's a bloody good hangover cure.'

'I've seen it all now. Jesus! Tell me, how the hell did you get that in your case? I bet you learned that at the bank.'

They both look at me.

'Private joke.'

'Honestly, he will be fine in the morning.' Scott says.

'He never drinks like this – if he's out of it tomorrow, I will murder Declan.'

'Kate, Luke can take his drink; I've seen him far worse.'

'Worse? He's out cold.'

'He's asleep. Trust us, OK?'

'I don't have a choice. Now leave me to deal with my fiancé.'

James and Scott roll Luke to his side, wedging his body with cushions so he won't choke.

Alone, just the two of us. So much for a lustful pre-wedding night. I might be pissed off with Declan, but the other part of me has to laugh at the man who wants to be in control of everything. Well, he's not tonight.

The next morning, my eyes open to brilliant sunshine streaming through the French doors, and a smile creeps across my face. Our wedding day is finally here! After today, my life will never be the same again. My hand sweeps across the bed, which is empty. I hear the shower running: my drunken fiancé must be washing away the memory of last night. I climb out of bed.

'How's your head?'

Luke looks at me through the glass panel of the shower.

'Surprisingly good.'

'That's because the men you worked with at the *bank* injected you with some form of antidote to alcohol!'

His hands run through his hair. 'Good boys.'

'So, you had a fun evening?'

He turns to assess my words, knowing the ridiculing has only just begun. Before I have time to speak, he yanks my arm, pulling me into the shower to join him and drenching my T-shirt.

'This needs to go.' He slides the wet T-shirt over my head and throws it to the tiled floor.

My arms link around his neck. 'Oh my God, you looked so funny last night. I've never seen you lose control before. You were passed out on your back... Declan got you well and truly pissed.'

'Yes, I love my brother dearly... Payback will be a bitch.'

I giggle at him, trying to remember his evening.

'Now then, we are getting married in a few hours. Am I allowed to fuck my future wife?'

'Only because you asked so nicely.'

Afterwards, we sit alone in our suite, trying to eat some breakfast, in matching white robes and 'just fucked' faces, with damp hair and tingling skin.

'How was your evening?'

I nod, finishing my last mouthful of scrambled egg. 'It was fun. OK, I know what happens on a girls' night should stay on girls' night, but...'

Quizzically, Luke looks at me.

'Your mum was really drunk. She was dancing on the bar; I've never seen anything like it... She is so refined and elegant, and last night she was—'

'Grappa.'

'What.'

'Was she drinking grappa?'

'Yeah – a lot of it.'

'When she drinks grappa, you need to run.'

I move to his chair, placing myself on his lap, locking my arms around his neck.

'In case I forget to tell you, I love you. Thank you for today, but most importantly thank you for asking me to be your wife.' Our lips meet.

A knock at the door makes me smile.

'I'm glad it's you; I thought you were never going to arrive.' I pull Mr Jones into my room.

He looks at his watch. 'You said eleven-thirty.' He moves further in to the suite. 'Are you OK?'

'Yeah, it's just been a crazy morning.'

'Weddings normally are.'

'I guess. Anyhow, I told Mum and Dad to go and get ready and come back at one. I need some time alone.' I walk towards the dining table and retrieve two glasses of bubbly. 'Cheers – here's to us, Harper Jones.'

'Sutton Jones, perhaps.' He smiles.

'Never – always Harper Jones. You seem to have the very last piece of me, Mr Jones.'

'So I do.'

I scan his flawless three-piece suit. 'You look fab.'

'Why, thank you. May I introduce to you my most treasured suit, handmade by my father from fabric he bought while in Italy?'

'Wow, and it still fits!'

Mr Jones laughs. 'Yes, it fits very well.'

'Let's sit down.' I reach for the gift bag on the coffee table. 'I have a gift for you – a very small gift. I thought…' I pass him the bag. 'Open it – you'll understand.'

'Kate, why have you got me a gift?' He opens the bag

and removes the box of handkerchiefs. 'Spectacular.' He examines them closely.

'I wouldn't go that far... We have a matching set.' There are three white hankies with *HARPER JONES* embroidered across them in blue.

'These will remain my favourite from now on... You are a special young lady.'

'Ready to zip me into my dress?'

'I would be honoured.'

We stand in front of the mirror. The dress looks perfect.

'I'm not sure what to say, Kate. You look beautiful... Luke's grandmother's veil matches perfectly, and I agree, your hair down is stunning.' The ribbon round my waist and the Sutton family heirloom complete my look.

I take a deep breath and move to the dressing table. 'You have one last job.' I pass him one of the Harper Jones hankies. 'Can you attach this to the underskirt of my dress?'

He takes my hands as I look at his eyes.

'No crying, Mr Jones; I'm barely holding it together.'

He kisses my cheeks in turn. 'Something blue?'

'Thank you.'

'For what, Kate?'

'For Luke – you helped me find him.'

A knock at the door dispels our moment.

'Allow me.' Mr Jones opens the door to Mum and Dad. 'Your daughter is waiting for you.' He moves, allowing them to see me.

'Kate.' Dad moves towards me first.

'Don't you dare start crying, Dad. Mr Jones nearly had me gushing. Tell me a joke, make me laugh.'

He squeezes my hand.

'Mr Jones, the dress looks even more stunning than when I saw it last. Thank you,' Mum says.

'It has been my pleasure, Susan. I will leave you to it.' Mr Jones places one more kiss on my cheek before he leaves.

'OK, we have a few minutes to kill.' I move to the tray and pour two more glasses of bubbly. 'Here.' Mum and Dad each take a glass.

'To one of my best girls in the world.'

'Dad – no.' I blow air through my lips to stop my emotions escaping.

'I know I don't talk about—'

'Malcolm, not today,' Mum says.

'Susan, I need to. The day it all changed.' His eyes rest on mine. I'm not his daughter – and it kills him. 'Kate, you make me so proud. You're so strong, and you've been through so much.'

'You too, Dad – we nearly lost you.'

I look at Mum, who has tears running down her cheeks. 'Dad's right, Kate: you held us all together when he was in hospital, and Harry would be lost without you.'

'You have never once complained about what we did, and I know you're angry.'

'I'm not angry, Dad. Maybe I was then, but not now. Sometimes I feel—' I look at Mum.

'Katenka? Kate, you can say her name: she gave me two precious gifts, and I owe her everything.'

Dad wipes the tear from my cheek. 'Your mum is right. You look like her, Kate, and she had a good heart too.'

I shake my head and take their hands. 'You gave me that. You gave me and Harry the best chance in life. I hate

527

that I never met her, but I don't blame you.'

'We want you to be happy, that's all.'

'I am.'

'Mum keeps telling me to open up to you girls.'

I nod. 'I know how hard that is for you. I love you, Dad; I will always be a Harper.'

He places a kiss on my cheek. 'You'll always be my girl.'

I can't take any more. 'Are you ready to hand me over to Luke?' *Am I ready to give him all of me?*

The three of us arrive by boat at Palazzo Cavallis. The weather is fairly warm and the sun beams down from a bright blue sky. There is a comfortable silence between us; maybe our long overdue conversation has released some hidden tension. In my heart we have barely scratched the surface, but for Dad it was a huge milestone and I respect him for that.

We move towards the room where we will marry. I take Dad's arm and hold a small posy of lily of the valley. Mum enters first.

'Ready?' Dad looks at me.

'As I'll ever be.'

The room falls silent and the music starts: Usher's 'Scream', played by the string quartet Luke used on Valentine's Day. It's perfect.

We reach the pathway to my future. All eyes are on me and my dress. But my eyes are solely on one person: dark and mesmerised meets dark and entranced.

How can a short walk feel like an eternity? Dad releases my arm as Luke takes my hand. I can just about breathe; I'm close to losing control, as my emotions fight for release.

He leans towards me and gently kisses my lips. 'You look breath-taking – like an angel.'

'I love you,' is all I can muster.

I hear a cough, and turn. Barney points to a laptop he's holding. I can see Molly crying.

I look at Luke. 'I knew you wanted her here; this was the only way it was possible,' he explains.

'Thank you.' I kiss him again. 'Wait a minute.'

I move towards the screen. 'Can you hear me?'

'Yes.' I receive a delayed response. 'You look beautiful, Kate – be happy.'

I look at Harry, who has tears streaming down her cheeks, and Barney is sniffing.

I kiss the screen. 'Love you, Molly.'

'Love you too. Now go and get married. I'm watching.'

I return to Luke's side. 'Thank you... Sorry.'

'Can we get married now?' He smiles, knowing he has my heart and now my undivided attention.

'Yes.'

I slide Luke's ring on to his finger, as we are declared man and wife.

'I want to say something.'

Luke looks at me, puzzled.

'I know my timing is off, but I have to say something... in front of everyone.' I squeeze his hand. 'You have blown me away since the day we first met, when you revealed your bossy nature...'

Luke smirks.

'Yes, you're definitely bossy, but I guess that's what makes you, you – the man I couldn't bear to live without. I love you more than you will ever understand. Your heart, body and soul belong to me – and they have done since the moment you said hello.'

He leans towards me, allowing our foreheads to meet, and rubs his nose across mine. I reach for his cheek, wiping away his tear. The only other time I've seen him cry was when he talked about Paul – and now my words have caused the exact same reaction.

'You've got me, baby – how am I supposed to follow that?'

'You don't. I just needed to tell you how I felt.'

Everyone remains silent, watching us both, then Luke takes a breath.

'*Hai cambiato la mia vita, dal momento in cui ti ho incontrato. Io non sono mai stato così aperto e onesto con chiunque, Kate siete il mio mondo. Io non sono nulla senza di te, ma con voi al mio fianco posso conquistare il mondo. Avete la mia anima e corpo – sempre.*'

Holy shit. Luke speaking Italian – I need to bottle this. It would be worth a fortune.

'I have no idea what you said, but please repeat it tonight in bed.'

'Words that I don't want everyone to hear. You have me – all of me, Kate, you know that. This is it, baby: us forever.'

I kiss him hard on the lips. God, I love him so much.

'How are you feeling, Mrs Sutton?' Luke takes my hand as we turn to walk down the aisle.

'Fab... and you, Mr Sutton?'

'Perfect, now you're my wife.' I giggle. Holy shit, I'm married. I am now officially Kate Sutton.

Finally we sit inside the restaurant, which is attached to an outside area suspended over the lagoon. The room looks perfect with hundreds of tea lights flickering on the tables, mixed with the delicateness of the flowers. I'm thrilled with how it looks.

Everyone is relaxed, which is exactly the sort of wedding we wanted. The food is fabulous. As each guest has ordered from the menu, the tables are filled with pasta dishes, steaks, fish – all sorts of wonderful food. I have to pinch myself. Being here, being married to Luke with all our friends and family here is a dream come true. I sit back and take in my special day, while the string quartet play classic club tunes.

As ever Luke's arm is placed firmly at the back of my chair, although today it feels different; today he is protecting his wife.

He leans to my ear. 'I knew you would look beautiful.'

'So do you, Mr S, my gorgeous husband.'

'Thank you for my shirt… and of course the socks.'

'Which ones did you decide to wear?'

He flashes his ankle, revealing his choice: *You & Me = Right*. 'Good choice.'

I hear the clinking of someone tapping a glass. To my absolute amazement, it's Max. I look at Luke. Max speaking in itself is a rare treat.

'Excuse me, everyone… I know Kate and Luke wanted a relaxed day without speeches, but I would like to say a few words. I know I don't usually say much…'

'No shit, Sherlock,' I say without thinking.

'Kate!' Mum looks across at me.

'Oi, Harper, let the man speak,' Barney shouts good-humouredly.

'Sutton, not Harper,' Luke jibes at Barney.

'Always Harper to me, babe.' Barney winks.

'Can I speak?' Max calls.

'Knock yourself out, Max.' All eyes lock on Barney. James and Scott seem slightly unsure how to take him.

'OK. Kate and Luke are like chalk and cheese. I know – I live with them both.' Everyone laughs.

I turn to Luke. 'Max does speeches… and he's funny… What the hell is going on?'

Luke shrugs in bewilderment.

'But they found each other. The day Kate arrived in Luke's life was the day I saw him change. He needed her more than he realised, and Kate… well, what can I say? She's loyal, caring, honest – too honest, sometimes – but she loves Luke. To watch them reach today has been an honour. I have never met two people more made for each other, two people who have found their missing link.' He swallows his emotional words, words he will never be able to say to his own son. 'Please raise your glasses for Kate and Luke.'

I stand up and walk towards Max. He needs a large dose of Harper affection. I lock my arms around him.

'I love you, Max. I can't believe you said so many words.'

'Watch it; I still have to drive you around next week.' He kisses the top of my head.

'Come here,' Luke says.

Max releases me and clasps Luke in a manly hug. God, this is so difficult for them. I know Paul is here in spirit; he walks with them both daily.

'Kate, Luke, they're ready for you to cut your cake.' Livy interrupts our moment with Max.

Luke and I stand next to the cake posing for pictures. He laughs.

'How appropriate.'

'Did you not see it when you first walked in?'

'No.'

'I emailed the hotel a picture… I'm amazed they got it right.' It's a white chocolate cake in the shape of a box, tied with a black sash and double bow with an edible label attached, inscribed: *eat me.*

The music plays, once again Usher's 'Scream' – it's our cue to hit the dance floor. Luke wraps his arms tightly around me as we dance slowly. I link my arms around his neck and kiss him cheekily, which pleases our guests, who cheer.

'So are you going to make me scream?'

'Yes – Mrs Sutton, every night.' He spins me around the dance floor. 'Have you enjoyed your day?'

'More than words can describe.' I finger my ring. 'Holy shit – Luke, we're married. It only feels like yesterday you asked me, and now I'm officially your wife!'

After a few turns, the string quartet up the tempo of our song, enticing everyone to join us. I could burst, I'm so happy.

It's my time to party with the pack: my Louboutins rest in the corner, my husband is relaxing with our family and friends, I have taken off my veil. Roller Girl has arrived – all that remains is to dance the night away, barefoot.

The dance floor is relatively small and instantly fills up, but I have a plan, one I have been thinking about for some time. I drag Max to join me. As he twirls me around, I take him over to my single Harper Jones colleague, Valerie. Max and Valerie – burly meets soft and gentle. They would be a perfect combination.

My next victim is my sister. We take hold of each other and spin joyfully. I pull her to my chest, holding her close.

'Love you, Harriet Harper.'

'You too, Kate Harper.'

What? I blink hard. The room slows to a second-by-second frame. I can hear the music, but I remain motionless. I can't breathe. My eyes fix to the doorway and the silhouette standing there. 'Ivor!'

'What?' Harry looks at me.

'Ivor!' I yell as I run towards the doors, hitching my dress up. My feet move fast as I search for him. All I can hear is Harry calling my name, and then Luke.

Ivor – I know he's here… I arrive barefoot in the hotel lobby. Still no sign of him. I move outside and run up and down the garden – nothing. He's here, my gut instinct tells me he's here. I return to the foyer, panting. People are staring at me; as I literally resemble the runaway bride. I rush past the reception desk and head towards the jetty.

'KATE… KATE!' I can hear Luke calling me.

My mind fills with fear – not fear of Ivor, but fear that he has disappeared from my life again.

I stop at the edge of the water. Darkness is everywhere, except for the lights twinkling in the distance.

'KATE… KATE!'

I turn as Luke runs towards me.

'Kate.'

I try to speak, but I can't quite catch my breath. 'I saw him. Ivor was here.'

'Are you sure?'

'It was him… I know it was.'

'Baby, it has been a long day.'

I look into his eyes. 'Don't stand there and tell me I didn't see him – I did.'

He pulls me to his chest. 'Shh…'

I hear footsteps behind us.

'Sutton.' James and Scott both arrive at the scene.

'Kate said she saw Ivor. If he is here, I want to find out where the hell he is.'

I look up. 'He is here. I know I saw him.' I move away from his arms. 'I want to go to our room.'

'I'll come with you.'

'I can go on my own.' My voice trembles.

'This is not up for discussion – if you saw Ivor, then I need to be with you.'

'I did see him.' I barge past all the men and make my way to the lift.

Luke joins me. He lifts my left hand and kisses my wedding ring, igniting my love for him and the safety he gives me.

Luke opens the door to our suite. He watches me closely.

'I need to freshen up.'

'OK.'

I head towards our bedroom and stop in my tracks. 'Luke!'

He arrives at my side. 'What's wrong?'

I point to the bed. 'Did you put that white rose on the pillow?'

He shakes his head. 'I haven't been back to our room since this morning.'

'He's been in here.'

'What? Kate, you're not making any sense.'

'Ivor's been in our room.' I move towards the closet

and collect a couple of items. The first is a photograph of Katenka and Ivor on their wedding day. I pass it to Luke.

'Look at Katenka – look at what she's holding.'

'A single white rose… Kate, the hotel staff may have put it here.'

'I don't think so.' I pass him the other item in my hand – the letter from Charles Morley. 'It was Ivor – I know it was.'

Luke begins to read it. 'Where did you get this?'

'Charles gave it to me when we were in Dubai… I wanted to show you but it wasn't the right time. He took it from his dad's office.'

Luke looks at me in disbelief. A knock at the door interrupts us. Luke walks out from the bedroom, and I follow him, feeling lost.

James Sullivan enters our room, carrying a laptop.

'I managed to hack into the hotel security – you might want to take a look at this.'

He shows us various images throughout the hotel – of Ivor. Crystal clear, in black and white – he was here.

'I knew it was him.' My body heaves; I rush to the bathroom to be sick.

Afterwards, I stand and move to the sink.

'I'm sorry.' He leans against the doorway.

I wipe my hands and face on the towel.

'It's OK… he's gone again.' I shrug.

Luke moves towards me. 'He's been here all day and probably followed you to the civil hall.'

'I don't understand.'

Luke holds his hand out. 'Are you feeling better?'

'Honestly? I don't know.' I move into his arms and look up at him. 'Today has been the best day of my life and I never want it to end… Is it wrong to feel pleased that he's been here?'

Luke gives a small smile, although I recognise the hidden signs of concern.

'No, it's not wrong.'

'How did he know about the wedding? You only booked it on Sunday, and there were no invites.'

'That's what concerns me.'

I raise my head from his chest. 'It can't be a coincidence that he's here.'

'No – he knew. I am positive he was here to see you.'

We return to the lounge area where Scott and James are continuing to search for images of Ivor.

'Anything?' Luke asks.

'It seems as though he disappeared into the thin air. The last distinctive image is by the jetty – he must have taken a boat.'

James stands from his chair, holding the information I received from Charles.

'Kate, Luke said a mutual friend gave this to you, and his father is the judge named at the bottom?'

I nod. 'We both agreed – that's the mutual friend and I – that something doesn't add up. Why would a chief coroner and chief justice work on a trivial case?'

'I agree.' He rubs his jaw. 'But where did he get this information from?'

Luke goes to the bar and pours four glasses of brandy.

'The mutual friend is not to be trusted, and is a fucking idiot.' Luke's eyes flick to mine.

'Luke!' My tone is harsh.

'Kate, we've discussed this.' Luke hands me a drink and

a kiss on the cheek. 'Drink it – you need to calm down.'

'Thank you.' I down it instantly. 'Charles snooped around in his father's not-so-secret safe. That's where he found the paperwork. I know it could be about anyone, as it doesn't say her name, but the date and location are the same. He also said that his father is methodical, so there must be a reason he's held on to this.'

'It's not the same post-mortem that I've seen for Katenka's death.'

'The chief coroner is George Williams. Luke knows his son, Matthew. Actually, George Williams and Joseph Morley are friends of Edward.' I look across to Luke. 'You know these men too.'

'Sutton, this doesn't add up.' James re-takes his seat.

Luke looks at his friend, disturbed. Although he would love to plead ignorance, he knows something isn't right.

'I grew up with their children. Our fathers are childhood friends.'

I move towards Luke, linking my arms around his waist.

'Charles told me to speak to Matthew; maybe his dad has some information.'

Luke's arms tense. I know he's angry at my mention of the name Williams.

'Under no circumstances are you to contact him. Do you understand me?'

'Luke, he may be able to help. I don't want to meet him, but I can't ignore what Charles said.'

Luke moves to a chair next to James, pulling me into his lap, where my dress takes up a fair amount of room.

'Kate, don't push me on this.'

'OK – let's take it down a notch. Christ, you've been married for a few hours, maybe go for a compromise rather than an annulment.' James looks at us both.

My lips meet Luke's. 'I love you. I would never upset you.'

'Good. You meeting Matthew would upset me, so please keep your word.'

'Anything?' Luke looks at Parker.

'No – he must have left on a boat. I have checked all the recorded images at all the exits… Nothing.'

'OK. So, what do we know? He's in Venice. Why? It must be for today, so how did he know about it?'

'Parker, can you trace any activities at the local airports? We know he has a jet. Sullivan, I want you to take the letter from Charles Morley and break it down, check dates and times, and look at what cases these two men were working on.'

'Already on it… Before I go, Kate, are Harry and your parents aware of the circumstances surrounding Katenka's death?'

I shake my head. 'No, I've never said a word.' I turn to Luke. 'We decided there was nothing to tell, since we have no proof that her death was anything other than a suicide.'

'Good – keep it that way.'

The men leave the suite.

I tuck my head in the crook of Luke's neck. He holds me gently as we sit in silence.

'Do you think you'll find him?' I look up into Luke's dark eyes.

'I don't, no. But one thing's for certain – he's watching you.'

24

My finger taps the arrow on my laptop, scrolling through the wedding photos.

'Are you looking at them again?'

I look at Luke, who has a towel wrapped around his waist.

'I wish we could do it again... I know it's only Tuesday, but it feels as though we've landed back with a bang.'

He moves towards me and rolls me onto my back.

'I know we haven't had any quality time together.'

'None.'

'OK, no time together. This time next week, you'll be naked in our very own private hut.'

'Hmm – I can't wait.' My hands move to the nape of his neck, enticing him towards me. As ever, his lips reach mine with desire.

'Christ, I wish I had time for round two.' He tilts his head towards the bulge pushing against his towel.

I unwrap the towel and reach for his erection.

'I have lots of time – are you sure I can't tempt you?' I

tighten my grip on his hardness and slide my other hand between my legs. He gazes at my amazing multitasking skills.

'Christ, I'm going to be late.'

'Blame your wife.' I giggle with excitement. I know I have him for the second time this morning.

I swirl my third mug of coffee. I need to think. I take a deep breath and pick up my mobile phone for the hundredth time this morning. However, this time I try to convince myself not to return it to the kitchen worktop.

I hit send, and wait. Three seconds later, the call is answered.

'Hello.'

'Hi Charles, it's Kate – Kate Harper, actually Kate Sutton.'

'Well, well, well, to say I am surprised is an understatement. Good morning, Mrs Sutton, and when did this happen? I assume when we had our chat last week you were not married?'

I can't help smiling at his voice. 'You're absolutely right, we weren't. Saturday. I'm now officially Mrs Luke Sutton.'

'Hmm, this is fresh news. I am so delighted to be one of the first to know, and I will have huge amounts of pleasure gossiping about you both.'

'Knock yourself out.'

'Oh, I intend to. So you have given me two surprises this morning. I assume you want something and this is not a social call?'

'Would you be hurt if I said it wasn't?'

'No.'

'Good. OK, after much deliberation I've decided that breathing isn't my main priority in life.'

Charles chuckles. 'Are you sure?'

'No of course not, but I need some answers, and if Matthew can get them, then I need to ask... Will Luke go mad? Hell, yes.'

'So your loyal husband is not in on your cunning plan? And I assume he's not aware of this conversation?'

'No to both... I'm seriously putting my arse on the line here – not to mention my pulse.' Bloody hell, I feel sick.

'My lips will remain sealed. I may act like an over-indulged human being, but you can trust me, so this call never took place.'

'For some reason I believe you... So this brings me to my next question: do you have Matthew's phone number?'

'Yes, I'll forward it to you.' There is a pause. 'You should receive it any moment. Well, Mrs Sutton, I wish you lots of luck and hope to see you very much alive – soon. Remember, if you need anything – call.'

'Thanks, Charles.'

Now what to text Luke's arch-enemy? I take a deep breath and begin to type.

Hi Matthew,
I wonder if you would meet me at Milsons Coffee House today at 1pm. I will explain why when I see you. Please let me know if you can make it.
Kate Sutton (was Harper until last Saturday!)

Without hesitation I hit send. My head is already going over the possible results of the meeting; the repercussions from Luke will be catastrophic. But what choice do I have? He said he would help me, but he's done nothing, and I can't help thinking he's avoiding the situation.

The bleep of a text arriving sends a shiver down my spine. Reluctantly I look – Matthew. Shit! He's quick.

Dear Mrs Sutton, Congratulations! Luke is a very lucky man. OK – I'm intrigued. I'll see you at 1!

Fuck, fuck, fuck... Crap. What will happen now?

Right – I have to think about my image today: what will I wear? Jeans with a matching denim shirt, topped off with a tweed blazer and tan ankle boots. *Hello, Mrs Sutton!*

Max drives my car to Milsons Coffee House – as ever, it appears to be jam-packed.

'I'll park the car and come in. What time are you meeting your friend?'

I check the time. 'In five minutes.' I look across to a happy Max. Make the most of it, Harper – pissed-off Max will most certainly be driving me home. I step out onto the pavement as Max watches me from the car.

The building is fairly large – it's an old granary with the original exposed brickwork and wooden beams. It feels rustic and charming. I am thankful I reserved a table. I take my seat and order a cafetière of fairly strong coffee – obviously, I need another injection of caffeine.

I catch sight of Matthew as he walks through the door; he instantly spots me.

'Hi.' I'm not sure how to act towards someone I punched a couple of weeks ago. He takes a seat and gives me his all-American smile. Still – he's not my type...

'I ordered coffee; I hope that's OK.' My hands feel shaky, and my heart pounds against my ribcage.

'That's fine. Let's cut to the chase, Mrs Sutton.'

'OK… First, I need to address my outburst the other week.'

He moves his jaw from side to side, demonstrating that I did in fact make contact with him. 'That was a surprise.'

'I know, but I'm not going to apologise; you were rude and out of line. I know what happened between you and Maddy… Anyway, Luke and I are married now, so it really doesn't matter.'

'Fair enough – besides, I didn't expect an apology.'

'It won't happen again – I hope!' I give a half-hearted smile.

I look beyond Matthew and see Max enter the building. Here goes! His face drops as he strides towards me. He takes hold of my arm.

'A word – now!'

'I won't be a minute.'

Matthew smirks.

Max drags me to a quiet spot. 'Are you out of your fucking mind? What the hell are you doing?'

'It's not what it looks like. Matthew's dad was the chief coroner at Katenka's inquest. Even Sullivan smells a rat, something's not right. I'm going to ask him if he can dig around in his father's documents.'

'You're playing with fire… Luke is going to hit the fucking roof. Jesus, Kate, what is wrong with you? You've only been married a few days and you pull a stunt like this.' He runs his hand through his hair. 'You know I'll have to call him.'

I nod. 'I know. But I have to ask, Max.'

'Not like this! I can't believe you… You've fucked up this time, Kate.'

'Christ, I'm not bloody shagging the bloke; I'm only asking him a question.' I sigh and roll my eyes.

'Don't roll your eyes at me… And don't talk like that in front of me either. Fucking hell, Kate.'

'Whatever.' I turn to head back to the coffee shop, but Max pulls at my arm, causing me to stop.

'You have ten minutes. If you don't move after that time, I will pick you up and move you myself… Do I make myself clear?'

'Crystal!'

I return to my seat, chastised.

'Problem?' Matthew asks, pouring himself a second cup of coffee.

'Yes, you're my problem. You may have guessed that Luke doesn't know I'm meeting you.'

He whistles. 'Do you like living dangerously?'

'Nothing I can't handle. OK – I'll get to the point.'

'The floor's yours.'

I place a copy of the partially completed post-mortem on the table. He draws it closer and begins to read.

'Charles took this from his father's secret safe.'

Matthew's eyebrows shoot up.

'I know – it's not that much of a secret. Well, anyway, we believe this relates to my birth mother.' I tap the bottom of the sheet. 'Your father was the chief coroner and Charles's father was the chief justice.'

'I don't see how I can help.'

'This is a long shot, I know, but does your father have a safe where he keeps – old paperwork? I was wondering if he

545

kept anything relating to my mother. I also wondered why two high-profile men would work on a case that involved a woman of no apparent importance who committed suicide. It all seems strange.'

He shrugs and rereads the paperwork. I sip my coffee while he digests my words.

'Can I keep this?'

'Yeah, it's a copy.'

He folds the paper in half and places it in his wallet. 'What exactly are you accusing my father of? If I find any incriminating evidence, this may affect him or Joseph.'

I shake my head. 'I don't think they had anything to do with my mother's death; they probably didn't even know her… But something isn't right.'

I look at Max, lurking in the background.

'I have to leave. Will you look?'

He nods. 'I will. But I don't know if my father has a secret stash of paperwork.'

I stand up. 'I appreciate it.'

'If I find anything, I'll call you.'

'Thank you… Now wish me luck dealing with my husband.'

'You don't need luck, Kate; you have most people under your spell at "hello".'

What the hell?

Max grips the steering wheel tightly, tighter than usual.

'How bad was Luke – mildly pissed off or full-blown demonic pissed-off?'

'What do you think?'

'OK – I thought I'd ask. You know why I met Matthew.'

He shakes his head. 'I normally back your decisions one hundred per cent, but not today. You're on your own dealing with Luke.'

'Fine!' I look out of the window, feeling hostile. 'I would rather go home.'

'Tough – Luke is expecting you, so I suggest you deal with it.'

Max and I stand side by side in the lift, but the emotional distance between us is huge. The doors open and I begin the long walk of shame towards Luke's office. The first thing I see is Stella.

'Hello, Kate.' She stands up to greet me. 'Are you OK? You look a little…'

'I'm fine, Stella. Actually, I've pissed off Luke, big-time, and now I have to deal with him.' My hand brushes against my stomach, which is full of nerves, knowing I have to enter his lair and deal with the consequences.

Her hand reaches for my face. 'You will be fine. He needs you too much; just allow the dust to settle.'

Dust! Bloody sandstorm, more like.

I open the door. Luke sits at his desk, on the phone. My feet carry me towards him, allowing me to absorb the darkness of his eyes – they're almost black. I stand corrected: they are darker than I've ever seen them. I sit in front of his desk.

He replaces the receiver and leans back in his chair, rubbing his jaw. The silence is deafening.

'I'm sorry… I was going to tell you, but not until after I met him.'

'You say you're sorry, but I feel it's an empty apology.' He tilts his head as his eyes meet mine.

'That's not true. I love you, you're my husband… but I needed to ask him. I *had* to.'

Luke laughs; obviously I am not remotely humorous.

'No, you didn't need to ask him.' He leans his forearms on the desk. 'I'm so mad at you, the truth is I'm struggling to even look at you… I despise this man more than any other. You say you love me, but if you do, then why would you hurt me? Do you really love me?'

'What? Are you joking?' Jerkily, I stand up, needing to pace the floor. 'You know I adore you – Christ, we only got married four days ago.' I hold my hand up to display my ring. 'Yes, I know you hate him, but even you should be able to understand that he may be able to find more information about Katenka's death. This isn't about you or us, this is about the truth. I know she didn't kill herself… I've always thought that.'

'You're wrong – and I'm furious with you. He may also not be able to help. I can only imagine his delight when you met – he's got one over on me again.'

'Oh, for Christ's sake, Luke, I saw him for ten minutes and drank one cup of coffee – I didn't shag him.'

He stands from his chair and slips his black blazer over his white shirt, collecting up paperwork and slipping it into his briefcase.

'Luke, I love you. I wouldn't hurt you.'

He stops to look at me. 'You have. Right now, I can't forgive you. I need some distance from you.'

My heart almost stops. 'What do you mean, distance?' I move towards him, but he brushes past me. 'Luke, please don't leave like this… I'm so sorry.'

He stops in his tracks. *Fuck, I've really hurt him.*

'I need some time.'

'Are you coming home?'

'I have a late meeting.'

'That's not what I asked.'

'That is all I can offer you.' He pushes open the door and he leaves. My body crumples to the chair and my tears begin to flow uncontrollably.

Back at home, there is no room left in the fridge, so I readjust the plastic food boxes, making space for my homemade chicken curry. The last few hours have been unbearable. All I want to do is cry, but instead I have cooked. Lamb stew, shepherd's pie, lasagne and chicken curry. These dishes have also overflowed to Jerry's fridge and to a very reluctant Max. I have no appetite to speak of, just nausea in the pit of my stomach.

'Kate.' I turn to see Max.

I offer him a blank expression.

'Do you need anything? It's six o'clock.'

'No.' I walk past him and head towards the staircase. He catches up with me.

'You need to give him time.'

Once again I remain silent.

It's ten o'clock, but Luke hasn't returned home. I walk into the kitchen and boil the kettle, knowing I need to drink, and perhaps eat, something.

Eleven o'clock arrives and I am still alone in the palace. My head and heart feels exhausted. How can I rest without talking to him? My only option is to leave him a note.

To the love of my life,
I am sorry for meeting him, and I would never hurt you.
You are my world. I knew that from the moment I met you.
Please don't ignore me, and please let me show you how
much I love you, today and forever.
Love, your extremely regretful wife x

I place the note on his desk, knowing if he comes home this will be his first port of call.

I lie awake, my eyes burning. It's midnight and Luke is still AWOL. I make one last attempt to communicate with him – a text.

Dear Luke,
I know you're pissed off, but I need you. Please come home and keep me warm. x.

I hit send and place my phone on the bed. I roll onto my side, knowing I should sleep. My phone bleeps, and I grab it. Caller ID: boss. At last!

X

One solitary kiss. No words or explanation for why he isn't home.

The next morning, my eyes open and my hands skim the empty space next to me. I'm positive Luke never came home. I feel the day stretching out emptily in front of me.

Washed and showered, dressed in skinny jeans, Converse and Luke's navy Abercrombie hoodie, I try to eat breakfast, but can't. Restless, I wander into Luke's office. The note has gone! He did come home! Feeling lethargic, and now a little pissed off that he's behaving so bloody ridiculously, I decide to call him. I hit send.

'Yes.' Wow – I wasn't expecting him to answer.

'Hi.' He may have answered, but I have no idea what to say now.

'Kate, do you want something?' His tone is abrupt.

'Only you.' Honesty is all I have.

'I'm busy.'

What? 'Right. I wouldn't want to interrupt you, then.' I hit end and throw my phone on the desk.

I sit back in his chair. Fuck – I feel like crap. My mood changes from remorseful to angry. He needs to get over it; my intentions were honourable. I know, if the roles were reversed, I would accept what he had done. I look around the room feeling twitchy. I need to be busy. I open Luke's office drawer and notice a set of keys with a tag: *Sandbanks*. Hmm, now there's a thought. After all, he wanted distance.

I pack. Soon, my rucksack sits on the desk and a small food bag waits on the floor. All I need is for Max to disappear – but not in my car. If he knows of my plans he will join me – not much of a hide and seek challenge with my sidekick in tow!

I dial Barney.

'Hello, my gorgeous girlie.'

I smile. 'Hello, light of my life – you sound puffed out. What are you up to?'

'Dancing – what did you think I was doing? You and your one-track mind. Jesus, Mrs Sutton, you're a little slut.'

'You're always on the job.'

'To be fair, I was earlier, but I won't go in to that. Hang on a minute, babe.' He returns, not so breathless. 'I couldn't hear myself think, let alone speak… What's up?'

'I need a bizarre favour.'

'Ooh, that sounds exciting.'

'Luke and I have… Well, we've had a disagreement.'

'*Already*? Jesus, you need some therapy, girl.'

'No, I need some space. That's why I need you. I'm going to send Max to the studio. I need you to give him a box with my name on it. I'm going to tell him to take it to my office for Valerie.'

'Have you lost your bloody marbles?'

'Not yet.'

'OK, you want me to give Max an empty box with your name on it… Can I ask why?'

'I need him out of the house so I can drive to Sandbanks. He won't let me go by myself, and I want to go alone.'

'Are you sure about this? If Luke is pissed off at you, he'll go mad that you're alone.'

'I'll be at Sandbanks. What can go wrong?'

He takes a deep breath. 'I guess.'

'Besides, you know where I am.'

'Great, land me in the fucking quicksand. OK. I've got this.'

'Thanks, babe; catch up soon.'

'Yeah. Drive carefully.'

'Barney has the box ready for you to collect. It's got samples of fabric he got from a friend, and Valerie needs them today. I really don't want to go out.'

'Does it have to be done today?' He frowns.

'Only if it's not too much trouble. With everything else going on, I forgot.' Bloody hell, my acting skills have improved – sort of!

'Fine.'

'Thanks, Max.'

I lean against Luke's office window, waiting for Max to depart – hopefully in the Range Rover, not my car.

Within five minutes the Range Rover drives past the window and heads towards the security gate. My plan is working. Quickly, I grab my bags and keys for Sandbanks, and move to my car. I push the start button and the engine roars. I search through the sat-nav memory. As I predicted, my incredibly methodical husband has stored the address – how thoughtful of him.

The traffic leaving London is fairly quiet, thank God. I have roughly an hour and a half, maybe slightly longer, before Max realises I'm missing. This will give me an advantage. The car detects the Bluetooth on my phone and our wedding song, 'Scream', starts to play through the sound system. Tears stream down my cheeks.

I look at the sat-nav. Fifty miles to go. Fifty long, lonely miles. Then the car phone rings, shattering my thoughts. Caller ID: Max. I can only imagine how pissed off he is. After another ten minutes, the car phone rings again. Caller ID: boss. I guess they know I'm missing. Let's see if Mr 007 Wannabe can track me. *Find me, Luke.*

At last I pull up to the gate of the house. I input the security code and drive down the gravel driveway. I open the front door and deactivate the alarm. It feels strange to be here without Luke. The last time we were here, he asked me to marry him. How things have changed.

After unpacking my bags and making a cup of tea, I check my phone. Fifteen missed calls, and five texts.

Text one. Where are you?

Sandbanks.

Text two. Max thinks you sent him on a wild-goose chase. Where are you?

Absolutely. Well done, Max.

Text three. Are you trying to make a point? I'm now fucking pissed off. Where are you?

Yes I am trying to make a point.

Text four. Answer your fucking phone. At least have the decency to let me know you're alive.

I'm definitely breathing.

Text five. When I find you, your arse will be fucking sorry. Where the hell are you?

Now, how shall I respond to such a romantic gesture?

Yes, I am alive. As I recall, you wanted distance and an obedient wife. Bingo – you have both. If you want to find me, I'm sure you can track me.

Love you forever, although I don't know if you feel the same.

I hit send and place my phone on the kitchen worktop. I have no intention of communicating any further with him unless it's face to face.

I switch on the new lamps in the kitchen. They look amazing and so too does the kitchen – coastal meets colonial. It actually looks like the room I imagined. I stop and pour a glass of white wine and eat a sandwich.

I check my phone: no calls or messages. My instinct tells me Luke is on his way; the feeling sends a shockwave through me.

The sound of the intercom buzzer startles me. Christ, he drove quickly. I stop to think. He can't drive that quickly... And why buzz? He knows the code!

I push the button. 'Hello?'

'Kate... thank God.'

I'm confused. It's a female voice, not Luke.

'Who is this?'

'Alexis.' There is a small silence before the revelation hits me.

'What?'

'Kate, let me in.'

'What the hell are you doing here?'

'We don't have much time... This is serious. Please, I'm not bullshitting you.'

My finger presses the button to open the gate. I lean against the wall, replaying her words in my mind. A cold burst of air washes over my body. The sound of banging startles me. I look at the glass panels on each side of the door. Fuck – it is her, and not a dream. I reluctantly open the door, and she barges through and shuts it behind her, shooting the deadbolts.

'OK, this is weird. What the hell are you doing here? I'm still fucking mad at you for kissing Luke.'

She pulls my arm, guiding me to the lounge. She moves to the windows, looking out towards the beach. She seems nervous.

'Alexis!'

She turns to face me. Her complexion is deathly white.

'What are you doing here? How the hell did you know I was here?'

'You need to listen to me…' She takes a deep breath. 'I had to go to B&C this afternoon to collect some paperwork. I walked past my father's office, and he was talking to two men I've never seen before. Even though they were smartly dressed, I felt uneasy about them for some reason, and hung back to listen. Kate, I don't know how to tell you…'

'What? Spit it out! You're scaring the shit out of me.'

'My father planted the bomb at your house – Luke's house. It was him who tried to kill Luke!'

I want to collapse, but try to be strong.

'Kate, I had nothing to do with this.' Her eyes are empty and lost. 'You know how I feel about Luke; I would never hurt him.'

Fuck. I believe her. She loves Luke.

'I shouldn't have kissed him. I apologise. I was drunk.'

'Jesus, this is madness. I need to call him.'

'We don't have time! The men I was telling you about are on their way here.'

'Here? How did they know where I was?'

'I don't know; they must have been following you. I overheard them talk about Sandbanks, and I put two and two together and called your housekeeper. I told her I had a delivery for Sandbanks, and she gave me the address. Kate, they're after you. My father has something planned for you – I don't know what. I'm sorry.'

I rush to the kitchen, grab my phone and ring Luke. My hands shake and panic is closing around my throat.

'I am so fucking pissed off at you…'

'Luke.' I nervously say.

'Baby, what is it?'

'Listen very carefully; I don't know how much time I have. Alexis is here at Sandbanks. She overheard Philip talking to some men, and it was him that planted the bomb at the palace. Luke, he tried to kill you! And he's on his way here now – he wants me.'

Silence follows my words.

'How long before they get to you?'

I stand next to Alexis. Bizarrely, she slides her hand into mine. I grip it firmly. 'She doesn't know – but they know I'm here. Luke, I don't know what to do.'

'I'm on my way, but I won't get to you in time.' His voice is dry with fear.

A sudden noise from the front door makes me jump. Suddenly it bursts open. I look behind me and scream. There are four men, dressed in black, on the decking.

'Run, Alexis – quick, upstairs.' Holding the phone to my ear, we charge upstairs. 'The bathroom.' We rush into the room and lock the door, knowing it will not hold off the burly intruders for long.

'Luke, it's too late – they're here.' Tears roll down my cheeks, and my heart pounds with fear. 'I love you, Luke Sutton – until the end. Please remember how much I love you.' I can barely speak through my sobs.

'I love you too, baby.' His voice cracks. 'You have your watch?'

I nod. 'Yes.'

'Then I will find you. Do whatever they ask, Kate. Stay alive. I promise I'll find you.'

The next second, the bathroom door is forced open. My phone hits the floor as four beefy men dressed in black come towards us. I hit out, over and over again, but they are too strong for me. One of them slaps my face, then grabs my arms and holds them behind my back, and another places a piece of fabric over my nose and mouth...

The world goes dark.

RUSSIA

Ivor moves closer to his captive, who is tied to a chair and has blood smeared across his face. He grips his chin. The man winces and opens his eyes. Unluckily for him, Ivor's team had been watching some of Chekhol's gang.

'Petrov, I will ask you again. Think very carefully before you answer. I will kill you if you lie – do you understand?'

The injured man nods.

'Good.' Ivor slaps him hard across the face, almost knocking the chair over. 'I know you work for Chekhol. I also know that you have information about his plans.'

Reluctantly, he nods again.

'Where are they going to take her?'

'Sss…' He tries to speak, blood running from his mouth. 'Sinyavino.' He whispers. 'Exchange.'

Ivor Varizin turns to one of his employees, who is waiting silently, and clicks his fingers. The black-dressed man walks towards him.

'Take him downstairs.'

The employee nods. He unties the man from the chair, roughly pulls him to his feet and drags him out of the room.

Ivor moves to a makeshift office next door, where other members of staff are waiting for him.

'We know that Chekhol is involved; they have paid a high price for Katarina. At least she will be kept alive until the transaction has been made. This gives us some time.'

One man hands Ivor a photo.

'This is the person delivering her to Chekhol.'

'Yes, sir. Philip Cooper.'

'I recognise the name.'

'The men are ready to move, sir.'

Another employee lays a map on the desk and begins to circle locations. 'We move to this point now; I have a team working north. There will be no exit; Chekhol's men will be surrounded.'

Ivor downs a glass of vodka and runs his hands through his thick hair.

'Very good – you need to go over the plan again. This must run smoothly. If anything happens to my daughter…' He inhales deeply and tries to compose himself.

'Boss, we will get her.'

He places his hand on the man's shoulder. 'Good. I trust you. Now tell me, where is her husband?'

'An airfield just outside London.'

'And his team?'

'We still have no way of tracking them, but I am sure we will meet them at some point.'

'Good. If we do, then we must work together – understood? Our war is with Chekhol, not their private military unit. He will get my daughter back, I know he will. I see the way he looks at her. He loves her.' Ivor rubs his forehead. 'Katenka, please help your baby,' he mutters under his breath.